For Bob, with love:
I hope you enjoy this
contemporary Colom-
bian novelist, one of
my favourites!

Fast Eddie

Bogotá, September 2022

ALSO BY

SANTIAGO GAMBOA

Necropolis

NIGHT PRAYERS

Santiago Gamboa

NIGHT PRAYERS

*Translated from the Spanish
by Howard Curtis*

Europa
editions

Europa Editions
214 West 29th Street
New York, N.Y. 10001
www.europaeditions.com
info@europaeditions.com

Copyright © by Santiago Gamboa
c/o Guillermo Schavelzon & Asoc., Agenzia Literaria
www.schavelzon.com
First Publication 2016 by Europa Editions

Translation by Howard Curtis
Original title: *Plegarias nocturnas*
Translation copyright © 2015 by Europa Editions

Library of Congress Cataloging in Publication Data is available
ISBN 978-1-60945-311-4

Gamboa, Santiago
Night Prayers

Book design by Emanuele Ragnisco
www.mekkanografici.com

Cover photo © Alexis Mire

Prepress by Grafica Punto Print – Rome

Printed in the USA

This book has been selected to receive financial assistance from English PEN's "PEN
Translates!" programme, supported by Arts Council England. English PEN exists to
promote literature and our understanding of it, to uphold writers' freedoms around the
world, to campaign against the persecution and imprisonment of writers for stating their
views, and to promote the friendly co-operation of writers and the free exchange of ideas.
www.englishpen.org

To Analía and Alejandro, walking to Farfa

Do not utter my name when you learn that I have died,
from the dark earth it would come through your voice.
—ROQUE DALTON

What remained in the end, however the world or life changed,
was the immutable fact of a universe abandoned by God.
—LOU ANDREAS SALOMÉ

CONTENTS

NIGHT PRAYERS

PART I

All cities have a fairly definite smell, but for most of the day the smell of Bangkok is covered by a dense blanket of smog that conceals it, making it hard to perceive. When it finally appears, well after darkness has fallen—when the city is quiet, when it has at last calmed down—it's a tangible substance that floats in the air, moves along the winding streets, and penetrates the remotest alleyways. It may come from the canals of stagnant water, where it's quite common to see people cooking or washing clothes; from the dried fish stands in Chinatown, the satay and fried food in Patpong and Silom Road, or even the live animals that wait in wicker cages in Chatuchak Market; or it may simply come from the vapors of the Chao Phraya, the brown river that crosses the city, invading it like an insidious illness.

Today it's pouring rain. The waters of the river heave and ripple, as if about to engulf the sampans and canoes that dare to navigate it. That's what I see through the window of my room on the fourteenth floor of the Shangri-La Tower at the Hotel Oriental. Shangri-La: the name means "paradise" but to me it suggests something else, "solitude," maybe, or just "waiting." Night has already fallen, and I'm drinking gin, my face glued to the window, looking out at a landscape distorted by rain: the Chao Phraya, the lights of Bangkok, the blue skyscrapers, the storm clouds streaked with lightning, the incredible metropolis.

When I switch on the air-conditioning, the grille gives off a strong smell, a mixture of damp and rust. What time is it? Almost eight. I'll go down soon, have dinner, then get through a few more gins. In spite of my age (I've just turned forty-five) I still believe in chance, the throw of the dice involved in going out into the night to look for a drink in a foreign city, an adventure we are less and less suited to with time, which is why, as the years go by, some prefer a bottle by the couch in front of the TV. But not me. I prefer to wander the city, refusing to sleep without having tried that first.

But what am I doing here, apart from launching these thoughts into the rotten air? Waiting, waiting, waiting. Or rather: remembering. I've made an appointment with memory.

I came to Bangkok intending to remember. To look again at what I lived through in this city a few years ago, but in another light. Sometimes, time is a question of light. With the passing of the years, while some forms become strangely opaque, others acquire brilliance. They are the same, yet they appear more vivid, and sometimes, just sometimes, we are able to grasp them. I'm not sure why. It may be no more than a wish, it may merely be words, but that's precisely what I'm looking for: words. I want to reconstruct a story in order to tell it.

Something—I don't know what, of course: perhaps an impulse, a creative élan, or simply an old sadness, I can't be more specific—made me feel that I had to go over all this in writing: the events that brought me to Bangkok that first time, and their consequences. An old story trapped inside a city, which opens up onto others. At that time (the period I'm trying to remember) everything was different and I was another person. Not better or worse, only different and a little younger.

Let's see now. Where to begin?

I'll begin with the worst of it, Consul. The worst thing of all: my childhood. Although at this stage, to be honest, I don't even know what the worst is.

I was born in Bogotá, in a lower-middle-class family, a family that was, as they say in the financial section of the newspapers, economically unsound and showing a marked downward trend. A family much affected by the crisis, down there at the bottom of all the indices and statistics, at the mercy of neoliberalism and the market economy. We also fitted the statistics in being a family of four. I was the second of two children, after an elder sister named Juana. We lived in the Santa Ana district, not up in the hills, where the rich live, but between Seventh and Ninth, which at that time was a mixture of middle-class people on the way down and what's called the "upper working class," in other words, the quintessence of pretention, frustration, and resentment. I don't know, maybe I'm being unfair, but that's how I remember it.

Mine wasn't a happy family, and, as in Tolstoy's novel, it was unhappy in its own way, although now that I think about it the only original thing was how all that frustration and resentment manifested itself. Anyway, that was where I was born. In an ugly old two-story house, similar to all the others in the neighborhood. Not far from an open sewer.

Mother made bouquets in a florist's on Fifteenth that specialized in senior citizens' parties, local festivals, and masses. Father worked in the national current accounts section of the

Usaquén Park branch of the Colombian Industrial Bank, and in spite of breaking his back for ten hours a day earned just enough to pay his monthly bills. He was a model employee, but with so much pent-up resentment that I think if he'd had the opportunity to torture—anonymously—any of his colleagues or customers, and of course his boss, without there being any consequences (like in one of those virtual experiments that universities do into the cruelty or cold-bloodedness of the average person), he'd have gone about it with genuine brutality, releasing great spurts of blood, sending megawatts of electricity into nervous systems, pulling out nails with a penknife, burning testicles with a cattle prod, crushing bones. He'd have been responsible for a real massacre if the city had suddenly gone crazy and descended into chaos, sending us back to the Stone Age for a time. I can imagine him shattering the skulls of colleagues with a stone hammer, decapitating his customers with obsidian knives, jumping from one desk to another, his body covered in skins, his hair long and dirty, emitting grunts. But he had to swallow this impulse and keep his head down. He had to smile and be docile, in his cheap striped tie and his shiny suit.

The managers took advantage of him, humiliated him gratuitously. "Always look on the bright side," he must have thought, gritting his teeth. Father had a real awareness of his class and believed it was his duty to wait patiently. Better times were around the corner. Times of revenge and justice. A happier era. In the meantime, they moved his desk to the most uncomfortable spot, gave him a chair that wobbled, placed him at the one counter window where the terminal didn't work so that he'd have to do everything by hand. But the managers never invited him to the office on the second floor where they had cable TV. He pretended not to notice, or not to care. How inconsiderate of them, he said to Mother once, sending me to Carrefour to buy a bottle of Tres Esquinas for the Barcelona game, and then not even inviting me to sit down with them!

"How inconsiderate," that was all. He didn't think he could express any other kind of anger. He had to keep supporting his family and it was best not to take risks.

Life wasn't easy for him, and the worst of it was that Mother despised him for that very reason, although at home he was quite the opposite, bossy and tyrannical, as if to say, I'm the king of this little world! here everyone does what I say! and Mother, who was a traditional wife even though she never lost the opportunity to humiliate him in front of his friends, would say to him, yes, of course, go sit down and watch the game and I'll bring you your food.

The frustrations of work had to be paid for at home. That's how it happens in poor families or unhappy families. And that was our way of being unhappy.

Mother always said we had to be grateful for the effort and the great sacrifice he made for all of us. And maybe she was right. But how could I accept that? Father never sat down on the floor to play with me, never took me affectionately by the hand, never did anything to make me happy or arouse any kind of emotion in me. And you know why? It's an old story, one that never changes. He only had eyes for Juana, my older sister. His heart couldn't stretch to more, and I was left out. It was a small heart, a dry heart, because, to tell the truth, Father didn't have many reasons to be brimming over with love. On the contrary: his life was a dusty expanse of scrubland, and there was nobody to support him. What love did he get, and from whom? Very little, almost none. Mother despised him silently, and he didn't really have anywhere else to replenish his stocks; my grandmother was dead and he didn't have any brothers or sisters. His father had been in a vegetative state for years . . . Did he ever have a girl on the side? I doubt it. Because of him, I've always believed that love emerges only when you get it from others, that it exists by contagion. It doesn't come about spontaneously, but through another person.

That's what happened to me. I spent my first years alone, a little ghost in a house where love was in short supply. It's what I thought the world and life were like, although from time to time I witnessed amorous scenes of which I wasn't the protagonist. The first time that someone came down to my eye level and gave me a hug, it was already too late. My world was irredeemably contaminated. I must have been about seven, maybe slightly older. And it wasn't my parents, but my sister.

Juana picked me up from the floor. She lived up there on her throne, a spoiled only daughter, but one day she decided to look at me. She saw me and I saw her, and we liked each other, and she gave me what I hadn't had from anybody up until then, in other words, understanding, or rather something more intimate: a mirror that fell from on high and reflected my soul back to me. Thanks to her, I survived childhood, although I can assure you it was very long. Long and painful. But how was that moment? How did it come about that Juana acknowledged me?

I think I was almost eight when, one morning, I started to feel pain and fever. My liver had become inflamed thanks to an unusual form of viral hepatitis that's quite rare in Colombia and could have killed me. By the time they took me to the hospital, I was burning with fever. I remember the hurried departure, racing through the streets in the middle of the night wrapped in blankets at an hour when everything seems terrifying. Because of my grandfather, who had been a lieutenant colonel, we had access to the military hospital. They even gave me a private room, and I swear to you, that's where I felt really free for the first time in my life. Through the window, I could see the lights of the city as evening fell. The sunset was like the end of the world, with those purple-colored dusks you get in Bogotá, which is an ugly city with a beautiful sky, something I've never quite understood.

I'd hunker down under the blankets and think, I want this

to be the last thing I see, I want to disappear now and forever, and I'd pray to God, I don't want to get out of this hospital, I don't want to go home or to school or to my neighborhood ever again, there isn't a single place in the world I'd like to go back to, and I'd drift into a peaceful sleep, protected by that childish hope, oh, what joy I felt! But I'd always wake up again to a rainy morning. And then my parents would arrive, and with them the horror, the frozen looks, the resentment that showed itself in everything, even in the way they breathed; the feeling of being trapped in a state of anxiety that wasn't mine. I'd sink back into my illness, look for protection in the fever and the pains and the dizziness I felt from the pills, and ask that it never abandon me. I just had to be strong, to bear up, because at a specific time, at the end of the afternoon, they would both go. Mother could have stayed and slept there but luckily she never did. The very first night she had apologized to the head nurse—because she thought she had to—saying that she had chores to do at home, and another child, a daughter, to look after, to which the nurse replied, don't worry, señora, that's why we're here, we'll take good care of him and spoil him, he's such a good little boy, so quiet.

Those nights in the hospital, lying in my adjustable bed and watching the lights of the city come on, were probably the happiest period of my childhood, although also the saddest. There's a strange joy in that memory in spite of the fact that today, when I talk about it, I feel a kind of pity. I don't know, Consul. If only I'd died.

One Saturday, Juana came with them. At first, although curious, she held back a little, but as she moved closer I noticed that she was staring at me, and suddenly she touched my forehead with her hand, a very light caress, and that was when the miracle happened. All at once Mother's agitated voice—she'd been looking constantly at her watch and talking about an appointment at the Wella hair salon that she couldn't miss—faded away, and Father, who was looking out at the city through the window, also seemed to disappear.

I don't know how she did it, but somehow Juana managed to turn that hospital room into a capsule. Only her, standing there in silence, and me. Nobody else in the world, and that, just that, was what I saw: that Juana's eyes were two caves through which you could gain access to a planet where we could live and perhaps be happy.

Then I had a vision.

A huge fire was spreading across the city from the mountains. In the midst of the spluttering concrete and the explosions, the screams and the collapsing buildings, beautiful tongues of fire appeared at my window, formed wild shapes, changed color, and vanished into the air. I didn't fantasize about the end of the world, but I felt strong. I heard the screams coming from the streets and stopped to listen to them. What a surprise! They weren't cries of pain but laughter. A resounding burst of laughter, as if there was something pleasurable in all that destruction. That's what that hateful city is like: capable of confusing us with pleasure when it's actually torturing us, a pleasure you can't imagine anywhere else, but since it's the only one we know there everybody believes that's how life is, that's what pleasure and happiness are like.

Poor people.

I saw the flames rise, heard them echoing ever more loudly against the roof, and my heart was pounding, will all this stop now? is this the end? Then I looked at Juana and started to fall into the sleep of illness and pills, but taking with me her eyes and maybe also something of her soul. I wanted that moment to last. I prayed again. But the sky was empty, nobody heard my prayers, Consul, and a few days later I had to return home, to that neighborhood of broken streets, and to my school, which was like a boil on the surface of the hills. Home was the center of my unease, something in it weighed on my mind.

What was it? Only Juana was able to understand it, and that was what united us. It was what we had discovered: we were part of something dark and sad that neither of us could change. The smell of cheap lotion, the floor polish, the aroma of raincoats and jackets, whatever. The intense smell of a humiliated family that thought it deserved a second chance but never got it. Only one thing had changed: I had a trench now, somewhere I could be relatively safe. My bedroom, Juana's bedroom, and the little corridor between them. When I got back from the hospital, that was my refuge.

Every morning the hell started again. At about six, we'd stand on the corner of the street, waiting for the school bus. I'd see the other children and feel profound contempt for them, and at the same time pity. They were happy. They chattered away nineteen to the dozen, talked over each other, laughed. Some sang, and clapped when the wheel of the bus hit a puddle and sprayed the pitted sidewalks; what sad happiness, Consul. There are some kinds of happiness that make your flesh crawl, don't you think?

At school I wasn't a bad student. I didn't like calling the teachers' attention to myself, so I made a personal decision to be a gray pupil, an invisible pupil. One more among many. It was a stupid matter of keeping up appearances, like so many other stupid matters I had to put up with during those years. Even now, in my nightmares, I return to my childhood and realize that period of pain hasn't finished. It's a wound that grows and opens with time.

The teachers were horrible women with torn pantyhose, varicose veins, warts, greasy hair, and sad clothes. It's because of them that I've always believed evil is ugly, even though that's not its exclusive property. These women, whose resentment, whose hatred for their mediocre lives, could be felt from miles away, were the people who were supposed to educate us! My God, what could these monsters, who exercised power over children in order to alleviate their own miserable existences, convey to us of beauty? Why did they have to be so revolting, with their mustaches and their stooped shoulders, rather than lively and beautiful? The explanation was obvious: they were there to take their revenge. Our youth and our liveliness and maybe our dreams were an insult to them, a cruel mirror of their own debasement, the poison that inflamed their brains and their spleen. And it was these devils who were supposed to teach us the value of life, love, and friendship!

So great was my revulsion that I frequently had to go to the bathroom to throw up, clinging to the water faucet. It was the only fresh clean thing in that place. The water. I let it run to cleanse my body and especially my soul of that hemlock, and absolutely the worst thing of all was seeing my classmates, children who should have been happy, who should have had the intuition to reject them, jumping all over them, telling them things or asking them questions, or doing that typical childish thing of boasting about what you did at the weekend, we went to and such a restaurant or museum or to the country. I never did anything like that at the weekend, but even so I never understood the desire for other people to know about your life, what was the point? Just telling them about something meant ruining it, contaminating it. And there were my little classmates, the poor dummies, talking over each other to tell the teachers, and the teachers would say, that's very nice, children, your parents love you very much, you must show your gratitude and the best way is to study, so for your assignment tonight learn about the second liberation campaign, and then they'd grab their chalk and their bags and walk off, clicking their heels, and a little while later you'd see them in the staff room sticking their mouths in cups of coffee, drinking red wine, and smoking, whispering among themselves, telling each other God knows what secrets or gossip, giving each other advice on how to humiliate us even more, how to take even better revenge on life through us happy children, because of all the things they wanted to be and never succeeded in being, having turned instead into what they were, hunchbacked old crows, because, believe me, Consul, the wickedness of the soul clings to the body and deforms it, covers it in calluses and warts and other excrescences, you can see evil and you can also smell it, I experienced it every day of my childhood and adolescence, and it's why most of my classmates ended up joining that system, that way of living in hatred and resentment, what else could they do when that's what they saw every day?

I had to make an effort and resist, since there was something inside me I didn't want to contaminate, something it cost me a lot to maintain. And how did I manage? Not too badly actually, just by fantasizing, letting my mind escape from that horrible prison, which was much worse than this one, Consul. Everyone thought I was there, sitting at my desk, but in fact I was light-years away, on a beautiful planet that belonged to me, in the foothills of a solitary volcano, surrounded by deep, menacing oceans, and nobody noticed, my mask was perfect because it was constructed in their image and likeness. The mask of an idiot.

The only moments of peace I had were sometimes at recess, when I went to the sport field to watch my sister play volleyball with her friends. I loved to watch them, they were so beautiful, Juana with her chestnut skin, dancing in the air. A streak of light. That's where I spent recess, watching the ball come and go, which for them was much more than a diversion or a sport and turned into something like the goal of their young lives. It was something clean and uncontaminated: six young girls playing and believing profoundly in what they were doing. How it hurt me to hear the bell ring! They'd play for another few seconds, waiting for the field to empty, and manage to throw two or three more balls until one of the crows came and said, that's enough, girls, go back to your classes.

That's how I grew up, Consul. That was my world, and the worst of it is that outside school things weren't any better.

In the city people talked and talked without stopping, gesticulating madly, expressing stupid and ignorant opinions about everything, yelling banal phrases to make themselves heard, to stand out or get one over on the others. Such vulgarity! Everything was an absurd comedy that seemed designed to grate on your nerves. Around that time I saw two episodes of a TV series called *The Twilight Zone*. The first was the story of an invisible man. The second was about a young man who found a magic watch that could stop time, not his time but other people's, so that he could move about as he liked among people who couldn't move. The invisible man was what I aspired to be and what, deep down, I had already been for a long time, but the idea of a clock that froze other people really grabbed me: to be able to stop reality with a click! People's breathing, their stupid chatter. To be able to stop all of it!

What silence, what peace.

I always hated the things that define life in that place: the social pretentions, the desire to impress, the hatred, the congenital stinginess, the envy, all that could stop! I dreamed of pressing a button and being alone, wiping out that gesticulating verbiage; I don't know if there's anywhere else in the world where so much bullshit is said simultaneously, where so much nonsense is spoken at such a frenetic pace, and all the people who believe we speak "the best Spanish in the world," my God, as if using lots of different words had some value, as if employing a few synonyms that other people, because they're worse than ignorant, don't use and probably don't understand, gives us a right to say we have "the best Spanish in the world."

And besides, you just have to look at the TV news any day to know what such a beautiful use of the language is used for: for cutting each other's throats, for making rude remarks and jokes and well-planned accusations, have you heard how most of our governors, congressmen, councilmen, and mayors speak? In their defense, they're drunk most of the time, which may be their most sympathetic characteristic, they drink on public platforms, in Congress, in their trailers, at meetings held in squares filled with paid deaf-mutes, wherever, if it wasn't so serious you could die laughing. I'm sorry to be so emphatic, Consul, they may be friends of yours and I'm offending them, forgive me, it's what I think. In any case nobody there realizes, nobody's bothered by all that buzzing. It's the noise of insects, all swarming together. Only an image of hell, a painting by Hieronymus Bosch, could account for that horrible sound.

That's what my life was like, but one day something happened.

One night I went out onto the street and walked as far as the open sewer on 106th, a stinking trickle of water that crossed our neighborhood and sometimes, when it rained a lot, turned into a river. I liked to go there to watch the water flow, even though it was dirty water. On one side of the sewer there was a park with a few trees separating it from the houses, and on the other a wall about a hundred feet long and twelve feet high, with bars on the top. For years I'd stopped in that place, attracted by something. The sewer, the wall. I'd pass it and stop there. I'd lean over the bridge and look, I didn't really know why. In the evenings there were people smoking grass between the trees or couples necking. Garbagemen taking a nap on the lawns. I'd look and look: at the sewer, the wall.

I only found out by chance. My sister's class had been making huge cardboard models of mountains, and to paint them they'd used colored spray paints. Days later I found the box of cans in the garage and took it to my room. I looked at them for a while and chose three, one yellow, one black, one red. And I went out onto the street, Consul. There was a cool wind, the air smelled damp, as if it was going to rain, but the sky wasn't very heavy. I walked as far as the park, jumped over the sewer, and stopped in front of the wall. I looked at it for a second, grabbed the can of black paint, shook it, and heard the little ball in the can, a sound that sent a quiver through me and made me feel dizzy. I looked at the wall and traced a straight line, about twelve feet long, and then a second one parallel to it. With the yellow can I made a thick wave and with the red filled the spaces that were left, like pregnant bellies. I stepped back and contemplated what I'd done. I was moved. I went back to the wall and painted curved arrow tips and a yellow shadow, and the colors, as they were superimposed, gave off a strange glow. I ran back to the house for the green and blue cans and added a kind of bubble to that strange figure, which now looked like a snake slithering through a tunnel, and when I'd finished, moving back to the edge of the sewer to get a good look at it, under the yellowish light of the lamppost, I felt it should be signed, so I wrote MAL in red. I didn't dare put my full name, I took three letters out. From the L I traced a curved line below the word, like a floating ribbon, and felt euphoric, I took a deep breath and said to myself, how will it look in the morning? how will I see it in the morning? I went back home and put the cans away. I washed my hands with soap and got nervously into bed. That night I dreamed about remote desert islands, filled with virgin walls crying out to be painted.

T he story I want to write, the one I'm now about to tell—
the one I'm remembering and putting into some kind
of shape here in Bangkok—happened at a strange time
in my life.

In those years I was working for the diplomatic service and
had recently moved to New Delhi, a city that seemed quite
unconventional to a Latin American, which was why, or at least
so I believed, it required a somewhat adventurous frame of
mind. That's how I thought in those days. I had spent a lot of
time in Europe—twenty-four years!—telling myself that if I'd
actually been a daring kind of person—as I wanted and even
believed myself to be—I should long ago have moved somewhere tougher and more remote, like Beijing, Jakarta, or
Nairobi.

Having spent a lot of time completing my education, then
searching for stability and reaching a certain level, I was now
ready to go out and lose myself, lose what I had acquired or
swap it for new experiences. That's why, when I was offered
the post of consul in my country's embassy in India, I didn't
hesitate for a second, but got ready to abandon sad old
Europe.

Arriving in Delhi and seeing the comfort in which foreigners lived—including the diplomats of our neighboring countries—I had high hopes, but the illusion only lasted until I
found out what my salary amounted to, a figure that tact for-
bids me from specifying, as Julio Ramón Ribeyro would say,

and one that didn't even allow me to dream of the traditional areas where expatriates lived, like Vasant Vihar, Sundar Nagar, or Nizzamudin East. Instead, I had to go somewhere cheaper, a middle-class area called Jangpura Extension, which struck me at first as dusty and a bit terrifying but which in the end, as often happens, I grew to love. A person can get used to anything, even the fact that two hundred yards from his home there's a corner filled with noisy rickshaws, sleeping dogs, clapped-out taxis, a foul urinal swarming with mosquitoes, and fried food stands that are like factories for typhoid or dysentery.

The offices of the embassy were in Vasant Vihar, a rich neighborhood, although one filled with dust and having the disadvantage of being just below the flight path of planes coming in to land at Indira Gandhi International Airport, which meant that every three minutes you had to shout in order to be heard indoors.

And that wasn't all: the front of the building faced Olof Palme Marg, where bulldozers and cranes spent an absurdly long time building an overpass—a flyover in Indian English—producing mountains of dust, the noise of pneumatic drills, and the horrific smells of drains, not to mention the traffic jams. It reached a peak one afternoon when, perhaps because of all the digging to lay the concrete, a snake some seven feet in diameter crossed Olof Palme Marg and reached the doors of the embassy, where it died, crushed by the wheels of a truck, whose driver, of course, stopped, took his head in both hands, and wept, since in India all life is sacred.

My office was on the second floor, with a view of the gardens of a dusty residence that was the embassy of the Arab Emirate of Bahrain; every time I looked through the window or went out onto my magnificent balcony I would see two guards and a dog snoozing in the sentry boxes, and a bit farther on, out on the street, groups of women in saris carrying bricks in baskets on their heads to a nearby site where their husbands were working and their children were playing amid the rubble and earth.

The principal task of the consular office was to issue visas, to Indian businessmen going to Colombia to make deals, to technicians, to students, and—rarely—to tourists. We also had to process documents from the National Tax Office legalizing the invoices of companies from India, Bangladesh, and Pakistan, and even from Iran, Myanmar, Sri Lanka, and Nepal, countries where we had no diplomatic representation but whose affairs we handled. On request, the companies had to send the originals of the documents and their registration by a chamber of commerce, everything duly authenticated and translated before a notary.

And naturally there were problems and requests involving our compatriots, of whom there were only a hundred and twenty in the whole country—one for every ten million Indians—plus visitors, those who came to India and got into all kinds of trouble, most of them through having a romantic and distorted image of the country.

My colleague, Olympia León de Singh, was a woman in her early fifties who had been working there for more than ten years and knew the ins and outs of the "consular function" as nobody else did. In addition, she was the only Colombian in the mission who spoke Hindi, since she was married to a Sikh and had lived in Delhi for more than twenty years. When I asked her, she told me she had met her husband in Moscow in the 1970s, at Patrice Lumumba University, where both were studying international relations. Her stories, which she kept feeding me in snippets and only when she was in a good mood, were amazing. She told me that at the beginning of the 1980s the embassies brought in toilet paper in diplomatic bags, since you couldn't get hold of it in India, and that at the airport, during stopovers, crowds of cripples and sick people would invade the runway and get on the planes to beg!

Olympia came from the Santander region of Colombia and had been raised a Communist. When she talked about Moscow in the seventies, her eyes shone. A city of abundance, culture, art. Delhi was quite the opposite: a vast village crisscrossed by oxcarts and unpaved streets, where people died of scurvy and diarrhea and where diseases that were rare in the Soviet Union, such as leprosy, were still common. This was basically true and is still true. My daily journey from Jangpura to the office took me through an intersection where you could see the following characters: a leper wrapped in a bloodstained tunic with three stumps instead of fingers and a pink orifice where his nose should have been; two eunuchs expelled from their neighborhood who begged for money in return for not cursing you; a woman walking a baby with a burned hand—according to Peter, my driver, the burn was false, made with butter and gelatin, which cheered me—as well as people selling magazines, umbrellas, pirated books, ties, and handkerchiefs.

One of the first images from soon after my arrival in Delhi was of a man in bustling Chandni Chowk Market, a very thin man displaying an elephantine testicle and an enormous rectal prolapse, two melons hanging from a skinny, twisted body, like the cams of a giant clock. Having already seen the human bazaar massed on the steps of the Jama Masjid Mosque, including a dwarf ulcerated and deformed by polio and various lepers in a terminal state, it was obvious that in Delhi, beautiful Delhi, disquieting Delhi, diseases provided those suffering from them with a stable way to earn a living.

But let's go back to Olympia.

She was the one who, every day, brought me the problems of our community of compatriots, mainly composed of pilots for Kingfisher Airlines, young people who had come to do internships with Indian companies, and, above all, adepts of "spiritual tourism," most of them rich ladies who found relief

in the teachings of Sai Baba, Satyananda, Osho, and other contemporary philosophers who dispensed advice about life and
uttered wise sayings about peace and love.

Everything my colleague hated.

On one occasion she came into my office very upset, and
said, come and look at this, boss. Don't call me boss, I begged
her, and we went out to the reception room, where a middle-
aged Indian was waiting nervously. He had brought with him
the passport of a Colombian woman who, according to him,
"had problems." When I asked him what kind, he told me she
was a follower of the guru Ravi Ravindra and that, ever since a
particular "spiritual seminar," her mind had been confused, as
if she had a screw loose. She was twenty-seven years old.
Problems of what kind? I asked again, and the man lowered
his eyes and said:

"She wants to go out naked onto the street, she can't sleep,
she's obsessed with Ravi, she says she's going to be his wife and
wants to go with him to Indonesia."

"Indonesia?" I said, thinking it was one of the countries
whose affairs we dealt with. "Why Indonesia?"

"Ravi is going there today to give some lectures," he said.

I immediately set off to deal with the case.

They were keeping her in an apartment near Green Park.
On seeing me, the young woman said, hello, would you like a
drink? something to eat? sit down, how are you? how nice of
you to come. This volley of words made it clear how serious
things were; when I asked her how she was, she said, I'm fine,
how nice to meet you, would you like a drink? something to
eat? my taxi will be here soon, I'm going to the airport, I'm
going to meet Ravi, we're going to Indonesia, how nice to meet
you, would you like a drink? something to eat? It looked like
it could be complicated. I managed to persuade her to come
with me to see a doctor. The friend who had been putting her
up, Amrita, said she was suffering memory lapses and I wanted

her to be checked over. I was afraid that she'd been drugged, maybe even raped.

Talking to her a bit more I found out that she had met the guru in Canada and that this was her third journey with him to India. She also said that she was deeply in love with him. Do you love him in a spiritual way? I asked, and she said, yes, but also as a woman, something very beautiful has grown up between us. Amrita looked at me with eyes popping out of her head and, in an aside, assured me that these were ravings, that it couldn't be real, it was only her obsession with Ravi. I was even more perplexed. Some gurus are accused of raping Western women, weak-minded women who are easily dominated and give themselves up body and soul. Body above all. Fortunately this wasn't the case here, at least not according to the doctor in the hospital where she was under observation for a week. Then her mother came and took her back to Tokyo, where she was studying for a doctorate on a scholarship from the Japanese government. When she left, the doctor told me they'd found psychotropic substances in her urine, had she been drugged? I was never able to find out.

Another day I was in my office, I don't remember if I was reading a visa application or writing a letter to the tax authorities, when Olympia burst in saying, boss, boss, you're about to get a call from the Ministry, it's an urgent case!

When I looked at her inquisitively, wanting to know what it was about, she whispered: get ready to go to Bangkok, boss.

"Don't call me boss," I said, lifting the receiver.

Where I'm from is the least of my concerns, because people are born a number of times in the course of their lives. I might have read that somewhere, but I can't remember where. If anyone knows, please tell me. When it comes down to it, I don't really care. I've learned to live in front of my screen, traveling the world. This is my true home. Sometimes I get fits of nervous laughter, but that just indicates that I haven't taken my pill. I have problems with recent memory, like the little blue fish in the movie *Finding Nemo*. The doctor who's been treating me since my illness started tries to scare me, saying: you'll lose consciousness, fall off your chair, and you won't be able to get up. One day you'll find yourself in a world you don't know and you'll have no idea where to go, so you have to look after yourself. But I don't take anything. I'm anorexic about food and pills and things that have come through the thick, filthy air of cities.

My best friend, or rather, my man, lives in a blog called *Sensations*. His name, or the name he calls himself, is Ferenck Ambrossía. It may be a false name. It almost certainly is a false name, he wouldn't be so silly as to put his body into the scrapyard of this topsy-turvy world. I don't know where he's from or what he looks like. I don't care. Is he black, yellow, white? Is he a humanoid like those in the movie *Blade Runner*? Is he "Jewish, quechua, orangutanic, Aryan," to quote León de Greiff? Is he one man, or many men? Is he a woman, or many women? Is he a group of convicts with time off for good behavior in the penitentiary of Moundsville, now exclusively inhabited by ghosts? Is he a mental patient with access to the Internet in some Scandinavian sanatorium, who dreams of living on the same bridge along which the character in Munch's *The Scream* is walking? Or a conclave of pederast novice monks who exchange photographs of Burmese and Kenyan children on the net? Or a nervous lawyer in Edinburgh afraid of meeting the specter of Robert Louis Stevenson in the doorway of his house? Or two hysterical sisters born on Rhode Island who want to emulate Lovecraft and are getting ready to kill their parents with an ax, burn their house down, and flee north, to the country of ice? Or maybe a seller of secondhand Bibles on eBay, the pages of which are ideal for rolling joints in prison? Or a Russian porn star, who, in her free time, masturbates with an old Soviet TYPNCT-3 telescope, while weeping for her lost youth and lost empires? Is he maybe a sad young Latin American poet postponing his suicide in the hope of an unlikely signal from Rubén Darío? Or a Cameroon Airlines stewardess disappointed and angry over a French passenger on whom she performed fellatio in the toilet while the plane was flying over Chad, who promised her the earth then abandoned her? Or an Adventist priest, a follower of Lewis Carroll's brother E. H. Dodgson, who, like him, lives in the community of Edinburgh of the Seven Seas, on the fearsome island of Tristan da Cunha? Or a young Spanish teacher at the Cervantes Institute in New Delhi, born in Bihar, who reads Lope de Vega on the Internet? Or a Norwegian assistant at Río Piedras University in Puerto Rico, unwittingly made pregnant by a Ponce taxi driver, who's hesitating between calling her future child Grunewald or Hectorlavó? Is he perhaps a group of Chilean transvestites who escaped with their lives from Pinochet's dictatorship and are now composing their memoirs in verse and pursuing their apocalypse in the faculties of letters? Is he a great Mexican novelist of the post-boom generation who includes dwarves, bicycles, and Leonardo da Vinci in his books, and who could well be the author of this crazy list? Is he a young Romanian female psychologist working in the psychiatric emergency department of the Hôpital de Marne-la-Vallée, who reads Cioran surrounded by the screams of the inmates in the high-security cells? Is he the illegitimate son of a chambermaid on the seventy-eighth floor of the Mandarin Oriental Hotel in New York, where nine years ago a German rock star left syringes filled with blood in the washbowl? Is he the enemies of a dramatist raised in Salzburg whose memories are of bombing raids, floors collapsing, and cities in flames? Is he all of the previous, united in a transitory Confederation of the Stateless, chaired by the switchboard operator of a five-star hotel in Jerusalem the name of which we omit for security reasons? Or simply a novelist writing alone and against all hope, his one desire being to hide his face and be forgotten?

I don't really care who Ferenck Ambrossía is, because I love him anyway. He's my man, my male. Real life ends with the first filter. Those of us who get to my stage are pure, volatile, subtle, diaphanous, ethereal. A new race of angels. A newly born angelic militia. Oh, how happy I am on the infinite steppes of my screen! In the sugar plantations of this delightful and perfect world! The true Orplid.

From now on, I'm going to tell you a few dreams or hallucinations, subdivisions, transformations of my psyche. What does it matter what they are? Postmodernism, as Bakhtin said, is defined by its abolition of the frontier between genres. That was what Ferenck whispered to me one night, before we launched into a violent fuck via the screen. My maelstrom is inflamed just remembering it, moistening my *légèrement culottée* pantyhose and lavender Intimissimi panties, because in spite of the fact that I never leave this rhomboid space I'm not one of those who wear Victoria's Secret. I'm an elegant woman.

Anyway, dear friends. Listen to me. Hear the desperate,

anxious voice of this woman whose one objective is love, words, life. In short, poetry. Let yourselves be led by my soft round hand that knows about the affairs of men, exemplary stories that have sometimes been and may continue to be of interest to the muses.

5

The following day, before getting on the school bus, I looked at my painting on the wall. A bright snake, an almost psychedelic wave. My heart beat faster on seeing my signature, those letters in red, and I wanted to talk about it, but I restrained myself and didn't say anything to Juana. Better to keep the secret for a while and see what else there was inside it.

At school, in that boring, unhealthy classroom, I'd found something better to do than listen to those monsters croaking away: make sketches that I would later reproduce on walls. That was how I first came to draw an island surrounded by a fierce ocean. In the middle there was a huge volcano, and in its foothills a little man sitting on his own, gazing at the fury of the ocean. I made a sketch in pencil and another one in color. The volcano was a dark blue cone at first, with red and yellow edges. Then I darkened it with ocher tones. It must be a volcanic island, I thought, but I also put in a little vegetation. My arms seemed to move of their own accord. I was thirteen years old, Consul. I had just made an important discovery, which I hoped would give me strength. That's why I decided to keep it secret, not expose it to anything or anybody, for the moment.

Sometime later, another little miracle happened.

We'd come to the first year of the high school diploma course and a new teacher asked us to get some books. *Five Go to the Mystery Moor* by Enid Blyton. *The Nightingale and the Rose* by Oscar Wilde. *Five Weeks in a Balloon* by Jules Verne.

A couple of years earlier I had read a number of Blyton's books about The Five, so I thought it was a good sign and I felt quite cheerful when I went home.

Of course, the last thing my parents thought to do was buy them. As far as they were concerned, books had to be borrowed, so Mother made a few calls and managed to get hold of the one by Enid Blyton and the one by Verne. For the one by Wilde, they sent a note to the teacher saying they hadn't been able to get hold of it, and asking her to excuse me, because it was strange that my sister didn't have it among her school things from previous years, but the teacher replied with the names of bookstores where we could get hold of it and a recommendation to give the boy his own library. Mother read it and turned green with anger. That night she told Father, who blinked in disgust, but said, okay, we won't impoverish ourselves over a wretched book, how much could it cost? Hearing them, I felt nauseous. Then he looked at me and asked, what's this new teacher like? I didn't know what to say, and shrugged my shoulders. She's like the others, Dad, I replied. And is she young? he wanted to know, and I said, I don't know, Dad, I don't know how old she is, but he insisted, already with a throb in his voice that presaged anger, I'm not asking you her exact age, I just want to know if she's young, it's not such a difficult question, is the teacher young? Yes, I said, younger than the others, and she's new, she started this year.

Father snorted and said, of course, that explains it! She must be one of those silly new graduates who come into a job and want to disrupt everything, turn it all upside down, I've seen them in the office, I know what they're like! the ones who think that just because they're good with computer programs and files they know it all, and because they're young and pretty their bosses agree to everything. I hate them. Anyway, Bertha, buy the boy his book tomorrow, we're not going to give her the pleasure of humiliating us.

The next day we went to the National Bookstore in the Unicentro Mall, Mother resignedly and me secretly happy, and when one of the assistants brought it I couldn't help giving a nervous laugh, it was really beautiful! Mother looked at the price, made a face, and asked if there was a cheaper edition, so the assistant went to the back room and I stayed with her by the counter, feeling embarrassed. It was strange: Mother stood there with her mouth pursed, looking dignified and even proud, as if demanding compensation for an insult, as if the assistants in the store ought to be paying us to be there. After a while the young man came back with another edition, an illustrated one, which fortunately was more expensive, so Mother decided to buy the first one. Of course, when we got home, she made sarcastic remarks about the price, and said, we'll have to cover it so that it doesn't get damaged, that way we'll be able to sell it next year, if that stupid teacher is still at the school. I was so happy to have it, even if only for a few months, that I didn't care about the pettiness of it all, and I ran upstairs to my room. For the first time, I had a new book! I clasped it to my chest and said to myself, this one beautiful object will help me to pull through.

But life goes on and gets to us, Consul, and unfortunately things start all over again, so that after that little joy there I was once more, sitting at the table in the dining room in front of an unappetizing dish. I had to make a great effort to eat anything, and to put up with Father's comments, because by now he was already starting to proclaim, ever more insistently, the country's need for a savior, someone who would come in with a firm hand and restore order, reestablish harmony, clear the air. Change the atmosphere in which we were living.

I don't know what was going on in his work or in his inner life, if he had one, but it was clear that suddenly, without anything particular happening, Father had started to change. Having previously had few political opinions, and moderate ones at that, he now spoke passionately about what he read in the press or saw on the TV news. Whatever he was thinking just had to come out, and it came out in the strangest ways. It's very likely that what he said to us at the dinner table was what he would have liked to say at work, but nobody there listened to him. His opinions didn't interest anybody. At home, on the other hand, we were obliged to hear them and that's what we did, stoically, hear that endless droning, that litany of rancor toward reality and the present day, that ultimate in resentment, depicting a country in a situation of chaos and moral collapse from which it could only emerge thanks to a true patriot, and who could else could that be but that soldier of Christ and champion of order, Álvaro Uribe, who at the time, very close to the elections, was already flying high in the opinion polls?

Father was mesmerized by Uribe.

It was that enthusiasm that turned him into a man with strong opinions, a secret amateur columnist, and Mother, hearing him talking about topics she considered of major importance, must have thought her husband had at last stopped being a resentful but docile bureaucrat and had turned into something new, a citizen whose ideas were appreciated and discussed by others, and which he shared generously with his family in order to show them the way, an ideological and moral beacon who filled her with pride.

I guess that's why we had to put up with that pantomime and listen to him talk about politics, economics, recent history, as if instead of being in the dining room of his house he was on a TV show, debating with experts, and so he kept giving us arguments and counterarguments, without anybody contradicting him. He would present objections and answer them, interrupt himself and take over, a horrible spectacle that made me feel ashamed for him, a spectacle designed to exacerbate my sense of the ridiculous and my own self-esteem.

It was like being hit in the stomach, squeezed by pincers, it was my own Loch Ness Monster starting to emerge and I closed my eyes, trying to escape, to go far away, but when my hallucinations finished and I came back to the table he was still there, endlessly spouting his opinions, quickly gulping a mouthful of rice in order not to lose the thread, saying things that sounded false even though they might have been right, ideas that, uttered by him, were pure bullshit: that in Colombia the terrorists had become stars, that everyone wanted to have their photographs taken with them, that it was incredible that anyone could still be talking about negotiating, that Tirofijo's empty seat next to Pastrana was a mockery, a symbol of a total lack of principles, and he'd repeat ardently, the blood rushing to his cheeks, what we need here is a firm hand, we have to make sacrifices, if you don't believe me look at Chile, which is an example now to the whole of Latin America, here we have to take over the helm and change direction, and we have to do so with resolution, a sense of duty, and a love of our country, and Mother, feeling obliged to support what he said, as if we were on *Big Brother* or some daytime quiz show, would say to him, oh, Alberto, I hope God hears you, Álvaro Uribe is the only one who isn't talking about making deals and handing the country over to the guerrillas, quite the opposite, he wants to fight them, that's the only language the terrorists understand, fight them and keep fighting, he's going to stand up to them, oh, yes, and let's hope those other crooks, rich kids, and traitors just go away.

And Father would say, yes, Bertha, the other candidates are the spoiled children of this country, they're all from foreign schools, always looking outside, people who feel ashamed of being Colombian, that's how they are and that's why they're handing over the country, whereas Uribe comes from the middle classes and from the mountains of Antioquia, with all the moral values and traditional courage of the countryside, that's what we need, a man who loves Colombia, who if you opened his veins would ooze Colombian blood, with pride, and that's something we've never seen in a candidate, Uribe is the first one to talk about true patriotism, national dignity, to glorify the flag and stand up to terrorism, and that's why I say, Bertha, that if Uribe doesn't win, we'll have to scoop this country up from the floor with a spoon, and we may even have to ask the gringos to send in the Marines to sort out our problem for us, the way it happened in Panama, and we'll have to swallow the humiliation, how can there be people who don't realize? You just have to see his slogan: "A firm hand and a big heart."

They would talk and talk for more than an hour, and since Juana was always studying at the house of one of her friends, I had to face it all by myself, unable to get up from the table until they'd brought their pathetic show to an end.

I often dreamed of running away, Consul: going out one morning and not getting on the school bus. Or rather: the two of us not getting on the school bus. I couldn't run away unless it was with Juana. I couldn't leave her behind, in our everyday life. Sometimes I'd say to her, Juana, when are we leaving? why do we have to wait so long? and she'd reply, you don't have to do anything, just wait, I'm going to arrange everything and when it's ready we'll go away forever, far from this hell. We'll go away without leaving anything that'll help them trace us.

Hearing her, my heart would thump in my chest. All that sacrifice was going to have an end, and that end was near. The two of us were working for the same thing: she with her intelligence and her strength and I with my capacity to resist. We'd get away from this rabid world and build a better one.

Books helped me, but I still had to get them.

A neighbor on the block had an enormous library, but didn't like to read. His parents were teachers and they bought him children's books, but he was only interested in football, Internet sex, and American cable TV series. He was fourteen years old. His name was Víctor and one day I suggested a deal: if he passed them on to me, I'd read them and then tell him the story, and that way we'd both be happy: he could devote himself to football, RedTube, and HBO, and I could do all the reading I wanted.

He agreed.

That was how I came to read Mark Twain's stories of Tom Sawyer and Huckleberry Finn, *White Fang* and *Call of the Wild* by Jack London, and things by Joseph Conrad like *Lord Jim* and *Heart of Darkness*, and the sad, exotic adventures of David Balfour by Stevenson, and *Ivanhoe* by Walter Scott, and the works of Rudyard Kipling, especially *Kim*. Soon after, little by little, came Salgari's series about Sandokan and the Tigers of Malaysia, *The Count of Monte Cristo* by Dumas, and *King Solomon's Mines* by Rider Haggard.

Usually, we got together in his room.

Time passed.

One day he was in the back garden of his house, kicking a ball at the wall, while I told him the story of the latest Salgari novel he had been given. Without our noticing, his mother arrived and heard everything from upstairs. When I'd finished the story, which if I remember correctly was *Sandokan Fights Back*, Víctor said, good, let me bring you the latest. I stayed out in the garden, waiting for him, and saw his mother come out.

Hello, Manuelito, I heard you telling Víctor the story of a novel, do you read his books?

I froze. We'd been discovered.

Goodbye, novels.

But his mother said: you can take whatever books you like. I'll lend them to you. And it isn't necessary for you to tell Víctor the stories. If he doesn't want to read them, we'll see about that.

A moment later Víctor arrived with a book in his hand, and when he saw her he hid it under his jacket, but she said, don't hide it, give it to Manuel. Books are for those who read them.

That's how I gained a library.

In my house it was the opposite, I had to hide them or pretend they came from school in order not to draw attention to them, because Father said with pride that he couldn't just sit there doing nothing and that's why he didn't read novels or watch movies, why he only read biographies and newspapers and watched the TV news, that way he could spend time sitting in his chair, sometimes with a notebook in which he wrote things down that he later used in his speeches at the dinner table. Father despised the world of culture. He hated it because he felt excluded from it.

When Uribe won the elections, Father was so pleased that he went to the neighborhood store for a bottle of Molino Rojo champagne and that night, that Sunday night, he uncorked it at the table, and served all of us, including me, and raised his glass saying, this country has been saved, dammit, it's been saved, long live life, there's a future, now those terrorists are going to see. I gulped down that horrible drink and didn't say a word. Juana did the same, not caring very much, but Father and Mother gave each other a big hug and when they separated I saw that they had tears in their eyes. The country has been saved, Bertha, he kept saying, emotionally, and Mother repeated, it's been saved, Alberto, and they hugged each other again, and so on until the bottle was finished. Then they went out on the street to watch the parade of cars going along Seventh, celebrating with music and honking horns, the buses making a great din, that cloud of joy rising into the air and coming to rest on the hills.

The country had been saved.

Father bought bracelets with the flag of Colombia and decals that said *I am a Colombian*. He felt proud. My only concern was for him to stop making his speeches, so I distanced myself from all that, which deep down I didn't care about, and devoted myself to my wall.

With my spray cans I painted another island surrounded by

ocean, with protective cliffs and a little house near the shore, where I imagined Juana and I were living, and below the island, which floated like a cork, I painted dragons with huge jaws trying to swallow it, and a beautiful smoking volcano, and at the side I again put my signature, MAL, of which I was very proud, just like father with Uribe. It was the fourth time I had painted something big near the sewer, and I thought, when would I dare to paint on other walls, far from the neighborhood and my house? One way or another, going out into the city meant breaking through the protective shell of childhood.

The truth is, I was nervous.

I also started to experiment with the shapes of some letters. The S a viper of fire in the sky, biting the night. The M a mountain, the feet of a strange Martian. The U an old cabalistic sign, a horseshoe in reverse, the imminence of fire and pain. The J a seahorse because it was Juana's letter, in other words, it meant my freedom, my hope. I foreshortened them, gave them depth and volume. Some shapes I made were kitsch, others classical. I imitated Garamond and Boldoni typefaces. I painted sunrises. I painted an image of the seabed that came to me in dreams, thick darkness with one open eye, the eye of some fish or other.

The history of the country was moving forward.

Not much time passed—a year, six months, do you remember, Consul?—before the joy of Uribe's victory started to crack and sunlight to filter in through the cracks. As often happens, it was a few intellectuals who sounded the alarm. They criticized Uribe for behaving like a provincial Messiah, always talking about the Virgin Mary, and started alluding to his relationship with the death squads and the paramilitaries.

Father closed his ears, he couldn't accept it. His rejection of the intellectual world became a matter of national security—as he put it—and when he saw what was happening he overflowed with justifications and reasons.

I told you! he would cry, what this country doesn't need is that herd of pundits, and not just them, the whole mob of intellectuals who live from one cocktail to another, rich kids, idlers who spend their time criticizing the president without suggesting anything better and talking ill of the country, because let's make no mistake about this, they're the ones who really give Colombia bad press, what do they care? most of them come from foreign schools, they're brought up to admire France or England or the United States, so what does it matter to them? That's why they criticize the president and only talk about the bad things that happen here, talking about them in Europe and the United States, why do they never talk about the good things? why do they never mention the heroes of our history, or the martyrs? why don't they say that Colombia is a power in biodiversity, in flora and fauna, that it has every possible climate and lots of greenery and clean water and blue skies? why don't they talk about how good it is to live in Bogotá, in spite of the problems, and how great it is to have a temperate climate like the climate in Melgar or Girardot just forty minutes away? oh, no, they can't say that because nobody's interested, speaking well of Colombia doesn't sell, don't you see? that's why they keep talking about the murderers in this country and the drug traffickers in this country and the hit men and the prostitutes and all the dead in this country, as if those things didn't exist everywhere! that's the truth, the sad truth, Father said whenever for some reason somebody, usually my sister, mentioned what some writer or intellectual had said against the government.

And as the years went by, he got worse and worse.

He just had to hear some name mentioned by Juana and he immediately came out with the same old story: on one side there's us, standing shoulder to shoulder with the president, waging war on FARC and on Chávez and on all the Communists in Latin America, and on the other side there's them, always criticizing, as if they didn't know that what they're saying helps our enemies, how many of those hippies are really Communists, Chavists, or even members of FARC? If they like it so much why don't they go into the mountains or to Venezuela or Cuba! let's see if they're allowed to criticize things there, oh yes, I'd like to see that! If they said in Caracas or Havana half of what they say in Bogotá they'd be thrown in prison, and as most are columnists, worse still, that's why decent people have to rally around the president, who's an upright man and, what's more, a believer. This country has always been Catholic, there's nothing new about that, why does everyone criticize him when he mentions the Virgin Mary in his speeches? what's wrong with him praying on television? It's normal in a Catholic country, haven't they seen how Bush goes to mass and talks about God and nobody says anything? Why keep saying that about the president? I mean, even Chávez quotes the Bible at every opportunity! It makes them angry and they criticize, but the truth is that we've never been better and we've never been respected so much in Washington.

Juana, who was already in tenth grade and had gotten used to answering back, would retort and say, what do you mean, Dad, respected? on the contrary, we're a pure banana republic, I feel ashamed when I see Uribe going to Washington to show the figures for the Free Trade Agreement, which they're never going to agree to while he's president, and you know why? because there they have reports about crimes, about the State's responsibility for massacres, reports they compiled themselves, or do you think the gringos rely on our local columnists to judge Colombia?

Father would lose his temper and say, what crimes of the State, no way, since when is fighting terrorism a crime? If the gringos had allowed the same NGOs in Iraq or Afghanistan that they've set up here, they'd all be in prison, from the Secretary of Defense down, but that's because the terrorists, how shall I put this? aren't students throwing Molotov cocktails, that's why the army has to act like any other army in the world and when that happens there are always victims, so what? Whatever those idiots you read say, nothing is happening here that hasn't already happened in all the countries where there's ever been a war, but because it's us, we're asked to do it with surgical gloves on.

Daddy, you're a fascist and a paramilitary! Juana would yell, like most people in this damned country, what a dumb country! gross!

Then she'd grab her jacket and go out, slamming the door, simultaneously with Mother crying, what a rude girl! but Father would intervene, leave her, Bertha, she's always trying to pick a fight, these teenage years of Juanita's will be the death of us, but we have to understand her, let her go for a walk and calm down, when you're young you're rebellious and you like to argue.

I'd sit there, glued to my chair, wishing I could take out my watch and freeze them, and as soon as I had the chance, I'd creep up to my room, grab a book, and start reading fervently, as if those signs were magic words that could take me out of that place and carry me far away, forever.

When I turned fifteen, Father and Mother decided to throw a party, and although I begged them not to, they insisted on inviting the family and a few friends. You wouldn't believe they did it for me, Consul, obviously not; it was for them, to satisfy that ridiculous social fiction that obliges people to celebrate their children's fifteenth birthdays. Juana had a study trip and couldn't cancel it, so I was going to be on my own. As they wanted me to have friends of mine there, I asked Víctor, the guy from the block, because I refused to invite any of my classmates from school.

It was horrible, going with Mother to buy clothes for the party. In every shop she'd complain about the prices, tell off

the assistants, and ask for discounts, or ask if they didn't have
the same thing but cheaper. The assistants all looked at her
with a mixture of mockery and commiseration. Until the day of
the party came. I don't know how to describe it to you, Consul.
I spent the afternoon praying that seven o'clock would never
come, that was the time the guests started to arrive, uncles and
aunts and cousins of Mother's, and a couple of colleagues from
the bank, all with their gifts, ridiculous things, a plastic photo
frame, an Avianca Airlines toiletry bag, two pairs of socks, a
spectacle case, a box of handkerchiefs with strange initials, a
tie with the word Carvajal at the bottom, things they must have
been given for Christmas or birthdays and that they were getting rid of, until Víctor arrived with his father and gave me two
gifts. The first was a pair of goalkeeper's gloves and some
kneepads, and the second was a box of books. Inside there was
a note that said:

> For the young reader of the neighborhood on his fifteenth
> birthday. A dozen novels. With pride,
>
> P and C

Mother looked at it scornfully and said, how stupid of me,
it was such a big box, I thought it was something good, and
Father, who thanked the neighbors, looked and said, hmm,
funny, they must be clearing shelves! but anyway, you don't
look a gift horse in the mouth, we can keep these for other
birthdays, you always have to look on the bright side, isn't that
right, Manuelito? and I said, no, Dad, these books are mine,
and he said, having already had a few drinks, all right, keep
them if you want, son, but you're not going to turn into one of
those long-haired intellectuals, are you?

I still remember the titles.

Four of the twelve were a single novel, *The Alexandria
Quartet*, by Lawrence Durrell; *The Time of the Hero* by Mario

Vargas Llosa; *All Fires the Fire* by Julio Cortázar; and *Aura* by Carlos Fuentes; the rest was Colombian literature: *Big Mama's Funeral, Que viva la música!, La nieve del Almirante, Sin remedio*, and *El desbarrancadero*.

Víctor helped me get through that horrible party, in which, for the first time, I drank soda laced with Cordillera rum, the cheapest there was in the supermarket. I had to make an effort to tolerate the tide of relatives and friends, who were all there out of obligation. It wasn't hard to catch them exchanging mocking glances. Father's colleagues from the bank made faces when they tasted the rum, looked scornfully at the glasses, and held back their laughter, as if saying, what is this concoction we're being given by this nobody at his son's birthday party? The worst of it was seeing Father go up to them and say, with a stupid smile, is everything all right? how about a toast, and the two guys would raise their glasses, hugging him and giving him the finger behind his back with the other hand. Mother's female cousins, who only drank soda, fingered the cheap fabric of the curtains or passed their hands over the shiny covers of the furniture and looked at each other, trying hard to contain their laughter.

Everyone at the party was making fun of Father and Mother, but they didn't realize, on the contrary, they kept proposing ridiculous toasts, requesting silence to make speeches in which they congratulated their son and thanked the guests, and Father even said, absurdly, that he "felt honored" by the presence of his work colleagues, who by now were laughing at him quite openly, to his face, but he didn't get the message and continued with his pathetic farce, he and Mother, both thinking themselves great hosts, serving a horrible sweet wine with the food that made everybody laugh.

Watching that unbearable spectacle, I felt as if a monster had gotten into my stomach and was tearing it to shreds; I was tempted to side with the guests and make jokes, but how could

I? An hour later, Father was completely drunk, demanding friendly hugs from his colleagues, who continued making ever more unpleasant jokes at which he laughed uproariously, anyway, Consul, I'm sorry to go into such detail about that night, I don't know why I remember it so clearly now.

Juana wasn't there, as I already said.

Around that time she started spending more and more time away.

Sometimes she'd get back very late, in the early hours of the morning, and come to my room. She'd take off her clothes, which smelled of cigarettes, alcohol, and sweet things, put on one of my T-shirts, grab me, and whisper in my ear: embrace me with all your might, you're the only person I love in this damned world, and I'd embrace her and she'd keep saying, you're the only person I'd protect, the only one I'd give my life for, you don't know what a pigsty it is out there, don't go thinking it's better than this; there too there are sharks and stagnant waters, frozen skies and clouds, but we're going to fight and we're going to take off for a country where nobody knows us and we can be happy, and then she'd start crying, because she was a little drunk.

I'd embrace her and say, I'm ready, when you say the word I'll go blindly, holding your hand. Suddenly I'd realize that she was asleep, that I'd been whispering into her deaf ear for some time, and I wondered what worlds she had returned from, so fragile and yet so brave, so full of things she preferred not to talk about and I preferred not to know.

After a while I too would fall asleep, listening to her heart.

6

I t was a call from the Foreign Ministry, specifically from the Department for Consular Affairs. I don't remember the name of the assistant director or deputy director who told me about the case, but he did so in a tone that seemed a tad sardonic. I was to fly to Bangkok that same evening. The Thai police had reported to the Ministry the arrest of a Colombian national with a small consignment of opiate pills in a hotel in the city; since Thai law was somewhat draconian, he would need legal and logistical help, even though there wasn't much hope for him. For this type of felony, thirty years was common, although the public prosecutor would ask for the death penalty, which made it a delicate matter.

"In other words," the man said, "another fellow countryman who's going to rot in a foreign cell, nothing to write home about, except that in this case it's a bit more dramatic, what with snakes and huge mosquitoes and unconventional languages. We don't have an embassy in Thailand, and normally it'd fall within the jurisdiction of Malaysia, but the post of consul is vacant there. Nobody in Kuala Lumpur can deal with it, so you see, that's why we thought of you. We've already arranged travel expenses and tickets. I think they have a reservation for you for today, what time is it there?"

Almost all flights from Delhi leave after midnight. That's why the Thai Airways one to Bangkok was a night flight.

I boarded at two in the morning and, three and a half hours later, the screeching of the plane's wheels woke me. A policeman stamped my passport and welcomed me. I underwent the formalities for diplomats. Then I walked through the huge glass doors and was hit by the first wave of heat.

Thailand is the tropics of Asia.

A taxi. Crossing the city at dawn to the Hotel Oriental. A pretty postmodern roof deck over the river, a room on an upper floor with a view of the skyscrapers. Just time for a shower before I dashed to the Thai Foreign Ministry, where they were expecting me.

The head of protocol greeted me at the door of the building with a copy of the case file, we walked up a flight of stairs, and he showed me into the prosecutor's office.

"Don't go thinking this is *Midnight Express*, right?" the prosecutor said in fairly refined English.

He was a short man. His face seemed to occupy half his bodily mass, and had no doubt seen better days (the marks of his acne were even more pronounced than mine). An employee in a white uniform brought in a tray with tea and biscuits. Everyone was smiling. It was the land of smiles, even if, in his case, the smile concealed a certain nervousness.

"We've had all kinds of things here," the prosecutor said. "Let me confess something to you."

He took me over to the window and pointed to the center of the city.

"Do you think I like knowing that most of those who come to my country don't do so because of its heritage or its history, but to sleep with our women? Oh, sure, they visit the Reclining Buddha and they go to Phuket and the temples of Ayutthaya, but first things first. They take an interest in the country only after they've had their way with one of our women, a woman who might be from my own family, anyway, I'm sorry if I strike you as crude or impolite, you're a diplomat and I'm not, I'm only an officer of the law, but how would you feel if your country, known for its drugs, turned into a whorehouse? wouldn't you try, in every way possible, to at least make sure the law was enforced? The law, the law," he said, his mind wandering a little, "is the only thing still keeping us from going crazy."

Before sitting down he looked me straight in the eyes and said:

"Let me tell you a joke. An Australian joke. To Australians, Thailand is a paradise, and I'm not surprised: young women, parties, casinos. They buy fake branded goods, they dirty our beaches, they live like kings, and they pay almost nothing. An Australian dies and goes to heaven. There, God says to him: you've been good, you're entitled to have one wish granted. The man thinks it over for a while and says, I'd like to go back to Thailand! So God, being understanding, lets him go back to Thailand, only transformed into a Thai, ha ha, do you get it? The Australians laugh a lot at that."

The prosecutor took out a handkerchief and wiped his eyes. Not a single muscle in my face had moved in response to his joke, and he appreciated that.

"This whole situation, I'll tell you right now, doesn't help to make us especially understanding toward strangers, at least not me. Bangkwang Prison may seem to you somewhat . . . harsh, yes, that's the word. There isn't a prison in the world that isn't, is there? Violence is the midwife of history. This kind of history, at least. They call Bangkwang the Bangkok Hilton. Even I'm shocked by it, but I never forget that its 'guests' aren't there because they talked at a religious retreat or drove through a red light. Yesterday I lifted the body of a young woman who jumped from the fourteenth floor of a tower in Bangkok Central. Her body, if you don't me saying this, looked quite horrible lying there on the asphalt surface of a parking lot, like a piece of nonfigurative art. She was nineteen years old and her stomach was stuffed full of pills. Those guys are murderers, shall I describe to you how her parents looked? I don't have to, see for yourself."

He held out the local paper and there they were, a couple my age, both with expressions of horror on their faces.

Then he said:

"Now then, let me show you your compatriot's case."

He opened a copy of the same folder I had and read out the facts:

Manuel Manrique, 27 years old, Colombian, passport number 96670209, visa number 31F77754WZ, entered Thailand by plane, coming from Dubai, on Emirates flight 1957, on . . . 22nd, checked in at the Regency Inn Hotel, a three-star establishment, room 301, Suan Plu Soi 6, Sathorn Road, Thungmahamek, Silom, Bangkok. He was arrested there on . . . 24th in possession of a bag containing four hundred ecstasy pills made in Burma.

The accused had been planning to leave the country on . . . 24th for Tokyo on Japan Airlines flight 2108. His contacts in the country are unknown, as is the way in which he obtained the drugs. Given the weight of evidence the prosecutor is asking for the death penalty or thirty years' imprisonment if he pleads guilty.

I was surprised that he had planned to go to Tokyo, and I said to the prosecutor, why Tokyo?

"I don't know," he said, "and frankly, I don't care. There are Mafias and drug addicts there too, and countrymen of mine and yours who live off that, and get up to all the dirty business they can. The Japanese are strange at first sight and you may think for a while that they're different, but deep down they consume the same shit as everybody else. They just have more money, that's all."

"And where was he going after Tokyo?" I wanted to know.

"I don't know, look in the attached documents, I think there's a photocopy of the airline ticket."

I leafed through and saw a copy of his passport. He had a visa to enter Japan. The ticket was a return ticket. His return flight to Colombia was from Bangkok via Dubai and São Paulo to Bogotá. Strange.

"When can I see him?"

The prosecutor stroked his beard, looked at his watch, and said: "Let me make a suggestion: go back to your hotel and sleep for a while, you look tired. Oh, these night flights . . . I don't suppose you'll find the heat and humidity too excessive, coming from Delhi. Nobody can explain how human beings with spines and brains ever thought to build a city in that place, with those temperatures. As I said, you should rest. Then treat yourself to a copious lunch and try our traditional cuisine. In the afternoon, cross the river and have a look at the temples. Go to an English bookstore, buy something, have a stroll around, then go back to your hotel at the end of the afternoon. Have a light dinner and go to sleep. I'll come and pick you up at seven in the morning to take you to Bangkwang."

I went back to the hotel and sat down at the bar. I hadn't seen much of Bangkok, but had a sense of a slow, endless traffic jam, concrete bridges between the buildings, fast food stands, markets. The deafening din of the *tuk-tuks* (cousins to the rickshaws of Delhi). It wasn't the first city in Asia I'd visited.

It was about eleven in the morning.

I took out the file and switched on my laptop. Opening my e-mail, I found a message from the Consular Department with Manuel Manrique's record as an attachment: it was clean! No legal proceedings, no run-ins with the police. Nothing. A poor rookie who'd tried it once and fallen in the attempt. That wasn't so unusual. After all, he was only twenty-seven years old. And something else that I'd seen in the file: the only stamps in his passport were from this journey. He had never been outside Colombia before. The passport had only recently been issued.

It was hot and the gin was good. I carried on reading and the surprises started.

According to the Consular Department file, Manrique had graduated in philosophy and letters from the National University and was studying for his doctorate. A philosopher? Now that *was* unusual. With what I had, I went on the Internet and started searching. I asked for a bite to eat, ravioli or the kind of meat snacks I'd seen on the street. Something that could be eaten with one hand. Various things appeared: his graduate thesis on Gilles Deleuze and three articles in the faculty review: one on Spinoza, another on post-Fordism, and a third on Chomsky. Hell. He was an educated guy, what the hell was he doing in Thailand? Why was he on his way to Tokyo instead of returning to Colombia with the pills? Who on earth was this Manuel Manrique?

The snack was good, with an aromatic sauce and a touch of sesame in oil. I tried to open some of the articles but the portals of the philosophy reviews weren't very modern. You could only consult the index, the rest was in grey. I looked for him on Facebook, but there were 1,086 profiles with the name Manuel Manrique. Philosophy, though? I immediately wrote to my philosopher friend Gustavo Chirolla.

Do you know someone named Manuel Manrique who studied philosophy at the National University? He's twenty-seven now. He may have finished three or four years ago. I'll tell you why later.

For a while I looked at the Chao Phraya, its brown waves, the canoes and sampans taking the tourists across, the oily reflections of the sun. The river moved at a thick crawl. The water wasn't clear. Something painful seemed to flow in it.

Much to my surprise, Gustavo's answer arrived immediately, what time was it in Colombia? barely midnight of the day before.

Gustavo said:

Yes, I knew a Manuel Manrique. He was a postgraduate student of mine at the National four years ago. A shy boy, rather quiet. Very intelligent. He was very interested in literature and films, and in the image. That's why he was studying Deleuze. I remember talking to him about the poetics of Rimbaud, and about Godard and Bergman. I was struck by how thin he was. He looked like something out of a painting by El Greco or a sculpture by Giacometti. With a gleam in his eyes, as if he was on the verge of asking something urgent and sensitive, but which he never managed to ask. He finished his postgraduate studies and I never saw him again. Let me make some inquiries and see if I can find out anything else. Have you met him? Is he in India? Let me know.

I wrote back:

I haven't seen him yet, but he's in prison in Bangkok. Pills. Don't tell anyone, this is confidential. I'm trying to find out who he is, because I have to deal with the case. Ask what circles he moved in, who he mixed with. We have to handle this with caution. I don't know if his family has been informed.

All the best.

I kept searching. What the hell had a philosopher come to Thailand for? At first glance, I couldn't believe he might be guilty. I remembered the prosecutor's advice, that I should look at temples. Nothing could have been farther from the way I felt, but I decided to go out anyway. Better not to be seen spending too much time in the bar, this was a business trip, and I had to stay for a few days. It wasn't at all unlikely that the prosecutor was investigating me, even spying on my movements at that very moment, obsessed as he was with protecting his country from undesirable elements. I went out.

It was hot on the street and I hailed a taxi.

"Bangkok Central," I said.

I stopped near a commercial area and started walking aimlessly. Before long, I came to a hotel, and I went in and headed for the bar. The light was pleasant there. I ordered a gin and tonic and got down to business. Deleuze. University of Vincennes. It rang a bell.

Years earlier, when I was a correspondent for the newspaper *El Tiempo* in Paris, the French writer Daniel Pennac, in an interview, had told me that he had been a pupil of Deleuze at the University of Vincennes and that in his classes, where political and aesthetic issues were hotly debated, Deleueze had decreed the death of the novel. But Pennac had in his bag, well hidden, the recently published translation of *The Green House* by Mario Vargas Llosa. If they had discovered him he would have been the laughingstock of the year, but he couldn't wait to lock himself in the bathroom and carry on reading.

Later, still in Paris, it had fallen to me to write about the suicide of Deleuze. He had jumped from the balcony of his house onto Boulevard Neil. Another "nonfigurative" death, like that of the young girl the prosecutor had told me about. Deleuze was ill and the pain had become unbearable. If I remembered correctly, it was a respiratory illness, perhaps emphysema. I took out my laptop and searched my files. The article was there, dated November 1995. I reread it:

DEATH OF A PHILOSOPHER
Paris

In despair thanks to a progressive respiratory infection, the French philosopher Gilles Deleuze dragged himself to the window of his house in the seventeenth arrondissement of Paris and threw himself out, bringing to an end seventy years of life and philosophy. The last journey of this nomad lasted barely a few seconds, crossing the air until he slammed into the sidewalk of Boulevard Neil and lay there in the cold, at eight in the evening. Passersby gathered around the body and minutes later an ambulance carried it to hospital, where he died. It is unlikely that those who tried desperately to save his life knew that in that bruised body lay one of the most unorthodox thinkers of the century, the great agitator of the University of Vincennes in the 1970s, author of such key works as *Anti-Oedipus* and *A Thousand Plateaus*, the thinker whom Michel Foucault called "the only philosophical mind in France."

He was born in Paris on January 18, 1925, and his life was spent in classrooms and cafés. He entered the Sorbonne in 1944 and from 1948 worked as a teacher in various places, a high school in Orléans, another in Amiens, until he obtained a professorship in Lyons in 1964, and finally arrived in Paris in 1968, at the University of Vincennes, where he left his mark on a whole generation that experienced May '68 alongside him and remained in a state of permanent revolt. Those who were his pupils remember his classes as veritable explosives launched against morality and tradition. The young women who began the year in patent leather shoes and tartan skirts ended it converted into agitators for free love, raising their voices against the establishment and cohabiting with Palestinian guerrillas, refugees from Cyprus, rebels from Guatemala, Nigeria, or Pakistan. Deleuze was the great time bomb of Vincennes, and his classes, which ended in the neighboring bars, were aimed straight at the heart of Conservative morality. The two crucial encounters of his life took place in 1962 and 1968: the first with Michel

Foucault and the second with Félix Guattari, his collaborator on much of his work.

His work began in 1953 with *Empiricism and
Subjectivity,* where he sketched his theory of the "multiple,"
and continued in 1962 with *Nietzsche and Philosophy,
Kant's Critical Philosophy* in 1963, and *Proust and Signs* in
1964. One of the characteristics of Deleuze is his rereading
of classic philosophers, so that he wrote about Bergson,
Bacon, Spinoza, and Leibniz, but also about Kafka,
Melville, and other writers (*Essays Critical and Clinical*).
Deleuze's vision is neither conformist nor explanatory: it is
a flashlight that shows us something previously unseen, that
tries to clarify a moment. It is difficult to grasp the work of
Deleuze as a totality, since it encompasses cinema, literature,
history, science, music, daily life, politics . . . Everything.

After the death of Michel Foucault from AIDS in 1984,
that of Louis Althusser in 1990 after being confined to a
psychiatric hospital for strangling his wife, and the suicide
of the situationist Guy Debord, the death of Gilles Deleuze
brings the Parisian school of philosophy to a tragic end,
establishing a macabre statistic. The ideas nevertheless
remain, resting on this definitive assertion by Michel
Foucault: "One day, perhaps, the century will be Deleuzian."

I read it twice.

I was surprised to realize how much I'd known about
Deleuze at the time. I'd never been comfortable with abstract
thought, and most likely I'd turned to Gustavo for help, but I
can't remember now. Nor can I explain how it was that it was
published in the section *Life Today,* because the article isn't
exactly exciting from a journalistic point of view.

It was time to get moving, so I went back out on the street.
Night was falling.

I walked aimlessly until I saw, on an upper floor, a sign that read "Bangkok Rare Books." I went in without thinking. They had travel books from the beginning of the twentieth century and a literature section with editions of Graham Greene for $850. I passed my hand over the spines of *The Power and the Glory*, Heinemann, London, 1940, and *The End of the Affair*, Heinemann, London, 1951.

Except for the temples, I'd followed the prosecutor's advice. My budget forbade me from buying any of this, or even sniffing it. But what a pleasure. I left old Graham Greene happily enough, and went down to look for a last drink before going back to the hotel.

D o you want to know, O mortal, what my most unmentionable desires are? Friend: those are precisely the ones you will never know, that's why they are unmentionable, but I can tell you others, simple things, did you know that there are cities in this vast world through which, some days, I'd like to wander? I'm dying to do that! To be part of the crowd, even if only for a few hours or minutes, to lose myself in the streets and subway stations, attend their help centers, look for relief in their help lines for lonely people.

What are these cities?

I will talk to you about one among the many in my nocturnal constellation, because there are stars that shine with greater intensity. Let's see, let's see, what is that beautiful, coppery, not-quite-golden light on the right-hand side of my map? What's the name of that star washed up close to the sea, at the beginning of a wide arm, like a baby's inert limb?

It's Bangkok.

The Asian capital of smiles. The capital of foot massage and other kinds, like the "body to body" (which may include a "happy ending," just imagine), multiple relaxation, anti-depression, and anti-jet-lag massages. There are 36,874 registered massage parlors. The body is connected by nerve endings to the soles of the feet and from there you can control and remedy deficiencies and boost energy. A strange machine, the body! You can help it to be happy.

Bangkok resembles that old TV series, *Fantasy Island:* "Its possibilities are limited only by the imagination." And so you ask yourself: imagine? imagine? But . . . What do you imagine? How do you imagine that place of pleasure and also of pain?

Bangkok is one of the most polluted cities in the world. Pedestrians breathe through masks that are sold at the cash registers of supermarkets. Some afternoons, the sky seems to be closer to our heads. The alleyways of Sampeng are difficult to walk down without a mask. Everything is on open display and the air is the same: fried crickets eaten with salt, monkeys' brains floating in jars, stomachs of dried fish boiled in water (good for gastritis), sharks' fins. Men drink snake's blood to combat impotence (divine impotence, mother of drunk poets!). In Chatuchak Market live cobras sleep in baskets. Their blood can cost three dollars. If it's a queen cobra it can reach a hundred, and if it's an albino as much as five thousand. *C'est plus cher, mon vieux!* Once you've chosen your snake, the vendor takes it out of the basket, slashes its jugular with a knife, and collects the liquid in a glass. He mixes it with a spoonful of honey and a small glass of whiskey. The customer drinks it in one go.

Bangkok, in the Thai language—a tonal language with 48 vowel sounds and 41 consonants—means City of the Island, but it has a second name: City of the Angels (Krung Thep). Its traffic jams are famous throughout South-east Asia. In addition, it's too hot and the waters of the Chao Phraya aren't sufficient to cool it down. On the contrary: its dark color resembles that of stagnant lagoons and many of the canals that divide up the city are filled with black water. Is it conscience? Beneath every living city is a city of the dead, a necropolis, and in it its unconscious, its tormented opium dreams. No city can be realistic and maybe for that reason Bangkok moves in dreams. The proliferation of canals gives it another nickname: the Venice of the Orient. Here we need music, maybe something by Haydn.

Bangkok, the unique. Buddhism recommends a veiled indifference toward history, but the Thais are proud of never having been colonized. Neither the kingdom of Siam, with its former capital Ayutthaya, nor present-day Thailand ever fell into French, English, or Dutch hands. Unlike its neighbors. Laos, Cambodia, and the two Vietnams formed French Indochina. Burma, Malaysia, and Singapore were English. Maybe they smile because they feel proud, and it may be that all this is true (even though it sounds somewhat forced to me).

And now comes something marvelous, incredible! One of the strangest discoveries of humanity! A case that kept the eyes and attention of science focused on my beautiful kingdom of Thailand! By one of its lakes, at the beginning of the nineteenth century, an English doctor found a child with two heads. After careful observation he discovered that it wasn't one, but two, two children with a single body. From them, that strange genetic anomaly took its name: Siamese twins.

With their oval eyes, dark skin, and low stature, the Thais are, in fact, very smiley. "Welcome to the land of smiles," you read at the airport. The king is considered a god and his subjects lie down on the ground before him (they don't kneel). The Royal Palace of Sanam Luang, with its brightly colored pagodas and stupas, is beautiful, as is the imposing 150-foot-long, gold-plated Reclining Buddha. He's a smiling Buddha. Strange to see millions of people worshiping someone who smiles.

Bangkok, capital of paid sex in all its forms, even the most despicable or circus-like. Sex in all its cruelty and misery. The district of Patpong is the brothel of the European middle classes. Here, a modest waiter from Berlin or Madrid becomes *The Mambo King!* For very little (coming from his paradise of the euro) he can buy himself a wife-lover-masseuse-slave who knows the Kama Sutra back to front, who can cook and agrees to play the game, who kisses him on the mouth and says, darling,

I've missed you, will you take me with you next time? The fiction of love (but isn't love always a fiction? Oh, Mr. Ambrossía, don't read this). The European male looks for sexual tourism in Thailand, Oriental punctiliousness, while the European woman goes to the Caribbean, to Cuba and Jamaica (some to Colombia), where she finds the anthropomorphic intensity of the black man without having to go to Africa, which is less amusing than the Caribbean and has malaria.

But attention, future customers! The Thai sex industry involves twenty-five percent of the women between fifteen and forty, and there are boys too. It's the paradise of novices and virgins, but can lead to unpleasant surprises: gonorrhea, hepatitis, herpes, AIDS. Many of the young girls (even virgins) are heroin addicts. They inject themselves in the knuckles or in the groin so that the marks can't be seen.

Smokers of heroin are called *moo*, which means pig, because when they smoke it they grunt. Those who use syringes are *pei*, in other words, ducks, "because they live in stagnant water." The white man is *farang*, a word that has traveled through several continents, all in the southern part of the world, and which basically, in its origin, means "Frenchman," and by extension "European" or even "Western Christian" (*al-Faranj* in Arabic, *farangi* in Farsi and Urdu and even in Amharic, the language of Ethiopia).

An old Thai chronicle gives the following description of the *farang*: "They are excessively tall, hairy, and dirty. They educate their children for a long time and devote their lives to accumulating wealth. Their women are tall, sturdy, and very beautiful. They do not grow rice."

8

My passion for walls continued and one day, I don't know as a result of what, I summoned up the courage to tell Juana. We went to the sewer and she stood there for a while in silence, a few paces ahead of me, facing the images. My islands and volcanoes glittered; my igneous snakes, my red crocodiles and dinosaurs, everything that I felt in my stomach and in my soul. She gazed at them in silence and I left her quietly meditating, not daring to breathe in order not to disturb her. After a while I put my hand on her arm and she turned.

She was weeping with joy.

You're an artist, she said, moved. She gave me a hug, clinging to me with her whole body, and I could feel her trembling. Then she looked me in the eyes and said: from now on, I'm going to work so that you have what you need.

Juana did her classmates' assignments for them, earned money for it, and began to bring me cans of spray paint. Montana Gold were the best, although Belton were cheap, and easier to get hold of. Ten thousand pesos per can, depending on the dollar exchange rate. Of course, Consul, the revaluation of the peso during those years helped me a lot and I never knew what it was due to, but anyway, I mustn't be distracted from the story. I liked the Montana for the way they penetrated the wall. As if the concrete, the brick, or the stucco had been created out of that color. You have no idea how it felt, shaking the can and hearing the little ball, and then, when I had the image clear, pressing the valve and almost touching the color expelled by the spray.

I started to look at Keith Haring's lonely and slightly hysterical dolls, and the designs of an Englishman named Banksy, a pioneer, someone who simply wanted to put on the street what he thought that street lacked, police officers kissing one another, windows in industrial walls with a view of the sea, playful rats, anyway, my work wasn't like that, I dreamed of other things, not populating the city but giving a little reality to what I had inside me. As I've already said, mine was an art of escape. Everything in me tended toward flight. I wanted to leave, I hated my life.

My sister started studying sociology at the National University. She had been given a scholarship because of her average grade in the high school diploma and the SAT tests, and because she did well in the entrance exam. That was the only reason my parents let her study that subject, because for them, as for most Colombians, studying sociology was like studying to become a member of FARC, a kind of apprenticeship, especially at the National. We were deep into the government of Uribe and anyone who wasn't a fascist and a patriot was suspect, all kinds of people were accused of being with the guerrillas, you just had to defend human rights or the Constitution to be considered a terrorist.

Every time Juana brought her university friends home Mother would say, are they guerrillas? are they all like that in your class? Father would barely greet them, he would put the newspaper in front of his face so as not to see them. Once he said to Juana, you see, princess, I can't pay for you to go to a university like the Rosario or Los Andes or the Xavierian, but at least try to change to economics and in the meantime I'll save, and then, when you graduate, I'll pay for you to do a decent doctorate in Argentina, okay? It's just that with these hippies you're going to give your mother a heart attack, do it for her sake. He told her he was going to ask for a loan to send her to Europe, or the United States. Once he went into debt to buy her an iPod and a new cell phone. He loved her but didn't understand her.

From that time I remember another argument at the dinner table.

It was very violent, and left me breathless for several days. Mother said something about the pre-Independence period, known as the Foolish Fatherland, and Juana, who already felt stronger for being at the university, said, well, it can't ever have been more foolish than this, we live in a country of fools right now, a really dangerous and corrupt country.

Father looked at Mother and felt obliged to respond. This country may be foolish now, he said, but it's the safest and the best we've had in all the time I can remember, with more security and peace and with more well-being. At least since I was born and since the two of you were born.

The best? Juana retorted, oh, Daddy, what are you, one of those snakes in Congress? it's a horrible time! A Mafioso president, an army that murders and tortures, half the Congress in jail for complicity with the paramilitaries, more displaced people than Liberia or Zaire, millions of acres stolen at gunpoint, shall I go on? This country maintains itself on massacres and mass graves. You dig in the ground and you find bones. What can be more foolish than this brainless and insane little republic?

Of course, my parents jumped on her, gesticulating like wild animals, is that what they teach you at university? to insult authority and order? what side are the professors who say these things to you on? who's giving you these analyses of what's happening in the country? do the rector and the Ministry of Education know you're being taught this? do the professors go around in uniforms and boots? how many have warrants out against them for capture and extradition? do they sit down with weapons on their desks? do they demand ransoms from the cafeteria or the Plaza del Che? do they give their classes with Venezuelan or Cuban accents? or in Russian? or directly in Arabic? Show some respect to our president, young lady, who's the first Colombian to get up and go to work! do you hear? when you're relaxing from your evenings out or from reading anti-Colombian texts with those aspiring terrorists you go around with, or when you're fast asleep, he's already in his office, studying and making decisions, giving orders and analyzing what's best for this country, and I tell you one thing: you may not like it but the reason you can sleep easily and continue going to study in that nest of idlers is because he's there, watching over your sleep, and not only you but forty-five million Colombians, do you hear me, young lady?

Oh, yes? watching over my sleep? said Juana, you're kidding, and does he watch over the sleep of the murdered trade unionists, does he watch over the sleep of the negro leader in Chocó who was shot by those who helped his campaign? does he watch over the four million displaced persons? or the anonymous corpses in the mass graves this damned country has so many of? No, Daddy, don't be taken in. The only ones who can sleep easily here are the paramilitaries, and not just sleep: they can continue killing trade unionists and governors, mayors and left-wing students, young unemployed people and drug addicts; they can continue making money and making deals with the State to steal its money; they can continue terrorizing the peasants, taking their lands away from them just by accusing them of being guerrillas, Daddy . . . The paramilitaries are the only ones who can sleep easily in this country! Not the decent people, not the humble people who, ridiculous as it seems, keep supporting the president out of ignorance or because they've been bought off with subsidies, the State money he gives away as if it's a gift! Because never before has so much been stolen, never before have the paramilitaries been able to speak in Congress, forcing the congressmen to listen to them, have you already forgotten that? do you remember how the security service threw out a representative of the victims who was raising a banner? don't you remember? well, I do, that happened in this respectable country, the representative of the victims kicked out so that the murderers could speak! what kind of democracy is that? what do you call a government that allows that, eh? The reason I can sleep easily, Daddy, and who knows for how much longer, is because, thank God, there are also decent people in Congress, like Senator Petro, who put their lives on the line to make the country open its eyes.

Father restrained himself from banging his fist on the table or throwing his glass at the wall and said, oh, Juanita, better keep quiet, okay? you don't know what you're talking about, you're just repeating what the terrorists at the National teach you, but that's because you're very young and you don't know where everyone comes from, that's why you don't know that senator's a Communist and used to be a guerrilla, a terrorist! he has blood on his hands so he can't come along now and give lessons to anybody. The president himself has already said that, did you know that? and Juana, who was a student leader in her year, said, Daddy, the M-19 wasn't communist, because being a Communist, at least in this world, means adhering to the thoughts of Marx or Lenin or even Mao, and the M-19 wasn't like that, it was a Bolivarian, Latin American socialism, and in any case being a Communist or having been a Communist isn't a crime, as far as I know, where did you get that from? On the other hand, being a paramilitary, supporting the massacres of peasants and the parapoliticians in Congress is being a decent person, who loves progress, his country, and the Virgin Mary, is that right? That's the problem, Daddy: everything here is back to front, but if anyone says that the top paramilitary leader is the president, people scream and cross themselves.

No, young lady, Father retorted, if that were true they wouldn't have been extradited, they wouldn't be in gringo prisons paying for what they did, how do your teachers at the National explain that? and she said, everyone knows they were sent there to shut their mouths, to stop them accusing him, him and his buddies, basically he betrayed them, because the characteristic of true Mafia bosses, and this is a well-known fact, is the ability to get rid of those who helped them rise to the top, haven't you seen *The Godfather*, Daddy? you should watch it again, it's obvious you didn't understand it. In Colombia *The Godfather* is an item on the local news.

They argued and argued, screaming at each other.

Mother kept quiet, watching them angrily. I was analyzing the stains on the ceiling or the tip of my shoe.

You see, Consul, how hellish the days and nights were in that horrendous lunatic asylum.

Apart from books, my sister and I loved the cinema. We dreamed about movies. We'd see them and then go smoke a joint in the park, next to my sewer and my drawings. Or we'd go up on the roof of the house and there we'd comment on them, relive them, bring them into our secret life. The most important thing for us, of course, was auteur cinema: Wong Kar-wai, Fellini, Scorsese, Tarantino, George Cukor, Cassavetes, Kurosawa, Mike Nichols, Tarkovsky. But sometimes, weirdly, the movies that contributed most to our games were the commercial ones, the ones from Hollywood. I'd imagine I was Edward Norton and she was Helen Hunt, for example, or we'd choose characters from other movies. She liked *Sabrina*, a remake they did with Harrison Ford of a film by Billy Wilder, and I liked Tom Hanks in *Charlie Wilson's War*, in which Juana chose to be the character played by Julia Roberts, as long as she could change it and not be a right-wing millionairess but an activist, the leader of an NGO, but I said to her, Juana, if you change it you throw away the story, better to choose another character, but she'd insist, what we have to do is change the bad things, so that the movies are better, and I'd say to her, why are you so radical? not everyone can be good, for there to be goodies there also have to be baddies, and she'd answer, that's silly, I don't have to be bad if I don't want to.

One of our idols was Wong Kar-wai.

In his films we found the sense of abandonment, the terrible need for affection, that was so much ours, and he made us dream of other worlds: Asia! Hong Kong! We knew those cities existed on maps, but when we watched Wong Kar-wai we realized that people like us lived in them: lonely people in phantom cities, fragile people on avenues and in cafés, with an imperious need to invent reasons to carry on and the feeling that they'd lost even before they started, that there was something terribly wrong from the start, anyway, all the things you can see in *In the Mood for Love*, *Chungking Express*, *2046*, and even *My Blueberry Nights*; we saw them at the film society and the others we rented or downloaded from the Internet, and it was amazing, a recognition and a pleasure in that recognition that was beyond us, but he wasn't the only one, we also loved the movies of Cassavetes, *Opening Night* and *Shadows* and *The Killing of a Chinese Bookie*, where the characters were even more desperate, and when we saw them we understood that only in the world of art could our lives be transformed into something beautiful, an enormous contradiction, Consul, but that's how it is: that great frustration we felt could generate something durable, we'd understood that ever since we were very young and that's why we believed that, deep down, our lives had something of value, provided we could stay together.

Seeing the films of Cassavetes we felt that other people, in the 1970s, had lived through similar things, and as they were New Yorkers they went to theaters and to empty bars, like those in Hopper, where people drink whiskey without ice or soda, late at night, and there are actors, and depressed dramatists, alcoholics, and so, from movie to movie, we went further into that world, and also in Martin Scorsese's movies about New York, from *Mean Streets* to *Casino*, characters who weren't completely well-adjusted, who had a desire to escape and a great fragility, the uncertainty of having been wounded very early in the ring, of coming out almost mutilated, hiding a blow or a cut that makes us feel ashamed and wretched, as Sartre wrote, that's how life appeared to us, and when later I read *Huis Clos* I understood perfectly what it was saying, as if a missing piece, a piece I had longed for, had become part of my cells, a fierce understanding of the ideas, the certainty that something is true, and that's why one of his phrases echoed for years in my brain, "Hell is other people," you can't arrive at such concision without having felt and lived what I did in those years, Consul, I can assure you.

The roof of the house was one of the places where we felt free. Watching the planes cross the sky made us nervous because we knew that one day we too would leave, what kinds of things happened up there, inside those little moving lights, what questions were those who were traveling in them asking themselves? where were they going? We would invent stories for the passengers: one who's going to study a long way away, who's just wiped away his tears because his girlfriend, at the last moment, told him that in spite of their passionate farewell she didn't think she'd wait for him, a poor boy who was think-ing, as in the poem by Neruda, how threatening the names of the months are, and suddenly Juana would interrupt me, listen, Manuel, do you think a lot about sex? have you lost your vir-ginity? and I'd say, come on, Juana, who am I going to lose my virginity with if I don't have any girlfriends, and she'd say, okay, I'm going to find you a really pretty girl who'll guide you, or do you also like guys, eh? I'd like that even better, a gay brother, we could share boyfriends! but I said, I don't think so, at least not for now, I'll let you know if there's any change.

9

The next day, the prosecutor arrived punctually at seven in the morning, in a brand-new black Toyota Crown with smoked windows. Drizzle was falling, and it was hot. We left the center slowly, negotiating a noisy wall of cars, *tuk-tuks*, bicycles, and buses. Asian cities are always like that, colorful and chaotic: signs above the streets occupying the visual space, banners on both sides of the avenues. At that hour the smell was different: exhaust fumes, overheated tires, fried spicy meat, boiled coconut. Each time we stopped at a traffic light, the vendors came to the window to wave their offerings: fake watches, bags of cardamom, Montblanc pens for ten dollars, leather jackets by Armani or some other brand name.

The traffic was heavy, but it flowed.

"It used to be much worse," the prosecutor said. "Ten years ago there was a jam that lasted for eleven days. We had to lift the cars out by helicopter. We built overpasses and this is what came after. As you can see, the bottle is filling up again and they'll have to do something. If we didn't have so many of the underclass coming to the city, things would be better."

The air-conditioning was going full blast. One of the vents, the one above my leg, was dripping. At last we got onto a fast-moving lane and, with the siren on, we were able to advance. The city was left behind, and the landscape filled with poor farmhouses, plane trees, paddy fields, and palms. From time to time, we'd see an artificial lake with lotus flowers. After a while, the driver turned onto a main road that seemed to move away from the country and go back to the city, until we hit a suburb, and finally came to a wall of concrete and stone. On top, it had barbed wire and watchtowers.

This was Bangkwang Prison.

"There's an old legend," the prosecutor said. "Before, when all this area was wilder, chimpanzees used to come and climb the walls. They liked to walk between the security cables and get into the watchtowers. Some even went down into the cells. The guards discovered it was fun to shoot them, and the prisoners would keep them and eat them. They were full of protein. Then they stopped coming. Now everybody misses them, and they say the ghosts of the chimpanzees run about the roofs. We're a superstitious country. How about yours? I've seen that you don't have the death penalty, but that there are more executions than there are here, how can that be? You'll have to explain it to me."

Fortunately the questions were rhetorical, since he continued speaking, gesticulating, explaining.

It was already nearly nine and the thermometer was still rising. The fact is, I would have given my life for an iced gin (even at that hour). The prosecutor parked to one side of the gate, and, after saluting the guards, we went up to the offices. There he introduced me to the warden, a man with a face full of scars and warts who shook my hand without looking at me.

He knows why I'm here, I thought, he must have received hundreds of diplomats asking for the same thing.

He made no attempt to be polite, and deep down I was pleased. If anything annoyed me about my job, it was unnecessary smiles and feigned interest. Then he led us along a corridor without air conditioning, from where you could already hear the sounds of the prisoners. Heat rose in a kind of thick steam.

"Please sit here," he said when we came to a kind of classroom. "We'll bring him."

I waited, beating my fingers on a table perforated by termites. Then came the sound of a barred door opening, the jangling of keys.

I saw him come in, dragging his feet, his ankles chained together. It was true that he was thin. Gustavo had given a good description: he was indeed like a figure out of El Greco.

As he approached, I noticed he was very nervous, although he said nothing until the guard let go of his arm. We introduced ourselves, and he looked at me with surprise.

"The writer?"

I nodded, feeling rather uncomfortable.

"I haven't read your books," he said, "but let me say something that may surprise you. This isn't going to be a crime story, it's going to be a love story. I'll explain why later."

He seemed to sway, looked around nervously, and continued:

"They told me I have to plead guilty, or they'll give me the death penalty, is that right? When am I going to get out of here? You have come to get me out, haven't you?"

I nodded. Then I looked at the prosecutor.

"Leave us alone, please."

"I don't understand your language," he replied irritably. "Nobody here understands it, it's the same as being alone."

"His feet are chained, he's not going anywhere."

"Good for him," he said. "You have ten minutes."

He lit a cigarette and walked reluctantly to the end of the cellblock. Then he made a noise—I don't know if it was a word, I wasn't listening—and the others too moved away.

The prisoner looked at me insistently. "Have you come to get me out? Will I leave here with you?"

"I wish that were possible," I said. "The charge against you is a serious one. They're going to ask for the death penalty, and there's not much you can do, except plead guilty. If you do that, they'll give you thirty years and then you can apply for a pardon or the king's mercy. That can take eight or nine years. This afternoon I'm going to hire the best lawyer in Bangkok, but I know from the prosecutor that acquittal is impossible. There's a bag of pills as evidence. I'm going to consult with Bogotá so that the Ministry can ask officially for your sentence to be served in Colombia, but that takes time, and there's nothing we can do if it's a death sentence. Do you understand? Once it's been pronounced it can be carried out at any moment. The lawyer and the prisoner are informed two hours in advance."

"Are you telling me to plead guilty?" he said, shaking his head, clearly upset. "The first time I saw that damned bag of pills was when the police showed up. I don't know where it came from. I was doing something else, Consul, not that."

"I believe you, but that's not the problem. We're going to investigate to see if we can find out what happened. It may be they'll catch someone. In any case, until the day of the hearing there's nothing to be done."

Manuel looked at me without blinking and I asked him a question. The dumbest and saddest of questions.

"Are they treating you well?"

He didn't answer in words. His face clouded over and his eyes filled with tears.

"Do you want me to call someone in Colombia?" I said.

He moved his head, saying, no, no . . . A scared, staccato no. I put a hand on his forearm and said, what about your family?

"I don't have anyone," he said. "It's best if everything stays here."

His fear seemed to go back a long way, even before Bangkwang and the bag of pills. A fear that had become part of his bloodstream, his cells. In his expression, I recognized what Gustavo had said: it was as if he had questions dammed up inside him and was afraid to bring them out into the light, to give them reality.

"I'm a friend of Gustavo Chirolla," I said.

A light shone deep inside. He took a deep breath and said, "Old Tavo! Such a good teacher. A pity I didn't often dare talk to him."

Our time was almost up, and the prosecutor was starting to get impatient. He gave me a sign, a click of the fingers.

"I'll be staying here and going over the case with the lawyer," I said to Manuel. "It's going to be all right. I'll be back in three days. You can send for me if anything happens. I'll be here for you."

He sank back into himself, like an animal retreating to the far end of its cave. The same curt expression as at the beginning. He moved a few steps forward and turned, without saying anything. I waved goodbye, but the prosecutor came between us and pushed me outside.

"Let's go," he said, "I have to be in my office by noon."

Back at the hotel, I sat down to put my ideas in order. He's innocent, there's no doubt about it. What could he have meant by those words of his? "Let me say something that may surprise you. This isn't going to be a crime story, it's going to be a love story. I'll explain why later."

A love story? What kind of love can there be in all this?

I sent the Consular Department an e-mail, saying that I needed funds to hire a lawyer because of the complexity of the situation. I also asked for legal advice and precedents. It was just after noon. I left my jacket and tie on the chair in my room, put on something more comfortable, and went out again.

Hotel Regency Inn, Room 301. Suan Plu Soi 6, Sathorn Road, Thungmahamek, Silom.

It was a fairly ordinary street. If you replaced the signs in the Thai language with ones in Spanish, it could have been in Bogotá, Lima, or Mexico City. A car missing a wheel at the side of the street. A bakery. On the corner, a pharmacy with a wooden counter painted blue. A wall with old faded signs and posters. Maybe advertising, maybe electoral propaganda.

The hotel was at number six, an old building, dirty, but with pretentions. The Regency Inn sign hung from the second floor, although the "n" in "Regency" had fallen off. Its three-star status seemed a bit excessive, although I hadn't yet gone in. I preferred to wait a while. Wait for what? I had no idea, but I killed time in the bakery. I walked past twice, looking furtively inside. In the end I made up my mind and went in. A dark, damp lobby. Carpets with cigarette burns. A smell of cigarette butts and stale air.

"Welcome, sir, how can I help you?" said a young man with rotten teeth, with MP3 earbuds in his ears.

I looked at him for a moment without knowing what to say.

"I'd like to see the rooms, how much does a night cost?"

"Twenty-five dollars, wait, I'll give you a key," he said.

The smell of his decaying teeth knocked me out. I looked at the board where the keys were, 301 was free.

"I'd like 301."

"Oh, that one? Very well, take it, sir. Don't forget to hand it in before you go out. How many nights would that be?"

Already on my way to the elevator, I said, without looking at him: I'd like to see it first, then we'll see.

It was the room where they had arrested Manuel Manrique. I didn't think I'd find anything, I just wanted to take a look. Room 301 was the last room in a corridor that ended in a window, looking out on a rough, damp courtyard, with plants that clung to the wall and climbed the pipes.

I opened the door, thinking that the police must have recorded everything many times. I was greeted by the same damp smell as in the lobby, but more concentrated. The air conditioner started up, filling the space with the gas from its condenser. That happens with old machines. The bed was small but decent, and next to it was a wardrobe of laminated wood. The carpet seemed in a better state than the one on the stairs. The window was at the same level as a curved overpass.

At night, the lights of the cars must filter in through the blinds.

I imagined Manuel sitting on that bed, the room receiving the intermittent flashing of the car lights projected on the wall. Maybe eating a chicken sandwich and a Diet Coke. The image of someone who wants something to happen, or who is protecting himself from something lying in wait for him. The smell of the room seemed to suggest: here he suffered in silence, in solitude. It struck me that in the middle of the night a place like that must have been populated by demons, at that cold hour when the birds call sadly to the sun. How long did Manuel spend here? I'd have to ask him. There were yellowish tiles on the bathroom floor. A mosquito was fluttering around the shower curtain, which was blackened and broken. I put my head in, but there was nothing. A mirror. The washbowl faucet was dripping.

I went back to the corridor, the elevator. I descended to the lobby. I handed back the key and went out on the street, realizing that I was sweating. It was an oppressive place, or maybe it was me, or the story. I walked to the intersection with an avenue, hailed a taxi, and went back to the hotel.

When I opened my e-mail, there was already a reply from Colombia: "Send budget to authorize funds. Write detailed report on the situation."

I called the Mexican embassy to talk with the counselor there, Teresa Acosta. I'd been told she could help me, and sure enough, she gave me an appointment for that same afternoon.

The offices were in the Thai Way Tower, not very far from my hotel, an unusual granite and glass building in the business district, North Sathorn Road, the face of Asian capitalism, the most conspicuous, most strident face of modernity.

"We haven't had any cases of prisoners," Teresa said, "but I've known of many, especially Australians and Brits. The best option is for the defendant to plead guilty and beg the king for clemency. That's what they'd interpret as a proper show of respect for their legal system. Diplomacy is important. Sometimes, you can arrange for the defendant to serve his sentence in his own country. The hard part is doing all that without having an embassy. I'll be honest with you. They'll listen, but they won't pay you the same attention, because they aren't obliged to."

She gave me the telephone number of the lawyer. I called him from her office, and on Teresa's recommendation, he agreed to see me the following day. In addition, Teresa offered to go with me, a gesture I greatly appreciated.

She was a friendly, attractive woman, who looked good for her age: about forty, or maybe slightly more. I liked her, she struck me as a generous person. I suggested we go down on the street and have a drink while I heard her advice on what to do. She accepted, and we went to a bar near her office.

She had been in Bangkok for three years, she was a career diplomat. The problems of her compatriots mostly revolved around robberies and the usual tricks played on tourists. Only once had there been a minor case involving possession of a small quantity of drugs, and it had resulted merely in provisional detention. That was how she knew the lawyer, who helped them with everything.

I told her Manuel's story and she listened to me with a surprised expression.

"A young philosopher?" she said. "That's the strangest thing I've ever heard! There have been cases of people accused of things in order to keep the police or even the press quiet and give breathing space to those who are really involved. It's a delicate matter. You'll have to handle it with kid gloves."

We kept ordering gin and Cuba Libres until we felt pleasantly drunk and a tad hungry. She suggested we have dinner in a place typical of her neighborhood, Sukhumvit, which turned out to be a very lively area full of restaurants and bars, with tables out on the street and neon signs.

"Do you like fish?" she said as we sat down on the terrace of a place called Bo Lan. "Because if you do, you can try this, look."

She pointed to the menu: red snapper in turmeric curry with coconut milk, a Renaissance dish that's called *geng guwa pla dtaeng* in Thai. We ordered it, and as we drank our aperitifs I thought of the great Manuel Vázquez Montalbán, who died in the airport of this city as he was changing planes and who actually wrote a novel called *The Birds of Bangkok*. I mentioned it to Teresa.

"I know the book," she said. "There's an episode where Pepe Carvalho has dinner in a Chinese restaurant called the Shangri La, eats duck, and then goes to the Atami massage parlor, which if I'm not mistaken still exists. You can go there later, if you like. The women are supposed to be stunning."

"It isn't Vázquez Montalbán's best novel," I said. "There's something very eighties Spain about it, the way it depicts Asia as a ridiculously exotic place. The characters talk like in Tintin: 'Velly nice city, we visit?'"

The food was delicious, and we drank more alcohol, including the *Mekong*, a cocktail mentioned by Vázquez Montalbán (it was through reading him that I'd discovered the Singapore Sling and Lagavulin whisky). After the check, Teresa invited me to have one last drink on the terrace of her apartment.

"I'll offer you a tour of Bangkok in one minute," she said.

She lived on the top floor of a huge building, from which, sure enough, there was a 360-degree view of the city: the metallic purple lights of the skyscrapers, the black silhouette of the river, the congested roads in the distance, the luminous profile of a never-ending metropolis.

Her apartment was a pleasant *deux pièces* with antiques, designer objects, and an original José Luis Cuevas on the wall, *Portrait of a Woman*. We continued talking.

"My husband and I separated rather abruptly," she said, "but there are people who get married at the point at which we parted. I loved him a lot. I still do."

Her elder daughter was completing a doctorate in human rights and lived in Aguascalientes. The younger one was about to graduate in political science from the Sorbonne. She was a career civil servant but she liked literature and, of course, kept under lock and key a few poems of her own that she wouldn't have shown anybody for anything in the world. She talked to me about Bonifaz Nuño, Octavio Paz, Gerardo Deniz. I told her I had read *Gatuperio* and she could hardly believe her eyes. "You know Deniz? You're kidding! He's hardly known outside Mexico!"

When a conversation turns to literature, there's no end to it, so we refilled our glasses. I tried to sum up for her what I admired about Mexico. A sea of letters that comes and goes in the Gulf, that rocks and sways through the jungles of Chiapas and the deserts of Sonora, Ciudad Juárez and the north. Mexico was the country of Colombian writers. That struck her as amusing. Others say the opposite, that people go to Mexico to die.

"It's the same thing," I said, quite merry by now. "Where we live, we die, don't we?"

She asked about Octavio Paz in Delhi. I told her that from a literary point of view India was Pazian or Octavian, I'm not sure of the word, Paztec? Octavian? Octopazian? We laughed.

The residence of the Mexican embassy is a tourist attraction, I told her, I was shown it by your colleague Conrado Tostado, the cultural attaché, the same person who gave me your telephone number, of course. It's on Prithviraj Road. The nim tree is still there, where Paz married Marie José in 1964, a year before I was born, and she cried out, '64? then we're the same age, that's something to be celebrated, before you go you have to try a tequila, and she took out a colored bottle, pulled the cork, and said, wait and see, this is really fantastic stuff from Mexico, and she showed me the label, José Cuervo, Special Family Reserve, it's like brandy, better even, and I added: if we talk about the development of the human spirit, the most influential personalities of the twentieth century are Johnnie Walker, Smirnoff, the Bacardis, and José Cuervo, don't you think it's strange that there are no women? and she said, there is a Japanese woman, Banana Split! she cried, laughing drunkenly, letting drops fall from her mouth, but I said, that doesn't count because it doesn't have alcohol, and she said, then you just have to pour a little in, right? and what about Bloody Mary? and I said, we're forgetting the most obvious, Margarita! and a very important lady, Veuve Clicquot! then she stood up and said, look, listen to this, but only one, I swear, and she put on José Alfredo Jiménez.

I remembered Fernando Vallejo's words: "If Mexico were the center of the world, José Alfredo would be classical music." That's quite a salute, he was an intelligent man, Vallejo, all honor to him, and she put on "Ella" and raised the volume, and seeing that I was worried about the neighbors said, don't worry, the Thais are even-tempered people, and anyway I don't have people above me or on either side, just offices.

We listened to two more songs until I looked at my watch and saw, to my horror, that it was two in the morning. I'm sorry, Teresa, I have to go, what a wonderful evening, could you call me a taxi? And she said, you just have to ask the doorman, there's a taxi stand opposite.

When I got to my hotel I found another message from Gustavo:

Hello, old man, I found out that Manuel lost touch with the philosophy people when he left university, but that a few weeks ago he was asking questions. His sister disappeared a few years ago and apparently he was investigating.

I'm going to get hold of the telephone numbers of these people and ask them what he wanted, what they talked about. Would that help you? Not that such things are easy here. Keep me up-to-date.

I answered immediately:

Thanks, Tavo, and if you can find out who his sister was, what kind of people she had dealings with, and when she disappeared, all the better. Thanks, brother. Have a hug from me.

10
INTER-NETA'S MONOLOGUES

I divide myself and I am many, contradictory, wild, clandestine. Today I'm dedicating this space to a friend of mine so that he can tell his story, so that he can talk to you directly, dear bloggers, who is he? is he a projection of me? is he you? Guess, read, invent.

I have a thousand nicknames, but the one I like most is Tongolele. That's the one they gave me in the Splendor, a karaoke bar in Culiacán in the north of Mexico, where I went to sing once with a boyfriend I had. Or let's say a friend with benefits, since he was married, not that that kind of thing bothers me. I sang "Ella," by José Alfredo, and my friend whispered in my ear: you sing like Tongolele, and so that's how I stayed. I hope you like it. I love it. I've seen that part of the public is like me and that's why I'm going to talk to you quite openly: the name I was born with is horrible, decadent, demeaning: Wilson Amézquita. I had to put up with that horror, God forgive me, until I came of age, when they finally operated on me, as if it were a deformity or a tumor. I feel a knot in my stomach just saying it. Amézquita, that's gross! I changed it to Jennifer Mor, which is so much more elegant and romantic, suggesting a woman sitting in a drawing room reading the classics, something like Racine's *Phaedra*, while outside, in New York, it's pouring rain and you hear the muffled sound of taxis hooting their horns. I mean, Wilson! I wouldn't call a tennis ball

Wilson! The name suggests a urinal with sawdust and flies in a chichi bar in Choachí. I'm a lady, I have delicate and beautiful things in my mind.

I changed sex in the Tarabaya Memorial clinic in Bangkok, at the age of twenty-one, after I'd recognized a great truth: I liked being with men, not with fags. Forgive me, I'm well-read and I know such words shouldn't be used, but they told me I should talk as if I were in my own home. So if they bother you, I'm sorry. As I said, I had my operation in Bangkok. A long way away, but safe. A lot of people have sex changes there, they're used to it and it always goes well. I read about it in a magazine and then made inquiries. My girlfriends told me I was crazy. Tongolele, you've gone crazy! You've really lost it! But I was sure. Scheherazade, who's like a sister to me, was the only one who looked at it a bit scientifically and told me it wasn't worth it, that it was an unnecessary risk. According to her, women have three pussies: one in the mouth, another in the vagina and the third behind, in the you know what, right? And so she said and still says: of those three I have two and I'm happy with that and I make my men happy, those who also like cock. For Scheherazade that's enough, but not for me. I wanted real men, the kind who fuck but won't let themselves be fucked. When I'd recovered from the operation, which takes time—but of course, Bangkok is wonderful!—I went to see a physical trainer, because now came the external transformation. . . I showed him a photograph of Pamela Anderson, the stunner I wanted to look like, and said: I need to be like that, what do I have to do? how much does it cost?

He didn't say it was impossible, although he looked at me sadly. Couldn't you have chosen an easier model? I said no, Pamela Anderson was the woman of my dreams: if I'd been a man, a man in my soul, it was a girl like her I'd have liked by my side. I'd have liked to find her every morning between the sheets, in the shower, look after her when she had a cold, or see her sitting on the toilet, taking her morning leak. That's why I want to be like her. Not that it was such a stretch. What I mean, my friends, is that I was already a woman, men gave me the eye when I stood up, when I went out for a walk; I felt that look, the kind that lifts miniskirts, goes through panty material, and burrows away inside, like a termite but really nice, it's great to be looked at like that, isn't it, my *tongolelos*? But let me carry on with my story: with the photograph of Pamela I went to see the best plastic surgeon, a really nice Colombian, Tomás Zapata, who's the one who beautifies the women who matter in this world, beginning with Amparito Grisales and Fanny Mikey, I'm talking about the body, not the soul, and not only in Colombia but also in Spain and Brazil, where the major leagues are, and I said, Tomasito, my dear friend, this is what there is and this is what we want to have. Then I took out a photograph of Pamela who was originally wearing a thong but who I'd stripped using Photoshop, since I needed to make things clear. Tomás grabbed it from me and said: we're going to make you very similar, or rather the same, my darling, and the rest is up to you, with that grace and intelligence God gave you. Oh, I love that Tomás! Because as the classics say: there is no beauty without brains.

But anyway, I've been invited here to talk about aspects of my life and my relationship with Pamela, not to philosophize, so I'll carry on: first came the silicon, the Botox, the nips and tucks, and then, when I'd recovered from it all, I started the physical work. Three hours a day in the gym. The tanning I do with P.A. products, which are the best, the acronym is like an amulet. I attend to everything, every detail, because the body is a painting. Let's say, for those of you girls who are cultivated, like Rembrandt's *Night Watch*. Every fold of the clothes is perfect. That's how a girl should be if the aim is to be the most beautiful woman in the world, or at least in my world, let's not be presumptuous. If you want to be a lady and not a floozy. Every tiny thing has to be perfect because otherwise the whole effect is ruined. This lovely hair I have, for example, is natural. You see what I look like today. The day after tomorrow, I'll be thirty-five and nobody believes me. They all think I'm in my twenties. And some men even confuse me with the original, after a few drinks, but I always say to them: no, darling, I'm the other one, the number two, the original is unattainable! The other day a boyfriend of mine, to make me mad, said I was the poor man's Pamela. How dumb can you get? If only he knew that I've won seven beauty contests in trans bars, at the Latin American level, and have been Miss Wet T-shirt Trans for 2007, 2008, and 2009. In 2010 it was stolen from me and given to the girlfriend of a drug trafficker, a filthy bitch who bribed the judges. When it's a clean competition, I always win, I'm the most beautiful because I'm identical to Pam. I can imagine you must all be wondering if I know her. Well, I have a little bit of gossip for you: yes, we did see each other once. At a charity parade. She was in her dressing room and I was in mine, but I preferred not to say hello to her. I was scared. What if she'd said something rude to me? What if she'd looked at me anxiously? When it comes down to it, she and I are the two faces of one and the same person. That's why I prefer not to know her and to continue dreaming. What could I do? I'd either keep quiet, or I could say simply: I always wanted to be you. But that, my darlings, is something you don't say to anyone. Not even a goddess.

11

In those years I had just one friend, Consul, a friend from school who was quite eccentric, and lived a strange life. A quiet guy who spent his evenings reading. His name was Edgar Porras, but sometimes, to play around or to be provocative, he liked to call himself Edgar Allan Porras. As you might imagine, his favorite author was Poe, and he always carried a book by him in his coat, which was a kind of very theatrical olive green overcoat.

He lived in upper Santa Ana, the rich part, and his house was a palace with nine bedrooms and lots of floors, in the last row before the hills. He knew English and French because he'd lived in various countries, but almost never spoke them. He said he was only interested in languages for reading. I was impressed by his library, it made me feel small. I only knew the little English and French I'd learned at school, which wasn't enough to read seriously. He on the other hand had, and had read, books in the original language by Céline, Malraux and Camus, Poe and Lovecraft, Salinger and Dylan Thomas, Roth and Bellow, and even authors I had barely heard of like David Foster Wallace, Kurt Vonnegut, John Cheever, and Thomas Pynchon.

I went to his house at weekends and sometimes slept over. The pretext was studying. My parents didn't usually allow such things, but since he was from a rich family he impressed Father, who always ended up agreeing. Like the social climbers they were, they thought it was an achievement that their son was spending time with rich families, and Mother, who was addicted to "aspirational" soap operas, talked proudly about the Porras family at the florist's. Of course Edgar and I never studied, being there was an excuse to do other things, because his family was always going out to dinners or cocktail parties, and the few times they were at home it was because they were throwing parties or dinners for lots of people, and since the house was very big we could be in his room and not hear a thing.

Señor Porras represented a French oil company, although I never quite understood what exactly his job was. A kind of diplomat in his own country. Edgar's siblings were older, two brothers and a sister. They were almost never at home, or when they were they almost never left their rooms, I already told you it was a strange house. There was no obligation to be together for meals, so everyone went to the kitchen, served themselves, and went to their rooms to eat as they chatted on Facebook, listened to music, or hung out with other friends. The kitchen was a little restaurant with a bit of everything. The sister's name was Gladys and she was older than Juana.

As well as being crazy about books, Edgar was also sex-mad and once told me that he knew how to spy on Gladys when she was having a bath. One Sunday he insisted that we go look at her. The bathroom had a high window that looked into a lavatory. If you climbed on the toilet you could see the shower cubicle. I said no but he insisted, saying she was really something, that she had huge tits and a fabulous ass. I found it strange that he should talk like that about his sister, and I told him that, but for him it was normal. Life is life, he would say, you have to take things as they come. He confessed to me that he'd steal her used panties and thongs, smell them, and jerk off. Finally we went to look at her, and to our surprise, she was with a guy and they were fucking like crazy. Standing with her back to him, her hands clutching the faucets, lifting her ass, and then on her knees sucking his cock, which was incredible. Edgar wanted to make a video and ran to his room for his BlackBerry, I'm going to put it on YouTube! he said. I preferred not to look, thinking of my sister.

In that family everything was strange, out of proportion, but I liked him, plus he was very generous. He passed on to me half the things they brought him back from their travels. The only time I ever had a Lacoste T-shirt was thanks to him, also a pair of Adidas and a Nike T-shirt. At that age, things like that are important. Later you forget, but at the age of seventeen they mark you.

His eldest brother, Carlos, would give us matchboxes filled with marijuana and say: take it nice and slowly, don't overdo it, kids, okay? and if they catch you don't say a word, if I saw you I'll say I don't remember. His father locked the bar, but Edgar knew how to open it by removing a wooden panel, so on Saturdays we'd steal bottles of wine or whiskey, whatever we could find, and take them with us to the parks in Santa Ana and Santa Bárbara, where we'd read poetry, especially Barba Jacob and León de Greiff, and of course, poems by Poe in English that Edgar knew by heart, and would yell at the quarries and the hills, cursing them, challenging Bogotá like a Colombian Rastignac.

Sometimes he'd read me things he'd written himself, and that surprised me. I'd never before met anybody who wanted to be a writer, an idea my father would have thought sinister. Edgar used to say that being a writer was the greatest thing a human being could aspire to. As far as he was concerned, anything in book form was sacred.

He had a text about vocation that he read to me every now and again and which I remember word for word, I don't know who he copied it from or if it was actually his, but it stayed with me for a long time. It more or less went like this:

You realize you're a writer when the things that swirl or echo in your head won't let you concentrate on anything else: neither reading nor watching a movie nor listening to what other people are saying, not even your teacher or your best friend. When your girlfriend yells: you're not listening to me! and slams the door and takes off, and you exclaim, what a relief, and keep thinking about your things. It's a relief when our loved ones leave us alone. If what's happening inside your head is more powerful than what's outside and can be translated into sentences, you're a writer. If you don't write, then you should think about it, it might suit you. If you are a writer, the worst thing is not to write. The bad news, given the times we live in, is that you can also tell yourself you're really fucked.

I, on the other hand, never told him I painted graffiti. That was a secret world, the one closest to my heart, and I could only share it with Juana. Several times he asked me, what about you, man, don't you write? how can you not write if you like novels so much? not even poetry? and I'd say, I prefer reading, I'm very passive or very cerebral, I like to contemplate the world from a distance, to see without being seen, it's an idea of the sublime I read about later, Consul, the sublime as the terrible seen from a safe place, that was the kind of thing I said to Edgar when, guessing that I had secrets, he started asking questions.

When we heard that David Foster Wallace had committed suicide, Edgar dressed all in black and invited me over to his house. He looked pale. We stole a bottle of Martini from his father's bar, along with four packs of salt and vinegar potato chips imported from England, a jar of high-quality tuna, and a Dutch cheese, and went to Usaquén Cemetery to throw a dinner in his honor. Edgar took with him a couple of original editions. I had managed to get hold of Spanish versions of *A Supposedly*

Fun Thing I'll Never Do Again and *Brief Interviews with Hideous Men,* which according to Edgar were amazing in the original. As I already said, I had a complex about the fact that I didn't know English. Or rather: that I didn't speak it as naturally and resonantly as the people from bilingual schools. I could say everything, using few words, but reading literature was frustrating. On every line I'd find things that I understood well enough from the context, but that left me with the feeling I was missing the most important part.

To get into the cemetery you had to go around the wall and along a side passage until you came to a garage door that was always kept shut. It was a barred door and you could climb over it and jump down on the other side. That's what we did.

Edgar liked the upper part of the cemetery, toward the hills, adjacent to the parking lot of a supermarket, because there was a series of graves without stones, with names written by hand on fresh cement. One of them said: "My son." There we sat down and opened the bag of food. We ate and drank toasts to the soul of David Foster Wallace, inviting him to this poor, simple cemetery in a poor, simple country in one of the poorest and simplest regions of the world. We kept passing each other the bottle of Martini until we were drunk. We staggered around, sang, cried out the titles of Wallace's books, and, incredibly, I felt free, so free it made me dizzy. I would have been capable of anything, however absurd or impossible. I could have run to the top of the hill and left that city forever.

To make things more exciting, Edgar rolled a joint and we took great puffs at it, and when we finished it we read out loud, and at that moment a gust of wind knocked over our plastic cups and Edgar cried, he's here! it's Wallace! We welcomed him with a bow and a few more drinks.

My head was spinning and I started throwing up, which forced me to move away; being young, that kind of thing embarrassed me. He was rich, free, brought up to do as he pleased, while I concealed a little hell in my house. I was shy. When he appeared, I told him I'd gone to take a leak and had felt the need to be alone. He said, sure, brother, I understand, but we finished the bottle and the joint, and we went home.

His brothers and sister were in their respective rooms, but they gave us more grass and half a bottle of aguardiente, so we started consuming all that while listening to "Bohemian Rhapsody" by Queen. I loved that song and I confess, Consul, that in those years I thought it had been written for me, just for me.

You remember the bit that says:
Is this the real life?
Is this just fantasy?
Caught in a landslide
No escape from reality
Open your eyes
Look up to the skies and see,
I'm just a poor boy (Poor boy), I need no sympathy

I never understood why Edgar, who was neither poor nor unhappy, liked it so much. He played at being a tormented, anguished spirit, at odds with the world, but in reality there was nothing to torment him, let alone anything to be at odds with, in the world or anywhere else. Reality was generous to him. When I told my sister, she said: rich people always think up ways to be depressed. They like being unhappy. It's very elegant to be sad.

To go back to that night: at two in the morning, listening to Queen and reading David Foster Wallace, drinking aguardiente as if it was water, already drunk, until I realized I was about to faint. So I went to the bathroom, turned on the shower, and stuck my head in, hoping the water would cleanse me, and in fact it did me good and I even felt pleasure in those cold drops running over my neck and down my chest. When I finished, I had the shock of my life: there was Gladys, watching me. She was wearing a short T-shirt that left her navel free and a blue Gef thong.

Are you very drunk?

It's passing, thanks, but she said, come to my room. I repeated that I felt better but she insisted, grabbing my arm and pulling me down the corridor. Her room was bigger than Edgar's and looked out on the garden; music was playing that I didn't know, some kind of French rap. With her was a guy, also in underpants, different than the one we had seen in the shower. Gladys told him I wasn't feeling well, that I was drunk, and the guy took out a little bag of coke, prepared a line on a mirror, and offered it to me. Take this, breathe it in well, he said. Then he prepared four more lines for the two of them. At first I didn't feel anything, but then a wave of well-being swept over me. I left the room, thanking them, and went back to Edgar's room, he'd fallen asleep with his flies open, wearing a pair of dark glasses and the headphones from his iPad, connected to the YouJizz porn site, the Asian Amateurs section.

In spite of the fact that, deep down, Edgar and I knew we weren't equals, it was a respectful friendship. I told him all about my life, and the only thing he said was, shit, if I'd experienced all that I'd be a novelist, and a poet for sure. Basically, you're very lucky, brother. An unhappy childhood is the best gift a writer can have. I'm going to have to approach it from the other side: either do things in the style of Carlos Fuentes or reject my family and my class, like Bryce Echenique. Those are my two options. Otherwise, I'm fucked, but you're made for life.

I looked at him sarcastically and said, the problem, brother, is that I'm not a writer.

Because Edgar, Consul, was fully aware of his vocation, even though he hadn't written a thing yet or only short fragments. He liked to say, quoting Monterroso, "fragment: genre much used in ancient times." To me, it was all a great mystery: his self-confidence, his amazing cultural knowledge given that he was so young, his extravagant and sometimes brilliant ideas, ideas he didn't share with anybody but me, which can't have been very stimulating for him. That's how he was, Edgar Porras, young millionaire and intellectual who wanted to know a suffering he didn't have, and maybe that's why, Consul, he chose me, his exact opposite, as his friend. But I couldn't choose. A poor person can't choose to be rich, not even as a game.

I remember one of his stories. He told it to me several times, changing a few details. I don't know if he wrote it in the end. It went like this: A young man from Bogotá was having a sex chat with a woman named Asaku, presumably Japanese. Asaku put the computer on her windowsill and sat down there, opened her legs and put things inside her, the necks of bottles, cucumbers, plastic dragons. The young man was jerking off like crazy, excited by the fact that Asaku, unlike the girls he knew, had lots of pubic hair, which seems to be a tradition in Japan, or at least that's what he thought.

Behind her, in the next building, he could see a window that was like Asaku's backstage area, and which in spite of being lighted had a curtain in front of it. The story really gets going when the young man, still jerking off while Asaku is sticking a Gormiti action figure in her vagina, sees that curtain open; behind it, a man raises his hand, with something sharp in it, and brings it down seven times into the figure of a woman, who's shorter and frailer than him, until she falls to the floor, clearly dead. Asaku doesn't see or hear anything, since just at that moment her orgasm starts; the murder is happening behind her back; the young man lets go of his cock and yells into his microphone, but Asaku, drowning in an ocean of endorphins, takes her time in reacting, and when he tells her there has been a murder she laughs and doesn't even turn around, she tells him he's drunk or stoned, but he insists and says, you have to report it, where do you live? in what city? She refuses to tell him, saying: you're making all this up to poke around in my life, don't even think about it, you'll never find out.

Edgar's story began with that murder. He wanted to write it to find out who the murderer was and who the woman was and why he killed her by the window, in full view of anyone who was having virtual sex with a stranger.

I told him I thought it sounded like something by Murakami, and he thought this over for a while and said, it's possible, but I believe in unconscious influences.

At school our classmates could never understand how Edgar, a guy from a good family, handsome, knowing lots of languages, could be my friend. That's why they started to spread gossip, people said cruel things, that I was his servant, that his parents paid me to help him with his studies and whisper the answers to him in exams. I heard about all this gossip and never said anything, but Edgar was affected by it. During recess he would say to me, what a bunch of jealous sons of bitches, and the girls? what a herd of loudmouthed bitches.

One of these bitches, Daniela, was about to turn eighteen and was organizing a big party in her house. She lived in a very comfortable apartment near the beltway, and to spice it up announced that her parents weren't going to be there, which meant it would be a really long party, and that got everybody excited. Of course it didn't even occur to me that I might go to something as dumb as that, and I kept my distance. Everybody commented on what they would like to do, which girls they'd like to make out with, and what drinks they'd like to get drunk on. The girls wondered what clothes they would wear, and with what shoes, what necklaces and earrings, the kinds of things that get people like that all worked up but just depressed me, so that I sunk into my shell and at recess opted to take shelter in the toilets.

As I'm a polite person, as soon as I received the envelope with the invitation—a ridiculous card, of course, with emoticons dancing under the words "be with me for my eighteenth April"—I hastened to respond with a note in which I thanked her for the invitation but declined it on the grounds that I had a family get-together on the same date.

Daniela didn't give a damn about my refusal, of course, but when she found out that Edgar wasn't coming either she started to panic. Swallowing her contempt, she made up her mind to talk with me during recess, escorted by her best friend, a girl named Gina, a really nasty girl who loved to spread horrible gossip about Daniela—that she slept around with guys from other schools, that she popped pills, that she'd had an abortion—when the truth is that both of them were crude, dumb girls, real sluts, both obsessed with being the beauties of the class when they were actually pretty average, Daniela with a boob job and her face always smeared with makeup, like a high-class escort, and Gina short and fat, an Indian-looking face with slanted eyes, which in that city meant she was the kind of girl that all the guys ended up with at parties when they were already drunk and stoned and none of the other girls would put out, anyway, Gina and Daniela sought me out during the long recess and found me in the place where I was reading, on the waste ground at the far end.

Manuel, said Daniela, I felt really bad when I found out you weren't coming to my party, I mean, like, that's terrible, the whole point is so we can all be together! So I asked my mother to call your house and speak with your parents, and guess what, she's just sent me a text saying that she talked to your mother and there's no problem about you coming.

I hated them, Consul, because of the stupid importance that women give their birthdays, but I restrained myself, I didn't want to give them the satisfaction of insulting them, so I said, look, Daniela, I don't like parties, I won't be good company, don't take it badly, but she glared at me and decided to lay her cards on the table, of course I take it badly, she said, very badly, not because I give a damn if you come or not, it's your life, right? nothing to do with me, but it's just that Edgar says he won't come either and of course that's because of you, so I have to ask you to come, I'm asking for a favor, just one little favor, nothing more, I'll give you whatever you want, I'm quite serious, it's important to me that he come, when he arrives you can go, if you like I'll get the chauffeur to drive you home or wherever you like, but don't spoil this for me, all right? it's my birthday, dammit!

I told her it was too much: if I left home I couldn't go back half an hour later, so she said, all right, then tell me what the hell you like to do and I'll treat you, maybe you'd like to go see a late-night movie? would you like to go to a restaurant? I really will treat you, whatever you say, ask me for whatever you like, shit, there must be something you like, isn't there?

Deep down she was suffering, so I said: I'll try to persuade Edgar but stop fucking me around. You already screwed things up for me calling my house. And don't worry, you'll never understand what I like, not in a thousand years.

Before the end of recess I talked with Edgar and told him he should go to the party, it mattered a lot to the girls. Then he, being the unpredictable person he was, said: I have an idea, man, a great idea! I'll take my mother's car and we'll go to Daniela's for a while. And then we'll go whoring, okay? The hour has come to live the life of the Parnassians, to explore brothels, which is where real life is, the real world, are you up for it? I told him I was.

And we went there, Consul, in a Citroën I'd never seen before. I was very nervous because Edgar didn't have a license, although with his contacts and his luck it was unlikely anything would happen. When Daniela opened the door her face lit up. The pounding of the music hit us full on. She hugged Edgar and gave him a kiss as we went in. She was wearing a tight miniskirt, fishnet stockings, and very high heels. The perfect drawing-room whore. Edgar handed over his gift and, without looking at me, she grabbed him by the arm and pulled him inside. I stayed back, with my gift dangling from my hand.

I preferred not to go where everyone else was, so I went and sat down in the living room, by a window. A minute later a waiter passed with a tray of drinks and I gestured to him, but he didn't stop. Then I moved to a second living room from where you could see the parlor. All my classmates were there, and people from other years. Some weren't from our school. They had set up a big screen to show videos. I thought to go out on the terrace and smoke a cigarette, but at that moment a woman in an apron approached and asked me if I wanted to eat something.

I said yes, but then didn't see her again.

Sometime later I saw Edgar among the others. He was dancing with Daniela and around them there were other girls raising their glasses and drinking toasts in time to reggae or rap or some other kind of music. I looked at my watch: an hour and a half had gone by. I felt hungry and was starting to get impatient. It didn't look as if Edgar wanted to leave. Slowly I walked back along the corridor, opened the door, and walked to the elevators. When one of them opened, two classmates who were arriving late came out, laughing loudly.

How's the party? they asked, is it good?

Very good, I said, and pointed to the door at the end of the corridor. They didn't even register the fact that I was leaving.

I went outside. It was drizzling.

I didn't have money for a taxi so I started walking without worrying about the drizzle. I'd have liked to have my paint cans with me, and I thought that if it stopped raining I'd go to the wall. I had an urgent need to express something: revulsion, anger, humiliation. I missed my colors, but there was still quite some way to go. After a few blocks I noticed something in my jacket pocket. I put my hand in, it was the gift I hadn't managed to hand over. I opened it to see what Mother had bought, and to be honest I was pleased I still had it with me. A box of hand-kerchiefs. I threw it in the nearest trash can and carried on along Seventh. If I was lucky I could find a bus that went to Usaquén.

When I got home the lights were still on, so I decided to wait. Father and Mother were watching television in the living room. I took out my cell phone, thinking I might call Juana, but then remembered she was traveling. Under the eave of the garage there was a dry spot and I sat down to wait. It was still raining, more heavily now. I was cold and tired, but I'd received a lesson that was more important than the cold and the tiredness.

I never went back to Edgar's house, in spite of his repeated invitations. We'd see each other at recess and he'd ask me, what's up, brother? but I'd say, nothing, problems at home, I'll tell you later. He told me about the party, how the time had passed and they'd gotten him drunk.

I fucked Daniela in the bathroom, man, he said, on all fours and against the washbowl, and I almost fucked the other whore too.

But I didn't listen to him, just smiled and shrugged. With time he got tired of seeking me out.

It was better that way.

Losing my only friend strengthened me, Consul. Solitude accentuates what you have inside you, so now I devoted myself to walls. I had already seen one in the upper part of Usaquén, more than three hundred feet high. It was on the edge of a lot where they were going to start building something. It wasn't completely clean, of course, it already had a few things on it, rude drawings, the odd word, hearts, a few old posters, but, far from bothering me, this gave me strength, as if the soul of the wall was in a crude state, just waiting for an image.

I went the next day, still feeling revulsion at the previous night. My hands were shaking as I grabbed the spray can. It was my first wall outside my own neighborhood and that was tantamount to a conquest, to pushing back the frontiers, broadening my horizons. I looked at it for a while from the opposite sidewalk and felt it palpitating, so the first thing I painted was just that, the silhouette of a palpitating heart, a heart that was at the same time a small continent drifting, and as I contemplated it from the sidewalk, it acquired relief, its veins and folds emerged, along with the outline of the surrounding water, the devouring monsters, the storms that lay in wait for it.

The cans sped through my fingers as if everything already existed, in the spirit or the soul of the wall, until I could do no more and I sat down to look at the stars, the lights of the houses. Then, already calmer, I contemplated my drawing, that small piece of my world in a distant street, at the beginning of night, and I felt comforted. I turned and looked at it again from the corner and it filled me with resolve. Suddenly I felt something on my cheeks, what was it? I was crying.

When I told Juana about Edgar, she listened to me calmly, without judging anybody, and in the end repeated her old question, are you still a virgin?

I had turned eighteen and couldn't even imagine myself seducing women, so I replied, what do you think? when have you ever seen me with a girl?

But you do want to? she asked, and I said, yes, of course, that's all I ever think about, it's bubbling up inside me, so she said, come with me to a party next Saturday, a gorgeous friend of mine will show you what to do, all right?

I spent the week thinking, but not only about the party and Juana's friend. It was the end of the year and school would soon be over. What would happen to my life? What would happen to Juana and me? Painting gave me strength, but reality opened up in front of me more broadly, with vast dark spaces to cover. I thought and thought. I would have liked to be a poet, to direct all that emptiness and those questions forward, project myself into the future, and even have visions. I had read Schelling and wanted to fully understand my own experience, luck, destiny, good and evil. I felt I was outside that reality and needed to understand it, to outline a little theory that would allow me to carry on. What was happening to me and my sister was tiny compared with the great ills of the world, but each person experiences things individually. Hence the absence of enthusiasm, that terrible clash with life, pure and simple. What to think? I liked being alone, going out to the fields, sitting down between the furrows, and waiting to hear the bells ring.

The following Saturday Juana took me to the apartment of a very unusual guy—although these days, Consul, he would only have made me laugh—with earrings, tattoos on his arms, and a sleeveless T-shirt clinging to his body, as if we weren't in Bogotá but Acapulco. The music playing was Metallica, 80s rock, and Kiss. Juana introduced me and poured me a whiskey. She told me to drink slowly and that if I felt bad I should tell her.

Don't worry, I've been drunk before and even snorted coke, so don't worry.

She almost fainted, coke? who gave you that crap? Edgar's sister, I said, but only once. I swear. Typical of those rich kids, she said, then she shrugged and joined in the dancing. She reached out her arms to me and said, come on, dance with me, but I refused, I'd never done it, it wasn't something I enjoyed. She insisted, you have to learn, when you learn it's fun, you'll understand music in a way you can only do by dancing, so I joined her and tried to follow, making clumsy steps as I clung to her waist and looked her in the eyes, and little by little, very slowly, the rhythm appeared and a certain balance I could absorb, and then I danced seven songs in a row and drank two more glasses of whiskey until I felt merry, euphoric, which was something I had never felt in all the times I'd gotten drunk with Edgar.

Then I found out that the hosts were two friends from the university, both homosexuals, one from Sociology, the one who'd opened the door, and the other from History, a professor, a guy of about forty who not only didn't have tattoos or earrings or anything like that, but in addition was fat, not obese, just reasonably fat, and quite calm and relaxed, who'd seen it all before, all the fights and debates.

What I liked most was his home.

An apartment on Sixth and Fourth full of books and antiques, some pre-Columbian and some brought back from Asia and the South Pacific. The first thing I did when I came in, before greeting the other guests, was to look through the library. Heidegger, Deleuze, Virilio, *Flesh and Stone: The Body and the City in Western Civilization* by Richard Sennett, the works of Lacan in French, the works of Michel Foucault in French, Chomsky, the *Mahabharata*, an edition of Gaddafi's *Green Book*, three biographies of Mao, *Del Poder y la Gramática* by Malcolm Deas, *The Intellectuals and the Masses* by John Carey, the biography of Che by Paco Ignacio Taibo II, *The Idea of Justice* by Amartya Sen, the collected poems of Rubén Darío, the collected poems of León de Greiff in three volumes, the complete works of Mayakovsky, Rimbaud in French, Baudelaire in French, books that later, as time passed, I sought out and bought, and of course read, you can't imagine, Consul, how important it was for me, going to that party, especially after Daniela's fiasco.

In the dining room, around a huge pitcher of pisco sour, there was another group from Philosophy, some postgrads, some from other universities. That was where I met your friend Gustavo Chirolla. I was struck by the way he argued, with his coastal accent and his enormous affection and respect for those who argued with him. That night they talked about various subjects and I stood listening in a corner, hypnotized by what they were saying, I can't remember it in detail but I'm sure they talked about politics, that was the great topic in those horrible days, local politics, everybody felt concerned, everybody thought they had to make their position clear, do you remember, Consul? it was an implicit duty, we were like Cubans, and out of that emerged loves and hates, something that ended when Uribe went and Colombia became a normal country again, or rather, went back to being a shitty country but a normal one, and people went back to the old grayness and lobotomy, which by comparison seemed like a sign of balance and even of progress.

They talked of all that and also of very specific things, Leibniz, social structures, the new critical thinking. I was dazzled listening to them, especially Gustavo. This man knows about everything, I told myself, and at one point, very shyly, I asked him where he taught, and that was when he told me a couple of things about his work and his classes at the Xavierian University. I told him about my interest in philosophy and in the National University, and he said that he recommended it to me, that we were sure to see each other there.

For some time now I had liked philosophy. It was the only thing that might have an answer for my failed existence, that frustration that only disappeared with painting, books, or movies. Art and its human stories helped me to understand that I was not alone, but studying literature struck me as unnecessary, and the cinema was a utopia. Juana wanted me to make a movie, but I said to her, for that you have to be a millionaire or the son of millionaires, don't kid yourself. Kubrick had a rich uncle who paid for his first film, don't you remember? And if we find a producer, which is highly unlikely, we'd have to forget about making art. You can't make the movie you want if the money isn't yours.

She believed in me blindly and said that she didn't mind spending her life working to pay for it. I let her fantasize, but I knew it was impossible, among other things because the movie I carry inside me is so tough that nobody would go to see it.

There remained philosophy: Anaxagoras, Epictetus, Peter Abelard, Saint Anselm, Scottus Eriugena, Emmanuel Kant. They had thought about everything. How to explain that profound sense of rejection? the certainty that something in life was wrong, profoundly wrong? what to call that feeling of insubstantiality, of emptiness? These were the answers I was looking for.

Hearing those people confirmed me in my decision to study at the National, although the truth was, I didn't really have much choice. Los Andes was out of reach, as was the Xavierian.

Plus, I'd be close to Juana.

At midnight, after a few whiskeys and a joint, a woman named Tania came up to me and asked me to dance. She whispered in my ear: are you Juana's brother? I didn't know you were so young and handsome. We danced for a while, she clung to me as soon as we took the first step, kissed me on the mouth, sucked my ear, and said, well, darling, shall we fuck? I'd heard people say that kind of thing in movies, so I said, nervously, yes, of course.

We went to one of the bedrooms on the second floor and without needing any words she opened my fly and started sucking my cock. She had a piercing in her tongue and she rubbed it hard against my glans. Then she took off her clothes, sat down on a hassock, and moved her thong aside. We fucked and it was really great, she made me feel as if it wasn't the first time. She had experience, she moved well, and she knew how to guide me. Thanks to that, I didn't come in the first thirty seconds, but by the time we had finished I was another person. She got upset because she couldn't find her bra, then she wanted to light a cigarette and the lighter didn't work. In the end she found her clothes, dressed with her back to me, and then snorted a line of coke through each nostril. I asked her for her phone number, but she didn't even reply. Suddenly she looked at me, as if surprised to see me still there, and said, are you planning to sleep here or what? Then something happened that made the atmosphere even tenser than it already was: bending to look for her huge Dr. Martens boots, she let out a loud and unmistakable fart. Not vaginal wind, but a classic fart. A fart that resounded through the room, and really annoyed her, although she didn't even say "sorry" or "it just came out." I asked her for her phone number again, but she said:

Look, there's no point our seeing each other again. I have a boyfriend, a really great Spanish guy who's traveling right now. I'm thirty-two years old, I'm not going to get involved with a child.

With those words she left the room, through which a sharp, foul-smelling wind was already blowing.

I felt very sick and didn't know what to do.

She left me alone in that stinking room that suddenly seemed like the saddest, most squalid place in the world. I searched for my clothes and got dressed. Then I opened the window and breathed in the clean night air. From some star or from the mountains there came a voice that said: get used to losing everything. I was puzzled. It sounded like a phrase of Edgar's, the kind he invented without it coming from his guts, for the pure pleasure of combining sounds. Then I thought it sounded more like Paulo Coelho and I decided to erase it.

I walked downstairs and went back to the party.

Seeing me, Juana came up to me, well? did you like it? I told her it had been great, and so as not to hurt me she said, Tania wanted to fuck you as soon as she saw you. She's the one you have to thank. I hugged her and said, let's dance, let's forget this, teach me some more steps.

12

I woke up at nine, somewhat the worse for wear after that mixture of drinks the night before, but a couple of aspirins with Alka-Seltzer and a furtive swig of gin revived me.

I ran down and took a taxi opposite the hotel, with the lawyer's address in my hand, but very soon fell into the paralyzing hydra of the traffic, the great ill of Asian cities. Or of modern cities. You go so slowly that the road fills with intruders.

My head heated up again and the pain returned.

I got to the address with two minutes to spare. Teresa was waiting for me on the street outside the building.

"Thanks for coming and for being punctual," I said, giving her a kiss. "How do you feel?"

"A bit rough, to be honest," she said with a smile, "but it'll soon pass. It's been a while since I had Cuba Libres and tequila one after the other. It was worth it."

I did mention that I'd give my life to postpone the appointment and have a Bloody Mary, which at that hour of the morning has the virtue of grabbing hold of your body, messing it up, and putting it back together again without any of the pieces missing.

The lawyer was an elderly man of about seventy. His venerable appearance seemed like a good sign.

"Sit down, welcome."

He made a gesture with his hand and a second later a servant appeared with a tray. Cold water, an orange-colored soda, tea, and coffee. Biscuits and pistachios. I missed something more aggressive in terms of alcohol content. I grabbed a coffee and a glass of water. Teresa did the same.

"Good," the man said, "I don't suppose you'll be upset to know that this morning, first thing, I myself called the prosecutor and asked for a copy of the report on your compatriot Manuel Manrique. You should know that the prosecutor was my pupil at university and has great respect for me. There's nothing illegal about that. I told him that I'd be dealing with the case and that you'd be coming to see me later."

That struck me as an excellent omen. I told him that I was grateful, that I had a mandate from the Ministry to hire him as of now. We were convinced of Manrique's innocence. I suggested trying to find previous cases in which the accused had been the victim of an injustice.

"Don't worry, Consul," he said. "I know what you're thinking, and I'll tell you something: you're not on the wrong track in any way. This very day I'll begin to put together a solid number of cases. In addition, and this too is, let's say, somewhat privileged information, I know that the police are hot on the heels of a network of amphetamine traffickers from Burma. It may even be that between now and the trial we'll have some good news."

I told him I had to go back to Delhi that weekend, but it was only Wednesday. In any event I would be dealing with the case and would be coming frequently.

We signed documents, he gave me his particulars, and, just as I was about to get up, he gently held me back by the arm.

"Go and see the young man," he said, "it'll do him good. I'll make sure they respect him in Bangkwang and don't mistreat him, but it's good that you see him regularly. These little things make all the difference. The prison warden is merely a functionary who wants to do well by his country. This kingdom may appear small but it's big, Consul. The eyes of the king cannot reach into all corners."

"I'll go see him tomorrow," I said. "Today I have to ask the prosecutor for authorization."

"Don't worry about that," the lawyer said. "I'll make sure that nobody stops you going in. Go tomorrow about ten, I'll arrange everything."

We left after reading, sealing, and signing an interminable series of documents that the lawyer would send by courier to the embassy in Delhi just a few minutes later. Then he let me use his telephone and I called Olympia. I asked her to make sure that as soon as the documents arrived they were passed on to Bogotá by diplomatic baggage.

By the time we left, it was almost noon, and we saw a sign on the other side of the avenue: Lobster's Bar, Wine & Cocktails.

I said to Teresa, "Let me buy you a soda, or whatever you like. It's just midnight in Colombia and I'm dying for a Bloody Mary."

But Teresa said, "Oh, yes, Mr. Consul, and what time do you think it is in Mexico?"

We had two Bloody Marys each, to which she added a Singha beer. I looked at her in silence, but she hastened to say:

"Don't make that face, my rule is not to drink before twelve o'clock, and look, we're past that. Some people wait until two in the afternoon, but there are times when that's simply not realistic. Right, I'm off to the embassy, let's talk later. Call me."

She got in a taxi and disappeared into the traffic.

I hailed another and went back to Suan Plu Soi 6, Sathorn Road. I had the impression, or rather the intuition, that the Regency Inn Hotel still had something to tell me. Again I walked around before making up my mind to enter; if someone saw me, I thought, they might alert the true criminals ("but this isn't going to be a crime story").

This time, the young man I had seen before wasn't at the reception desk. Instead, there was a woman my age, so I asked her if I could see room 301, which was still free. She handed over the keys. As I went in, I saw myself reflected in the closet mirror. I sat for a while on the bed, without thinking of anything specific. There was nothing new, only the dense air. This was all so unfair. Something dark seemed to be making its way through the air, without seeing reason, without listening to the words of a young man who had already known, before arriving here, what it was to suffer and be very alone.

I went back to my hotel and locked myself in my room. I wanted to read, to think, even to forget. To prepare myself for the following encounter. The next day I would go early to Bangkwang.

The time had come to start listening to him.

On days like these, dear internauts, I feel the need to do something intimate, to expose another small corner of my mind to your eyes. I'm going to talk to you about the liquid of purity and madness. The most important creation of the soul in alcoholic terms. Can anyone guess? You're not even warm. Because it's a drink that's served very cold.

Like so many things in the world and in life, gin was invented in the seventeenth century (some say 1550, who is right?) by a distinguished member of the medical profession, the Dutchman Franciscus Sylvius de le Boë, and as he was a physician its original use—as you can imagine—was very different than the one we give it today: it was a diuretic. It helped us take a leak. De le Boë's ambitious idea was to relieve constipation and stomachaches according to some, gallstones and liver complaints according to others, with a mixture of distilled barley, rye, and corn, and in order to increase its potency he added berries of juniper (French: *genièvre*; Dutch: *genever*) to the brew.

Did Shakespeare drink it? If De le Boë did indeed invent it in 1550, then old Will would have been in time. It's highly unlikely that he never suffered from constipation or needed to provoke urination.

John Cheever wrote: "A lonely man is a lonesome thing, a stone, a bone, a stick, a receptacle for Gilbey's gin, a stooped figure sitting at the edge of a hotel bed, heaving copious sighs like the autumn wind."

When the recipe crossed the English Channel and reached the British Isles, at the time of William of Orange—who was Dutch, like Rembrandt and van Gogh and Rip Van Winkle and Heineken beer—the legend was born that the name *genever* came from Guinevere, the wife of King Arthur of the Round Table, an intelligent woman generous with her private parts, who cuckolded the king with Lancelot of the Lake. (I would have done the same, with a name like that!)

By the way, do you know why the Swiss don't drink whiskey?

Because they have a lake of gin (Lake Geneva, get it?).

Before then, the English used to get plastered—what a crude word that is, how much more refined is *se soûlaient la gueule*—on pear liqueurs and French wines, but the closing of trade with France led to authorization being given for the distilling of grains native to the British Isles. When it comes to binges and benders, you have to be independent.

Gin was a "smash hit." Two and a half million gallons in 1690, five million in 1727, and twenty-one million ten years later. With a population of six and a half million, that makes, let's see, three and a half gallons a head per year! Not bad. Alarmed, in 1736 Parliament passed the Gin Act, levying high taxes on sales, thus restoring order and saying: "We're Protestants! We have to defer gratification!"

The English say, with their English sense of humor: "There's always someone trying to stop us from getting drunk," but the producers continued bottling the stuff secretly and consumption increased. Bernard Shaw would say much later: "Alcohol is the anesthesia by which we endure the operation of life."

In 1742, there were twelve thousand arrests. Faced with this landslide of prisoners—drunks sleeping it off in prison cells—Parliament lowered the taxes. Life is short and drink is long and plentiful. The producers went back to making legal gin, of excellent quality. The first to have a registered name, in 1749, was Booth's, the oldest distillery in England.

As Frank Sinatra says: "Alcohol may be man's worst enemy, but the Bible says love your enemy."

It was normal to drink it without ice. Sometimes with a little sugar. Lord Byron said that gin and water was the origin of his inspiration. In a grim period it was recognized as the drink (not bitter but sweet) of the lower classes. Charles Dickens, being a puritan, denounced the "gin palaces." Prime Minister Gladstone tried to limit its sale to certain bars and lost his seat. "I was buried under a torrent of gin," he said.

The favorite son of gin is the dry martini, which takes us to the other side of the Atlantic.

Humphrey Bogart's last words were: "I should never have switched from Scotch to martinis." They were his doom, as they were for many elegant drunks with their tuxedos and their cigarette cases. A martini in the hand was a symbol of success in the country where success matters. We are in the United States, friends.

Someone once said that the martini was the only American invention as perfect as the sonnet. Is that possible? At the Tehran conference of 1943, President Roosevelt gave it to Stalin to try. Stalin looked at the glass, drank it cautiously, looked at his advisers, then licked his mustache and asked for more. Later, Nikita Khrushchev would say that the martini was the true "lethal weapon" of the United States.

"When I get to heaven I am going to ask St. Peter to take me to the man who invented the dry martini," wrote William Buckley. "Just so I can say thanks."

Who was that man? Not an easy question to answer.

There are three hypotheses. The "San Francisco theory" attributes it to the bartender Jerry Thomas, born in New Haven, Connecticut, in 1825, who worked in the bar of the Hotel Occidental in San Francisco. In 1862 he published his

Bartenders' Guide, in which he includes inventions such as the Tom & Jerry and the Blue Blazer. *Et voilà!* In a later edition, in 1887 there appears a new cocktail called the Martinez. Martinez was a town in California and, according to the legend, Thomas made it for a man who was on his way to Martinez. "Very well, friend, this is a new drink I've just invented for your journey," he said. Martinez became Martine, and then Martini.

But the citizens of Martinez have their own theory (the "Martinez theory"). It's this: in about 1870 there was a bar owned by a Frenchman named Jules Richelieu, who had moved there from New Orleans. On one occasion a miner came in and asked for a whiskey. Richelieu filled his hip flask, but the man, on trying it, spat it out and cursed. Ashamed, the Frenchman is supposed to have said: "Wait, I'd like you to try something different." He made a mixture and served it in a glass with an olive. The miner tried it, smiled, drank it all down in one go, and asked Richelieu: "What is it?" Richelieu replied: "It's a Martinez cocktail."

The final hypothesis (the "New York theory") is that of a mysterious bartender named Martini di Arma di Taggia, an Italian immigrant, who worked in the bar of the now-defunct Knickerbocker Hotel in New York (on 42nd and Broadway). According to this version it was invented in 1912, and became popular because it was the favorite drink of John D. Rockefeller, a hypothesis supported by one of the best known experts on cocktails, the Englishman John Doxat, author of *The World of Drinks and Drinking* (1971).

For sad Jack London, the martini was a symbol of social ascent: going from whiskey to martini was like jumping from the frozen wastes of the Yukon to the drawing rooms of the Upper West Side.

Oh, no! What do we do now?

We close the bars!

On January 16, 1920, thirty-six states ratified the Eighteenth Amendment to the Constitution, prohibiting the sale of alcohol.

Buñuel, who was in Los Angeles around that period, wrote in his memoirs: "I have never drunk as much as I did during the period of Prohibition."

It lasted until 1934, when Franklin D. Roosevelt signed the decree repealing it in the Oval Office of the White House, in front of the press. To drive home the point, he mixed the first legal martini for the cameras and the flashbulbs.

The dry martini entered literature and the cinema. Hollywood grabbed hold of it and the actors drank it like crazy. David Niven always had a glass in his hand. Marlene Dietrich only chose lovers who drank martinis (as she admitted once to Hemingway), and its short glass, like an upside-down umbrella, was reproduced in paintings, photographs, and advertisements. The one by Mel Ramos is famous: a naked woman sitting in a glass of martini.

The best verse was written by Dorothy Parker (hers is the brilliant phrase: "brevity is the soul of lingerie"). Her poem says:

I like to have a martini,
Two at the very most.
After three I'm under the table,
After four I'm under the host.

14

I graduated high school at the end of that year and enrolled to study philosophy at the National University. Mother took her head in her hands and started crying. Father said angrily, oh, my God, first the girl becomes a guerrilla and now this fool wants to become an intellectual, it's like a disease! what did we do to have children like this, Lord? why are you trying our patience?

Whenever we were out on the street and Father saw beggars under a bridge, he would say, look, Manuel, a philosophers' convention, is that what you want from life? you're going to die of hunger! To stop him bugging me, I showed him an Internet page that said the philosopher Fernando Savater had been paid twenty-five thousand euros for a lecture. Father looked at it suspiciously and said, it isn't possible, it must be a mistake or a fake, Manuel, you faked it, you can fake anything with the Internet . . . Who is this Savater?

The university! At last I was leaving that absurd high school behind. Getting out and spending my time with people similar to me was a blessed respite. Although not without its drawbacks. One mistake we make when we're young is to believe that people who are interested in the same things as we are must necessarily be similar to us. Nature does its work, the spirit blows where it will. There are envious and wicked people even in worlds that we would think are dominated by clarity and beauty, but be that as it may, at the university I began a period of calm, intense reading, and for the first time felt that I was finding some kind of harmony.

The first semester passed, then the second.

Apart from my own classes, I loved to wander around the fine arts department, sometimes sneaking into one of the studios to see what they were doing. There too, surrounded by the smell of turpentine, in those spaces dominated by the sensual qualities of color and volume, I felt a great sense of peace, although I never regretted my choice. I was getting to know the world. Sometimes, when I left my classes late or stuck around for a talk in the lecture theater, I'd paint secretly on the walls of the faculty: letters, islands, storms, skies.

It was a period of long silences, Consul. My life had settled into a pleasant routine, and repeating it daily, without any upsets, was a genuine relief. Attending my classes, reading in the library, going to seminars and lectures, reading on the bus, reading on the lawns of the university, reading at home, going to the movies, scribbling in exercise books, taking notes. Life at home was the same as ever, but now I could also be a long way away. As I got used to the outside world, Mother and Father came to seem as if they belonged to another era, like an old sepia photograph.

Another semester passed, and another.

Sometimes Juana would come and find me after my classes and we'd have a glass of red wine in the cafeteria or go up to Chapinero for a bite to eat. I can still see her on the sidewalk, her hands deep in her pockets, shivering with cold in the wind coming down from the hills or avoiding the fumes from the buses. We'd eat whatever, Chinese food, fried chicken, pizza, and talk about my courses, the things we were both reading, movies, and sometimes also about politics, but while I talked or listened to her talking I felt something strange, a kind of premature nostalgia, as if in those chats of ours I already had a premonition of what was soon going to happen: her disappearance, the way that suddenly, without anything unusual happening, she stopped being among us, without a word, which was worse than if she'd died, Consul, because when someone dies you're there, you witness their deterioration and are aware of the advance of death, its progress, and there even comes a time when you want it to come and set everyone free.

Juana disappeared without anything to suggest it was about to happen, although later, remembering those afternoons at the university, it seemed to me that a wind of anguish was already blowing our way, the urgency of something that was about to fall, because sad and tragic things do announce their coming, I believe, they don't come just like that, they aren't mere chance, don't you agree? At least that's how I remember it now, how I imagine it, even though I always end up wondering, what could she have feared in those years? I knew very little of Juana's life. Her constant absences, coming back early in the morning, bursting into tears for no obvious reason, all that was a mystery. That's how we remember people who disappear or die, everything that happened before seems bathed in a symbolic glow, an aura that, with hindsight, appears to be the forewarning of a tragedy.

I've observed that there are two ways to die.

The first is an illness that causes us to deteriorate and submerges us in a slow agony. That's sad, but in a way it's good for the relatives and friends, who have time to get used to the idea, although it's painful to the dying person himself, because of all the pain, decay, and indignity it carries with it. The second is the opposite: a gunshot in the back of the neck, a brain hemorrhage, a traffic accident. Your relatives suffer but you go quietly. You go quickly to the other side. That's the best way.

But there's a third way, at least in our country, a way that's cruel for everybody: disappearance. For everybody? The victim suffers from imagining the anguish of his nearest and dearest. The relatives suffer because they cling to any hope they can, and when it's lost they suffer even more when they imagine the terrible loneliness of the death: someone kneeling in a patch of waste ground, in the early morning, shaking with fear, pissing in his pants, then two or three flashes and, already, a lifeless body falling into a hole, the earth covering it, vegetation growing over it and hiding it, the long suffering of those who spend years investigating, searching for that place, that horrible, monstrous place, trying to understand the reasons, the still inexplicable reasons, for what happened, why he was killed, to find his bones and clasp them and kiss them, trying to relieve the loneliness, to bathe it with tears.

When Juana disappeared I felt all that: grief, hatred, sadness, pity, resentment, guilt.

There wasn't even a date, at what moment did she go? We didn't know, we didn't even realize. She would go on her travels, giving vague details, and the family got used to it. I got used to it. Juana would ask me to understand, tell me that she was still working on our escape plan, that I shouldn't ask questions, that I should trust her blindly. That's why I didn't know at what moment it happened.

One day I simply noticed she wasn't there anymore.

And so began that succession of ideas, of intolerable images, of hurtful words. My first reaction was to grab my bag of spray cans and paint her on all the walls of the city: her eyes, the palm of her hand supporting her chin, her smiling face, her figure walking towards me, and a question, where are you? For me it was inconceivable that the world should continue to turn without her, that the sun should rise and shoots should emerge from the trunks of trees and there should be disasters in distant places, how could the wheel not stop? One day, on Thirtieth, I walked past one of my paintings and saw that someone, an anonymous graffiti artist, had written beside it: "Why don't you come back? can't you see how he's suffering?" Somehow, the city was answering me.

She's been murdered, I thought, she must be in one of those mass graves in this country that's rich in cemeteries, our beautiful national territory, the body must be rotting, her bones must be starting to separate without anybody caressing them, without my having had the chance to kiss them.

Where are you, Juana?

I thought it would be enough to love her and walk about the city, reproducing her and calling to her on streets and avenues; I thought that intuition or a ray of sunlight, as in the poem by Salvatore Quasimodo, would indicate a place, but that didn't happen. We reported her missing, and the small amount of information we were able to obtain showed that she hadn't been arrested or murdered or kidnapped, of course the disappeared have no record of their disappearance, that's why they call them disappeared, but you have to start somewhere, and Father, with that blind faith of his in the country that, according to him, "we had at last," went to police stations, prisons, courthouses, hospitals, the ombudsman, and, finally, to his hated NGOs.

That's when he started to change: his admiration for Uribe weakened and one day I heard him say that human rights weren't being respected in Colombia, that our family had already lost the war, and that there had been enough raised fists and hot air. With bloodshot eyes and an expression that might well have been weariness, he said, we have to do things differently, we can't carry on like this.

One Sunday, much to my surprise, he came and woke me early. Get dressed quickly and come with me, Manuel, your mother doesn't want to come. I got up without knowing what it was about and had the shock of my life: Father was going to a demonstration for the disappeared! He was wearing a T-shirt that said *Where are they?* and holding a banner with a colored photograph of Juana. I had taken that photograph, Consul, and it was one of the best ones we had of her. On it she was smiling, just about to puff at a cigarette, looking out of the corner of her eye, as if keeping a humorous eye on someone, and raising a glass of wine. Father had chosen that photograph, and below it, in black letters, he had written *Juana Manrique, twenty-four, disappeared November 2008.*

I got up and took a quick shower, put on a white T-shirt, on which I wrote my sister's name, and went out with him, by his side for once, feeling that for the first time something united us. How strange this is, I thought, after a life spent not understanding each other, with me thinking him mediocre, always judging him harshly, but that morning, seeing him advancing along Seventh to Plaza de Bolívar, raising the banner with his daughter's name and shouting, where is she? I admired him, for the first time in my life I wasn't ashamed of him and I felt proud to be by his side, absorbing his cries so that his voice and mine should be one, and so I also raised my fist and cried out, feeling less alone, cried out for what we had lost that now made us both the same person.

Juana Manrique! where is she?

A mass of people was advancing, yelling slogans, holding up flags and banners with bloodstained silhouettes of the country, patterns of bones, mounds of corpses, crows with military hats, an enormous skeleton with a scythe in its hand and the presidential sash across its chest, saying, "Colombia, I will liberate you." And the cry went up:

"Uribe, watch out, the people are coming!"

The demonstration reached Plaza de Bolívar, where the organizers had set up an enormous dais for the main event just in front of the steps of Congress. For a couple of hours there were orators citing testimonies and giving analyses, declarations of support from some senators and political personalities, songs, and even a mime show, the mimes weeping in silence, swallowing their sighs and their tears just as we were all doing in that square, a couple thousand sad, angry people, some still hopeful, until slowly it started to spit, the sky darkened, and the rain came down, in a neutral, subdued way at first, but then, after some terrifying claps of thunder, the downpour really began, forcing some of the people to run and take shelter in the colonnades of the cathedral or under the eaves on Eighth Street. Others took out umbrellas and remained in front of the stage, where the mimes were looking up at the clouds and making gestures of surprise. That's how the rain is in Bogotá, it always arrives at the worst or saddest moments.

We started walking back along Seventh looking for some transportation heading north, but the street was closed because of the demonstration so we had to go on foot, dodging puddles, from eave to eave, avoiding the rain. Father didn't care about getting wet, but jealously protected the banner with the photograph of Juana, maybe he was trying to protect her; and so we walked side by side in silence in that ghostly city that is Bogotá in the rain.

Without knowing how, absorbed in our thoughts, we reached Chapinero, just as the black clouds dispersed and you could finally see a piece of the sky.

As we crossed Fiftieth and Seventh a black Mercedes passed us. One of its wheels hit a puddle and the water it threw up splashed our pants, making them even wetter than they already were. The driver turned and looked at me, just for a second, but long enough for me to recognize him. It was Edgar Porras.

The Mercedes moved away and I saw him looking at me in the rearview mirror, I hesitated for a moment, but then I grabbed Father's arm and said, let's carry on, old man, let's walk a little more, it's only just twelve-thirty, we should be in time for lunch.

Mother didn't change. Whenever she mentioned Juana's disappearance her voice was sad, but the tragedy didn't seem to have shifted anything essential inside her. She carried on the same, and had her problems with Father. Luckily, I was almost never there at mealtimes.

Sometimes, Father would come into my room in the early hours. He would apologize and say, I saw the light was on, Manuel, can I come in for a while? I can't get to sleep, dammit . . . He'd sit down on my bed, take a quart of aguardiente from the pocket of his dressing gown, and have a few slugs. He'd offer it to me and I'd say, I can't sleep either, that's why I'm reading. But he'd say, if only I could, Manuel, if only I could stop thinking. He'd sit there for a while in silence. Then we'd hug and he'd go. Seeing his resigned expression, I knew he would spend the night awake. His prayers, like mine, drifted up into the darkest part of the sky and faded away. There was nobody who could listen to them.

I told you that we never found out exactly when she disappeared, because she had gotten us used to her being away for long periods, and this was just the latest one; only when too much time had passed without her coming back did I decide to call her on her cell phone, and not getting any reply or any e-mail message, I realized that something was wrong. So I said to Father, do you know when Juana is coming back? And he looked worried and said, I was just about to ask you the same question, son, I don't have any idea, how come you don't know? That's how it all started. That's when we reported her missing and began the round of police stations, prisons, and hospitals.

Sometime later Mother said something that stayed in everybody's heads, but which nobody dared to repeat. She said it to Father when he had come back from one of his fruitless visits to some hospital or courthouse.

Oh, Alberto, maybe she ended up with FARC.

She said it, and Father immediately put his hand over her mouth, a gesture that was meant to be strong but in fact was merely desperate.

Never say that again, Bertha. Ever.

Then he took out his handkerchief and dried his eyes.

I sought out her classmates, the friends who had known her. It was a long and difficult process, since I didn't even know their names. It's incredible how little we know of the people we love. Little by little, I tracked down some of them, but nobody knew anything. They told me vague things, that she had gone on a journey, that she was doing fieldwork. None of them thought it possible that she had gotten involved with the guerrillas, who were very discredited in the university. I said that one night to Father and he moved his head, as if to dismiss the thought, and said, I knew, I knew that, but thanks anyway, Manuel.

Father ended up lodging an official registration of her disappearance with the help of the NGO Caritas. From that day on, he devoted himself to studying disappearances in Colombia in the hope of finding some clue, some lead that would show him the path to follow. He also devoted himself to aguardiente for a while, but the pain from his ulcer soon put a stop to that. He and Mother didn't talk much, at least not in front of me.

The worst thing about such situations is that life goes on.

A year passed, then another year. Father aged about ten years and Mother started taking control of things at home. The bank, knowing what had happened and seeing what bad shape he was in, told him he could take early retirement, and he thought about it seriously. But he preferred to carry on working. At home, the memory of Juana was just too strong and too sad.

I finished my philosophy degree and started a doctorate, and that's when I studied aesthetics with Gustavo Chirolla. It was the best course I ever took. But although Gustavo was fond of me I never dared to talk to him about anything personal or try to be his friend. My fellow students were on friendly terms with him, they even went to his house, he was very open, a great guy. I was dying to do that but I never dared.

I don't know why, Consul. What had happened with Juana made me feel distant, and also guilty, very guilty. Because of everything I had lost, I wasn't like the others. Without her, life wasn't worthwhile. Mine, at least. I decided to wait a little while to see if a miracle would happen.

With time, the suffering turned into something secret, a little fire that united my father and me, even though we almost never mentioned it. I knew that it was there, nothing more.

But early one morning, I was woken by some kind of light, and I sat up in bed.

Juana was alive.

I could feel her presence, as if a wind filled with words had burst into the room, and in that magma, in that invisible net, there was her voice. I heard it. It was a voice surrounded by many voices, cries surrounded by many cries. I heard it. She was alive and I had to start looking for her again. Almost three years had passed.

Of course, I didn't say anything to Father.

I decided to begin with Tania, the woman who'd initiated me into sex, and with whom I hadn't spoken since. It took me two weeks to find her, but in the end I did. She wasn't studying anymore, she never completed her course in systems engineering, and was now working in the IT department of the *El Tiempo* publishing group. On my way there, I remembered her Spanish boyfriend. The newspaper had been bought by Spaniards and I put two and two together. In the course of looking for her, I'd discovered that her real name wasn't Tania but María Claudia. Tania was her student name, a very common name in her generation, I suppose because of Che Guevara's girlfriend.

She received me in an office with a view of the hills, and I told her what had happened. Every now and again we heard the planes taking off from the runways of the airport. To persuade her to help me, I showed her the list of offices that we had scoured in the search for my sister, the civil and legal actions I'd started with my father. She was touched by all that, and decided to speak out.

Listen, I liked Juana very much, she helped me in lots of things and was always great to me. You can't even imagine what I owe her. That's why I'm going to start by telling you something you may not like, but it's important that you know.

I looked at her nervously, swallowed, and said, tell me, please, whatever it is.

Juana was working for a former Miss Colombia who ran a modeling agency, she said, and after clearing her throat added: but it was more than just modeling, what the girls did was go out with men who had money. It was actually an escort agency, you know what that means?

Yes, I said. High-class prostitution.

I think Juana's disappearance has more to do with that than with anything political, Tania went on. I didn't know her that well either. Look, this is the telephone number of the agency. That's all I know.

Now she was the one who was a little nervous.

Did you also work as an escort?

I'll be honest with you, she said, after all, you and I know each other. At that time I was in financial difficulty, I'd just broken up with a real son of a bitch, a slacker, an alcoholic, a junkie, and I had a three-year-old child. I was on the fucking street, I didn't know what to do. Your sister threw me a life-line, it was legal, she introduced me to the former Miss Colombia and I started working and earning good money. Soon afterwards I met a Spanish executive with a good position who became my boyfriend and is still my boyfriend. He helped me to get out, but I owe it all to Juana. Call this number and tell them it's from me. I'll talk to them today to make sure they see you and help you, all right? And please, when you find her tell her I'm dying to see her.

I left with a strange mixture of emotions. I couldn't believe that Juana had gotten herself involved in that world, but at the same time I was overcome with joy. She was alive, or might be. My intuition had been correct.

But after I'd taken a few steps, a shadow fell over me, bringing with it some terrible words, terrible because they had no answer: she would never have abandoned me! I couldn't imagine a situation that would have stopped her getting in touch with me. Apart from death, of course. But I had a lead, and in such cases a lead is worth everything. The following day I would go and see this mysterious former Miss Colombia.

Juana always said: I'm working so that we can escape, so that we can get out of this wretched city and go somewhere where nobody will find us, so you must believe blindly in me.

There was a light at the end of the tunnel.

Maybe desperation was part of it, and I just had to wait. But three years had passed.

The following day I called the telephone number, introduced myself as Tania's friend, and a voice gave me an appointment for six in the evening. I left the university early, feeling nervous. It was on 78th, just below Eleventh. As I was walking to the bus stop, it struck me that on a day like this I would have liked to have a friend, someone I could tell the hopes and fears I felt. It was difficult always being alone. Although I wasn't alone, I told myself: my sister is somewhere and I'm going to find her.

The building was in the process of being refurbished, although the workers appeared to be taking a break. On the first floor, with an entrance from the street, there was a drugstore that also sold stationery. I walked as far as the lobby and found a doorman dozing over an issue of *El Espectador*. I asked him about the modeling agency and he pointed out a plaque next to the entry phones: School of Modeling, third floor.

The elevator isn't working, he added, grouchily. You're going to have to use the stairs.

I walked up the three floors feeling a bit intimidated, filled with doubts, afraid of what I was about to hear. The door was opened by a woman who didn't look like a model and who turned out to be the school secretary. She smiled and said, yes, yes, the director is waiting for you, sit here a moment, we'll be with you shortly.

On the table there were copies of the magazine *TV y Novelas* with pages missing, and cards advertising a plastic surgery clinic selling various comprehensive beauty "combos" in a three-in-one offer: lips, breasts, and hips, or breasts, bottom, and thighs. The offer had expired the previous September.

The secretary came back and said, follow me, and she admitted me to a large office piled high with fashion magazines. A woman who looked familiar was sitting behind the desk. She was probably around fifty, maybe slightly less. You could see the effort she made to keep herself young, the gym and the operations, the diets and implants, the dyed hair.

When she smiled, her name almost came back to me. She gave me her hand and invited me to sit down, a soda? she said, I have Colombiana Light, which is really good. I said yes. Then we sat for a while in silence until she said: Tania tells me you're looking for Juana and that you already know what she was doing with us. I nodded. Tania thinks you may be able to help me, I said. I took my folder from my backpack with the list of places where we had been looking and the missing persons report.

The former Miss Colombia let me read to the end, listening attentively, and then said, look, I'm going to tell you something, what happened to Juana has nothing to do with that, she hasn't disappeared, and she certainly isn't dead, let me explain. What we do here is absolutely confidential, we never give out details of what our models do, but in this case, because it's such a delicate matter, I'm going to break the rules. I want you to know that it's the girls themselves who ask that no information be given to family members or friends, real or supposed, let alone to clients. Those are the rules of the game. Oh, would you mind waiting a second, please, I forgot to take my pill.

She stood up and went into the adjoining bathroom. I started leafing through a magazine, trying to contain my emotions, Juana was alive! I didn't care about the circumstances, any situation, however disastrous or degrading, was redeemable, my God, my heart was almost coming out of my chest, one of my arms started shaking, and I wanted the woman to take her time coming back.

Suddenly I heard a loud sniff from behind the bathroom door; five seconds later, a second one, even louder. Then the woman came back to her desk.

Sorry about that. Now then, before anything else I want to make it clear to you that what I'm going to tell you you mustn't repeat anywhere, let alone in front of a judge or anything like that. The reason I'm telling you this is because I want to help you and your family, but in a confidential way, without it leaving these four walls, do you understand what I'm saying?

She looked me in the eyes. Her own eyes were beautiful. One of the few things in her body that didn't appear altered. I told her she needn't worry. This was a totally personal search. If Juana's disappearance had nothing to do with politics there'd be no need for legal action. That seemed to reassure her.

Well, what I can tell you is this: she went to Japan to work. Three years ago.

Japan? I was stunned, incredulous. Japan? You mean she went there to . . . ?

Yes, to work as an escort. She's making tons of money. At that time I had a good contact, a Colombian woman who received them and put them in the best houses. Everything is very select there. I can tell you my associate was called Maribel, I don't know her surname, and to tell the truth I haven't heard from her in more than two years. I think she was detained by immigration, and I don't know what happened, if they sent her back here or if she's in prison over there. Apparently her papers weren't in order. Since that time I haven't heard from Juana. Look, I can give you this: a copy of your sister's ticket and travel itinerary. She left from Quito, not from Bogotá. I never knew why and I didn't ask. I'd already talked to her about the possibility of Japan, and one afternoon she called me up and said she was interested. She asked me to get her a ticket, leaving from Quito, and told me it was critical she didn't give me any explanation. Here's the photocopy.

From Quito to São Paulo. From there to Dubai. From there to Bangkok and then to Tokyo. I was puzzled. I didn't know you could do that route. I asked, why such a long way around?

To avoid visas, darling. You don't go through the United States or through Europe, you see? A Schengen visa is very difficult to get, and as for the United States, forget it. This way you pass under the radar, if you see what I mean.

I thanked her and put the paper in my pocket. And when did you last hear of her?

The last time was when Maribel wrote to me from Tokyo saying she had arrived and that they were finding a place for her. That was a week after the flight, November 3, 2008. Up until then, I was responsible. From that point on, everyone makes their own life and doesn't owe anyone an explanation, because we're talking about adults here, free, independent adults, right? That was the last I heard. A month later I tried to talk to Maribel about another girl who wanted to go, but she took a long time to reply and then, three months later, she wrote and told me she was having legal problems and had to stop. I never heard any more after that.

I looked again at the photocopy of the ticket, and read my sister's name about ten times. The letters danced in front of my eyes, I couldn't believe it. At last I had something concrete.

The former Miss Colombia stood up and went back to the bathroom. Again I heard two sniffs. Then she came out and said:

It's possible your sister was arrested along with Maribel. That's where you could start looking.

I asked her again if she had any contact information for Maribel in Colombia, but she said no. She didn't even know her last name. Well, I said, you've been an enormous help, do I owe you anything? No, come on, said the former Miss Colombia. Go find your sister and when you're with her tell her I miss her and she should give me a call.

When we said goodbye she gave me a kiss on the cheek.

I went back out on the street, feeling strange. Japan, Quito, what the hell did it all mean? I took the copy of the ticket from my pocket and made two photocopies in the stationery store. On the way home, I read it again at least a hundred times. At the traffic light on Eleventh, a couple looked at me in alarm from their car and I hid my face. I was crying.

When I got home, I locked myself in my room.

I switched on my computer and started searching: Japan, escorts, Colombian women in Japan. There were lots of names and telephone numbers, and I didn't know what to do. I looked for the Colombian embassy in Japan and the Japanese embassy in Colombia. I copied down all the numbers, a very long list. Also the codes and the time difference. It was eight in the evening in Bogotá, nine the following morning in Tokyo. The timing was right, I was sure to get through. But I didn't have any money. My heart was still pounding. When I went down to the living room I saw Father on the couch, with his head thrown back and a newspaper open on his lap. He was asleep. As soon as I took one step, he opened his eyes, are you going out at this hour? Yes, I said, and I need money. He looked at me in surprise. How much? About ten thousand pesos, I said. He pointed to his jacket and said, take it from my wallet. With the money in my hand I said goodbye. Thanks, Dad, I won't be back late. He didn't reply, but as soon as I opened the door I heard him from the living room, it isn't to buy drugs, is it?

No, Dad. It isn't for that. I swear.

That's good, son. Take care.

I took a bus to the Church of Lourdes, because I'd seen a few call shops in the vicinity. I found one on Eleventh and asked how much it cost to call Tokyo. Seven hundred pesos for a minute. Hell, that's expensive, I thought. I could only talk for about fifteen minutes. I went to one of the booths, dialed the number of the Colombian embassy, and waited. When the ringing started, my heart began pounding, and a drop of sweat ran down my back. Six rings, seven. They finally answered, and I explained that I was calling from Bogotá, that I had a sister who was lost in Japan, and gave the name and her identity card number. I was about to repeat it when a voice said, please hang on, I'll put you through to the consulate; there was an internal switchboard noise, followed by some music by Vivaldi. I looked at the digital counter, three minutes and forty-six seconds, and then they answered at last, and I quickly explained that I was calling from Bogotá and that my sister was lost in Tokyo, and the name, and then the official said, can you repeat that, please? one moment, and left me waiting, and I looked at the counter, seven minutes and fifty seconds, my heart was stopping me from breathing, and then the man came back and said, no, there's no record of anyone with that name, so I asked, what if she's in prison? and they said, oh, one moment, and again Vivaldi, ten minutes and five seconds, more Vivaldi, twelve minutes and fifty seconds; the voice returned and said, no, there's nobody registered under that name, all right, thanks, I said, and hung up, fourteen minutes and forty-eight seconds. I paid the ten thousand pesos and went out with my head about to burst.

I went up to Seventh and started walking back, looking at the expanse of the hills, the darker areas between the lights of the buildings and the lampposts, and I was filled with reproaches, questions, guilt: why didn't you tell me? did you think I was going to judge you? do you think I'd have tried to stop you? It's possible, it's possible, where are you at this precise moment, while I'm walking along a horrible avenue filled with buses and vulgar people rushing along the sidewalks?

I got home at eleven. I didn't want to meet Father in the living room, let alone Mother, so I made a few detours. I was grateful that he hadn't asked me what the money was for. Ever since Juana had disappeared, he had become more generous toward me. Mother, on the other hand, continued with her suspicions and her silences, and those horrible ironic remarks of hers, a way of dealing with problems that consisted of not discussing them at the time, pretending they didn't exist, and then bringing them out in front of other people and ridiculing Father. What most bothered me about her was her apparent insensitivity toward what had happened to Juana. I say apparent, Consul, because I'm giving her the benefit of the doubt, after all it was her eldest child, but the truth is, she didn't give a damn, I'd even say she was pleased. That's how she was, resentful and evil.

In my room, I went on the Internet and started to look at images of Tokyo: it seemed to me a strange, unreal city. Then I looked out at the night from my window. In Japan it was already the following day, which meant that Juana was in the future. She ran away to the future, I thought. She's intelligent.

That was the moment, Consul, when I decided to go to Japan and look for her.

The next question, obviously, was, how to get there? Of course the decision was connected to another one, the decision to leave home forever. I couldn't turn to Father, because if I did I'd have to tell him everything and hurt him even more. I

felt that now was the moment, that, as they say in romantic stories, fate was knocking at my door. Knock, knock. The hour
had come for me to go. Deciding to do so made me euphoric
and I started with the most complicated thing. I took out
Juana's plane ticket, went on a website offering cheap flights,
eDreams, and checked the fares. The journey from Bogotá—
Juana's was from Quito—would cost seven thousand dollars.
In other words, to find her, I would need at least twice that.
About fifteen thousand dollars, thirty million pesos, which was
in the realm of fantasy, even for Father.

Where could I get hold of that kind of money? I fell asleep
making calculations. Working and saving, it would take at least
two years. Out of the question. Sell something? I had nothing
of value. Rob? I couldn't think whom. A sliver of an idea
crossed my mind: Father worked in a bank, couldn't I rob it?
After all, Brecht taught us that it's a worse crime to create a
bank than to rob it. But these were idle thoughts, it would be
like planting a dagger in Father's heart, and he'd already been
hurt enough.

What to do, then?

I spent a week thinking and nothing occurred to me.
Everything that came to mind was impossible or ridiculous. I
actually imagined I was robbing a supermarket like the
Pomona on Seventh, not far from my house, but I calculated
that I would have to rob it at least three times to get the full
amount together. It was impossible for someone like me to get
hold of that much money.

After a while I hit on an idea that was also fairly desperate,
but was the only one that didn't seem impossible.

The former Miss Colombia.

Maybe she could think of a way for me to make that journey. Without asking for an appointment I went to the modeling agency. The secretary said, oh, you're back! Obviously you
like it, and winked. I wasn't too sure what she was referring to,

but she announced me and the former Miss Colombia received me in the same office, looking rather more of a mess than the first time, maybe due to the fact that there were a half-empty bottle of aguardiente and a plastic cup on the desk. When she saw me, she smiled and said:

How did it go with Juana? did you find her?

I said no, I'd barely started. I told her I'd called the Colombian embassy in Tokyo and that they had no record of her. Nor had she been arrested. I don't know why I felt the need to tell her all that.

The former Miss Colombia looked at me with interest and offered me a drop of aguardiente. I accepted. Then she went to the bathroom and came back ten seconds later, rubbing her gums with one finger.

So what are you planning to do, darling? she said.

I'm convinced Juana is there and I want to go and find her, I said. I've already made up my mind, but I have a problem: the money. The journey costs fifteen thousand dollars and I don't have it. That's why I came here. Maybe you can think of a way to finance me, make me a loan, something like that.

The former Miss Colombia didn't say no immediately, but moved her head up and down.

Okay, okay, she said. It's difficult, and it is a lot of money, but let me see. Write your cell phone number on this piece of paper, and if I think of something I'll make sure they call you, and you'll come, all right?

I thanked her and went out on the street. That she hadn't said no, or laughed in my face, seemed to me already a success. She was the only person who could help me. Now I just had to wait.

And that was what I did: I waited and waited, nervously watching the display screen of my cell phone. Five or six days went by, I can't remember exactly, until at last it rang.

Manuel Manrique? a voice asked. You have an appointment

at the modeling agency on Friday night at seven. I said I'd be there on time.

Three nervous, frantic days passed. When you're waiting, time is heavy, impossible to get hold of. I don't know anything about time.

By 6:40 on Friday evening I was at the door of the building, looking insistently at my watch. I smoked a cigarette, then another. 6:49. I went in slowly and walked up to the third floor. The secretary was more jovial than usual. How delightful of you to come back and see us, she said loudly; but as she said the last words drool ran from her mouth. Very strange.

This time the former Miss Colombia had a bottle of vodka and a cooler. With her was a man who also looked familiar, an old TV heartthrob whose name I couldn't remember.

They poured me a drink. She was the one who spoke first.

I've been thinking over what you told me about Tokyo, but the truth is, what we might be interested in is Bangkok. I told her that my sister's journey had taken her through Bangkok.

She and the man looked at each other for a moment and nodded. Then he spoke.

We'd be prepared to pay for your entire journey, to give you the fifteen thousand dollars, but you have to bring us back a small case some friends of ours in Bangkok are sending us.

And what's in this case? I said, although, Consul, you'd have had to be an idiot not to realize that it was something to do with drugs. I knew where I was and who they were, but my need was great and required me to take risks. Beggars can't be choosers.

Some pills, the kind that people take in discos, the man said. It's no problem, my friends there will help you to pack them. We've already done it lots of times and nothing ever happens.

It was my only chance and I thought I'd be able to get away

from them. Or that I'd come back with her. When I was with Juana, we'd find a way to get out of this. So I said yes.

I accept. What do I have to do?

A relatively simple process started. I had to go to 100th Street to get a passport. Then decide on a date. The Holy Week holidays would be ideal in order not to arouse suspicion. They agreed. That was less than a month away. They gave me half a million pesos for the preparations: a suitcase, vacation clothes, things for the journey, a diary, a camera, I had to make my journey credible. They asked for my address in Bogotá and my parents' names. That bothered me, since I knew that if I didn't do what they wanted they would go looking for them. But that would be after Juana, and with her the problems of the world would cease to exist. Together we could face anything, so I gave them the dates, the names, I told them where my father worked, the telephone number of his office.

They checked it in front of me, calling him, telling him it was a special offer of a trip to Cartagena de Indias, to which he, of course, answered no and told them to go to hell and hung up on them, insulting them for calling him and bothering him during working hours, which was very much like him, of course, a trip to Cartagena de Indias? what an idea.

I couldn't keep the things at home, so I left them at the modeling agency.

One Thursday, I arrived after five in the evening to leave a digital camera that I had gotten hold of, secondhand, at the Lago shopping mall, and the secretary opened the door to me, smiling from ear to ear. She was more cheerful than usual and said, come in, darling, can I help you?

I explained it to her and she came with me to the office of the former Miss Colombia, who wasn't there. I bent down to open the suitcase and put in the camera and a memory stick.

When I turned around, I saw that she was lifting her skirt and showing me her shaved pubis; the strange thing is that she was laughing and at the same time drooling, a strange expression, either of stupidity or anal dilation, so I said to her, are you all right?, and she said, oh, darling, don't you think I'm pretty or what? look how sexy I am, and she reached out her hand and said, here, take this and she came up to me and gave me a red pill, take it, handsome, and just see how good you feel.

I put it under my tongue without swallowing it and straightened up, but she threw herself on me and tried to kiss me, and in the struggle I ended up swallowing the damned pill; a minute later I felt a tickling in my blood, a great calm, and a desire for lots of things, as if my body and my skin couldn't cope, and then the woman led me over to a couch, pulled down my trousers, and started to suck my cock. A mountain of sugar dissolved in my veins, and I lost all notion of time. Suddenly she turned, put herself on all fours, kneeling on the couch, and said, will you fuck me, darling? I stopped seeing her, there was nothing in front of me but a spiral of colors, like fireworks.

I regained consciousness on the street, walking to Seventh with the sun behind me, in the middle of a violent sunset that brought out the outlines of the hills and turned them into masses of color, like paintings by Rothko; I walked along, feeling strong, and told myself, all this is about to change, for the first time my life is going to be truly mine.

When I got to Eleventh I had a hallucination: Juana was sitting in the branches of a willow tree, next to a shop selling cell phones. With her hand, she said to me, come, Manuel, come, and she whispered, I'm waiting for you, you'll find me if you follow the signs I left, a path of shiny leaves in the wood, a symbolic wood, like the one in Baudelaire, you'll see, it'll be easy, and when we're together we'll go to another planet, the one you're going to create with your imagination for the two of us, so that both of us can be happy.

Five days later, I left my home forever.

I said goodbye to Father, who was in the dining room underlining and analyzing the newspaper, which he did every morning before going to work. I put my hand on his shoulder and said, goodbye, Dad, look after yourself. He looked at me for a moment, a little surprised, but didn't say anything; then I waved goodbye to Mother, who barely responded, just lifted her chin slightly.

By ten, I was at the airport. The flight to São Paulo wasn't leaving until past noon. The former Miss Colombia and her friend went with me as far as Immigration. In the Juan Valdez Café, before boarding, the man gave me an envelope with five thousand dollars, which I put in my jacket. I already had a list with the telephone numbers and names I had to contact, and in any case, they said, someone would be waiting for me at the airport. In Bangkok I would spend a couple of days making those contacts. Once that was done, and everything was ready, I would go to Tokyo for a week to look for my sister. Then I would go back to Bangkok to pick up the merchandise and make the return journey to Colombia. They agreed that, in that way, I would arouse less suspicion. It was a simple plan.

My secret plan was different: once I found Juana in Japan, I'd get lost. Nothing else mattered to me anymore.

They went with me to the international departures entrance and said goodbye with big hugs, as if they were my parents. I was trembling slightly as I walked to Immigration.

I was leaving Bogotá, leaving Colombia. I couldn't believe it.

The Immigration officer asked me a routine question, where are you traveling to? São Paulo, I replied, showing my boarding pass. He stamped my passport. I passed through baggage check, where they searched me a couple of times. I went into the duty-free shop. Then I sat down in the departure lounge and looked at the other passengers, the hustle and bustle, the rush.

When I got on the plane everything was new. They gave me

a window seat, just behind the wing. Was I nervous? Yes, a little. The movie of my whole life passed through my mind, the way they say it happens when you're about to die. Next to me sat a young Brazilian girl with an iPod. She smelled good and was very beautiful. When she leaned forward she revealed the top half of her tanned ass. She asked me if I was going to Brazil on vacation. A few moments later, the plane started moving and taxied to the runway. It gathered speed and I sank into my seat. I felt a strange pleasure and a second later saw my hated city from above.

Poor, wretched Bogotá, I thought, I'm never going to see you again.

The plane did a number of turns until I lost sight of it. I felt something strange running down my cheeks. I was crying again.

I crossed the world. I flew over the Amazon and the Atlantic. I passed over Africa and reached the Persian Gulf. Then Asia Minor, India, and finally, the Malay Peninsula and my first destination, Thailand.

At Bangkok airport I was absolutely determined to get away from the former Miss Colombia and her partner, so once I'd collected my baggage, I slipped away through the crowd, hailed a taxi, and went to a hotel that I had chosen over the Internet with that in mind. It wasn't the one they had booked for me and I thought that this way I could evade them. To avoid upsets, I stayed in my room after registering. The plan was not to go out until three days had passed, during which time I would wait before carrying on to Tokyo.

I'm not naive, I knew they would look for me and raise the alarm. The only thing I could do was remain hidden, not move, and each day would be a small triumph. The first one was like that. There were no strange movements. That night, I went down and ate in the cafeteria and didn't see anything threatening, although the service people looked at me with strange expressions. Twelve thousand miles from my city, everything was bound to be strange, I told myself. The second day was the same, and I ventured outside. To be on the safe side, I took the money, the passport, and the ticket with me. If they came to my room they could keep everything, nothing that was in the case mattered to me. I went down to the river and crossed it in a canoe. I saw the skyline of the city in the sunset and it struck me as sad. The river was sad too, as if it was carrying along with it something that never get completely clean, as if it was running through a membrane that was about to burst painfully.

When night fell I had dinner in a restaurant that had a terrace over the Chao Phraya. I kept looking at it, hypnotized by that desolation. I should have listened to what it was telling me, but I couldn't understand it. I got back to the hotel at eleven that night and lay down to sleep, thinking that the following day, very early, I would go to the airport. At six in the morning someone knocked at the door. I was scared and stayed in bed, hoping they would go away, which was highly unlikely. They knocked more loudly and I got up and looked through the peephole. They were police officers and that calmed me down. I opened the door and asked what was going on, but instead of answering they pushed me with my face against the wall. Then they handcuffed me and took me out into the corridor.

They brought me here and the rest you know. They found those pills in my case, but they weren't mine, I didn't put them there. I was trying to escape and they caught me, and that was the punishment. The police know that. I haven't committed any crime.

15

M anuel stopped speaking and sat there in silence, in the darkest corner of his cell. I supposed it was the first time he had spoken so much, the first time he had told his life story in such an extensive and desperate way. It was clear to me that he wanted to save himself. That was the deep meaning of his story: a cry for help. Then he said:

"Consul, the reason I told you all this is because I want to ask you something. Find her for me. Go to Tokyo and bring back Juana. That may seem a lot to ask, but it's my last request. Think of it as the final wish of a condemned man."

I was silent for a moment, looking at him. In spite of everything, he still believed in something. He was barely twenty-seven years old, that must have been it. We soon forget our youth and what it entails. I noted down a few names. This wasn't really my role, I was thinking, but I'd once written: "When you know the right thing to do, the hard thing is not to do it." That phrase had acquired a new meaning, its eloquence was showing me the way, there in the hot, dirty air of Bangkwang.

I said yes, I would go and find her, but in return he had to plead guilty to save his life.

"If you find her, my life is hers," Manuel said. "I'll do whatever Juana says."

When I left, it was pouring rain. Another of those tropical downpours that arrive suddenly and obscure the air. I refused the tea offered me by one of the prison trusties and walked back to my taxi. The driver was asleep in the backseat.

We returned to the city beneath columns of water and roaring clouds. The paddy fields glittered, illuminated by a slanting sun that came from another part of the sky. I went straight to see the lawyer, thanked him for arranging my visit, and again asked him to take personal charge of the case. As he spoke, I saw that he had an open book on the table. It was *The History of Rome* by Jules Michelet, in an English translation. Once again he had surprised me.

Noticing that I was looking at the book, he said:

"You know what I've always thought? It's curious that your culture, Western culture, comes from that crazy empire, with its Caligulas and its Heliogabaluses. It's no surprise that you're living through such an incomprehensible era today."

I looked at him with approval. I thought to say something but preferred to keep silent, now was not the time to start a historical discussion.

"The day after tomorrow I'm going back to Delhi," I said. "I'll call you frequently, and keep in contact. It's important to know the date of the hearing in time. My compatriot is ready to plead guilty, but I'd prefer things to be cleared up before that, I hope the police can get at the truth. He's innocent, I have no doubt of that."

The old lawyer looked at me in silence. "It's good that he's innocent," he said, "that'll make things easier. The truth always comes out in the end. Don't worry, Consul. You can go knowing I'll be taking up the reins of the case and keeping you informed."

From there I called Teresa, I wanted to say goodbye. We arranged to meet at seven that evening in the bar of the Blue Elephant. Then I went down onto the street and walked aimlessly until I reached a place called Paradise Tower. It was a shopping mall. On one of its avenues there was a little bar that looked out on a park and there I sat down and watched the people. The rain had stopped. I ordered a double gin with lemon and ice. A second later, a young girl sat down beside me. She was wearing white hot pants that looked like cream against her skin. The color of her nails and heels didn't match. She asked me what my name was, where I was from, if I was alone, and if I'd buy her a drink. I told her she could order whatever she liked, but that I wasn't looking for company. She ordered a Singha beer and moved slowly away, looking back at me.

I kept thinking about Manuel's story. "Let me say something that may surprise you, this isn't going to be a crime story, it's going to be a love story." Now I understood those mysterious words of his, and he was right. It was a love story.

Listening to him, Bogotá had come back to me, the city I, too, had fled, although for other reasons. I knew Manuel's neighborhood well, lower Santa Ana. My friend Mario Mendoza lived there. Did he know the family? It was possible.

Soon afterwards I went back to the hotel and wrote to Gustavo:

> I already have the story, you don't need to search further. I talked to him and he told me everything. It's a real mess. I'll tell you the details later. He remembers you with affection. Big hug.

I reread my notes: Maribel, Colombian Consulate, November 3, 2008. I didn't even have her passport number.

I had accepted the mission to find her, and, somehow, I had already started. What did she look like? I put her name on the Internet and found an old and probably invalid Facebook membership. There was no photograph of her, just the image of some native children, maybe Wayuu or Paez, the picture wasn't clear.

At seven I went out and hailed a taxi.

Teresa was waiting for me in the Blue Elephant, drinking a pink cocktail. What is it? I asked. A Singapore Sling, she said.

I had tried it in the bar of the Raffles Hotel in Singapore, where it was invented. It appears in Somerset Maugham's story "The Letter." I still have a poster with an image of a bartender and some special glasses. But I preferred a very dry martini.

The place was very grand, with high ceilings, large windows, and leather chairs. The walls had gold veneer. It reminded me of the Coupole in Paris, with wooden window panels and fans with blades. Like the Long Bar of the Raffles or the Batavia in Jakarta. British colonial architecture.

Obsessively, I told her Manuel's story, the way in which, in spite of the difference in age—I was almost twenty years older than he—he took me back in his story to the Bogotá of my adolescence, to those walks on foot through dark streets, in the early morning cold and the drizzle.

"So he was looking for his sister," Teresa said, "and now you're going to look for her."

"Yes," I said. "I'll have to go to Japan."

"You've spotted a good story and you can't resist it," Teresa said, biting the olive as she spoke. "That's fine. I assume I'll read it eventually."

"It's possible," I said, "but it isn't going to be a crime story. It's going to be a love story. That's what Manuel said."

"All the better," Teresa said. Then she turned and asked the bartender for another round. I gave her a grateful look.

"Each person drinks what he needs, and in your case what you need can be read on your face. We'll have dinner later."

"Jesus," I exclaimed, "you're my ideal woman."

"My ex-husband said the same, but as soon as I had my daughters, I crossed the imaginary line of forty, my tits started drooping, and he went off with a twenty-eight-year-old, so you can shake hands."

We laughed.

"Not all bad men are equal," I said, "there is no solidarity of gender."

"I know," she said. "I'm speaking in double entendres."

We drank until three in the morning in two different bars. Before we parted, Teresa took my arm.

"And what about you and me? How are we?"

I gave her a big hug and said, "You and I are very good."

Then I got into a taxi and went back to my hotel.

The next day, at three in the afternoon, I caught a plane back to Delhi.

PART II

1

Ah, Bangkok.

The rain and the solitude bring back memories. My notebook is filling up with question marks, arrows, parentheses. I long to reach a point of no return. I already reached it, but in life, where there is no return possible, where could one return to? Nowhere.

It's 10:32 in the morning and I'm sitting in a bar on Silom Street with a somewhat extravagant name, Mr. Oyster, a Singha beer in my hands. It's hot. The bottle still has little strands of ice from the refrigerator, tiny stalagmites around the label. I stroke the cold glass and feel a shiver on my skin.

I'm very happy.

The notebook (I'm already on my second) makes me look like an expatriate: an exiled industrialist or even an old actor who's been forgotten by everybody, someone who's come down in the world in spite of having been on a winning streak years earlier, before things like drugs, divorce proceedings, and alcohol took him away from the screen. I'd like to look like an intellectual, but that doesn't exist anymore. The gloom of this place protects me and the other customers, that fat man between fifty and sixty, that ancient, toothless woman, that young man trembling as he drinks something that, seen from here, looks like—and I sincerely hope is—a Bloody Mary, any-way, all of them will be my company, though I don't think I'll talk to them. I like to drink alone, to slowly immerse myself without anybody interfering.

Through a side window I can see the sky, rough at this hour, the few clouds laden with something dense. Clouds presaging thunder and lightning. Will they add something to my notebook?

The infinite shapes of clouds.

Anyway, my one wish, in this cool corner of Mr. Oyster, is to be alone. If certain precautions are taken, there will be no surprises. It's easy to avoid everything I hate, and now I have to carry on before this page bursts.

2

As if somebody up there was manipulating the threads of this story, the day after I got back to Delhi, as I was sorting through the mail in the office, I received an incredible proposition: the Cervantes Institute in Tokyo was inviting me to take part in a symposium on Colombian literature two weeks later. I would be there with the writers Enrique Serrano and Juan Gabriel Vásquez. I almost fell off my chair! I accepted immediately, incredulous at the happy coincidence (someone else must have declined the offer at the last moment). I wrote to the Colombian consul in Japan to tell him I was coming and, in passing, asked for information about Juana Manrique, giving the date of arrival that Manuel had given me. He said he would check on the list of people registered with the consulate and get back in touch.

Two days later he replied saying that the name was there, but that they had no recent news of her. Why had they told Manuel she wasn't registered with them? Maybe they'd been negligent, maybe the page hadn't been very clear, or they'd simply acted in haste. Things done and said on the telephone are usually vague and imprecise, but how happy he would have been if they'd told him she was on their list.

The consul went on to say that Juana Manrique had given the address of a hotel, and that she had never voted in elections. He added something that I already knew: many leave the country without bothering to inform the consulate, the fact that someone is registered only means they were here once.

All of us were here once.

The consul was a religious person and ended his letter with a biblical allusion: on his list, he said, he didn't know who was who, or what they did, which was why we would have to wait for the last day, when the Lord—he wrote it with a capital letter—came to separate the good from the bad. I didn't have a Bible to hand to check what exactly he was talking about, but I was impressed all the same.

I flew to Tokyo soon afterwards, feeling nervous and excited.

What a strange city. My first, fairly rapid, observation led me to the conclusion that it was in the future, but then, thinking of Delhi and Bogotá, I realized that Tokyo is indeed the future, but only of Tokyo.

Tokyo is the future of Tokyo.

On this kind of trip, I'm always in the habit of referring to literature, to see what other people have written and said. Books and poetry are my Lonely Planet. And so I found, for example, that when Marguerite Yourcenar arrived in Tokyo in 1982 she exclaimed: "My God, eleven million robots!" She couldn't get past that caricature, that paternalistic image that Europeans have of Asia. Not the case with Richard Brautigan, who married a Japanese woman in 1978. Americans are (or were) better travelers, demanding nothing of the places they visit. The marriage lasted only two years, but Brautigan remained in Tokyo, until his life, as his biographers say, "dissolved into alcohol and insomnia." An interesting dissolution. Brautigan liked haiku and wrote this:

I like this taxi driver,
racing through the dark streets of Tokyo
as if life had no meaning.
I feel the same way.

We were being put up at the Sheraton Miyako on Shirokanedai

in Minato, near the residence of the Colombian embassy, a luxury hotel with a beautifully tended inner garden opposite the lobby, reminding one that gardening is one of the Japanese fine arts (through it you can learn about Buddhism).

The dinner to welcome us to the symposium was at seven-thirty in the evening, so I had time to get organized without having to rush. I went to a 7-11 to see what I could find of interest, and ended up buying a liter of gin for the same price as a little bottle at the hotel. I asked room service for some ice and soon afterwards they sent up the most beautiful ice bucket I had ever seen in my life, with cubes that looked as if they'd only just been invented, as if they came straight from Plato's Cave: aseptic, perfect, symmetrical. I suppose these things happen to everybody on their first visit to Japan.

At the dinner, after the formal greetings and expressions of gratitude, Enrique Serrano gave us a wide-ranging talk about Japanese culture, including historical, political, and economic aspects, and then, at about eleven, we were driven back to the hotel. Once in my room, I asked for a little more of that Swarovski ice and sat down to read a novel by Kenzaburo Oe, but found I couldn't concentrate. I was extremely anxious about the chances of finding Juana and, of course, taking her to Bangkok.

The consul was waiting for me the following day.

The branches of the trees swayed in the wind, and the cold of winter was already in the air. A leaf dancing, an empty sidewalk, the dark cherry trees, the drizzle. Everything seemed made for a haiku.

The office was next to the residence, a big, impressive building surrounded by gardens that evoked the Japanese forests with their spirits and demons.

I told the consul who Juana Manrique was and why I was looking for her. He ordered two cups of coffee, we sat down by the window, and he pointed to the clouds. They move very fast here, had I noticed? No, I said. He was a friendly man, a bit out of the ordinary. He was interested in the story of what had happened to Manuel Manrique in Bangkok, and wanted to know if we had hired a lawyer. In his experience as a jurist, he thought that the most desirable thing would be to transfer the sentence to Colombia. The problem, once again, was not having an embassy. Countries look at these things with a lot of suspicion. Then he told me his own suspicion, or rather his hypothesis: Juana Manrique hadn't come to Tokyo to study Japanese, as she had stated when she registered with the consulate, but to work as a prostitute; that was why they'd had no further news of her. I agreed, omitting to tell him that I already knew that.

"They get them here through deception," the consul went on, "although to be honest, the deception has more to do with some of the details than the basics, if I can put it that way. They know they're going to work as prostitutes, but they think they'll be high-class escorts, working a few times a week, and above all, that they'll be able to decide the terms. That's what they're promised. But when they get here, things are very different. They're forced to work on the street, which makes them very frustrated. If they show promise and gain the trust of their bosses, they get promoted to working in hotels. The trade is controlled by the Japanese Mafia. The girls are known as 'talents'; they work in places called theater bars, where they have to do striptease, pose for pornographic photographs, and have sex with men who win draws for them. The rest of the time they're kept in residences and aren't allowed out, not even one day a week. Their clothes are taken away from them, they live in the nude."

The consul was well-informed. He said there were about a thousand Colombian women doing this. That was a rough calculation, because they weren't usually allowed to register with the consulate (the case of Juana Manrique was unusual, which suggested she was at a higher level). Naturally, their passports were taken away.

"It's a kind of slavery," he went on. "They're considered to have incurred a debt, but it's one they never stop paying off and that keeps growing at the discretion of the lender, which in this case is the Mafia. It's like Rivera's *The Vortex* but in Japan, have you read *The Vortex*?"

"Yes," I said. "It's very good. And where do you think she might be?"

"Hard to say. A lot of girls go to Yokohama or Kyoto. Here in Tokyo, there are different zones. It's like looking for a needle in a haystack, but it isn't impossible."

I made a copy of the registration document for the sake of Juana's photograph and went back to my hotel. Before I left, the consul took me by the arm and said, almost conspiratorially, look at the color of the leaves on the trees, try to spot the differences, it's a real source of peace. I told him I would and thanked him. When I'd turned the corner, I pulled out the document and took a good look at the photograph: Juana had very dark, very expressive eyes, and a tense smile.

My God, that was her.

The first thing to do if you're looking for someone is to use the Internet. I typed in *Juana Manrique* and got 11,600 results. It's a very common name, like her brother's. Adding the word *Japan* reduced it to 190, but none of them were her. I looked at the kind of people they were but that wasn't any help either. I tried *Juana Manrique + Japan + sexual services*, and the figure shot up again: 9,345 results. Then I tried something a little more specialized: *Colombian women + sex + Tokyo*. Again, an absurd figure: 560,689. Then I thought of another angle and wrote *Tokyo + escorts*. The first site I clicked on had a telephone number, which I called. Much to my surprise, there was an answering machine and multiple options, with questions I didn't know how to answer. I replied at random and carried on until I got to an operator. Looking for company in Tokyo? Yes, I said, making it clear that I wanted a Colombian girl.

"A Colombian girl?"

There was a silence and after a while the voice said: "That's possible. Do you want her now?"

I calculated that I had a few hours free. "Yes," I said.

"All right, sir, we'll send her to your hotel right now, she'll cost five hundred dollars."

Five hundred dollars? I swallowed and said, looking at Juana's photograph:

"All right, but she must have natural dark hair and dark eyes, be five and a half feet tall and thirty years old. I don't want a teenager."

"Don't worry, sir, we'll send someone with the characteristics you're looking for. Will you be paying by credit card?"

"No. In cash."

I poured myself a drink and lay down on the bed, feeling nervous. Would it be her? It was absurd to think it would, but whoever came might know her or know something about her, it wasn't unlikely that the Colombian women here were in contact. I'd seen that in other countries. Economic migrants meet together, organize, support each other. Were there organizations of Latin American women in Japan? There had to be. It could be another lead.

Knock, knock.

My heart skipped a beat. I got up and opened the door.

It was room service, with more ice, so I continued with my deliberations. I tried to think of other possible points of contact. All at once a light came on in my head: a church with a Colombian or Latin American priest who held masses in Spanish. That was the place! Knowing her history, it was most likely that Juana was an atheist, but there might be someone in that church who knew her, or who knew where else in Tokyo you could look for a Colombian girl.

Knock, knock.

This time there was no room for doubt, and I opened the door.

It was a woman of about thirty, with dark skin and dark eyes. About five and a half feet tall. I asked her what her name was and she said, I'm Cindy. Are you Colombian? Yes, she said, from Cartago. From her northwestern accent I realized she wasn't Juana, but physically speaking, even though she was a bit different than the photograph, she could have been her.

She didn't react when I told her we were compatriots, only asked me to pay her and then walked to one side, with her cell phone in her hand.

"I'm sorry, I have to call my *mamiya* and confirm, it won't take a moment."

Mamiya? That must be her protector. Then she sat down on the bed and told me that for that price I was entitled to a blowjob and complete "frontal sex." Anything else would be extra, which struck me as fair. I asked her how long and she said, thirty minutes, forty maximum. I said that to start with we could talk for a while, that I preferred to use the time asking her a few things.

"You aren't going to ask me difficult questions, are you?"

"No," I said, "only easy ones. Do you know a Colombian girl named Juana Manrique? She lives here in Tokyo."

She looked up at the ceiling and shook her head. I explained to her that she was from Bogotá and I showed her the photograph, fully aware that in a situation like this, even if she knew her, even if she was her best friend, she'd be most likely to say no . . . out of fear, or because she didn't know who I was, or didn't know the reason for my interest.

Cindy looked at the photograph and said she looked like a number of Colombian women she had known, but she wasn't sure, and the name didn't ring any bells. She had been in Japan for six years and had seen lots of girls come and go. I offered her a drink and she accepted; by the second sip, she seemed more trusting, so I told her who I was and why I was looking for Juana.

"I'm a consul," I said, "and I'd like to help her. She doesn't know it, but she's involved in a problem I'd like to help solve."

My explanation convinced her and she started to lower her guard. Juana did sound vaguely familiar, but she really wasn't sure, all the same she'd think about it. I asked her if she was happy with her life and she said she was lucky; it had been hard at first, but now it was better and she could send money to her mother, who was bringing up her son in Cartago. She began by working on the street, like the others, never knowing who the guy was who was taking her to the hotel on the corner, or sometimes into his car; she'd feel scared, or disgusted, or even amused at the things Japanese men asked her to do: spit in their mouths, urinate on their faces, hit them with the heel of her shoe.

"These people are so regimented that the only time they let themselves go and enjoy life is when they have sex," she said, "but they aren't violent, I'll say that for them. The thing is, the language sounds very abrupt and you always think they're telling you off, but deep down they're affectionate, they help you, they have feelings, they even give tips."

In the two years she was on the street, her knees frozen with cold from lowering and raising her stockings so much (that's how she put it), nothing untoward ever happened to her.

I asked her if there was a group of Colombian friends and she said, yes, but not an official one, just a bunch of Latin American girls who got together in a Latino restaurant called La Caverna, in the Shinjuku district.

Then I gave her my telephone number and e-mail address. She promised to call me if she found out anything. As I poured her a third drink, she got a call on her cell phone and she stiffened again.

"It's my *mamiya*," she said.

She spoke with her hand over the phone. When she hung up she said, I have to go, but if you want me again I can arrange it. I walked her to the door and said: I can't now, but I'll be here until Sunday and I'd love to see you again. She smiled and walked down the corridor to the elevators.

I opened my notebook and wrote: La Caverna, Shinjuku district.

That night we had a presentation at the Cervantes Institute. We talked about literature, our careers, and our relationship with the work of Gabriel García Márquez, which is an obligatory question. As I listened to either Juan Gabriel or Enrique talking, I can't remember which, I looked out at the audience and, suddenly, I was almost certain that Juana was in the hall. A sociology student from the National University wouldn't miss an event like this. My heart started pounding and I began looking along each row. The lights in the hall had been dimmed, and there were two spotlights shining directly at the platform, blinding me. But I did the best I could, starting from the front rows and moving back.

It's a well-known fact that audiences for this kind of event, and for literature in general, are made up mostly of women— there are authors with a great practical sense who aim their writings at them—which is why that night, at the Cervantes Institute in Tokyo, there were at least three possible Juanas in every row.

But as I was scrutinizing the upper part of the hall, where it was darkest, I spotted a woman sitting alone in the left-hand corner. She had taken a seat some distance from the others, as if afraid to be recognized. Her age was right for Juana, so I looked straight at her, seeking out her eyes, trying to establish a modicum of contact, but at that very moment I heard the voice of the presenter saying my name and I realized it was my turn, so I started talking. I spoke a little about everything, about my life and the things I'd read and what it might mean to be a writer in this strange era, to be a Latin American writer and as if that weren't enough a Colombian, if that still made any sense at all, if it meant something in aesthetic terms or was only an avatar that bound us to a series of landscapes, problems and complexes, to a common frame of mind and a fairly grim history, a fast-paced reality and a way of speaking, and all this transplanted to literature, where, for many, to be a Colombian seemed to oblige us to deal with certain themes and above all to deal with those themes in a particular way, which was why my generation and the ones after us were trying to escape all that, trying to be just writers, and I added that in our part of the world, being a writer was a highly uncertain and probably unhappy existence because of the helpless state, the neglect and poverty in which most of our writers grew old and died, or because of the fact that, once you reached a certain level of recognition, that became an excuse to ridicule you on the part of those who hadn't made it or had made it some time ago and had seen their own success devalued by newcomers, not to mention the critics, most of whom were writers or frustrated writers, although as my friend Jorge Volpi says, "a literary critic isn't a frustrated writer. A literary critic is a frustrated literary critic."

These last words I threw out as a provocation, to see if they generated a debate, but instead of that there was laughter. I looked anxiously at the top left-hand corner of the hall and saw that the woman was no longer there. Could it have been Juana? I was starting to get impatient, I wanted the discussion to be over so that we could go up to the restaurant, where we were supposed to be having cocktails, since I assumed that the "shadow woman"—as I dubbed her—would be there to have a drink and a bite to eat before leaving. That, at any rate, was what I'd done in Paris in the years before I made it: I'd go to parties and receptions and eat and drink whatever I could, storing up the calories for harder times, which usually started when I left and walked out onto the street.

After an amusing story by Enrique about his years in the Colombian merchant navy, in which he called the ships "floating monasteries," ideal for the study of philosophy and religion, the audience finally applauded and we started for the top floor, where wine, Serrano ham, and Spanish omelet awaited us.

In a state of great excitement, I managed to get away from those members of the audience who were trying to ask more questions, and went up to the restaurant. Oh, the relief! The mystery woman was there! But when I approached her, the mystery dissolved into thin air, because she was Spanish.

Hello, she said, how are you? What an interesting symposium, really, it's been ages since we last had anything like this, do you live in India? Sadly, I couldn't stay to the end, I had to come up here to make sure everything was ready.

She worked for the Cervantes Institute.

I quickly had a look around the other women present in the hope of spotting Juana, but none of them really looked like her, they were all exchange students, young girls who of course were a long way from the kind of life I was investigating. I did actually ask three of them if they knew a restaurant called La Caverna, in Shinjuku. They said no, but one of them took out her iPhone and within a second was writing down the address in a notebook.

I thanked her, then slowly, trying to emulate the invisible man, walked to the door. But just as I got there, I ran into the hosts and felt obliged to ask them if anything else had been arranged. They said yes, there was a dinner after this aperitif, so I had to wait.

At eleven at night, when it was all over—luckily things there finish early—they dropped us at the hotel and I immediately left again. I called a taxi, with my paper in my hand. Then I sank into the seat and watched the streets pass by, the flamboyant neon signs, that other nocturnal sky, an apocalypse of facades, skyscrapers that seem to burn, covered with lava or igneous winds, small planets in collision.

The taxi pulled up outside a low door with a descending staircase. Restaurante La Caverna. The street was narrow and there were lots of people on the sidewalks even though it was late. I got out of the taxi and was taken aback when I converted the price of the ride into euros (this investigation was going to ruin me!). I entered the restaurant, which now that it was after midnight was already turning into a bar, and ordered a pisco sour. There were couples sitting at tables and on high stools. Everything seemed totally normal. Latin women? Of course there were, lots of them. Almost all of those here. So I approached a waitress.

"Hello, are you Peruvian?"

"Yes," she said.

She was about twenty-five.

"Have you been working here long?"

"Yes, to pay for my studies."

The pisco sour was good, I finished it in one go and asked for another. When she brought it, we carried on talking.

"A friend from Colombia recommended this place to me," I said. "Her name is Juana Manrique, do you know her?"

She thought about it for a moment, then looked up and said: the name sounds familiar, is she dark?

"Well," I said, "that depends what you mean by dark. She has white skin, and dark hair and eyes. Here's her photograph, do you recognize her?"

She looked at it, smiled, and said, yes, I've seen her, but she hasn't been in for a while.

"She was always with two Colombian girls and a Japanese man," she added. "A guy who never laughed, he looked like a bodyguard."

I asked her for a third pisco sour.

"I'm sure he was a bodyguard," I said. "Do you know what she was involved in?"

The waitress stopped and looked at me inquisitively, as if putting two and two together. When she spoke again, her tone of voice had changed.

"You know something, that sounded strange . . . I don't think she recommended this place to you. I don't think you know her, you're looking for her, that's it, who are you?"

"A friend of Manuel, her brother," I said. "Juana has to go back to Bogotá, there are things she has to resolve urgently. I'm a diplomat. Do you remember the names of the Colombian girls who came with her? What did they look like? Do you remember anything about them?"

She looked at me with an earnest expression. "I'm not getting into trouble by talking to you, am I?"

"No," I said, "I've already told you who I am. You'll actually be doing Juana a favor if you help me find her."

How difficult it is to persuade someone to do or say something they have no interest in doing or saying. You have to appeal to feelings like curiosity or a wish to save someone, if they have them. It's exhausting. If this were a movie and the screenwriters had given me the role of an interrogator with a suspect to question, it might have been easier. There are codes and clear identities. You can hit the table or make the suspect laugh. But not here. I was nobody to her. Just a stranger coming late into her restaurant, ordering drinks, and asking unusual questions. Obviously, our paths might never have crossed in the first place, and now that they had her life would still be the same if she didn't save anybody tonight. I realized she was reading my thoughts when she said:

"And what do I get out of this?"

It was an enormous relief to hear her say that. "It depends on what you want to get out of it," I said.

She thought this over, then looked at me slyly. "This city is very expensive, I could give you those two names for a hundred dollars, and if you want me to go to your hotel that'll be another two hundred, as long as you pay for the taxi rides."

I loved her.

When we got to the Sheraton she went straight to the bathroom. I heard the water running in the shower. After a day's work, I thought, a clean, warm place like this must have been paradise. It certainly was for me. I took advantage of her being in the bathroom to call room service and ask for one of their artistic ice buckets, and when it came I looked at it for a while. Each cube could have been a diamond.

Finally she came out with a towel covering her shoulders. She was wearing a thong. There was a slight flaccidness below the navel, and her lined belly hung over the elastic. She had been pregnant. I fantasized for a while about her pussy, but preferred to have a drink, so I said to her, put on one of my T-shirts, it'll cover you better. Oh, and what's your name?

"Aurora," she said.

Then she gave me the names of the Colombian girls: Susana Montes and Natalia Collazos. She called on them for work at weekends and they helped her out, but she had never seen Juana again.

"Can we call them now?" I said.

"Of course, but wait, aren't you going to offer me a drink?"

I poured it for her, adding two slices of lemon, while she dialed the numbers. Then I heard her talking:

"Hello? Susy? Yes, it's me, how's it going? Listen, a friend wants to talk to you, it's something important, could you see him tomorrow? Yes? He's Colombian, I'd like to introduce you to him, can you come to La Caverna?"

She held the telephone away from her and said: what time? I looked at my diary, it would have to be about midnight, is that possible? Aurora told her and nodded. Perfect, midnight tomorrow.

I hadn't thought it would be so easy, let alone so quick, to arrange it, and neither had Aurora.

"And now what? Do you really not want me to do anything for you?"

I poured myself another gin. "Nobody said that, but for now let's drink."

She left just before dawn, when the subway opened. I lay in bed thinking about everything that had happened since my arrival in Bangkok.

Through the window I saw the night at its darkest point and imagined Manuel in his cell, hoping that my strength or my intuition or even my lack of scruples would help me find Juana and take her away with me.

The following day, there was an arranged visit to the National Museum. An imposing place, surrounded by red and sepia-colored trees. All totally symmetrical and perfect. They explained to us the rules of battle and code of honor of the samurai. Also that it took them three days to dress for those battles. I remembered Kurosawa's film *Kagemusha*, in which a simple archer fires off a blind shot in the middle of the night.

After this we had the afternoon free, then in the evening a debate with pupils and teachers of the Faculty of Hispanic Studies at the University of Tokyo. Much to my surprise, the Salvadoran writer Horacio Castellanos Moya was in the audience, there on a grant from the Japan Foundation. One of the teachers, a friend of his, had told him we were coming and he wanted to say hello. I had met him years earlier, in Madrid, along with Rodrigo Rey Rosa.

When the talk was over, the professors invited us to an informal dinner at a beer hall in Shibuya, which pleased me, because it was near La Caverna (or so I assumed). We drank beer from pitchers, ate dozens of little dishes of exquisite fish, talked about the divine and the human, and, of course, about Japanese literature: about the writer who was the most widely read and most fashionable outside Japan, Murakami; and about Oe, who for me was the best; as well as Tanizaki, a classic, as was Kawabata—his story "First Snow on Fuji" is a masterpiece—the indescribable Mishima, much admired by Marguerite Yourcenar; or the strange Osamu Dazai, who led a dissolute life in Tokyo. Of course nobody knew the Burns Bannion novels, all set in Japan and with openings like this: "I've never seen a bottle of beer broken into so many pieces of *chiisai*. A bottle of Sapporo beer, large size."

When dinner was over, I asked Horacio if he'd like to go somewhere with me, without being any more specific than that. He was surprised that I knew a place in Tokyo, but he said nothing, so we went, and as we walked down the steps at the entrance Aurora approached and greeted me.

"Give us two pisco sours but make four," I said.

"Sure," she said.

Then she leaned toward me and whispered in my ear: she's already in the room, she's waiting for you, you can talk to her now. I saw her from a distance: a pretty woman, but one who looked as if she'd lived through wars and shipwrecks. Aurora introduced us, brought the drinks, and started talking to Horacio.

Susana's northwestern accent was even more marked than Cindy's. I bought her a drink and got straight down to business.

"I'm told you're a friend of Juana Manrique, that you know her. I'm a friend of her brother Manuel. I'm here on his behalf."

She gave me a guileless look and said, Manuel? Juana never stopped talking about him, day or night, he was the love of her life.

"That's why I'd like to know about her, is she still in Japan?"

Susana frowned. "Why are you asking me that? Don't know where she is, or what?"

A light came on, a warning light. I'd have to take it nice and slowly. The natural defenses of a woman injured by life had been activated. I ordered another pisco sour.

"Manuel's in prison in Thailand and I'm trying to get him out. Or rather: the Colombian Foreign Ministry is trying to. I'm a diplomat. I've come to Japan on personal business and I'm using the opportunity to look for Juana, it's urgent she should know what's going on. Manuel's desperate to see her. He was on his way to Tokyo when he was arrested. He'd been searching for her, did you know she hadn't been in touch with Manuel for more than three years? did you know that?"

For a while she sat pensively sipping her pisco sour. Then she opened her handbag and took out a pack of menthol cigarettes. She lit one (I was surprised to discover that smoking was permitted in bars in Tokyo).

"Look," she said, "I knew Juana was running away from something. She loved her brother but didn't want him to know she was here, especially that she was in this line of work. They kept a close eye on her. When she was working on the street, she always had someone close by, never letting her out of his sight. I don't know why they treated her like that. We lived together for about eight months. Or rather: they kept us in the same room, locked up. That's not living. They always had their eye on her. Juana had style, she was well educated and spoke English; she earned a lot of money for them and they didn't want to lose her."

I was starting to get impatient. At the other table Horacio was chatting with Aurora.

"I need to talk to her, where is she? It'd take me a long time to explain, but right now it might be a matter of life and death."

Susana gave me a strange, almost angry look. "She's not here anymore, she ran away eleven months ago."

"She ran away?" I cried.

Fortunately the bar was noisy.

But Susana was afraid to say too much, to go into details. She may have been questioned many times, maybe threatened. I felt as if I was stepping on shifting sands. I ordered another two piscos and took out my diplomatic passport.

"You don't have to believe me if you don't want to, here's my passport, I have nothing to hide. You can tell me where she went and nothing will happen to you. As soon as I know where she is I'll go find her, that's what her brother would have done. I promised him."

Susana breathed in deeply, then took a long sip of her drink. "She went to Tehran with her Iranian bodyguard. They fell in love and he tried to pay her debt. They wouldn't accept it and one day they disappeared. We never heard from her again. They kept me locked up for a month because of it."

Tehran, Tehran, I thought. And what was the bodyguard's name?

She thought for a moment, lit another cigarette, as if calling on her memory, and finally said: I don't know his name, they called him Jaburi.

La Caverna closed at two o'clock, but we went and had a last drink at a nearby bar that was like a doll's house, with a very low ceiling and a kind of little wooden balcony around each table. Japanese beer is very good. While we were in this second bar, we heard ringing. It was Susana's cell phone. She spoke for a while with her hand over the receiver and when she hung up she said she had to go. I told her that if she was going to the Sheraton I'd take her. She laughed and said, no, cheeky, it's another hotel.

It was already after three, so I called a taxi and gave Horacio a farewell hug, thanking him for the company.

The following day they picked us up early to visit the Buddhist temple of Asakusa, and then Kamakura. It was said the French writer and traveler Pierre Loti had been there, and he was an old traveling companion of mine (especially on journeys to Peking, but also to Jerusalem, Turkey, and Morocco). Displaying his proverbial racism, Loti says the Japanese smell of "rancid camellia oil." All the same, his descriptions of the Buddhist temples are remarkable. I was so upset by what I'd heard about Juana that I barely noticed Kamakura. The temple of the great Buddha is beautiful and harmonious, and surrounded by a colorful garden, but to be honest, having seen the ancient city of Pathan, just outside Kathmandu, it didn't strike me as anything much. What I liked most was the ride, and the fact that for most of the time we were held up by the heavy traffic on the way out of Tokyo.

That night, my friend Satoko Tamura, the translator, and her silent husband invited me to see the majestic view of the city from the tower on Rappongi Hills—an ocean of lights—and then to have dinner in the Ginza district, with its elegant commercial streets, luxury department stores, and buildings that are screens of liquid glass.

Back in my hotel room, already packing my bag to go back to Delhi, I asked myself why I had been so startled to discover that Juana was in Tehran, until I realized something incredibly obvious: Iran was one of the countries our embassy dealt with! so if, for example, she had requested a new passport or some other consular procedure, it would have had to pass through my hands. I myself would have signed it. I felt dizzy, thinking that I might be close. Unable to wait—it was Friday, I wouldn't get to Delhi until Saturday—I sent Olympia a message asking her to look through the Tehran files for the name Juana Manrique and saying that we'd talk about it first thing on Monday.

When I got to Delhi, the heat was overpowering.

Every time I traveled anywhere else in Asia—perhaps with the sole exception of Kathmandu—I had the feeling when I got back that Delhi was a real slap in the face: its polluted air, smelling of smoke and kerosene; its streets filled with earth, garbage, and waste, its human anthills, the maddening noise of car horns and sudden accelerations; the permanent dust cloud and the sense that dengue and tetanus and malaria, in other words, everything that's sickliest and most despicable, float in the very air you breathe; the fecal matter on the walls, the gobs of spittle, the humidity, the horrific diseases and deformities, all these counterpointed with the indolent look of those who survive, the absurdly insulting conspicuous spending of the rich in a country with eight hundred million poor, whose economy, roughly speaking, is based on the fact that two thirds of the population earns paupers' wages, in short, all this became even more obvious on returning from a city like Tokyo where you don't encounter unpleasant smells, not even in the fish market. Of course, its equivalent in Delhi is a place so dirty that the flesh of the fish is covered by a layer of several inches of flies.

I was tempted to go to the office on Sunday, but I wouldn't have gained anything by it, because Olympia keeps her things under lock and key, so I spent the time organizing what I needed for the journey and in the afternoon went for a walk in Lodhi Gardens, a park that reconciles you with the city, being one of its few unconditionally beautiful and clean places, where you can lie down on the grass and listen to the cawing of the birds of prey, the parrots, the crows, the eagles, in other words, the birds of all sizes and types that are the real masters of the city.

By about seven on Monday morning, I was already on my balcony drinking a cup of strong coffee. Eagles were flying over the pines opposite and a group of workers was digging in Jangpura Park, converting what had been a very green lawn into a dusty stretch of earth. I couldn't wait for Peter to pick me up and take me to the embassy, which, after a recent move, was now at 85 Poorvi Marg, still in Vasant Vihar but further back, far from the terrifying Olof Palme Marg and its crazed traffic.

As often happens in such cases, an element of suspense now crept in. Olympia wasn't there, she had gone off with the chauffeur to deposit the monthly income from consular activities in the bank in Chanakyapuri, and wouldn't be back until noon, so I went to the office to deal with other matters, such as studying visa requests and approving them—in the whole time I was there, I only ever denied one, to a Mephistophelian guru—answering mail, or discussing new cultural projects with my good friend Professor Aparajit Chattopadhyay of Jawaharlal Nehru University, a specialist on Neruda.

At noon, Olympia arrived and came up to my office, which was on the second floor of our three-story building.

"Look, boss, here's your girl," she said, and placed on my desk a passport renewal application from two months earlier, already signed by me.

I looked at it with genuine excitement. There it all was: telephone numbers, address, a recent photograph.

She had changed. Her hair was shorter. She was using her husband's surname and was now called Juana Manrique Hedayat. Attached to the form was a request for a birth certificate and passport for a newborn child named Manuel Sayeq Hedayat Manrique, her six-month-old son. Everything seemed to be all right, so why had she forgotten her brother? when was she thinking of contacting him? Communications aren't easy in Iran, but what was stopping her from sending an e-mail, a Facebook message, or making a long-distance telephone call?

All this was a mystery.

The form had the telephone number and a note that said: please call only between 9 and 11 A.M. I looked at the clock. It was after nine in the morning in Iran so I asked Angie, the secretary—the only member of staff with an international line—to call her and put her through to me in my office.

It isn't easy to call Tehran, as I knew from having tried months earlier to send a batch of Colombian books to its book fair. Something as simple as talking to the person in charge of Latin America at the Foreign Ministry was impossible.

The telephone rang and I rushed to answer. I heard Angie say: "Madam Juana Hedayat? Please stay on the line, the consul wants to speak with you."

"Juana?" I said.

At the other end of the line, through a storm cloud of electrical noise that sounded like a swarm of mosquitoes, I heard her say, yes, that's me, is there some problem with my application?

"That's not why I'm calling," I said. "I'd like to talk to you about your brother Manuel."

There was a silence that seemed even longer thanks to the heavy interference. I prayed that the line wouldn't be cut off.

"Did you hear me?"

"Yes, Consul, what's happened to my brother?"

"He's in prison in Bangkok," I said. "There was an incident and he was arrested. He was on his way to Japan to look for you."

"What?" Her voice broke and there was more noise on the line, and sobs. At last she recovered and spoke again. "Manuel in prison in Bangkok? he was looking for me? but . . . is he all right? how did he know . . . and you?"

I took a deep breath and told her everything, from the beginning: the journey, the arrest, the pills. The communications with Colombia, the fact that Delhi had had to deal with the case because of the post in Malaysia being vacant, my own journey to Bangkok and Manuel's version of events, his pressing need to see her again after three years, the urgency of her coming to Bangkok, all in all, I spoke for about ten minutes without interruption, without hearing anything at the other end except that noise like a failing engine on the line. When I stopped talking I heard her crying. Not broken sobs, but sustained weeping, as if a muddy current had found an outlet.

I let her cry without adding anything. Then she asked, sobbing, are you sure he's all right? I assured her he was, Manuel was strong and was being well protected, the lawyer was influential and knew the warden of the prison, but I insisted: it's vital that you travel to Bangkok, he needs to see you.

"Yes, Consul, but I have two problems. My husband won't let me leave Iran and I don't have a passport. Or rather, I have an Iranian passport I can't use and a Colombian one that's out-of-date. And besides there's my son. I can't leave without him, and he doesn't have a passport."

I told her the passports weren't a problem, we'd deal with them immediately. She had presented the forms and they were already signed.

"Can't someone come to Delhi," I asked, "like other Colombians who live in Iran?"

But she said that was impossible.

"I already told you I can't leave, Consul, you don't know my husband, he barely lets me go to the market. We don't have an international line or the Internet. If anyone calls when he's there I'm not allowed to answer. This is the only time I can receive calls, don't you see? I depend on him for everything, he's paranoid and jealous. The application for the passport and the birth certificate I did in secret, a Colombian friend helped me."

"If you had the passports in your hand, could you travel?"

"Well, I could go to the airport without his knowing and get on a plane, but I don't have the money for a ticket."

I told her I'd think of a solution and call her again the next day, at the same time. Before she said goodbye, she thanked me and asked again, are you sure Manuel is all right?

"He'll be better when you get here and he can see you."

After lunch I called the lawyer. He told me there were no new developments yet, but that the police were still following a lead about the pills, and that we might be getting some good news very soon. He was sure of it. I told him I'd tracked down Manuel's sister and made him write down her name, spelling it for him.

"Please," I said, "let Manuel know that I'll soon be coming to Bangkok with her. It's very important. Get in touch with the warden and make sure the news gets through to him today."

"Count on it, Consul. As soon as we hang up I'll call Bangkwang. I already told you the warden was a student of mine."

I hung up and joined Olympia. I told her everything. We couldn't do bank transfers to Iran, and the passport couldn't be sent by mail, so what to do? As in many other things, she had a ready-made solution.

"Organize a mobile consulate in Tehran, boss," she said. "That way you'll kill something like ten birds with one stone."

A mobile consulate? and she said, yes, we take the books, the stamps, and the forms with us, and we attend to the community in the offices of the Argentine Embassy. The last time it was done was three years ago. It's about time we did it again.

And she added:

"I know that kind of case well. In Tehran, there are a hundred and thirty Colombian women married to Iranians they met in Japan. They all went there to earn a living by sweat, but not the sweat of their brow, and ended up involved with Iranians, who are there as economic migrants and do all kinds of jobs."

We drew up a letter to the Consular Department, saying there was an urgent need to take a mobile consulate to Tehran and pointing out that there were thirty-seven minors waiting for birth certificates and forty-nine of our countrymen and countrywomen who had applied to renew their passports and were waiting for an identification document sent by an office of the State, which was a constitutional right.

The problem with urgent communications between the consulate and the Ministry, as I said before, was the time difference: an exotic figure of ten *and a half* hours. I waited until nightfall and then called the Consular Department. Luckily they had already read my dispatch and were considering it. They would give me an answer by evening (Bogotá time), and I would receive it the following day.

That night I could barely sleep. It was hot, and I was anxious. Several times I got up to drink something cold and finally sat down in the living room, watching the moon come in through the window and cast strange shadows.

At moments I seemed to hear the voice of Juana, also at home, also unable to sleep, maybe embracing the child, watching over him in the darkness with attentive eyes. The voice was barely a murmur, a soft breath trying to cross the sky over Asia and reach the ears of Manuel, who must have been told by now and would be very attentive to her words. A young man in a damp, dirty cell in Bangkok, a woman lying next to a man she didn't love, in Tehran, pretending to sleep.

Words, words, words.

Night prayers.

Those they had not said to each other and now were thinking, words that in their minds were heartrending screams, cries of anxiety and love. Two silent litanies, and me in the middle of that strange storm, near a planet created by those who never lived on it. Two fragile creatures who longed to be together and to be forgotten, and life, like a wall, coming between them.

When I got to the office the following day, Olympia said to me:

"Good news, boss, we're going to Tehran."

"Did the authorization come through from the Consular Department?" I asked, and she said, yes, I printed it out and it's on your desk.

Again I asked Angie to put me through to Juana Hedayat. Two hours later, after many attempts, I was at last able to talk to her. "Your brother's fine," I said. "I spoke to the lawyer in Bangkok and told him everything. He already knows I met you and that you're going to see him."

I told her the strategy: I would go to Tehran the following week to catch up with all consular matters relating to the Colombian residents there. That same afternoon, a public announcement about the mobile consulate would be made.

"You have to be prepared," I told her. "The ideal thing is for you to leave Iran with me."

And she said:

"Oh, don't worry, Consul, by the time you come I'll have everything ready."

I spoke with the Argentinian Embassy, which confirmed its traditional offer of lending us its premises for three days. I also wrote to the head of protocol at the Iranian Foreign Ministry announcing the journey and its purpose. We asked the travel agency for tickets. By the following Tuesday, everything had been prepared and we left on the Wednesday. We would attend to the public on Thursday, Friday, and Saturday. The mission consisted of Olympia, the second secretary, and myself. We were received by a delegation from the Iranian Foreign Ministry, which put a car and a chauffeur at our disposal for the four days.

I won't be in this story of split personalities and dreams either. And what grandiose, histrionic character will you adopt on this occasion, *chère* Inter-Neta? Wait, don't be so impatient, remember what Rimbaud, your beloved poet of Aden and Harar, wrote.

Je est un autre.

My name is Beauty and I am dreaming. I dream and dream and while I do so I prefer to talk, to say what I see in my mind and pursue images, which are also words and sometimes smells or fears. It's what I have in my head, which is tantamount to saying: what I have in my heart.

As I said, my name is Beauty or Belle or maybe Bella, depending on where I am, given that the vast world is my bed. Who am I? Let's take it piece by piece. I was deflowered for the first time—when the moment comes I'll explain what "first time" means—at a Guns N' Roses concert, in the back of a milk delivery van (it smelled of milk), by a man whose mouth gave off a strong odor of raw onion and sausage and who was certainly as drunk and probably as strung out on drugs as I was, nothing very strong, nothing injected into the veins, you know me by now, I love men but I hate needles.

Oh, God, it was a needle that started this long story, this rebuke, this strange coming and going that is my life, you must know my story, it's very popular among children, let's see, how does it go? There were some good fairies and one bad one, and of course a curse: my finger would be pricked when I was sixteen with a spindle and I would sleep until a prince kissed me, that's pretty much the story, and for me the best part, the funniest part, is the bit about the prince. In actual fact, I wake up with a desire for someone to stroke my skin or talk in my ear (it doesn't matter if it's a prince, there are no princes anymore), I wake up and die of anxiety: the flower breathing inside me, its retractable sting, or that similarity to the Virgin that we women have when we're born—our destiny is to lose that similarity—is reconstructed in dreams, the tissues come together again, the membrane is reborn and there am I, with eyes wide open, awake and filled with desire, oh, God, the world trembles, the universe turns to jelly every time a woman is seized with the desire that I feel, a ray that descends my spine and lodges between my thighs and buttocks, and there is nothing I can do but leave this bed in which I have lain for days and nights, while the miracle of reconstruction is performed, and go out into the world.

The last time, the deflowering was intense: it was one of the doctors in the clinic where I woke after being asleep for twenty-two weeks. I don't know what his rank or position was—maybe he was an anesthetist, because it didn't hurt—but he liberated my body, brought it back to life in a little room filled with medical supplies, bottles of alcohol, gauze, and hypodermic syringes, where there was also a photocopier—a strange place for a machine like that—and to be honest that was the most enjoyable part of it, because the doctor sat me down on the glass, and as he deflowered me—was it the twenty-seventh or twenty-ninth time?—he kept making photo-copies, images of my backside flat against the glass and a cylin-drical shadow lying in wait, a chisel striking the mass, I won't go into detail, I'm dreaming now and losing certain nuances of reality, which is my closed garden, the place where my hand-some men, my lovers, live, those who with their breath and their words take me out of this vegetable dream and take away my treasure, always restarted—*toujours recommencée*, like in the poem—which, when you come down to it, doesn't have any more value than a counterfeit coin, something beautiful but not unique, and I think, why should unique things be better? I, at least, enjoy what's banal, but that's another story.

Where am I? where am I? Dare to look for me. Leave everything for me. Look for me. Look for me. Maybe I am that woman on the publicity hoarding that you long for so much, the one who sometimes pays you a visit at night. My bare legs emerge from a martini glass and move about. I am the only one who listens and attends to your prayers, because I live in your imagination.

Saying this, I remembered a man, one of the few I have loved and who was called, what was the name of my Beautiful Man? I've forgotten, but I'm going to give him a name in this dream, his name was Lars and he was a Danish sailor, he worked on the lower deck of a yacht that did cruises in the Baltic. Lars gave me the breath of life while I was asleep in the stern and took me to his little cabin where he lifted me onto his body, then, looking through the porthole, that circular window, he said, "We are passing a purple island, and on one of its plains there is a war, the soldiers are falling, their helmets are rising in the air, and their armor is bleeding." That was what Lars said and I listened to him while other blood bathed my thighs, the wound of his body in mine, and I longed for this man not to stop, longed for him never to take his sword out of me and that the story of the war would last all life long, in short, that that little circular window would be life, but very soon something happened and a bell rang, Lars had to go up on deck to make sure that the sea monsters of the North didn't sink the ship, or something like that, that's what he told me, and when I looked through the porthole I saw the battle on the purple island, but all this happened on the old Telefunken TV set in the kitchen, which was what there was on the other side of the window, and I understood something, I understood the smell of fried oil and fish, which is what should be eaten at sea, what the sea should smell like, that mixture of salty water and fish and plankton and the remains of shipwrecks, and Lars left and I understood also that the movements that were carrying me away into a state of intoxication (in case anyone has lost the thread, I'm talking about sex, sex is my storm) came not only from the fury unleashed in Lars, but from the sea itself, or rather, from the storm that was lifting the sea and I wanted to take him out of his bed, like the men who touch me, and so I loved him, Lars and the storm, and on returning to my own cabin I heard cries and knew that Lars had fallen into the tempestuous water and the waves had carried him away, oh, what pain, and I fell asleep again, the world saddened me, and Lars's face dissolved inside me and now nothing was left, that happens when I sleep and it's because the world goes away, people leave or go out one day onto the street and never come back, and what saddens me most is that the world carries on in the same old way without all those people, nothing changes because Lars isn't there, or because I'm asleep, because we are all dead, nothing changes, believe me, beneath the stones life emerges again, like a snake or a poisonous plant, and when it wakes there will again be poets and sailors and milkmen, desperate and solitary people, life will have the appearance of reality and some will cry out with pleasure while others decide to slash their wrists or go away forever, wandering about, kicking tin cans after being humiliated, and life will go on having that bitter taste until I open my eyes, and when I do someone will be happy, you can believe me, whom the sea will then take away, but I say, while I dream, that it's better to be happy just for one moment, and let ourselves be carried away, than never to be happy and to live like a rodent, that's what I say, that's what I think, I've been happy, and as I say it I ask myself, what will my next beau be like? and you, beau, ask yourself, where am I? would you dare to look for me?

4

I had never been to Tehran, and to be honest it surprised me. The airport is modern and clean—as I've already said, everything seems clean after Delhi—the design rather similar to Roissy, in Paris, with wide open spaces, metal ceilings, stained-glass windows looking out on the desert and the sky, glass staircases, friendly people, good signposting and a pleasant smell, maybe of lavender, at any rate not of cheap air freshener.

When we got off the airbus of Mahan Air, the Iranian state airline, we saw a plane of the Venezuelan airline Conviasa parked next to it, which does the Tehran-Damascus-Caracas route and which, according to the press, is always empty, although in this case the line of passengers seemed infinite.

Tehran, like Santiago in Chile, is dominated by snow-capped mountains, and you have the feeling that the city is on a slope. Our hotel overlooked a large part of modern Tehran, which at first sight, and leaving aside its heritage, reminded me of a Latin American city (an impression I've also had in some Arab cities). But as soon as I entered my room, opened the window, and breathed in the cool air of the mountains, I became aware of something rather inconvenient, which is that there is no alcohol in Iran, so that I couldn't carry out my usual ritual of asking for a bucket of ice, lying down, and having a drink while organizing my ideas. Those ayatollahs! I hate religions that ban alcohol.

That night, the Argentinian ambassador and his wife

invited us to dinner at their residence in an area in the upper part of the city, full of large buildings, identical to the rich Parisian suburb of Neuilly-sur-Seine, and, much to my delight, the ambassador, a refined man of great taste, opened his bar, a large wooden chest, and offered us an aperitif. I spotted a bottle of Gordon's, so I poured myself a generous measure, with a couple of ice cubes and two slices of lemon. The ambassador did the same, and so did the second secretary who had come with me, a pleasant young diplomat from Barranquilla, Mauricio Franco de Armas, whose posting to India was his first.

We were given an overview of the situation in Iran, how a process of reform was bound to be under way soon, given that 70 percent of its population was under forty and wanted to live in a system that was open to the world; we were also told why it was that Iran, which has borders with ten countries, was destined to be the leader of the region. Through its petroleum and other industries, it was an economic powerhouse. One example: 95 percent of the medicines they consumed were made internally. European companies were well established in Iran, as well as some Asian companies, especially Japanese and Korean ones. Thanks to the embargo imposed by Washington, there was no competition from North America. France built the freeways, manufactured the road signs, and assembled cars; the Spanish beer company Mahou, as well as the Dutch Heineken and Amstel, made alcohol-free beer that didn't exist anywhere else, flavored with pineapple, vanilla, and strawberry; Hyundai cars from Korea were assembled here, as were Toyotas and Suzukis; German cars too, Volkswagen and Mercedes. The problem of payment, given that they were not connected to the international banking system, was solved by going through a third country like Jordan, which had grown rich thanks to the embargoes on Iran and Iraq.

The ambassador's wife was equally enchanting. She worked

for the Department of Foreign Studies at the University of Tehran and immediately suggested I give a few lectures about Latin America. I could even come back and give a course now that a faculty of Latin American Studies was about to open. We had empanadas, delicious meat, and wine, and got back to the hotel just before midnight. Our mobile consulate would be opening at eight the following morning, and we needed to rest.

Back at the hotel I started thinking about Juana again. What ideas were crossing her mind now that she was so close to her brother? so close to fleeing Iran? I imagined her looking at it all with the eyes of someone looking at the things they are about to leave, which in her case included her husband: fearful eyes, anticipating homesickness; proud eyes, almost wild at the thought of what she is about to do, aware of what it will cost other people; hungry eyes that want to devour everything, swallow it up; predatory eyes that bite and don't care about the blood. What had her life been like? and above all, the strangest, hardest thing to justify, the thing that kept hitting my brain over and over like a drop of water (that old Chinese torture): why had she never tried to get in touch with Manuel?

One word from her, and none of this would have happened.

The following day, at eight-thirty in the morning, those members of the Colombian community with procedures pending started to arrive. Olympia sat with the second secretary in what would become the dining room, and I sat at a small desk behind a staircase. The only problem we had—and it was one that almost drove us to distraction—was getting hold of an electric typewriter to fill in the passports. A typewriter that was big enough to allow the books to pass through the roller and that also had an corrector; being an antiquated machine you couldn't use Tippex (I'd used Tippex when I wrote my first novel, typed on a Remington portable, and I remembered how it stayed on my fingers). In the end, the Cuban Embassy lent us one, which arrived just in time!

Most of those who came were women and, I have to say, almost all of them were very attractive. Apart from my own experience in Japan, I remembered what Olympia had told me about the Tokyo-Tehran connection. In the light of that, Juana's case was just one among many.

Every time the bell rang and the secretary of the embassy opened the door, I imagined Juana coming into the room. But she didn't. Even though I had her number, I preferred not to call her in order not to arouse suspicion. She must have had to invent an alibi to come. I continued waiting.

By three in the afternoon I had signed—and done by hand, with Mauricio and Olympia—twenty-two passports, sixteen birth certificates, and nine wedding certificates. Some of the Colombian women came with their husbands to ask for visas, but this was one of the few procedures we couldn't do, because Iran was on the list of countries for which the Foreign Ministry obliged us to send the forms to Bogotá to be authorized. At four o'clock, we received the last forms and announced that the following day would be the deadline for applications. With that, we shut up shop for the day.

At about five the chauffeur took me to see the Grand Bazaar, one of the attractions of the city: a beautiful medieval market that at times goes underground, with winding alleyways. I bought pistachios—the best in the world—admired the pastries, the leatherwork, the many veils; just as I had in the bazaar in Damascus, I took photographs of the splendid stands selling women's underwear ("brevity is the soul of lingerie," who wrote that?), with their daring multicolored thongs as thin as dental floss, decorated with plastic flowers and flashing lights, corsets and panties open at the front, a whole range of models that, at least in Europe, can only be found in sex shops, which can't help but arouse curiosity given the strict morality and Islamic modesty around women's bodies.

Then, at seven, I went with the second secretary to the

Foreign Ministry for a formal talk with the minister. His advisor for Latin America spoke excellent French and some Spanish, and the minister himself had served as ambassador in Cuba and Venezuela for ten years. Both agreed that Iran wanted closer links with our country, since they saw us as an economically prosperous area. Their friendship with Venezuela and Bolivia had opened their eyes. We returned the compliments. They insisted on their desire for Colombia to re-establish a diplomatic presence in Tehran, which it had not had since the Uribe government had severed relations in 2002. We promised to bear it in mind, ate more delicious pistachios with tea, and half an hour later were back out on the street.

That night we had dinner in a traditional restaurant: meat, kebabs, rice with saffron, mint, extraordinary flavors. It's difficult to enjoy a dinner of that caliber without any kind of wine. Instead, we drank tea and mineral water. A little later I saw a singular spectacle, when a customer wanted to show his appreciation of the singer by offering him money. The master of ceremonies changed the sum into small notes and threw them over the singer, one by one, a shower of dinars, a colorful custom that, if any of our drug barons had seen it, would surely have become established in our country.

The following day we opened at the same hour.

The wait was a long one, but at last, about twelve, Juana appeared. She seemed unreal to me, as if looming out of a fog: an idea that materializes and takes on form and body, that emerges from a wood or a lagoon, from something symbolic, and at the same time, profoundly human. Was she beautiful? Anyone preceded by a history like hers would have been. I greeted her, holding back the emotion I felt. She was in fact very attractive. All Manuel's words were in her: in her smile and her proud eyes, in her colossal expression of strength. She gave me a hug, then showed me her baby.

"This is Manuelito."

Something in her expression, a certain weariness or sadness, bore witness to the blows she had received. I offered her tea. When we had moved apart from the others, I looked her in the eyes and said, have you decided? are you coming with me?

"Yes," she replied, "everything's ready. Is the flight on Sunday?"

I told her she could come to my hotel and we would leave from there. For obvious reasons, I didn't put her name down as someone coming with our delegation, because that might cause diplomatic problems. But she would travel by my side. She said yes. We went to the office and she herself checked that the child's documents were in order. Her passport had already been drawn up, as well as the birth certificate (Manuel Sayeq Hedayat Manrique). Having done this, the second secretary proceeded to remove the adhesive from the passport for the signature, but when I went to take hold of it, Juana stopped me.

"No, please, you keep them. I don't want to take the risk of someone finding them. I'll get to your hotel at eleven o'clock on Sunday, with everything ready. Thank you."

I walked her to the door. She said goodbye with a sad, nervous smile. I watched her walking along the street in the direction of the avenue. Then I called my travel agent in Delhi to get his confirmation, and ordered him to send the tickets for her and the child on the same return flight that he had reserved for me. Foreseeing this situation, I had taken a return for Sunday, whereas Olympia and the second secretary were going back on Saturday. I trusted them completely, but I preferred not to have witnesses.

On the day of the flight, Juana arrived at the specified hour, with two small suitcases. Manuel Sayeq was asleep in her arms. She seemed nervous, but her eyes were hard and determined. She had swum in difficult waters, cold and deep; she was used to making definitive and even cruel decisions. I omitted to ask about her husband or to mention her life in Iran, the life she was on the point of abandoning. Now was not the time.

She was wearing a blue jacket gathered in at the waist and covering her hips, as is traditional, and a veil, which was also blue, but a little lighter. She clearly respected the hijab, which is obligatory in Iran. Her eyes were beautiful. They stood out. The day before, I had dismissed the chauffeur I had been given by the government, so I called a taxi. Toward noon we set off for the airport, and when we got there we checked in without incident. The only anxious moment was when we went through Immigration, but since she was with me and I had a diplomatic passport, nobody asked any questions. When we got on the Mahan Air plane, she clasped her son to her chest and wept in silence.

The flight lasted four and a half hours, but I preferred not to ask her any questions and she barely spoke during the journey. I only heard her making a fuss of Manuel Sayeq on two occasions when the child woke up and demanded her breast.

When we got to Delhi, Indian Immigration had a ten-day visa ready for her, which I had arranged the previous week, explaining that it was an urgent case. There were no problems, and around midnight we got to my house in Jangpura. Manuel Sayeq was asleep in his mother's arms. I told Juana where the lights, the refrigerator, and the pantry were, and settled them in my study.

Then she took off her veil and said, "Goodbye to that rag, goodbye forever."

She unfastened her bun and her hair fell over her shoulders.

"You really do have a lot of books, Consul," she said. "Can I take a look?"

"Of course, they're arranged by author, more or less in alphabetical order."

She walked slowly between the shelves and passed her finger

over a few spines. Suddenly she took one out, read something that made her smile, and looked at it again. Then another one. She also looked at my pictures. Her attention was drawn to an oil painting of Saint Sebastian.

"It's by my mother," I said, "She's an artist."

"I like them," she said. "They suffer and prefer not to see the world, and don't like the world to see them."

She continued walking around among the books while I switched on my computer to check my messages. I was hoping for something from the lawyer in Bangkok, but there was nothing. Then it struck me that people don't write work-related e-mails at the weekend.

Suddenly she said, "Do you have any art books?"

"Yes," I said, "anything in particular?"

"Anything, especially if it's classical."

I went to a shelf and looked at a few books. "How about Mantegna?" I asked.

"Yes, perfect."

Then I poured myself—I might say: threw myself into—a longed-for gin, a cold glass filled with ice and slices of lemon. I asked her if she'd like one too.

"Yes, please," she said. "I haven't had a damned drink for a year."

We drank, then she asked:

"When are we going to see Manuel?"

As she asked this, with the book of Mantegna open in front of her, she stroked the image of the dead Christ with the tips of her fingers.

"We have to wait for the okay from Colombia," I said, "but it's a matter of a few days. They're putting the pressure on from over there too."

I told her I would call the lawyer in Bangkok the following day, although the fact there had been no messages suggested nothing had changed. I asked her if there was anything in

Delhi she was interested in seeing. We had to spend a few days there before flying to Thailand.

"Yes," she said, "a Sai Baba temple. That's the only thing."

"Sai Baba?" I said "There's one ten blocks from here. It's like the Vatican of Sai Baba. I'll take you tomorrow afternoon, so you're interested in Indian religion?"

"I think so," she said, "although in all this time I haven't managed to believe in anything. At least Sai Baba isn't a god, just a guru."

The following day, at the office, we evaluated the results of the mobile consulate and sent the respective reports to the Consular Department, along with the supporting documents, and travel and other expenses. An exhausting job. Olympia went to the bank and paid in the money taken, the stamp duty, and contributions to the savings fund. But before she left she took me aside and asked: did she come with you? I told her she had, that she was in my apartment with the child. Do you think we'll have any problems with Iran over this? No, Olympia replied: she's an adult, she's a foreigner, and she has a valid passport. She can go anywhere in the world and do whatever she likes. If she does have any problems with Iranian law, it'll be with the husband, because of the child, but that's no concern of ours.

Then I called the lawyer in Bangkok. He told me they hadn't yet fixed a date for the trial but that he had exerted pressure on them to hurry it up. He added that we needed to think about the guilty plea, which had to be framed in such a way that we could gain time. If it was harrowing and dramatic enough, and displayed heartfelt remorse, we might impress the judges and obtain a shorter sentence. He concluded by saying that Manuel had already been informed about his sister.

I left the office early and went home. On the way I stopped at the Prya Market and bought a couple of model Ambassador cars for the child: a black taxi with a yellow roof and a white official vehicle with a siren. I was eager to tell Juana the news.

I found her on the balcony, giving Manuel Sayeq a bottle and watching the eagles circling above the park. As they flew overhead, two green parrots with red beaks hid in the branches of a plane tree. Below, on the street, a knife grinder was pushing a beat-up old cart and shouting something. Three children were playing cricket beside a mountain of garbage.

"Manuel knows we're together and that you're going to Bangkok," I said. "He must be very happy."

She opened her eyes so wide I thought she was going to faint. The emotion made her cry and she hid her face.

"I'll have to prepare myself," she said, recovering, "or I won't know what to say when I see him."

She started crying again and I hugged her. The crying made her body shake. Suddenly she pulled her head away and in between her sobs said:

"I feel so guilty . . . !"

She walked to the rail and stood for a while facing the park: the birds, the clouds of smog and dust covering the sky. I judged it best to leave her alone with her thoughts.

After a while, she came back into the study, already recovered. We had a quick gin, with a lot of ice, and went out to the temple of Sai Baba, near the India Habitat Center and the Jorbagh district.

The temple was a strange construction, with a staircase of white tiles and metal bars around the prayer room. From the upper part of the walls hung banners of saffron-colored canvas. The ground was covered with rotten rose petals, paper pennants, incense and aromatic substances, lighted candles, mountains of candle wax hardened and blackened by the dust, garlands of saffron flowers, trodden fruit peel, plastic bags, and outside, on the avenue, an infinity of fried food stands, sellers of pistachios, maize, a thousand kinds of fried and salted grains, chapatis with spicy sauce, and all around, scattered on the dusty ground and the pavement, hundreds of disposable plates with the remains of food, covered in flies, besieged by dogs and crows, generating a smell of decomposing matter that mingled with that of the fried food, the pollution, the kerosene, and the fumes from the buses.

"Exactly as I imagined it," Juana said.

She walked up very slowly, with Manuelito in her arms. When she reached the prayer room she knelt and remained like that for a long time, not changing place, only making slow movements from side to side, as if she were calming the child's tears, whispering the words of consolation and love that I imagined she herself would have liked to hear. She seemed more like a goddess in her own temple than someone who was praying.

Suddenly I remembered my conversation with Manuel:

"What makes me a fragile person is having been unhappy in my childhood," he had said.

I recalled that I had looked at him in silence and said nothing, but had thought: what made me fragile was the opposite, having been happy. What of it? Then Manuel had thought for a moment and added: Life, when you come down to it, always presents you with an unusual bill to pay. That's why Marx said that in history, events happen first as tragedy and then are repeated as comedy.

By the time Juana left the temple, she seemed transformed. Her smile was clearer, and you had less sense of storms inside her. It may have been an effect of the light or my own nervousness. I don't know. Then we went for a walk. I showed her a number of places: India Gate, Connaught Place, Gandhi's house, Indira's house, the mansions of Golf Links and the architecture of Sundar Nagar. That night we had dinner at the Balluchi, in Hauz Khas Village, because apart from Punjabi food they had Kingfisher beer in green bottles, the ones with the highest alcohol content.

I didn't want to pressure her, but I was intrigued to hear

about her life, what had led her to leave everything so drastically, her adventures in Japan, her relationship with Jaburi, who by now must have been desperate, hitting the walls and howling with anger. Had she left him a note? had she promised him she would come back after seeing her brother? what were her plans?

"When you feel up to it, you could tell me something about your life," I said to her, "whatever you like. I'm curious. Manuel told me a few things."

A shadow passed over her face. It only lasted a second, but it was noticeable. Her eyes were no longer at peace.

"Does he know I went to Tokyo to . . . ?"

I didn't see any point in hiding it. "He knows everything," I said, "that's why he went looking for you."

There was a grave look on her face now. She seemed about to say something, but no words came out.

"You decide, if you like," I said. "When it comes down to it, you don't have to tell me anything."

She looked at me. Her eyes were like rays.

"It's all right, Consul, but for now, do you mind if we sit for a while in silence?"

A couple of days went by. In the office I was still waiting for news from Bangkok that would make it possible for me to go back and deal with the case again. But everything seemed frozen.

The Consular Department continued its contacts with the Thai embassy in Bogotá, sending them a memorandum in which they asked if Manuel Manrique could be allowed to stand trial in Colombia. The embassy transmitted it to its ministry in Bangkok and we were still waiting for a reply, even if just a comment, anything that might allow negotiations to start. For the moment it was pointless to do anything, what with the travel expenses involved.

All I could do was wait.

The women servants in my apartment became fond of the child and one of them started taking him to the park in the afternoons so that he could play and see other children, thus giving Juana a bit of free time. She took the opportunity to read *Vislumbres de la India* by Octavio Paz. I would get home around seven-thirty, sometimes a little later, and we'd have a couple of gins until it was time for dinner. Then she'd lock herself in her room and I'd sit and read.

A week went by.

The following Thursday they were showing a Spanish film, Carlos Saura's *Cría Cuervos*, at the Cervantes Institute. I suggested it to her and we went. She liked it. Another day she went with me to a book presentation at the India Habitat Center. Then to a literature event at the Alliance Française. There is a great deal of cultural life in Delhi. The Italo-Indian cultural center offered a program linking literature and food, and invited a group of people to sample dishes that had a connection with some of their most famous films. Juana was starting to feel at ease, or at least that's what I thought. I was curious to know how she would justify having abandoned first her home, then Manuel, then her Iranian husband. How had her life in Tehran been? what was Jaburi like? would he put pressure on her about the child? would it be something like that sentimental film *Not Without My Daughter*, in which Iranian men were depicted as monsters? I had no idea. She still hadn't made up her mind to tell me anything.

Faced with the absence of news from the Consular Department, I had to write to the Indian embassy in Bogotá asking for an extension of Juana's visa and her child's, which fortunately was conceded without their having to leave the country. After the attacks on the Oberoi and Taj hotels in Mumbai, which the Indians, imitating the Americans, call 26/11, India had modified the legislation concerning foreigners, introducing more requirements for obtaining or extending visas. Those who had six-month visas could no longer simply go to Nepal and stamp their passports, but had to wait two months to reenter India. Fortunately, this was not the case with Juana, thanks to the recommendation of the Indian embassy in Bogotá.

One day, in the middle of breakfast, she asked if her parents had been informed.

"Manuel asked me not to," I said. "I passed that on to the legal department of our Foreign Ministry. Frankly, I don't know."

She was lost in thought, so I picked up the phone and offered it to her.

"Do you want to call them? Call them, you could talk for as long as you like."

She looked at the phone, but immediately put it back on the table.

"No, thanks, I only wanted to know. When I see Manuel we'll decide together what to do."

Two more weeks passed and Juana started to get impatient. That was understandable. According to the lawyer in Bangkok, things were going well and we would soon have news. His friend in the police had assured him that they were about to make a big arrest of drug traffickers. We just had to be patient.

Juana bought a sari at Fabindia, a shop selling traditional clothes, with good bargains, and one night my Nepalese maid showed her how to put it on. What a curious and beautiful garment: twenty feet of brightly colored cloth, folded until it covers the body, leaving the midriff free, which is a matter of comfort and at the same time provocative. In their saris, all Indian women looked like princesses. The men, in their common drill trousers or jeans, were more like third-class servants, except when they wore kurtas or Punjabi-style vests.

When I got back from the office, I found Juana waiting for me in her sari. I praised her fulsomely, we drank a toast, then we got ready to go out. First to look at books at Full Circle, in the Khan Market, where you could drink tea on a terrace over which crows and vultures flew; Juana looked at everything with a certain casualness, as if she didn't want to establish a close relationship with anything that she saw, or be too startled. Like a butterfly that flits from spot to spot. Later, we ate in the restaurant in Lodhi Gardens, which had good Indian lobster dishes.

Although her sari was compact, I thought I caught a glimpse of strange signs and images beneath it. Were they tattoos, I wondered, or a printed T-shirt?

Another day I invited some friends to the house. Among them was an unusual, very pleasant Colombian, Alexis von Hildebrand, who worked for UNICEF, and who had lived in Madagascar for ten years. He was the only person I had ever met who had been to the islands of Tonga. His grandfather was a Catholic philosopher, a German, a friend of Nicolás Gómez Dávila. I also invited Sudeep Sen, poet and editor of a literary review in Delhi, the aspiring guru and my collaborator at the embassy, Madhuván "Rishiraj" Sharma, who was preparing himself by interpreting the *Mahabharata*, and of course my friend Professor Chattopadhyay. The group was completed by a Spanish-Indian couple, Lola McDougall and Nikhil Padgaonkar, poets and photographers, and the Catalan Óscar Pujol, director of the Cervantes Institute in Delhi and professor of Sanskrit at the University of Varanasi.

I introduced Juana to them as a sociologist passing through Delhi, and the evening was unforgettable. Von Hildebrand told us of a strange tradition in the islands of Tonga: once a year the king has to go into the sea and offer a roast pig over to the king of the sharks. If the shark bites the king, it's a sign that he has been a bad ruler.

Then Von Hildebrand went into the kitchen and came back with a half-gallon pitcher of pisco sour, his specialty, which accompanied most of the meal.

Later, as we opened the third bottle of Bombay gin, between travelers' tales and literary quotations, Lola MacDougall suggested an amusing game: the construction of pagodas and ziggurats with books by favorite authors.

Juana, without calling attention to herself, built a simple one-story house using the poetry of E. E. Cummings, and roofed it with Rudolf Otto. I tried to build a Japanese temple out of Houellebecq (Nikhil told me, in French, *tu te houelle-becquises!*). We all did our work and ended up with a number of concepts: an art nouveau house made of aphorisms by Lichtenberg and prose by Edmond Jarrès, an Islamic temple shared between Raymond Roussel and Vikram Seth, a Hindu temple made out of Malcolm Lowry, and a great ziggurat of confessional works: the *Journal Intime* of Benjamin Constant, the diaries of Ernst Jünger, *La Tentación del Fracaso* by Julio Ramón Ribeyro, two volumes of Anaïs Nin, and the *Journal Littéraire* of Paul Léautaud.

Sudeep read some poems by Dylan Thomas, to whom we raised a toast, in memory of his untimely death at the age of thirty-nine, in New York, after a series of successful recitals. In connection with that, I presented (and maintained) my theory of an apoplectic seizure brought on by hypercholesterolemia: a sedentary life, alcohol, obesity, excessive smoking, hyperten-sion, high cerebral irrigation, and insomnia. A hundred mil-ligrams of losartan, taken on an empty stomach, and five of amlodipine at night, plus a diet of unsaturated fats, would have prolonged his life and his work for at least twenty years. Twenty-five if he had added thirty minutes walking a day. *Dommage!*

Chattopadhyay, remembering his days as a Naxalite guer-rilla, instructed us in how to leave my apartment in case of a police raid and where to go, and then recited various poems by Neruda, his specialty (especially "Tango del viudo"). We talked about Malraux in India (*Antimémoires*), Roberto

Rossellini in India (he married an Indian woman), and Romain Rolland in India (he was the French ambassador there in 1921, it's in his *Diaries*). Starting from there, the list of visitors became interminable: Paz (*Vislumbres de la India*), Pasolini (*L'Odore dell'India*), Herman Hesse (*Aus Indien*), E.M. Forster (*A Passage to India*), Alberto Moravia (*Una Idea de la India*), Michaux (*Un Barbare en Asie*), a long list of authors I have investigated and read for a book to which I am, of course, still hesitating whether to give the title *India: A Passionate Human Family* or the simpler one *Masala Tea*.

At four in the morning, after saying goodbye to the guests, and being reasonably drunk ("each person drinks what he needs," as Teresa said), Juana and I bade each other good night, but then, from my room, I heard her returning to the living room to collect glasses and empty bottles, arrange the chairs, and tidy up the books. Clearly, she felt at home.

The weekend came and I suggested that she and I and the child go for a walk in Nehru Park. I had been lent a stroller for Manuel Sayeq and it was the perfect opportunity. The park was crisscrossed by paths, between gardens and groves, a cool, clean place, ideal for a Saturday. As a memory of other times, it had a statue of Lenin.

Walking between flowers and shrubs, Juana suddenly said:

"Would it bother you if I told you something about my life?"

"On the contrary," I said. "I've been waiting for it for some time now."

She gave me an affectionate look, was silent for a few more steps as she pushed Manuel Sayeq's stroller along a path, and at last began speaking.

5
INTER-NETA'S MONOLOGUES

S ome nights, when the sky was ablaze with distance storms, the Virgin Mary appeared to me. My room lit up and at the same time filled with dense shadows. Of course, she was quite different than the Virgin Mary who appeared to the three shepherd children of Fatima. Judge for yourselves.

Mine arrived with a weary air and lay down on the couch in my bedroom. Pour me a whiskey, or whatever you have, Inter-Neta, hopefully above forty proof, which is the liquid temperature best adapted to my spirit. You know what I mean.

She drank slowly, looking up at the ceiling, as if making a complicated mental calculation. The last time, she said to me: 11,186,986 girls stopped being virgins today, oh, if only you'd seen it . . . The youngest was seven years old and was raped by a priest, a filthy fellow who first stuck his finger in, made her suck it, then penetrated her. Don't ask me for any more details, priests disgust me, they're reptiles in human skin, like that Dickens character, I don't know if you've read him, Uriah Heep, who always has cold hands.

The oldest was thirty-eight, a real record, and the curious thing is that she had been married for twelve years. Until now she always told her husband she didn't like frontal penetration out of respect for me, and the guy accepted it. Can you imagine? He sodomized her, and they performed fellatio and masturbation. He's a harbor technician and, curiously, he would tell his best friends about it, and even make jokes. My wife's tongue is fourteen inches long and she can breathe through her ears! And they would all laugh.

She also laughed with her friends: my husband has a small cock, no bigger than his tongue, and his semen tastes either of pastis or whiskey, depending on what he's drunk the previous evening. And that's how they've been all this time, but today she had a party at her office, drank to excess, and ended up fucking in the bathroom with one of her colleagues. This happened in France, in the offices of BNP. I can't give you any more details. Seeing the blood flowing down her thigh, the current accounts manager of the Sully Morland branch thought she was starting her period and exclaimed, *mon dieu!* at least you won't get pregnant, but she wept with pain and he thought she was weeping with love and pleasure, so he said something vulgar to her. They separated on a great misunderstanding. Later he went back to the bathroom to wash one of the tails of his shirt. She had been waiting so long for her husband and look what happened.

Pour me another, is this really whiskey? Never mind. At least you have alcohol, I'm tired, you have no idea, dear Inter-Neta, what it means to be what I am and the tremendous solitude in which I live. Up there, there's almost nobody left. I think that everyone, including him, drinks too much and is past caring. I drink too, but it's different. I drink because the pain of the world is too much for me, and I can't take another iota of pain.

Do you want another crazy and eccentric story? This might be the best one: a young woman of twenty-two decides to give her virginity to her philosophy professor, who is married. After a class on the pre-Socratics, he takes her to a motel—this happens in Latin America—penetrates her for the first time gently, softly, until she says, oh, do it stronger, so he penetrates her again and they both laugh and kiss and she, filled with ecstasy, cries out in French, *Je suis une sirène!* They fuck and fuck as if we had invented original sin exclusively for them—and for that night—and then, having already been penetrated through most of the orifices in her beautiful body, when they're having a beer and he's smoking a cigarette and she's preparing a line of coke, the young woman realizes she's lost a lot of blood and the sheets of the modest motel bed are soaked, as if the Red Sea had burst into that little space of adultery and pleasure.

As they're about to go, the young woman suffers an attack of modesty and says: I can't leave it like this, it's a shame and an embarrassment, I'll take the sheets away and wash them, and send them back by courier. The Dionysian philosophy professor, who's exhausted, says, don't worry, they're used to it, they've seen worse things, but she insists, she's had a French education and is stubborn, she thinks that faced with any situation in life there's only one way to proceed that's the right way, so she grabs the sheets and puts them on the back-seat of the car.

As luck or *fatum* would have it, that night, returning to the city—the motel was on the outskirts—there was a routine police roadblock, and when the officers searched the car they found the sheets. Blood! They arrested him on suspicion of murder. There was no point explaining that it was her virginal blood, and the tests would take a couple of days. They were taken to the local police station. The philosopher had to call a lawyer, and of course his wife.

6

I was a happy child, Consul, but in a sad, opaque world. A black and white world. And why? I still ask myself that. There was very little in that happiness, if you looked into it: clouded landscapes, gray people who hated their lives and dreamed of something different, people who never managed to live up to anything they thought was beautiful, banal creatures conscious of their own banality, prisoners of something that had no end and could never have an end. I was a little queen as long as I believed that the world was the same for everybody. Then I realized it wasn't and that made me angry. I'm still angry, but anyway, that's not what I want to tell you about.

As in children's stories or Russian novels, I'll begin at the beginning. Even though the beginning is boring. I was the spoiled child of the house until, when I was four, they told me I'd be having a brother. I felt as if they'd betrayed me and that triggered a hatred in me, a feeling of abandonment, even a kind of sense of being an orphan, and when the child was born I wanted him to die. He was an intruder, a stowaway. Seeing him crawling through my space, watching with horror as he took over my things, I had a lot of ideas: to push him down the stairs, to open the door so that he got out onto the street and was lost. But then I noticed that in spite of the novelty I was still being spoiled, and that saved his life. My position wasn't in danger and in order to be sure I forced them to choose. I put them to the test. Father always opted for me. So I kept quiet. My little world continued to function more or less as before, and the years went by. I continued to ignore him. Don't you love your little brother? they would say, and I'd say, yes, I love him, he's the king of my country, and I'm the queen, and everybody would laugh and say we were cute, but they didn't realize how much I despised him. His diapers, his talcum powder, his mournful crying. I hated him and told myself: God sent him to put me to the test, because in those days I believed in God, you know? I thought: he's only here to see what I do, but then God will get him out of my way. He'll have to be very careful. That was what I always thought, and I waited and waited, but God never granted my wish.

Father idolized me.

I never loved him as much as he loved me. He was a poor man whose neck had been wrung, whose wings had been scorched. What could I do? I decided to keep quiet and wait. My school friends were luckier, their families were rich and important and there wasn't that rancid taste in their lives, that atmosphere of desolation that lived in my house. What did I do? I kept quiet. I waited.

One day I thought God had heard me, because my brother got ill. They took him to the clinic, and I said, goodbye to all this, back to a world without him and it'll be better. I could see from my parents' faces that it was serious, but I noticed (and somehow knew) that it wasn't going to be a great loss for them. They had me, why did they want more?

One Saturday they suggested I visit him, and I accepted, all right, I'll make a little sacrifice, but looking up I said, God, I know what you're playing at, I'll go see him and then you'll take him away, right? As I walked into his room, I looked him in the eyes and something very strange happened. It was the first time I'd looked at him in that way, and what I saw changed my life. How to explain it? I realized that there was no God and that nobody had sent him to put me to the test; he was simply a little person who was terribly alone and fragile and who seemed to be saying: here is the other half of your soul. I heard that in his eyes, and there was more, a kind of path, or a world; in those days I hadn't yet read Rimbaud, but later I understood: "In the dawn, armed with an ardent patience, we will enter splendid cities." These were the words of the path I thought we had to take, he and I, alone, because deep down what there was in his silent eyes was a voice, the voice of a ghost that seemed to whisper: you too are here, we contain the same breath, my soul and yours are united, don't break it, so I reached out my hand and touched him, understanding profoundly who he was, and immediately, for the first and only time in my life, I felt love, a cataclysm that almost buried me, a storm that took my breath away, something so big that from that moment it filled my life and I could never again love anybody else, not even today, only my son who is also called Manuel because they are both made of the same matter: the flesh and the bones and the blood and the look of that love.

It wasn't necessary to speak. We didn't say anything to each other, we were very young! But we knew that we were together: we had recognized each other. That was why I devoted myself to protecting him. He was my younger brother. I protected him as much as I could from the wickedness of that city, and from that cruel thing known as childhood. I also tried to protect him from the family. I don't know if I succeeded. And later, as he grew, I became aware of his unusual intelligence. His opinions about life and the world, and later about art, were exceptional. Everything in him was like that: brilliant, enigmatic, superhuman. Inside him something was growing that was beautiful and I was there to look after it, like a lighted ember you have to cradle in your hands to turn it into a fire. That gave us strength. Sometimes two cowards together can produce courage. That was the case with us.

When I turned fifteen I felt that I had to find a way to escape.

One day we saw the movie *Papillon*, with Steve McQueen and Dustin Hoffman, and we told each other this was how it had to be for us, to get away from a prison island by taking advantage of the tides, to keep trying until we escaped, it was that or death, to leave our sad house, that middle-class neighborhood with its social pretentions, that sad, hated city. Our prison island. We had to jump when the tide was high, like in *Papillon*.

When he was very young Manuel started to read and to watch movies, thanks to a friend on the block. Later, much to my surprise, he started to paint graffiti. Beautiful things, islands, seas, storms. He had a beautiful world inside him that I wanted to know, to touch. That was why I had to get hold of money to buy him cans of spray paint, books, and DVDs, in other words, everything an elevated soul needs, so I started to look for little jobs at school. I did my rich classmates' assignments, whispered the answers to them in exams, or did their exams myself, putting their names on the papers. They paid me and I went off happily to look for the best for him; while my classmates looked at shopwindows full of clothes and asked the prices, I would stroll along rows of books, touching the spines, following the alphabetical order, discovering the immense pleasure of buying books, the smell of the shelves, that silence charged with wisdom that exists between books and the people who buy them, a dense atmosphere, and so I'd return home with two new ones, sometimes three, knowing that with them I was giving Manuel something of the life he didn't have, which was the space in which both of us would later be happy.

I need to tell you some intimate things, Consul, for which I apologize. At the age of seventeen one of my classmates told me on the bus: I've lost my virginity. It was a Monday. She'd been to a party with her boyfriend the previous Saturday and they'd gone on to a motel. These things matter to a young girl.

To me, at least. An army of ants ran through my veins, and I asked, what did you feel? and she said, I almost died, I think I fainted. And I said, inquisitively, but did it hurt? A bit at the beginning, she said, but it's so nice that it passes. From that moment on, it turned into an obsession, but I didn't have a boyfriend and didn't want one. At parties I danced and hugged boys, but they didn't take me seriously. I met one in the end, not long afterwards. He was from a foreign school and had money. When he asked me for my phone number, I said to him: call me, if you like. In the middle of the week he called and to tell the truth I really couldn't be bothered with him, because he was quite stupid, but on Saturday, when he picked me up from home to go out for an ice cream, I said to him, look, can I make another suggestion, let's go to a motel and you can deflower me, okay? The guy was surprised and said, you bet! he accelerated and we drove along the freeway to La Calera, and there, in a room with a jacuzzi and a disc player and a view of Bogotá, I lost my virginity, which was nothing special, or rather not very intense, but at least it was done, so the following week I said to my classmate, that's it, I also lost my virginity, and we started comparing notes, how big was it? what did it smell of? how long did it take him to come? did he wear a condom? that kind of thing.

In the middle of the week the guy called to invite me to a party, but I said to him, forget about parties, I'm not your girl-friend, if you want to fuck let's go and fuck, but don't talk crap, and the guy, who was sweet but a complete dickhead, said, all right, Juana, that's cool, we'll do what you want, and so I had a lover, but because he never listened he fell head over heels in love with me, guys are all the same, so he'd call me and say, hey, Juanita, I want to see you, can I come to your house? and I'd say, over my dead body, call me on Saturday, and don't be so mushy, and on Saturday he'd call and I'd say, no, I'm going to the movies with my brother, and he'd say, and what movie are you going to see? and I'd say, what nerve, the kind you don't like, and he'd go, no, Juana, on the contrary, I'm crazy about Fellini and Pasolini and all those Italian surnames, seriously, and I'd say, thanks a lot but no thanks, call me next Saturday, and then the guy would try to get to me through my friends, but since none of them knew where I lived, there was no way, and he'd call like crazy, send text messages and crap like that, and go on Facebook, until he really drove me crazy, saying that he was dying, that he needed to see me, that he couldn't stop crying, so I sent him a message saying, right, this bullshit is over, ciao, ciao, I'm going to block you out and I'm going to take you off my Facebook contacts and all that, okay? so it's best if you don't insist, thank you, and of course, the guy didn't take any notice and through friends sent me messages and gifts, and I sent everything back, marked him as spam, until he turned up at my school, crying, and got down on his knees, so I said to him, all right, stop, that's enough, let's talk on Saturday, and the guy left, and on Saturday he called and I said, pick me up at the Pomona and we'll go to a motel, but on the condition that you don't talk to me or tell me any more of that bullshit you've been telling me, and that's how it was, we fucked and the guy didn't say a word, which was how I liked him, so I continued seeing him, although one day I said to him, look, it'll be better if you find yourself another girlfriend, if you like we can carry on fucking until you get one, but I can tell you now it's not going to last because I'm going to university to study sociology and I don't want to go around anymore with spoiled brats like you or have anything more to do with people like you, do you understand me? I like you, I prefer not to be a bitch, and that's why I'm telling you right now not to start throwing tantrums like the other time, okay?

I got him out of my hair when I started at the National, where I met really fantastic people and found my world. In my school there had been rich people and middle-class people, like me, but the rules of what was good, what was cool, were dictated by the rich, whereas at the National it wasn't like that, there were other values. Being cultured, having courage or nobility, was much more important than a shirt or a pair of shoes. The opposite of the horrible world I had just left and had never belonged to.

My place was the National, with its lawns and its white buildings covered with graffiti, and its brick constructions, its middle-class and lower-class people preparing to go out into life like lions or crocodiles, with their stomachs to the ground, all equal in that enormous larder, a gnoseological throng, as a Cuban poet said, and that was why when I found out that they'd accepted me I felt my cheeks burn with pride, Colombia's in my image now, I said to myself, walking along the path that led across the lawn to the sociology department, and when they called out the names of those enrolled in the first semester my eyes started watering, I thrust my hand in the air when I heard my name, yes, here I am, so overcome with emotion that they looked at me, and I thought, this is my patch, I wanted to meet everybody, to love everybody, to tell them how long I had waited for them, it was wonderful, but of course, at home it was quite the opposite, the atmosphere was grim, to avoid problems I'd told Father that I was going to enroll in law or engineering, so I said that sociology was my third option and that was the one I'd been accepted for. They didn't believe me, but it was too late to do anything about it.

Father and Mother were conservatives, but not part of an erudite, aristocratic right wing; they belonged to that cheap, mean, jingoistic right wing that was so common there, people filled with hate and resentment who look for something or someone with whom (or through whom) to express that hate and resentment; with their admiration for the upper classes and their social aspirations; with their classism and racism. That was why Marx said that the middle class was the class least prepared for a revolution. He was only partly wrong, but if we're talking about my parents, he was right.

As I'm sure you remember, Consul, Uribe won those elections using words that got people heated up, words like motherland, everyone wearing wristbands with the colors of the flag and talking about one thing and one thing only: "security." The people wanted war and he promised them war. The people wanted deaths and he promised them many dead. The people wanted a patriarch, a sovereign, a satrap, and he promised them he would be a patriarch, a sovereign, a satrap. His victory was celebrated with shots fired in the air and chain saws roaring, do you remember? The paramilitaries celebrated and the left said: now we really are fucked. FARC greeted the news with a shower of grenades in Bogotá that killed a couple of junkies in a crack house near the Palacio de Nariño. FARC said, war is war, and Uribe replied, bring it on, let's see who has more guts.

Because he represented people with guts, and Catholics to boot. The Conservatives shouted for joy. The Liberals celebrated. Our Forbes-listed millionaires opened bottles of Veuve Clicquot and rubbed their hands saying, let's get ready to make more money. Those who didn't have anything got drunk on aguardiente or sweet wine and sighed, saying: oh, how proud I feel to be a good Colombian! The paramilitaries fired their mini-Uzis in the air, and it was lucky those bullets didn't land in the skulls or spines of peasants, trade unionists, community leaders, or native Indians. The Catholics bowed down before the new Messiah: "He has a picture of the Blessed Marianito that he carries sewed into his fist!" wasn't it his foreskin? no, his fist! The evangelicals said: "He worships the Virgin Mary!" The elegant Hindu ladies in Bogotá celebrated: "He gets up at three in the morning to say chakras and meditate!" The Jews hugged each other: "He may be a bit of a Fascist, but at least he's a friend of Israel!" The paramilitaries sang the national anthem with their hands on their hearts, and said: "Now you're going to see what's good for you, you sons of bitches."

Remember, remember how it was, Consul.

The country filled with tricolor flags, everybody shouted, long live Colombia! Or long live Colombia, son of a bitch! or even long live Colombia, fucking son of a bitch! Others said, that's enough of this crap about human rights! we're going to show those traitors! And others, the regions controlled by the paramilitaries are areas of progress! Or: the regions controlled by the paramilitaries are areas of progress, thank you, president! Now we're going to work and to love our country! And others, if you cut my veins, Colombia will come out! They'd even knock back aguardiente and sing songs about how patriotic it was to drink the national drink! Anyone who criticized Uribe was a supporter of terrorism; anyone who criticized Uribe was a terrorist; anyone who criticized Uribe was a fucking terrorist. Best to kill those fucking terrorists, bang, bang, you're dead. Let's wipe them out. They're anti-Colombian, dangerous people.

In many regions, starting with Córdoba, where the sovereign had his estate, they cried at the tops of their voices: long live the paramilitaries! long live President Uribe! long live progress and pacification! And over everything: long live Colombia, son of a bitch! and even louder, as loud as you could get: long live the Virgin Mary, son of a bitch!

That's how my parents were, Consul. Two small parts of that mass that felt ennobled. Nothing unites people more than hate and the desire to exercise that hate. And hate means you're scared. You're looking for protection and want it to be long-lasting, a military anthem all about death and battle that seeps into your soul. Every time something important or serious happened, in other words every day, my parents would say: "We have to stand by our president!" The word "president" stood in for many others: father, guru, leader, chief, benefactor, savior, liberator, god. Every time he insulted some neighboring head of state they'd say: "We're proud of our president!" He could have urinated over the country from a helicopter, and the country would still have worshiped him. He could have shouted from the highest peak, from the top of Pico Cristóbal Colón, which is eighteen thousand feet high: "Colombian sons of bitches!" and the people would have gotten down on their knees and begged him for forgiveness.

Apart from my parents, the rest of the family was also like that. Only a brother of my mother's, who worked as a clerk in an insurance company, said one day, during a family birthday: "Colombia is becoming a training camp for paramilitaries," and they jumped on him, if only it were, they cried, that's what's missing in this country of bums, discipline and order, and that's what we have at last, discipline and order, and my poor uncle retorted, yes, but how many people do we have to kill or disappear? and then they said to him, Omar, you're a bit old to become a Communist, and you know what? we'll have to kill whoever we have to kill, and good people have nothing to fear from the people who do the killing, because it must be for some reason, mustn't it? we can't carry on like this, anyone who gets in the way is useless, didn't you know that? it's a painful operation but it has to be performed, and that's what they're doing, thank God there are people who've decided to pull themselves together and do something about it, people who care about the future, and if you don't like it go to Venezuela and then you'll see, won't you? That uncle never again put in an appearance at family get-togethers, and the others said, Omar has become a communist, and that's his problem. But what they were actually thinking was: we hope they kill him.

Neither my brother nor I could stand that filthy atmosphere and that's why I started to try to earn more money. If Father had found out he would have killed me; he always said with pride that he could support his family, but the truth is that he couldn't manage, it wasn't his fault, although we weren't poor like 50 percent of Colombians, but he couldn't, he considered it a matter of dignity and I didn't want to hurt him, so I looked and looked, but of course, in the university you couldn't do other people's work for them like I had at school, people weren't rich and the work was complicated, I barely had time for mine, so I started to look at small ads. A friend who looked after elderly people told me it was easy, you could study while you did it, all you had to do was take them out for a walk, give them food, read to them, and if it was at night it was even easier, you just had to be there while they slept, administer their medication through a saline solution, then stay up and watch over them.

I started looking until I found an ad, it was for someone to look after an old man who had recently had an operation, he was looking for a night nurse, and I told myself, great, I'll dress up as a nurse, my friend could lend me her uniform, so I went and they hired me, he was a very frail man, just skin and bone, poor thing, lying in bed connected to a bag. I'd get there after dinner, when the other nurse finished her shift, and stay with him until the following morning. I had to replace the saline solution, give him his sedatives, put a damp towel on his forehead. It was three nights a week. At home I said I had study groups and had to sleep over at my friends' houses. The advantage was that my mother didn't like my fellow students, so I didn't have a problem; Father would say, fine, you can stay over, but if you see it's uncomfortable call me and we'll see what we can do, maybe you could come back in a taxi, all right? and I felt very tender toward him when I heard him say that, because in our house mentioning a taxi was like talking about a bottle of French champagne, only rich people took taxis!

I started to keep my money in a savings account that I opened secretly, and from it I'd make withdrawals to take

Manuel out, and to buy him books and movies and lots of acrylic paint so that he could paint all the walls he wanted, and to pay for his tickets at the movies. I was educating him and I wanted the best for him, he was my great pride. On those nights when I kept guard, listening to the labored breathing of the old man, I devoted myself to reading. The old man was a cultured person. I don't know if I mentioned that he was French, I think I forgot to tell you that. He was French but had been living in Colombia since the sixties. In his library there were French books, and I'd look at them admiringly. Some I understood, because I'd studied the language at school. Books by Jean Genet, Albert Camus, the whole of Proust, André Gide. He had *La Condition Humaine* by Malraux, with what looked like a dedication by Malraux himself, could he have known him? He lived in a big old house on Fiftieth and Eighth, in Upper Chapinero. He had servants and a chauffeur. His children came every day, but they needed someone for the nights. They didn't want to put him in a residential home. Or rather: they couldn't until he was completely well again. I became accustomed to that routine and to the university, to my studies and my new friends.

When the old man, whose name was Monsieur Echenoz, was better, we started talking. I asked him why he had chosen to stay in a backward, violent country like Colombia, a country everyone wanted to leave, and he said, not necessarily, would you leave? I told him I would, if I could I'd go that very moment, with my brother, and he asked, where would you go? and I said anywhere, any corner of the world must be better than this, I'd like to go to Europe, to a civilized country, and he'd look at me without judging me, the sheet covering half his chest, with white hairs coming out through the buttonholes of his pajamas, and he said, a civilized country? you don't want to leave Colombia, what you want is to get away from something you don't like but which you could find in lots of places, and he said, I know a lot of the world, especially Africa, when I was young I worked for French petroleum companies in Zaire and Rwanda, countries full of awful things, but beautiful, too. I could say the same about Asia. In spite of the difficulties, life is much more beautiful there than in "civilized" places, what does civilization mean? There's no future in Europe. A tired, bad-tempered continent that tries to teach other people how to live, but that's become frozen from looking at itself so much in the mirror. You're studying sociology, aren't you? Italy and France governed by clowns, what does it mean to be on the left in a place like that? not much, reading the left-wing press, owning an old Manu Chao CD and T-shirts of Che Guevara and Subcomandante Marcos, worrying about the environment, about human rights in some distant country, not much more; like any affluent society, Europe is going downhill. Just like a person who has everything, who's in love with himself and full of self-admiration, that's what's happening there, but what the Europeans don't know is that they aren't anybody's future. The opposite is true: the future is on the margins. How can you say that this country is backward and violent, as if that were a basic racial or cultural value of one nation and not of another? What's happening here is that it's a young country, a very young country, and is still looking for a language. What you see in Europe, the peace they have today, cost two thousand years of war, of blood, torture, and cruelty. When the nations of Europe were the same age as Colombia they were mutual enemies and every time they met rivers of blood flowed, lagoons and estuaries of blood. The last European war left fifty-four million dead. Do you think that isn't violence? Never forget it. Just in the capture of Berlin by the Russian troops, which only lasted a couple of weeks, more people died than in a whole century of conflict in Colombia, so get the idea out of your head that this is a particularly violent country, because it isn't. But it is very complex and has been beaten down, and worse still, armed. It has riches and a wonderful location, and that always ends up exploding. Violence is part of the culture, the history, the life of nations. Out of violence, societies are born and so are periods of peace, it's been like that since the dawn of time and Colombia is in the middle of this process; I assure you it will achieve it more rapidly and with less blood than Europe.

I listened to Monsieur Echenoz with skepticism and said, but in European wars people killed each other for an ideal, not here, here it's pure barbarism, it's money or land or cocaine, but he said, it's the same thing, the reasons someone who's about to shoot another man thinks he has may vary, but the deed is the same, someone will press the trigger, and when the lead breaks the skin and drills into the cranium and damages a lobe and perforates it and opens a path in the brain, a life with a history and past will be cut short and a body transformed into a bloodstained mass that will fall to the ground, and that fact, which is horrible in itself and can't in any way be explained or justified, makes all the reasons equivalent; in the middle of the twentieth century it was ideologies, then it was land or the control of resources, reserves of hydrocarbons. Politics isn't the reason, just the way politics represents a need to take the next step, which is to go on the attack. Ideologies are merely self-fulfilling prophecies. Force is the argument most often used by man in his history, whatever culture he belongs to, so don't worry, nothing is being done here that hasn't been done before in other places, and for the same reasons. What's happening today in Colombia, deep down, is the result of an imposed formula. Do you know the contemporary name for perversity? It's democracy. If a chimpanzee with a drum becomes popular and amusing, he could be elected president. Why are the votes of those who don't have standards or education or culture worth the same as the votes of people who do have them? Why is a vote obtained with a revolver to the head or by brainwashing people with advertising or buying them off with fifty thousand pesos worth the same as a vote expressed freely? Ask the defenders of democracy. That's the great perversity, but we're not allowed to say that. If everybody had education and the variations between high and low, in terms of culture, were smaller, democracy would be universal and we'd be in Sweden, but that's not the way it is. In Africa people vote for those in their own tribe and that's why the party of the biggest tribe always wins, and you know the only way a tribe has to reduce the number of voters for another tribe? The machete. In many countries in Africa, it isn't dictatorship that's led to civil war, but democracy. The small tribes hate the system that gives power to the biggest clan, and what is power? The right to take control of a country. Here, it's different because there are no tribes, but there are clans and, lately, tyrants. How, in an environment like this, can a candidate of the left, or an ecologist, for example, win? The one who wins is the one who has most money, like in Italy, or the one who has most arms and is stronger. The alpha male wins, because democracy, in terms of sexuality, is a masochistic relationship: power is given to the strong man so that he can exercise it over the weak man, who adopts an attitude of submission that consists of turning his back, lifting his hip, and offering his anus in order to avoid confrontation.

Monsieur Echenoz's reactionary opinions made me jump out of my seat, and, at first, I argued with him, but then I realized there was no point. In any case, it was more stimulating to disagree with him than to talk for hours and hours with my fellow students, who thought the same way I did. Maybe because his ideas came from his experience, not just from books or from political ideologies. He said what came into his head. His notion of utopia was a system in which the dignitaries of a society, the aristocracy of thought, took the reins of power. An old-established aristocracy guaranteed to avoid the one thing that seemed to him a real sin, which was to hand the land over to foreign countries or powers.

When I asked him about the advanced democracies of Sweden and Norway, he'd say: I don't know them, and they don't interest me. I'm not attracted by countries where life is quiet and fair, where everybody has levels of protection and stipulated good health and happiness. I'm not interested in perfect societies; I only deigned to look at them when I discovered, through mystery novels, that horrible crimes and tragedies happened there too, which gave them a touch of humanity. Those men of ice all have some kind of hell in their brains. But I prefer life in places where, from time to time, the streets are running with blood. That's why I've stayed in Colombia.

I didn't learn much about his life. He had always worked for French companies, but after his retirement he had decided to stay in Bogotá, where his children and grandchildren were. He was a widower. His wife had committed suicide while he was in a motel with another woman. He was forty-two when that happened. His wife found out through his secretary, who, I don't know why, although I can imagine, had promised to inform the wife when he had an appointment with his new lover. She did so and the wife, instead of showing up and causing a scene, cut her wrists in another hotel. The secretary broke down and admitted everything. Monsieur Echenoz assumed the guilt, gave up work, and never saw his lover again. His wife had left a note in which she asked just one question: "Why?" Several times he had a Browning pistol in his hand, but never summoned the courage. His wife was Belgian and had been in Colombia because of him, they had met in Africa. They had done everything together. When I asked him if his lover had been Colombian, he said no, she was Hungarian, and added: I'll tell you the whole story another day, but in the end he never did. What he did tell me was that a man needs the company of several women, and women, too, although for different reasons. Marriage and monogamy are really stupid, he would say, and above all, the biggest source of unhappiness; a mammal needs to exercise his sexuality, and in both men and women there is a very strong life principle: curiosity. Do you have a boyfriend? he asked, and I said no, I have lovers, people who come and go but nothing more, and he said, good for you, you're not tying anybody down, young people are quite stupid by definition, but it's not their fault; they're stupid because of something that's been inculcated in them by adults, which is faith in the future; they're stupid because they have hopes, something that sorts itself out with the passing of years; that's why the worst thing is for a young woman to marry a young man, because that's like two idiots uniting their idiocies; the best thing a young woman can do is be with an older man, but not get married, I'm not saying that, I'm saying be with someone older, and listen to my advice: use young men to enjoy yourself, for pleasure, and to obtain material things, let them flatter you, all that's quite normal, don't believe the feminists when they say that a woman defends her dignity by being independent, that's nonsense, women don't need money because they have something that's much more powerful than money, and you know what it is. I've seen the most powerful men on the planet go to pieces over a vagina: Kennedy, Onassis, Rockefeller, and what about Paris and Menelaus? Now that's power, and I'll give you a piece of advice: when you want something, use it, and don't be ashamed, many people are going to say horrible things to you, especially the feminists and the lesbians, they're going to insult you, they'll say it's because of people like you that women suffer, and maybe they're right, but you just keep going because we live life as individuals. Men do the same when they're lucky enough to be desired, especially by older women. Who are they harming? They attract those who are already starting menopause, and they obtain money, gifts, travel. Everyone is happy, but such cases are rare. The opposite is more common. Nobody asks a man to be handsome. They ask him to be powerful or rich. To be famous, to be an alpha male. When I was young and went to the seaside, in Europe, I'd look at the sports cars pulling up at the beach clubs. Their occupants were always rich men, usually fat and vulgar, and they always had beautiful women with them. It never failed. Almost all of them were blondes, even though their eyebrows and the down on their arms were black.

Every night, Monsieur Echenoz had a new story to tell, something to give his opinion about or to teach me, something to contradict, always with the same shameless cynicism. He asked me to tell him about my course, and I talked to him about authors like Mario Bunge, Ernst Cassirer, and György Lukács, especially *The Destruction of Reason*, and he knew them, reduced them to comprehensible phrases, rejected them, and criticized them in a lucid way that I'd then repeat in class, and the other students would look at me in surprise, where does she get these ideas from? Sometimes Monsieur Echenoz would be interrupted by a violent coughing fit that would drain the color from his face. He had pulmonary emphysema. He had been an alcoholic three or four times during his life. He was dying and would say to me: if only I could get up and go out to buy cigarettes and alcohol, nothing worse can happen to me, I'm going to die soon anyway; I thought to bring them myself, but if his children found out they might report me and I would go to prison for identity theft.

One day I asked him if he had known Malraux and he said yes: when he was very young, in Hong Kong, he'd had to accompany him during an official visit, when Malraux was minister of culture. That was when he had dedicated his book to him. And he added: an arrogant, unscrupulous man. He would have given anything to be richer, more famous, and more powerful than he was, but deep down he never stopped being a parvenu. He actually despised him, and the only reason he kept that book was to remember the irritation such people aroused in him. Who did he admire? I asked, and he said: Céline, a writer who had the courage to say what all of France thought, and who kept saying it right to the end, when saying it earned him a prison sentence. Or Jules Barbey D'Aurevilly, accused of being a pornographer and a monarchist in a country where everybody is a monarchist and a pornographer. He liked Jarrès and Pierre Loüys. Jean Genet too, except when he campaigned for noble causes, and he said, angrily: I can't stand writers who support noble causes! They're opportunists who thrive on other people's blood, hypocrites. When the streets are running with blood, the only sensible advice is that of Baron Rothschild: to buy property. Among contemporaries he admired Houellebecq, because in him he recognized that same spirit unconstrained by conservative morality. France had always had writers like that, according to him, because that crudeness and coldness was part of the Gallic chromosome. He took as an example the language itself, and said: French, which people think is a pretty, sonorous language, is one of the hardest and most hostile. You just have to look at its cruel expressions for referring to cruel things: *elle s'est fait violer!* ("She had herself raped" instead of "she was raped.") It's a language of brute peasants! Only the wicked and the homicidal can get beauty from it, people like Rimbaud or Baudelaire, or like the Marquis de Sade, who was confined to a dungeon and who, according to a very bad film, wrote with his own shit, which is quite ridiculous, of course.

As I climbed the steep, dark, gloomy streets of Upper Chapinero, I would ask myself, what will Monsieur Echenoz tell me about today? Then I started to do my classwork with him. He would tell me to reach him this or that book, and read it to him. Sometimes he himself looked at the index. Of course he couldn't read aloud, because he didn't have enough air in his lungs, but I could, and in this way we advanced. I would write and he would read. He would make comments, help me with my writing. He was very strict about words. He always said that ideas were an illusion of language and that's why in writing you had to be hypnotic, precise, and direct. That's the one truth, he would say: that which is well expressed, which convinces through its form. I took note of this and then read over what I'd written and realized the number of extraordinary things I was learning with him.

One night, about one in the morning, he had such a strong fit of coughing and choking that I had to call an ambulance. They gave him oxygen and took him away. I wanted to go with him, but one of his sons had arrived and they wouldn't let me get in the ambulance. I thought he was going to die and I felt really anxious. They kept him in the Andes Medical Center for three weeks; I spent them keeping my eye on my cell phone in the hope that they would call and say: you can come back, Monsieur Echenoz is home again.

It was then, during those days of waiting, that the story broke in the press of eleven young men from Soacha, first presented as "disappeared," and then reported as killed while fighting the army near Ocaña in Santander province. It was a great scandal, do you remember? Uribe went on television and said they weren't disappeared but criminals, who had fallen in combat against the army. The family said they hadn't been guerrillas, just unemployed young men. Uribe defended the army, but people started to protest, to go out on the street. Cases came to light in other parts of the country and there were more testimonies and accusations. The army put on a brave face: the safety of the citizens rests on our shoulders and our blood, the army is tireless in its task of building peace, these lies are being spread by terrorists and their accomplices, decent people have nothing to fear, we are an honest, humane army, our weapons are the basis of a new society, free from the scourge of violence, long live the state of law, long live President Uribe.

As was to be expected, Mother brought up the subject at dinner, saying, what's the problem? why all this fuss over a bunch of dope fiends? Father refused to take part in the discussion, in the hope that it would die out by itself, but I couldn't just bite my tongue, so I said, since when have we been on the side of the murderers? what's happened to this family? when are you going to realize what's going on in this country? and Mother lost her temper and retorted, what's going on in this country isn't what those terrorists at the National say, they only know what's going on in the country that belongs to FARC and ELN, not in ours; the president, who is actually the president and not just some journalist, already explained what happened on television, and so did the attorney general, and they already know that those guys really were fighting the army, and you know how it is, those who live by the sword die by the sword, and I said, those poor guys were murdered, that's social cleansing, like the paramilitaries do in other regions, social cleansing done by the army to earn rewards, it's a State crime and Uribe is covering it up, and then Father got into the discussion and said, oh, Juanita, stop talking bullshit, how can it be a State crime when the army faces up to bandits, on the contrary, it'd be a crime if they didn't defend us, Juanita, what they tell you at the university is really very twisted, you saw the president speaking, you saw the attorney general confirming that they had died while fighting, do you think they're lying? do you think the president and the attorney general, the two highest authorities in the land, are lying? no, Juanita, let's not exaggerate either, but I said to both of them, yes, they are lying, those boys were murdered, I believe the mothers, and then Mother said, oh, yes? and what would you have the mothers say about those lazy bums? they should have brought them up better.

I was so angry that the following Sunday I went with two fellow students to Soacha and we took part in a demonstration on behalf of the disappeared; I saw powerless women carrying pictures of their sons, raising banners, and weeping and shouting the names of those young men, some of whom had been brought back to them in bags, but not all; some said that their sons still hadn't come back, not even dead, and my fellow students and I started shouting, and I felt grief and infinite pity, because what these poor mothers were asking for, that is, justice and truth, seemed such a crazy idea, a princely whim, because, as my parents said, who was going to question what the president and the attorney general both said, but I thought, anyone seeing these women walking, so dignified in their grief, anyone seeing how some collapse and fall on the ground and the others stop the procession and lift them up, anyone seeing that can only believe in them, and so I grabbed the arm of one of them and started to call out the name of her son, a boy who could have been my age or Manuel's, I started to shout and she clung to me and we walked, and I noticed that she smelled of oil and onion and fresh coriander, and I thought, before coming to demonstrate these women left food ready for their other children and made the beds and washed clothes, and I felt something similar to the day I started at the National, and I thought again, this is my country! not the country of the hypocrites, not the country of those who close their eyes or the country of the murderers, and I was so moved that I started to cry and it was the woman who consoled me, saying, why are you crying, girl? and I said, I'm crying for all this, for what they did to you, because there are things that can never be made up for, and I'm crying with anger over the lies and the cynicism, and she passed her hand over my head and said, calm down, girl, keep walking, and I was able to do so, but at each step I told myself, it's important to know and important to take revenge, there must be something I can do.

The following week Monsieur Echenoz returned home, so I went to look after him. What joy to walk up the little streets, cross the park, and climb the steps that led to his big old house. It was only then that I realized to what extent he had become part of my life, my little life, the thread of a story that I could continue. He was very frail, his skin wizened and covered with purplish veins around his nose. He was very pleased to see me and, as had been the case before his attack, I noticed that he was waiting anxiously for the other nurse to go so that he could be alone with me.

I told him about what I had seen in Soacha and said that I wanted to do something, and he said, they murdered those boys and while they're putting together a story they come out and deny it, presenting details that deflect attention, and in the end there will be another scandal to distract people, but those women must keep going out on the street and you must support them, he said to me, and then, with a sly look, he added: you could try something else, do it from within. I looked at him in surprise, from within? Yes, he said. You're young and pretty, you could get close to whoever you want and find out whatever you want. It may be difficult, but not impossible. Try to reach as high as you can, you may be able to help them from there. I already told you once: there is nothing a woman can't get. Sex is the most powerful weapon on earth. I'm eighty-three years old and it's the only thing I miss, the only reason I'd like to be young again. Anyone who tells you the opposite is either a dreamer or a fool who confuses real life with ideas and suppositions about how life should be. Infiltrate the world of those criminals and destroy them from within, if you really do hate them. It's a world of men, of brute, unscrupulous males. If you manage to get close to it, they'll eat out of your hand. Remember that a silly young American woman, using nothing but her mouth, almost brought down the most powerful president in the world, don't you see? and I'll tell you something:

charge them a lot and don't have any scruples. Destroy them and get what you can from them, when it comes down to it money is the one thing that gives us freedom in this wretched world. They're going to tell you that you're a prostitute but you won't listen to them. Let them talk and shout. They're going to tell you that you're evil, a witch, let them bark. Never take your eyes off your goals. Your family will criticize you, forget them. Mothers tell their daughters: marry well, choose well, but that basically means "sell yourself well." It's the worst kind of prostitution, for a single client, and the payment is a lie called "respectability." Don't enter that world of insects, Juana, because you're strong and intelligent, and you can have a destiny of your own. If you choose freedom you'll be a truly lethal weapon. Destroy them.

In the mornings, walking down toward Seventh to go to the university and have breakfast, I would repeat to myself his stories and advice, and as I advanced, shivering with the wind you get at seven in the morning and already smelling the acid smell of the exhausts, I'd think that in spite of his cynicism and his distaste for life, Monsieur Echenoz was right: the world wasn't made for harmony and kindness, but quite the contrary, for confrontation. The world is a boxing ring, a battlefield. And you don't go to battlefields with smiles and soft words, no, sir, you go armed to the teeth. Seeing it any other way struck me as childish and stupid.

I remember that day, walking along Fiftieth and Seventh, I stopped at a breakfast eatery, asked for scrambled eggs with onion, coffee with milk, and orange juice, and started looking around at the recently awakened city: people cleaning their cars, beggars, a woman in uniform washing down the entrance to a pharmacy, the assistants from a cell phone store lighting cigarettes outside the door, people huddled together, shivering with cold, at the bus stop on the corner, and a black cloud over everything, bringing that wind that seems so damp. I took out a notebook and wrote: "Life is a fucking battlefield and you have to be armed to the teeth." I read the sentence about a hundred times. Then I tore off the sheet, rolled it into a ball, and threw it in the trash can.

I set off again for the university.

Time went by. One afternoon my cell phone rang. It was the daughter of Monsieur Echenoz. I have some news for you, she said, Father died yesterday. How? It was in his sleep, the doctors say he didn't feel a thing, he was wrapped in blankets, he seemed asleep. I was happy for him. He was already on the other side, far from this life that he had known and analyzed like nobody else. I asked about the funeral arrangements, they gave me the information, and I dropped by the undertaker's briefly to say hello to his children. I wanted to see him one last time but the box was closed. It was better that way, since I was left with the image of his eyes filled with anger, and his words that, even though subdued by his emphysema, had been pure fire. Instead of praying, I sat down to one side and, in a little book, started to write down what I remembered of him, his cynical phrases, his judgments and opinions. I wanted at least some of his ideas to survive, and that was why I proposed to live them.

"Ideas are not made to be thought, but to be lived," said Malraux. And Monsieur Echenoz was right: if the world was cynical and cruel, it was best to be cynical and cruel. My kindness and my love would, from now on, be hidden behind a thick iron door, and they would be only for Manuel. Reality was the place where Manuel and I had to survive, a lonely, arid steppe, a rocky desert, infested with vipers and scorpions, in which we had to search for water or weaker animals to feed ourselves on, and above all weapons; weapons to avoid others getting first to the valley, or the plain, the promised place where we could be happy.

Starting the following week, I began looking for other work

and, after a series of interviews, I was again hired to look after an elderly man. I was pleased. I liked old people. It would be hard to find another Monsieur Echenoz, but I was willing to take advantage of whatever there was. This one had also had an operation. He had a horrible scar on his side. When I arrived, an old woman gave me the drugs I had to administer to him, showed me the kitchen, the towels, how the house was laid out, and then went to sleep in another room. I had to bathe him. The old man sat down in a tub of hot water and asked me to scrub his skin and clean the scar. It was disgusting, but I did it. Then I helped him out of the bath and walked him to his bed. He lay there on the blankets, naked, and asked me to bring him something, pointing to a drawer. I didn't quite understand. I opened the drawer and found a whole lot of creams. I brought them over to him and he asked me to spread them on him. Then he pointed to another drawer and as I was about to open it he came up behind me. Inside the drawer was a black plastic dildo, and I realized that the old man, in the middle of his wrinkled and bruised body, had an erection. I ran out and hailed a taxi. I felt humiliated. When I got home, I washed my hands for hours and felt like cutting them off, like a salamander that gets rid of a limb to escape danger and it then regenerates, as good as new.

I remembered Monsieur Echenoz and I told myself, enough of this crap, now the war starts.

I knew of some girls from the industrial design department who went out with guys and charged them, so I approached them, determined to gain their trust, until they suggested going with them to a party given by some male students from Los Andes, the same age as us. There were four of them and by the time we arrived they were drunk and stoned. They gave us drinks, pills, coke. They had a bit of everything. On a trip to the bathroom I asked one of the girls how it worked, and she said, we charge them 300,000 pesos to suck them and fuck them, but it's okay, with what they've taken I don't think they'll be able to get it up anyway, so enjoy the party and don't forget to ask for the money as soon as you go in the bedroom, before taking your clothes off; otherwise, they'll fall asleep and forget about the money. The only rule is not to kiss them and not to agree to swapping. We already told them that. We left the bathroom and I sat down in the living room. These rich kids were studying philosophy and letters. I heard them talking about Wittgenstein and Clément Rosset, but they were so drunk that they got everything wrong, and besides, I told myself, what could these idiots know or understand of Rosset's tragic ideas? Everything was luxurious and I felt inhibited, but Monsieur Echenoz's words gave me strength. Suddenly, the owner of the apartment said, okay, guys, let's get down to business with the girls, I'm already horny, and the others said yes and put on *vallenatos* and pulled us up and forced us to dance, a dance that really drove me crazy because what it consisted of was the guy putting his hand under your skirt as soon as you took the first step, which I found disgusting, and I said to him, listen, honey, you're going to have to be a little more friendly if you don't want to be jerking yourself off tonight, and he said, hold your horses, what's the matter? I'm paying, aren't I? but I said, you haven't paid me yet and my cell phone has eleven missed calls, so if you want I can go, then he said, hey, wait, don't fly off the handle, who are you? I mean, what's your name? and I said, Daisy, like Donald Duck's girlfriend, but I'm no bimbo, got that? if you want to, we can go to the bedroom but pay me first, and the guy said, what a girl, yes, madame, anything else? and I said, yes, pull your pants down, I'm going to suck your cock, close your eyes and think about your professor of logic, or Paris Hilton or Ricky Martin, that's up to you, and he said, hey, what a generous girl, and can I think about you? but I said, no way.

That was my first night. I realized I could do it without

being fussy and so I carried on, almost always with rich kids from Los Andes or the Xavierian, or young executives celebrating birthdays or throwing parties; sometimes in apartments and other times in motels. I learned to despise all those daddy's boys, living off the country. My contempt was turning into hate. Every time I charged them more, and seeing them pay I felt strong. Monsieur Echenoz was reincarnated in me and I was happy. One day, taking advantage of everyone being out of it at a party, I stole a laptop and an iPad. I didn't care and then, when the guy called and asked, I told him he was crazy, it must have been some other whore, I hadn't been the only whore there that night. I switched it on to delete what was on it and found a collection of sexual photographs of boys and girls; little vaginas being violently penetrated, girls performing fellatio, boys being sodomized. I called the guy back and said to him, I have your computer but there's a problem, baby, I'm with the Secret Service. The guys started to stammer. No, I said, I'm lying, I'm not with the Secret Service but I have a really good joke for you: I'm one of the whores from the party and you're in deep shit because I found the photos. He asked me not to report him, and said he'd give me anything. I asked him for twenty-five million pesos in cash. He was an executive in quite a big insurance company. He told me that was too much money and that I was crazy. All right, I said, the price has just gone up to fifty million, otherwise I myself will hand this over to your bosses and to the police. I advised him to ask for a loan, there were banks that gave fast credit in urgent cases, and this was one of those. Very urgent. Fifty million. I made three copies on hard disk with everything he had on it including his personal details. I arranged to meet him at the Unicentro mall, opposite the entrance to the movie houses. I told him that if anything happened to me everything would go to the police. The guy handed over the money, nothing's going to happen to you, it's all here! I told him to put his cell phone in the bag, I didn't want him to call me again. He was puzzled. Hey, what about my sim card? Get another, I said. Then I went into the bookstore and bought the diaries of Luis Buñuel as a gift for Manuel, and a novel by Martin Amis called *Money*. I was nervous. It was the first time I had committed a crime. But I told myself, if that son of a bitch reports me, I'll kill him. What to do with the money? I'd prepared a hiding place at home, in the ceiling of the bathroom. It would have been suspicious to put it in my account. I went home and hid it really well. Then I went to the post office and sent the three copies of the disk in three envelopes: one to the Colombian Welfare Service, another to the director of his insurance company, and a third to his home address, in his wife's name. I fulfilled my promise to him by not sending it to the police. In case of doubt I kept another copy. I felt real pleasure imagining the guy confronted with the truth, having to explain things to his bosses and his wife. I know that life in general is quite horrible, but you mustn't go too far either. Of course, I erased what was on the iPad, recharged it, and gave it to Manuel as a gift.

One weekend, I went back to Soacha to see the women who had been demonstrating. Things had changed and it was now common knowledge that the young men had indeed been murdered. The army was announcing a purge. I met with Señora Martha again, the one who had seen me cry the previous time, and said to her, how can I help you? but she said, there's nothing to be done, they're going to put some of the soldiers on trial, but everything is slow and difficult and we're already getting threats, they say we're with the guerrillas. My voice shook, and my hands shook, and again I felt full of hate. That day I could have killed someone. I went back home on a crowded bus and enjoyed the smell of the students, the poor crowd: those who had to cross the city for a job and then run to a night class and have the strength not to fall asleep over their books. Poor people. Only hope and probably imagination gave them the strength to bear that shitty life. When did something pleasant ever happen to them? Almost never. I was going to be their avenging angel.

The next step was to get involved with the State and its yuppies, with its security apparatus and that gang of macho men, oh so macho behind their rifles and their checkbooks of public money and the complicity of the great alpha male, the supreme asshole of the nation.

Now they would see, the sons of bitches.

I sought them out, Consul. I infiltrated the Secret Service, and how did I do it? I became their whore. I was their whore because I wanted it. I preferred to sell my body rather than my soul, which is what everybody sold in that horrible country. Everybody except me, I did the opposite. I gave them my body. Look at me, I'm pretty and I can be a really attractive chick if I put on high heels, a miniskirt, a low-cut top, and hey, presto. I was told about a bar where people from the Secret Service hung out, so I went there and hooked one of the top guys, whose name was Víctor. He'd go around with a roll of dollars, a bottle of Blue Seal whiskey, and a bag of coke in his car. It all comes from the seizures, sweetheart. We fucked first at the Paracaídas motel, then at the Calera, and then at those in the north. He didn't like to stick to one in particular, for security reasons. They may be following me, he would say. Evil never sleeps, that was his motto. We often went out with a guy called Piedrahita who was his boss in the Narcotics division, and the parties would end up at the VIP room of the Francachela motel. It was always on the house, thanks to the owners of the motel, they never paid. They hired other whores to do striptease and played around with them, but in the end Víctor would have sex with me and Piedrahita with Mireya, a girl from Choco who looked like a transvestite, and he was crazy about her, in love with her, because he liked them black. Melanin and frizzy hair, that's how he put it. The parties would last three or four days, until they got a call from headquarters and went off to solve a case. When things went well they'd come back with fresh supplies for the party. We did coke, drank high-class whiskey, ate paella, and watched porn movies; Piedrahita, who must have been around fifty, would get very drunk and sometimes he'd go crazy and do ugly things, he'd give the whores hundred-dollar bills to perform cunnilingus on Mireya right there in front of him, and if one of them refused he'd take out his revolver and slam it down on the table, what's the matter, girls, don't you like her? don't tell me you're racists? racism is against the constitution! Don't be like that, darling, Mireya would say in his ear, let's go to the bedroom, and she'd drag him away. One day a shot went off that ended up in the ceiling and Víctor had to go out with his Secret Service badge to calm the neighbors.

Another night we were in the bedroom and he came and knocked, calling to Víctor: come on, brother, hurry up and get dressed, duty calls, this fucking country won't let anyone fuck in peace. Víctor went out into the corridor. Wait, let's get high before we go, Piedrahita said, and prepared four lines of coke, which they snorted. Now, girls, don't cry for us, when you're a public servant you have to make sacrifices, I'll leave you to enjoy yourselves but none of that dyke stuff, all right, my beauties? and he put half a bottle of whiskey, a roll of dollars, and what remained of the coke on the table. Mireya came to the couch and we talked. How is he in bed? I asked. She poured herself some whiskey in a cup of coffee and lit a cigar. What he likes is for me to jerk him off from behind; he takes tons of Viagra but it doesn't work for him; in the year and a bit that we've been together he's only stuck it in me about ten times, can you believe that? A girl always misses that. But if he finds out I told you he'll shoot both of us.

Víctor was married with three children. He wasn't a bad person, but I hated him. He told me he could share the stresses of his work with me, but he never talked to his wife about the atrocities he committed, out of respect for her. Son of a bitch. One night he arrived covered in blood. They had nabbed some dealers in a house in Modelia, young guys, on a tip-off from a former paramilitary who'd turned himself in. They found twenty kilos, three submachine guns, ten pistols, and a bag with two hundred thousand dollars. Piedrahita was high on coke and started slapping one of the guys around, asking him about the stash with the big money, where was it? He'd been told there was a lot more. Víctor tried to calm him down. That's enough, boss, let's hand some of it in and we're done, but Piedrahita went crazy and shot the dealer in the head, and then there was nothing else they could do, he had to shoot the others. There were five of them. Five young guys. Three Secret Service officers took them down to a garage. Víctor was shaking and Piedrahita said to him: let's load them in the van. He went to speak on the telephone and came back saying, nothing happened here, I'm going to send them to a buddy in the Lanceros battalion, they need them more than we do, and he turned and said to Yesid, the youngest officer, son, take these guys to Commander Suárez, I already talked to him and he's waiting for them, but be quick about it, and then call me, son, this is just between ourselves, okay?

That night Víctor arrived with rolls of dollars in his pockets, and when I told him he was lucky to have such well-paid work he replied, the hell I am, I can barely enjoy the money, just give it away or waste it on drink, not even buy a house because I'll be grabbed by the tax people, or put it in the bank, just buy gifts for my wife and kids, but only little things, and send it to my mother, but not too much, and that was really bad, one of the unfair things about life, according to him, after so much sacrifice. That day he was very drunk, and I asked him, what do the soldiers do with the dead bodies? do they bury them? and he said, no, sweetheart, they make money with them, but don't ask too much, it might put you at risk. You don't know the really ugly things that have to be done to protect this fucking country.

I played dumb, but I was thinking: I already know what you people do, you asshole, I don't need you to tell me, what comes out in the newspapers is true, you're killing people, it'll be your turn next.

I went out with him two or three times a month, whenever he celebrated a good arrest. The rest of the time I studied, read, went to the movies. Things happened and I sensed others about to happen. Life was passing like a wind that set my teeth on edge, gave me the shivers, soaked me. Everything was happening very quickly. One day a friend from the faculty invited me to a bar in the north of the city. Politicians go there, she said, really cool people, guys with money. I was afraid I might meet someone from the Secret Service, but it was an exclusive place, only people with style went there. By the time I'd had three glasses of rum, I already had a friendly man fluttering around me, smiling and winking at me. At last he made up his mind to speak to me. He invited me to do coke and I accepted, a long line. Shall we dance? He was an adviser to a senator, I can't remember which one. From there we went to an apartment on the beltway to continue the evening. A swanky place, belonging to a girl who had come with them. The strange thing was that I didn't go as an escort, since nobody had offered me money, but I had the feeling it was the same thing. The bozo's name was Juan Mario and when he asked me, what do you do, where do you study and that kind of thing, I told him at the National, and he laughed, seriously? oh, wow, really? he said, and I said, yes, I study sociology, and he said, wow, sociology at the National! you're not with FARC, are you? That's what my father thinks, I said, but I regretted having told him that because after a while a friend came, they hugged drunkenly, and Juan Mario said to him, hey, man, let me introduce you to this girl, let's see if you can guess where she studies? and the guy said, no idea, I don't know, I mean, where could it be, at Los Andes? and Juan Mario laughed and said, no, man, not even warm, it's incredible, at the National! and the other guy said, and what's so funny about that, it's cool, the National's a cool university, what's so funny? I liked that and I said, and what's your name? and he said, Daniel, wait, I'll give you my card, he took it out and I read, "adviser, Congress," so I said to him, what do all you people advise about? He laughed and said to the other guy, you see, man, the people at the National are cool, well, we study projects, we suggest the subjects to be proposed, we study the constitutionality of it, I'm a lawyer, of course, when you come down to it, those guys are really a pain, you do all the work and then the congressman comes along and finishes it off, and sometimes he fucks it up, or rather, he usually fucks it up, that's the way it is, and how is the National? Wow, it's amazing, I'm a big fan of Mockus, seriously, my dog's name is Antanas, a very intelligent Labrador, I swear to you, then he asked me for my cell phone number and I gave it to him, and a sixth sense told me that if I wanted to hook him I had to leave the party; I called a taxi and went home, but the next day, sure enough, the guy called me, hi, we met last night, do you remember? you left very early, didn't you like the party? well, to be honest, it was boring, a real drag, right? listen, do you remember me? I'm the adviser, no, the other one, the second one you met, Daniel, are you in class? will you call me when you finish? and so I started going out with him, kind of on the sly, because he had an official girlfriend but he told me I was a lot better, that he could be natural with me, say what he thought, so I asked him, and what kind of things do you think? and he said, I don't know, the kind of things I tell you, I like you a lot, babe, with you I can talk about movies and books, and I said to him, doesn't your girlfriend like movies or what? and he said, no, I mean yes, but only romantic movies or comedies, she spends her time watching YouTube videos and chatting, can you imagine? the other day we were talking about something and you know what she said to me? look, I can't stand talking with you, let's chat instead, can we do that? or else, how are you doing, darling? oh, shall we chat? and the worst of it is that she is right, we get on better when we're chatting, do you want to see her? and he showed me photographs of the girl on his BlackBerry, a pretty girl, he even had a photograph showing her backside in a nice little thong, and how's the sex? I asked him, good? and he said, yes but she's a hysteric, if I give her a hug she says no, it has to happen naturally, she doesn't like me to go close to her, wanting her, she says she feels dirty, and so I say to her, but, babe, if we don't get close how's it going to happen? and she says, it'll happen naturally! it should come from the two of us, not just you, as if we have to fuck, as if it's an obligation, no, we should just let things happen, and I said, okay, but I don't understand how they're going to happen if we keep miles apart, but anyway, that's how it is, and a second later she's already fallen asleep, she's always tired because she's always busy, and when we fuck, I don't know, I tell her, or rather, I think, that it's a new form of anal sex, you know, she looks such an asshole when we fuck, with the faces she pulls, for it to be okay you have to give her a whole bottle of wine, she's such a bore, that's why I like you, you don't make such a fuss about it, and I can talk to you and say the things I think seriously, that's what I like about people from the National, I love Mockus, did I tell you that?

We fucked in his apartment in La Cabrera, and I didn't charge him because what interested me was the Congress, finding out things, getting information. I asked him questions as if I were a silly girl, a student, who is this senator? why does that other guy have so much power? and he'd say, well, look, babe, that one is a hard man, the hardest of the hard, and so he'd come out with things and I'd put them together, and I'd tell myself, through this son of a bitch I'd get to others, I was patient and that's what happened. One day he said to me, how would you like to come to Buenos Aires with me, babe? there's a meeting of the Latin American Forum for Public Administration, do you know Buenos Aires? no? it's a great place, you'll love it, there are a million bookstores and people who are really intellectual, just the way you like it, babe, will you come? I traveled with him and there I met other advisers, among them the adviser to the presidential private secretary, and I said to myself, that's what you're after, the big fish. The opportunity arrived very quickly because Daniel's meetings finished late and he always arrived at the end, so one day I met the presidential adviser at a cocktail party at the hotel, a very elegant place in Recoleta, and I approached him, acting dumb, a woman knows how to draw attention to herself without being noticed, and the guy fell in the net, he saw me in the line at the drinks table and stepped forward, what would you like? and I said, a glass of red wine, and he said, Malbec? and I said, yes, it's my favorite, so he picked up two and said to me, my name is Andrés Felipe, I'm adviser to the presidential private secretary, and I said, yes, I know, Daniel has told me about you, and he said, have you come with Daniel? I said yes, but it was one of those women's yeses that mean: "yes until I find something better." The guy realized that and said, oh, what a pity, how sad, how envious I feel because I've come alone, so I said to him, alone in such a cold city? I don't believe it, with all those beautiful Argentinian women you see on the streets, and he said, you know something, my dear, they may be very pretty, but what I like is the national type, why look outside when we have such beauty inside, am I right? look at you, for example, and he pointed at the mirror I was reflected in, and I laughed, and just then Daniel came in through the door, looking for me, and I saw him in the mirror, so I told Andrés Felipe, it's been great, I really like people from the northwest, what room are you in? and he said, 711, come whenever you like, princess, 24-hour service.

Daniel arrived, looking tired, hi, babe, what are you drinking? oh, Malbec, great, wait while I get one for myself, have you already met Andrés Felipe? and I said, yes, he's very nice, and he said, yes, he's a really powerful man, highly educated, with a good agenda, and protected by Uribe, obviously, but I'm going to tell you something, babe, in Bogotá we're tired of all these people from the northwest! there's no room for any more in the Palace, anyway, there's nothing to be done, and I said to him, well, you people should have thought of that before, shouldn't you?

The next day, at eleven in the morning, I called room 711 and Andrés Felipe answered, hello, my dear, I got out of a meeting today because a little bird gave me a word of advice, it said, look, stay if you can, stay and something good will happen to you. I told him I'd be right there and a minute later we were kissing on the carpet; we fucked on the couch and sitting on the washbowl and finally on the bed, which most people say is the best place to fuck; he told me he was married, that he had two children and they were the only reason he didn't separate from his wife. His wife was a hysteric, and I said to him, seriously? and why is that? and he said, we almost never make love, whenever I want it she says, don't pester me, I want it to happen naturally, so I said to him, oh yes, I know that, and in the end she falls asleep, right? he laughed and said, exactly, she falls asleep, and you're left lying there, none the wiser.

I hooked up with Andrés Felipe and when we got back to Bogotá we started seeing each other, first in the airport motels and then at motels in La Calera; the ones at the airport were good but the noise of the planes wouldn't let him talk on his cell phone. One day I was with him and Daniel called him, but he didn't answer. Another day I got a call from Víctor, the

Secret Service guy, and he said to me, where have you been, girl? I have a little gift for you, we're going to party the whole weekend with my boss, and I said to him, okay, but I can't talk now, I'll call you in a little while, it's great to hear from you; I was dying with fear that I'd be intercepted so I switched off the cell phone and said to Andrés Felipe, I have to go, darling, ciao, and he said, has something happened with Daniel? and I said, look, I don't know if you know this, but I have a private life and sometimes things crop up, I'll tell you later, I kissed him on the mouth and ran out in a panic, Víctor had never gotten me so scared before; I went to my friend's house in Chapinero, changed clothes, oh, I didn't tell you that I had different clothes for this guy and that guy and couldn't leave them all at home; those for the advisers were high-class brand-name things that my friend kept for me.

I put on something simple and provocative, and called Víctor. He answered right away, hi, doll, shall I send someone to pick you up? tell me where you are, and so that he shouldn't suspect anything I answered, okay, darling, I'm at a girlfriend's, they can pick me up on Third and 66th, on the steps outside Cinelandia, and he said, okay, Yesid will be there in the black van, and soon afterwards I was with them, Piedrahita drunk with Mireya on his knees, Víctor really stoned, not in a motel but in an apartment in the north of the city, near San Cristóbal, so I said, pretending to be happy, what an elegant party today! you should have told me to wear a long dress, and Piedrahita replied, no, sweetheart, this is a real stroke of luck, we're going to hand back the apartment later, but for now we can enjoy it, it belongs to a fugitive we caught up with this afternoon, bang, bang! we took him down and found out he was loaded, isn't that so, Víctor?, yes, boss, he said, really loaded, and he took out a roll of bills and put it in my pocket, four thousand dollars, I counted them later in the bathroom, and we started to drink and do coke and they sent Yesid out to fetch roast chicken with potatoes and melted cheese, which kind do you like, girls, Kokoriko, Cali Mío, or Distraco? Piedrahita asked, and Mireya said, oh, no, they're rough, I heard Kokoriko gives you colitis, bring me Kentucky Fried Chicken, and with French fries please, and so we were there for three days more or less, Yesid going in and out with rib broth and oatmeal rolls and bringing bottles of aguardiente because, after a couple of days, Piedrahita and Víctor got tired of drinking whiskey and went back to the home-grown stuff, bring us some real hooch, Yesid! they screamed, and another day or two went by, I lost all sense of time, and there was also a jacuzzi and sauna and we'd get in them, all a bit messy with the chicken legs and the guacamole, but in one of our trips to bed I asked Víctor, was it a really good arrest? and he looked down at me and said, we hit it lucky, gorgeous, oh, yes? why's that? I played dumb while I sucked him off and he kept talking, we caught four of them, all loaded, and we killed two, and you know what? the two we didn't kill will be useful to us for something else, we have to deal with a journalist who's making the chief nervous, a man who's always sticking his nose in everywhere, the order came down from upstairs a while ago, we have to find something on him, but so far we haven't found a thing, the guy's cleaner than a nun's panties. With those two guys we're going to put something together to make sure he keeps quiet, what they're going to tell the prosecutor is already being written, anyway, don't go thinking this is some low-level thing, gorgeous, the orders come from all the way upstairs, that's why the prize is so good, they left the booty to us, and so I asked him, and the two men who are going to make statements, what will happen to them, will they be sent to prison? and he said, we'll hide them for a while and then bang bang, that's the safest way, or rather, that's what the order is from upstairs, my God, in this country life isn't worth anything, can you do me a line of coke, doll? and so he continued talking, about this and that, until we heard

Piedrahita yelling, and we went out to see what was going on
and he was in his underpants, with his gun in his hand, shouting, Yesid! open the other bag, Mireya needs more coke, and
then he turned up the volume on the stereo, some horrible reg-
gaeton, the apartment was like a dance hall in La Caracas, and
Víctor said to him, turn it down, chief, the neighbors are going
to complain, and that only made him worse, let those sons of
bitches come and I'll shoot them in the mouth, or in the ass,
don't be paranoid, Víctor, the walls are soundproof, or do you
think these dealers don't party? Maybe the coke doesn't agree
with you, right? what are you drinking? and he grabbed a
bottle of twenty-five-year-old Chivas or one of Blue Seal and
filled the glass to the brim, and said to him, go on, chill out,
and he went back to the bedroom where we could see Mireya
with a very strange thong stuck between her buttocks and with
a huge belly in front, and Piedrahita said, wow, what a big
black mama, did I tell you we're trying for a kid? and he went
back to the bedroom.

It's getting harder all the time, Víctor said, the chief's very
nervous, they're putting pressure on him from upstairs, he
went crazy again on this operation, he smashed the skull of one
of the guys with the butt of his pistol, I had to grab him to stop
him still hitting him when he was already dead, chief, chief, the
man's already gone, leave him, because Piedrahita goes crazy
sometimes, he acts like a lunatic, and I get scared, because I'm
his pupil, anyway, after the thing today they may promote me,
the top brass were very pleased and they're already giving out
statements to the press; there's a guy in the office who's a
champion with stories, we call him the poet: he's the one who
arranges things so that they look good, because in this country
you have to fight with everything you have, those terrorists are
worse than scorpions and they've been really hounding us, just
imagine, they got two friends of ours last month, you can't piss
around with these people, you fuck them before they fuck you,

you see? my language is getting damaged from going around with Piedrahita, I wasn't always this way, vulgar like him, a pity he's my chief because I can't correct him, and the worst of it is, I come out with these words in front of my wife and children, and so I asked him, for the first time, how old is your wife? and he said, twenty-nine, and the kids seven and five, a boy and a girl, the girl's the older of the two. He took out a photograph from his billfold and I saw them, two really ugly kids, to tell the truth, because that's typical of Columbia, Consul, how ugly poor children are, don't you think, I like them when they're bigger, and it wasn't that Víctor was poor, he had bags of money from the seizures, but he was humble, his mother had a grocery store in a little town in Boyacá, anyway, I didn't tell him what I thought about the children, but the opposite, obviously, how beautiful, the boy looks just like you, and he said, oh, gorgeous, now you really got me, and he took out another roll of dollars and said to me, look, doll, just to show how much I appreciate you, and he gave it to me, another two thousand, he must have been carrying six thousand with him, that was the good thing about big seizures.

Then I started searching on the Internet to see what had happened. In the case of that party that lasted for four days, plus two for recovery, they had taken out a straw man with money from drug trafficking, but fronting for FARC; not long afterwards it was said that one of the prisoners had accused a journalist, and that everything was corroborated in some e-mails, that he'd been paid I don't know how many dollars and that the Secret Service was still investigating why that journalist had attacked the government, especially a minister, they suspected that FARC was behind it, a conspiracy, in other words, that was the language they used at the time, do you remember that, Consul?

In spite of the atrocities, nothing ever happened to Víctor or his chief. They didn't feel they were in any danger, quite the

250 · SANTIAGO GAMBOA

contrary: they thought they were heroes, and the worst of it is, they probably were. Heroes of that horrible country. I listened to their stories, they whacked these people, took those out, charged this one, fabricated evidence against another, arrested someone they had previously protected, threatened others, and so on. One day they took me to a party with other people from the Secret Service and there I realized that they were all in the same game. They were playing to kill. They were plainclothes policemen and they felt protected. For the chief they had various nicknames: Big Boss or Chief White Feather.

Every time I heard of someone they'd killed, I'd tell myself, people like me or my brother, people who remain buried forever on patches of waste ground, abandoned, how solitary that is, dying on a patch of waste ground, without anybody knowing where, don't you think? That's what happened to most of those they caught because, according to Víctor, there were a hell of a lot of traitors in the country, and that's why they had to kill them. And, seeing him with Piedrahita, I'd say to them in my mind, you still think you're gods, carry on while you can, sons of bitches, because very soon you'll be singing a different song, and I continued paying attention and preparing my revenge, making accounts and calculations.

The first thing was to get Manuel out of the country and send him to Europe to study film. My dream was to pay for the education he wanted, not philosophy anymore but film, I wanted him to become a great director, and to make that possible I'd put myself through hell. I saved and saved, but of course, I also had expenses. I set myself the target of a hundred thousand dollars; I even thought to ask Víctor, telling him it was to help my brother to study, but then I had second thoughts: best not to tell him anything about myself or talk to him about our plans, which were the one beautiful thing in my life.

At home, I kept lying: that I'd been on a field trip to study a native community in the Montes de María, where there was still an ongoing situation with the guerrillas and the paramilitaries, and Mother would cry, oh, my God, Juana, and did you see terrorists from FARC? and I'd say, to pull her leg, of course, Mother, the work was with them, and Mother would lose her temper, and say, oh, daughter, you're proving me right, I said it from the first day you went to that training camp they call a university, didn't I? But Father would defend me, calm down, Bertha, can't you see the girl's pulling your leg? And then it was time to go to bed, and when there were no more sounds in the house I'd go to Manuel's bedroom and say to him, what do you think? what do you see? tell me those beautiful things you have in your head, and then he'd hug me and cover my eyes with his divine hands and say: there's a new constellation, a different sky where there are no stars, only volcanoes, and you and I are sitting on the edge of one of those volcanoes watching the others spit out lava, that's what I see; the lava looks like liquid gold; there's a terrible silence in the constellation and the eruptions boom, but we're calm, there's a refreshing wind and what reaches us is the echo, an echo that comes from a long way away, and then, Consul, I'd close my eyes and listen to him talking, and Manuel's words, those worlds he had inside him, existed because he existed, and I'd fall asleep, dreaming of those skies and those volcanoes, he and I in each other's arms. I could see him not only through his words, but because he painted them on the local walls, floating in the air, or in the water of the sea, solitary planets filled with volcanoes, that was his beautiful world. On those nights I was very happy, you can't imagine how happy, but it made me anxious, being so happy, so terrifyingly happy. That's why when I say that he liked movies I thought: finally I'll be able to see our story, more of what he has inside, and I'll be able to protect him, I was strengthened in the thought of making all these sacrifices, I'd do whatever it took to get there, even rob a bank.

I saw myself going with Manuel to the premiere of his first film, in Cannes or Venice or San Sebastian, and then I fell asleep, cradled by these fantasies, and the following week I continued with renewed strength, in order to save money, to live without fear, and I answered the calls from Andrés Felipe, who always came back on the attack when I was with Víctor, as if he had radar, and I'd arrange to see him and we'd fuck like crazy and I'd listen to his stories about his frigid wife, just so that he would trust me, because I couldn't forget the face of that woman in Soacha and the promise I made her, you know? I'm a person with fixed ideas and if I tell someone I'm going to do something I do it, that poor woman and her son, I could imagine all too well where he might be, or rather his bones, because that damned country is built over a grave, wherever you dig you find bones, we've spent years digging up bones and looking for their names, and even now they keep coming out, it's horrible, but you know what I'm talking about, don't you?

One day I called Andrés Felipe on his cell phone and said, what's up, are you getting bored with me? Quite the contrary, darling, he said, I was just thinking to call you and ask you to go with me to a convention in Cartagena, do you like Cartagena? and I said, oh, how wonderful, I have a new bathing suit, and he said, bring it with you because we're going to the Santa Clara, the most beautiful hotel, and so we went, what kind of convention? I asked, and he said, what do you think, darling, a convention of advisers, and I said to him, hell, it's pretty good being an adviser, but when we got there I realized that it was much more about security, a private thing, not open to the public, they were meeting with gringos, security advisers, and I almost had a heart attack when I heard Andrés Felipe say that the head of the Secret Service was with them, because the president was going to be there on the third day, he himself had called the meeting, that's why I had to stay in the hotel, a bit hidden, the meetings were in private places and it wasn't good for him to be seen with a strange girl, he explained to me, but I said to him, it's your loss, and I'd go for walks and buy crafts, although feeling anxious, hell, if the head of the Secret Service was coming, there must be a whole security setup, and what if Víctor and Piedrahita came there and saw me? No, no, I told myself, they're in Narcotics, but I was scared all the same, I wasn't doing anything bad but they were law enforcers and saw the bad in everything, it was best to be careful, so I spent the afternoon walking around and at night I went to the hotel to wait for Andrés Felipe, and when I asked him how it had gone he was angry, angry with the gringos who were giving them lessons and angry with the guy from the Secret Service, who said the problem was that they had to respect the rights of the people, and in a country like ours, a country at war, either you fought to win or you protected rights, and of course, Andrés Felipe, who had done courses at Princeton, felt bad, he didn't like that way of thinking, but he had to swallow it, because the order was to follow the instructions of the gringos, but then, when the gringos left, the very same chief had said to them, well, boys, now you know what you have to do, the terrorists are among us, not only in the mountains, if only they'd stayed there to be machine-gunned, but no, now they go around in ties in the corridors and offices of the Supreme Court, in the newsrooms of the press, in the universities, in the trade unions and NGOs, and there we can't machine-gun them, the war consists in bringing them out into the light, so we're going to spy on them, listen to what they say on the telephone, and since this struggle is relentless and has to be won quickly, it's important to hurry things along with witnesses and testimonies, we can't wait for the terrorists to fall by themselves, it's a way to save the lives of our countrymen, are you listening to me? does anyone disagree? And everyone said, no, no! dying of fear, that's what Andrés Felipe told me, because according to him that's what they felt when faced with the Supremo, fear, a guy so cold and authoritarian, with that icy look, devoid of scruples, like that of a snake about to bite, and they all went out to obey him. Nobody can say a word against it, he said, but later, with a few drinks in him, smoking a joint after we'd had an amazing fuck on the terrace, Andrés Felipe told me that the chief was a hard person, true, but he was also intelligent and loyal, and sometimes he made people do ugly things but the result in the end was good, what's that phrase? oh, darling, you must know it, for sure, the end what? and I said, the end justifies the means, hell, don't you know something as simple as that? God knows what the advice you give must be like . . .

Then, in his doped-up soliloquy, Andrés Felipe told me that his family had been friendly with the president for several generations, and that in spite of that there were things he didn't agree with, although he knew they were necessary, especially when it came to contacts with the people in blue, that was what he called them, and I asked, and who are the people in blue, darling? and he rolled another joint and took a slug of whiskey and said, who do you think, precious, do I need to draw you a picture? of course every time someone is denounced we put him under surveillance, we dig up what we can about him, because I do think there are moments in history, History with a capital "H," when you have to choose sides and take risks, you have to stand up and be counted, do you understand me? and like a submissive girl, bowing down before him, I said, of course, and I asked him how about you, what risks are you taking in this war? and he answered, well . . . do you think what I do is nothing? standing side by side with the chief, advising him about things I myself don't agree with, carrying messages, exchanging information, protecting the cause, all the things I wouldn't do, for example, if we lived in Switzerland or Costa Rica or the United States, countries that don't put you up against the ropes, but what can we do, we live in Colombia and this brave little country we like so much forces us to do complicated things, do you understand me? And I said, yes, of course I understand, I have a friend who says the same, and why do you like this country so much? I asked, and he said, well, because it's mine, why else do you think? I love this fucking country, or rather, if you cut one of my veins what would come out is . . . Colombia! no more, no less, isn't it the same with you? and I said, no, what comes out of me is blood, but I understand you, and to stop him looking at me suspiciously I lit his joint and slid over him and started fucking him again until he looked me in the eyes and said, all romantic, or rather all mushy, oh, Juana, you're the bright star of my soul, the light of my life, what do you call what we're doing? and I answered, fucking, and he said, oh no, that's vulgar, this is making love! really, don't you feel the same or what? and I said, of course I feel the same, we both have genital corpuscles in our mucous membranes, and he said, no, come on, are you giving me a college lecture or what? and he kissed me, and said, come here, my beautiful genius, if I didn't have those three kids I swear I'd leave my wife and I said to him, don't leave your wife, don't even think about it, those kids deserve everything.

At the end of the whole thing there was a cocktail party at the convention center, and after it, when the top brass had gone and the Secret Service people were already flying back to Bogotá in their private plane, Andrés Felipe took me to a party in a very luxurious apartment in Bocagrande. There I met other advisers, all in security. The party really took off around two in the morning, with the arrival of a former Miss Colombia who really spiced things up, sang *vallenatos*, and excited everyone with some very pretty girls who were with her. I was surprised that she'd arrived on her own, I mean without a partner, but then I saw her sit down in the lap of the guy who owned the apartment, whose face looked familiar, an old actor or a former TV presenter. Pills were passed around, the glass ash-trays were filled with coke. At one point, I saw one of the advisers pass a pill on his tongue to his girlfriend, and then the former Miss Colombia snort a line of something, a coffee-colored powder that didn't look like coke. I was surprised. I took whatever was going, but within certain limits. After a couple of hours, I told Andrés Felipe that I wasn't feeling well and asked him if we could go, but he didn't want to leave and he said, go to one of the bedrooms and lie down, princess, I'll call you. I went to the second floor, walked along a corridor, and opened a door at random, but closed it again when I saw the owner of the apartment in bed with a young black guy. At that point I recognized him and told myself, of course, he was an old actor! Farther down the corridor, in a kind of living room, I found a couch and fell asleep.

I don't know how much time passed but when I woke up dawn had already broken and the atmosphere was very unreal. I had a headache and my muscles felt lethargic. A group of employees was just finishing taking a table of fruit, eggs, and oatmeal rolls onto the balcony, next to the table of drinks. There were people in bathing suits coming out of a swimming pool and a Jacuzzi at the far end. I didn't see Andrés Felipe anywhere, but I didn't care. I went and ate a dish of fruit. Then I did a line of coke, because someone was regularly filling the ashtrays, and walked toward the Jacuzzi. I lit a cigarette and felt a little better. The former Miss Colombia was there, in her underwear, with a black thong that was like a thread. She had a glass of gin in her hand and was talking to two guys. I took my clothes off and went into the water, which brought me back to life. How delicious, a Jacuzzi at that hour. People said hello to me. Someone said they had seen Andrés Felipe on the other terrace, but I just shrugged. I heard them talking from a long way away, with the warm water on my body and the still cool breeze of the morning. They asked me who I was and I said

just anything, an invented name, and that I was studying sociology at the National. One of the guys offered me a line, but I
said I'd snorted not long before. The three snorted their couple of lines and continued talking, saying how difficult it was
to get credit because of the fluctuation of the dollar, and the
worst thing, said the former Miss Colombia, was the damned
revaluation of the peso, which has screwed us all up, right?
You put your savings abroad and now it turns out exactly the
opposite, the good thing is to have pesos. She had a modeling
agency in Bogotá, and from what I gathered some of the girls
at the party were hers. They talked about the reigning Miss
Colombia, she said she was betting on her this year for Miss
Atlantic, but Miss Universe was going to be difficult because,
according to her, Chávez had it fixed, and then the two guys
said, that clown, that son of a bitch, poor Venezuelans, I don't
understand how come the gringos haven't brought him down,
and the other one said: we should bring him down ourselves,
what bullshit it is always to depend on the gringos, and the first
one said, yes, but if anyone finds out, can you imagine? and the
former Miss Colombia said, what a pity that here in Colombia
the government doesn't help beauty queens and models, we
have to do it all ourselves, there should be subventions for
beauty, I envy the Venezuelans in that way, because they're
protected there, and then one of the guys said, well, what is it
you don't have? and she said, me, nothing, thanks to the agency
I have everything, my girls are the best and are in demand
everywhere, the problem is that sometimes they get damaged,
they get sent back to me with more weight on them or with
vices, and one of the two guys, passing her the little mirror
with the coke, laughed and said, what vices do they get sent
back to you with? and the former Miss Colombia put one line
in each nostril and said, with the worst of all, the vice of easy
money, that's the worst one in this country, the one that everybody has, including us here, on this terrace in Cartagena, in

this delightful Jacuzzi, without having to get up early in the morning to work like other people, and one of the guys, indicating me with his eyes, said, well, don't exaggerate, what will our guest think, we're entrepreneurs, we already break our backs building a heritage, generating employment and critical mass, making a country, so we deserve a little enjoyment, don't we? I laughed and said to them, of course you deserve it. I poured myself some aguardiente from a tray and said to them, cheers, this is my first of the day, and the three of them applauded and said, wait, we'll drink with you, and they poured themselves three glasses and we raised a toast, and the former Miss Colombia said to me, you're pretty, what are you doing, studying with those guerrillas in the National? I shrugged again, but she insisted, you should come to my office in Bogotá, you have a lovely body, let's see, do you mind standing up a moment? I did as she asked and she said, look, with a month of going to the gym you'll be perfect, I have teachers who can train you, would you like that? and I said, yes, of course, a thousand thanks, then she called somebody on her BlackBerry and soon afterwards a young girl came with cards and gave me one, seriously, you'll call me next week? I said yes, and they continued talking, one of them said to her, listen, you're the only one who works at parties and at this hour, but the former Miss Colombia said, that's because the talent and beauty of this country won't allow us to rest, you have to keep your eyes wide open, and they continued talking about politics, all of them wanted the President to be reelected for a third term, this country has never been better, they said, has it? and all of them said, yes, we have foreign investment, security, business is good, oh, we don't give a damn about the constitution of '91, why can't we change it? and again they filled their glasses and filled mine, and they said, a toast to our beloved president! We knocked back the aguardiente, me choking of course, but keeping quiet, and one of the guys held out the mirror and we snorted some more, and because it was finished they called a maid, a black girl with an apron, like something out of the nineteenth century, and they said to her, do us a favor and prepare some more lines, and they toasted again, to the president who's going to win the war for us! and another said, praise be to him! and if the neighboring countries kick up a fuss we'll take a stick to them, Chávez is just asking for an invasion, and Correa in Ecuador too, let them know that we'll enter their territory whenever we fucking feel like it to kill terrorists, that's why we have half a million soldiers and policemen, let them come, we're waiting for them.

From one of the tables on the terrace, a group of guests turned to look at us, raised their glasses, and said, to the bravest president we've had! And those who were leaning out of the windows on the second floor, hearing the toast, also raised their glasses, as did those who were in the bedrooms and the terrace roof, all together; the servants put down their trays, from other apartments they leaned out and lifted their hands and cried in unison, long live our president!! a resounding, enveloping, all-consuming cry that was repeated from building to building, long live our president!! as if a storm had invaded the sky, something dark and electric, a storm cloud laden with omens. Then the cry drifted off through the air and faded in the distance, in a cloudy area where the sky merged with the sea and which to me, from that Jacuzzi, seemed liked the entrance to hell.

Then I drank another aguardiente and the party went on.

When I got back from Cartagena I called the former Miss Colombia's number and went to see her. Her office was on Seventh and Eighth, below Eleventh. On the entrance door there was a plate: School of Modeling.

Oh, how good that you took the plunge, she said, remind me of your name, she gestured to me to come in and wrote something in a cheap diary, from next year, and then said, and what would you like me to call you? Oh, yes, I said, well, look, I'd like to be called Jessica, but she said, no, my dear, we already have three Jessicas, so I said, well, suggest one, like in Hotmail; we laughed, she looked at her notebook, all right, seeing you the way I saw you, seeing the brave and assertive person that you are, I'd give you a really cool French name, and the best one is Emmanuelle, you remember the movie? I said, yes, I knew everything about films, but then I said straight out, listen, I'm curious about something, do all the models have false names? and the former Miss Colombia said, well, that's for protection, dear, because you know how men are, and I said, but is the modeling thing mainly about going with guys or what? and she cleared her throat and said, oh, my dear, we have to do a bit of everything here, the way things are right now, with the economic crisis and the revaluation of the peso, with the fall of Wall Street, if there's any modeling work, then fine, but in the meantime, most of the girls take on what there is, obviously they're well paid and they know who the client is, we don't service drug traffickers or paramilitaries or guerrilla chiefs, none of that, just businessmen, sometimes foreigners, diplomats, highly placed people, the thing is, these days life has changed a lot, just imagine, at the party in Cartagena I took six girls and all of them were paid really well and were happy, because when you come down to it they're paid to do what they like doing, which is having a good time, doing their pills and their coke, having their drinks, doing a couple of fucks almost without realizing it, they earned two million pesos, sometimes three, which was nothing in dollars, and I thought inside me, poor girls, three million? is that what they need those asses and those boob jobs for? Víctor gives me on average three thousand dollars per party, but of course, he's middle-class, meaning he's more generous, so I said to the former Miss Colombia, look, I'll leave you my cell phone number, I'm not interested in modeling or any of that bullshit, just going out with really high-class guys, especially lawyers, I'm crazy about lawyers and they come in useful when there's any problem, right? and the former Miss Colombia, who looked at me in surprise when I said this, replied, right, boss, right, and how much do we charge them? to which I said, five million, minimum, the rest is for your office, and she said, no, girl, that's very high, so I said, okay, all right, four and a half, here's my phone number, nice to have met you.

Three days later I was in the cafeteria of the García Márquez Cultural Center, reading *Juego de Damas* by R. H. Moreno Durán, when my cell phone rang. It was her. My dear, I have your first client, and I asked, conditions okay? and she said, more than okay, are you presentable? and I said, that depends, who is he? And she said, he's a very dear friend, sixty-six years old but as strong as an ox! I told him about you and he said he'd like to meet you, he's a lawyer, this is the address; I went home, put on a black Punto Blanco thong and a pair of Diesel jeans, and changed my blouse; instead of the tennis shoes some low-heeled shoes, made myself up like a cat, and asked for a taxi. I looked at the address: it was in the Nogal building. Great. I didn't know it.

I arrived and he turned out to be a brilliant guy, a real old gentleman; he showed me into the library and there was something of everything, history books, literature, dictionaries of the cinema, he offered me a drink and as he was bringing ice for a whiskey I took down a book by Lévi-Strauss, *The Savage Mind*, that was always on loan from the university library, he had it in Spanish and in French; when he came back with the glasses he said to me, are you interested in Lévi-Strauss? and I said, I'm sorry, I just wanted to look at this book, I've been waiting for it for months from the library, and then he said, you can have it, come and take a look, and he took out *The Raw and the Cooked* and also *Tristes Tropiques*, books that seemed in the realm of fantasy in the university library, and said, take them, they're yours, I've already read them and I have them in French, these books are the kind you read and appreciate, it's been years since anybody took out those poor volumes, it'll give me pleasure to know that you're going to read them and lend them to your friends, that's what they're for, to be read many times and by different people.

We sat down on the couch and talked about literature and history, about the *Escolios* of Nicolás Gómez Dávila, the aphorisms of Lichtenberg and Elias Canetti; then he talked about life and read me a fragment of a poem by William Blake:

That Man should labour & sorrow, & learn & forget, & return
To the dark valley whence he came, to begin his labour anew.

That's what he was like, he said, trying to get back to a place, searching anxiously for it, but sometimes his valley was in his books or in his memory or in movies, he didn't have much left. He told me he was a widower, his children lived in Europe, and for the moment he didn't have a girlfriend. He was in recess. His verse from Blake had made me think of one by Mayakovsky, and he said, do you know it? can you quote it to me? and I said:

Without drinking even a drop
I have reached my soul's aim. My solitary human voice
is raised
between cries
between tears
in the rising day.

He gave me a hug, and suddenly I noticed that his eyes had glazed. It's very good, and he talked to me about Mayakovsky, "the unhappy Mayakovsky," as Sabato calls him. He said that in Moscow there was a Mayakovsky Museum next to the former

KGB headquarters, a strange, elliptical, theatrical museum that tried to reproduce his poetry and his world. One day you'll visit it.

He started caressing me and kissing me, it was really nice and I was enchanted, Consul, I swear, and we had a great fuck; then he asked permission to put the TV news on and I said to him that I didn't want to interrupt him, that it was already time for me to go, but he said no, stay with me, and we saw it there, lying naked in bed. Over our heads there passed that hurricane of horror contained in any of the news bulletins in that cursed place, with the massacres and the violence and the hypocrisy, and then those crazy women who present the final part, as if the news bulletin was about Disney World and not about a country with more displaced persons than Zaire and more executions than Liberia; reaching this point, Alfredo, that was his name, said to me, I can't bear these idiots, and he switched it off, and then I said, it's been really great to meet you, I have to go now, and he said, wait, he got out of bed and got dressed and as I was going out he handed me a roll of banknotes, but I said to him, don't worry, Alfredo, the books are more than enough and I'm indebted to you, but he insisted, and I stuck to my guns, you and this house are an oasis, I don't know why I'm telling you this, and he embraced me and said, I understand why you're saying that, can I see you again? and I said, yes, and gave him my telephone number, call me whenever you like, it doesn't matter what time, call me and I'll come right away.

I left with the strange sensation that I had touched something clean and unpolluted. Of course Monsieur Echenoz had been like that too, although in a way that was Luciferian and cynical. Not Alfredo, even though he was rich and from Bogotá. I walked northward along Seventh, glancing at the books by the light of the streetlamps, and when I got home Manuel wasn't there, he'd gone to the movies, so I shut myself in to read and take notes, remembering Alfredo's voice as he said: "It'll give me pleasure to know that you're going to read them and lend them to your friends," which was precisely what I was thinking to do, and I fell asleep with a smile.

A few days went by like that, going out from time to time with Víctor and with another couple of clients of the former Miss Colombia who turned out to be nothing special, until Andrés Felipe the adviser, as I thought of him, called me again. How's it going, precious? and I said, I'm bored, I guess you forgot all about me, and then he said, no, precious, not at all, I'm actually calling you to ask you to go with me on a really nice jaunt, it's to a ranch in Antioquia, how does that sound to you? it sounds great, I said, and when is it for? and he said, now, right now, get ready and I'll send someone to pick you up, give me an address. I told him at the entrance to the Andino mall and I went there with a hand case. A car came with official plates and took me to the CATAM military airport, near El Dorado. Andrés Felipe was waiting for me on one of the runways with two men dressed in dark suits who I didn't know; we got on a helicopter and took off; I was pleased because I'd never seen Bogotá from a helicopter, in other words, as the birds, the buzzards and the vultures, see it, and the truth is that as soon as the flight takes off and you rise into the air the city looks like a trough of sugar houses and winding paths; of course if you go further it already looks like a patch of vomit, next to the hills; then I started looking at the mountains and the rivers, those beautiful landscapes that the country has, and I imagined them full of guerrillas and paramilitaries, our beautiful fields, the paths and valleys filled with mines and bones and rifle cases, and so we continued, without anybody talking, until one of the guys, looking at a BlackBerry, said to Andrés Felipe, they've just sent the coordinates, sir, wait and I'll give them to the pilot, and then the helicopter turned and gained speed and two or three hours later we saw a clearing opening in the middle of the greenery and as we descended a ranch house came into view, with two swimming pools and well-tended, symmetrical, brightly colored gardens. A group of people stood beside a tree, signaling to us.

We got off and Andrés Felipe said, best if you don't say too much while we're here, gorgeous, you do understand?, and I said, yes, but who are these friends? and he said, don't ask too many questions, precious, I'll tell you later. We were received with hugs and taken to the guest room, which was like a suite in a five-star motel, with air-conditioning and a bathroom with a marble tub, porcelain containers, bars of Spanish Heno de Pravia soap, and mirrors with wooden frames. The only thing missing was Benetton condoms. We left our bags and were invited to sit on the terrace, next to the swimming pool, and someone said, would you like a nice cold aguardiente? I accepted, but Andrés Felipe asked for a Coca-Cola Light. He was nervous, kept looking around, and every now and again talked in a low voice with the people from the house. A very nice lady, who seemed to be the wife of the host, asked if I wanted to put on a bathing suit; I said yes and she took me to the changing room, and in the meantime I started talking to her, do you live here? and she replied, no, I just come here to relax, and so I said to her, what kind of work do you do? No, I don't work, I live with my husband. I felt like asking her, if you don't work why do you need to relax? but I preferred to keep quiet, you had to be blind and stupid not to realize that the house belonged to paramilitaries, or straight drug traffickers, so instead I said, it's a lovely house, I congratulate you on your good taste, and she said, thank you, we hired a foreign interior decorator, my husband didn't want to build the typical Antioquian ranch house, but something high-class, and it came out well, didn't it? Oh yes, I said, really high-class!

We went out on the terrace, and with the heat, I got straight into the pool. It was nice and cool. A waiter reached me my glass of aguardiente, but I noticed that the others weren't drinking, so I said to myself, this party is a little strange. Better to act as if I'm stupid and not ask any questions; then I heard one of the men say that the gentleman wouldn't be coming until the following day, we have to wait for him. After that Andrés Felipe relaxed and had a few whiskeys. The lady of the house started a conversation but I couldn't say anything because they were talking about Colombian soccer. Our soccer that's poor and ugly, like the country: poor and ugly, and that's why I don't like it. Like talking obsessively about a disease, the way most people only talk about accidents or madness. But nothing else seemed to matter to them, and they talked and talked, that if the Junior or the DIM, or something very strange called La Equidad, which sounded like a discount store for poor people, and the strange thing is that the one who most insisted on the subject was the lady of the house. I realized they were talking about all this because they didn't have any other subject and because the reason for this meeting was a secret and could only be touched on with the husband, who would be arriving the next day. Her role was to distract us. When they served the food she showed us into a very swanky dining room, with silver cutlery and a beautiful blue and white dinner set with embossed hunting scenes, and of course wine, not Argentinian or Chilean wine but French wine, Pomerol, a delicious red wine, though it was a strange thing to drink in that tropical heat; I had about four glasses with the first course, which was an asparagus consommé; then they replaced it with a white, a Sancerre, also delicious and very cold, and the main dish arrived, which was fish, a roll of salmon with fines herbes with a salad of leeks and purée, a delicious thing, and since I love to ask awkward questions, pretending to be dumb, I wanted to know if the salmon was from some nearby river, and the lady of the house laughed and said, yes, from the river Orkla, not here in Antioquia but in Norway, and everybody laughed and I sat there like a silly young busybody but she looked at me affectionately, since I'd given her the opportunity to tell her joke and look good.

When night fell it got cooler, and they lit the fire and served us brandy and offered cigars, Montecristo and Davidoff; now the talk was about Shakira, whether or not she represented Colombia well abroad. The hostess complained that she sang in English, she didn't think that was right because in Colombia people don't speak English, but I said, yes, they do, it's the mother tongue in San Andrés and Providencia, then she said, all right, and also the yuppies of Parque de la 93 in Bogotá, wasn't it? Again everybody laughed. Andrés Felipe looked at me gratefully, I was giving a perfect performance in my role as the pretty but dumb girlfriend.

After the brandy they passed around trays with a delicious dark whiskey, served in cognac glasses, without ice, because they said it was too fine, and they talked vaguely about how well the country was doing; around midnight we retired to the bedroom and I commented to Andrés Felipe, pretending to be dumb, what elegant people, nobody snorted coke or smoked joints, and he said, no, gorgeous, it's different here, that's why I told you that the best thing is not to talk too much and go with the flow, although you're doing it very well, precious, I'm really glad you came. I fell asleep after a good fuck, but before I did I thought: are they paramilitaries or just traffickers?

The following day, the host arrived at last, riding a sorrel with a high-quality saddle, surrounded by bodyguards. He greeted Andrés Felipe and said, how nice to see you, are they looking after you as you deserve? and Andrés Felipe answered, of course, Don Fermín, I wasn't treated this well even in my grandmother's house, and then the man said, come on, Andrés Felipe, don't exaggerate, I knew your grandmother's house, maybe you don't know this, but my mother was one of her maids. Andrés Felipe didn't know what to say and we all stood there nonplussed, there was a silence that seemed to go on forever, you could hear the air passing, so I stuck my oar in, out of pure intuition, and said, that's the good thing about this country, the opportunity it gives us to advance, I congratulate you on your house, Señor Fermín, we've been feeling as if we're in the Palace of Versailles, and then the man started to laugh and gestured to Andrés Felipe and said, and who is this very polite young lady? and he said, a friend, I invited her because I know you like to see friendly young people, and he said, good for you, come, my dear, and he took me by the arm and walked me as far as the terrace and said to me, before you leave here I'm going to give you a gift, and I looked at him and said, the only gift I need is this invitation, but I'll take it because it came from you, and he said, yes, I like intelligent sensitive people, but go get in the swimming pool because I have to work with Andrés Felipe until lunchtime, all right?

They came out around two on the afternoon. There was a moment when Andrés Felipe tried to switch on his BlackBerry but one of Don Fermín's security guys approached nervously and whipped the phone out of his hand. We had lunch and then another helicopter arrived. Before saying goodbye Don Fermín took me to his study, closed the door, and said: I'm going to give you your gift, just as I promised. He opened a drawer in his desk and took out a box wrapped in gold paper. Then he gave me a hug and said: take good care of that bastard and say hello to the chief for me. In the helicopter, on the way back, I opened the box and found a beautiful watch. It was perfect for me. When we landed in Bogotá, Andrés Felipe put me in a taxi and set off along the road. They were waiting for him at the Palace. I understood everything but said nothing.

I see I haven't told you anything about my friends at the faculty, Consul. One of them was Jaime, an Aesculapian priest who had special permission from the Curia not to study at the Xavierian but at the National: a strange-looking guy, who looked more Norwegian or Hungarian, or even Russian. Yellow beard and hair, and very white, sensitive skin. He lived with his community in an area near Usme, with a Dutch priest. Actually it was a home for street kids and he was studying sociology because he wanted to understand what he should do to change the world. He was from Santander. A good person, very committed. He said that if Christ were alive today, that was where he would be. He hated the little chapels in the north of the city where rich people had their weddings. He said he could happily shoot those who celebrated Mass in those neighborhoods, without his hand even shaking, although obviously not all rich people were the same, there were shades of gray, and even some rich people who were good. The real sons of bitches, according to him, were the priests who ministered to the rich and were all opportunists and liars.

Other friends of mine were Tamara, José, and Carlos Mario. All three from Cali, very together, or rather, good students. They liked having fun and sometimes I went with them to prepare work or exams, because in the end, when it was over, we always went dancing at Café y Libro or Son Salomé. They liked salsa, as did I, and also rock in Spanish. With them I went to concerts by ChocQuibTown and Aterciopelados and Side-stepper. They were all on the left but they hated FARC and ELN. We wanted a change, simply to aspire to something different. The guerrillas were corrupted by the money from drug trafficking and kidnappings, and because of their passive attitude of hunkering down in the regions and becoming like local chieftains. The university was an open space. Sometimes FARC or ELN people came and held parades in the Plaza del Che, but it was nothing, nobody paid any attention. Anyway, that was my group, we'd come out of class and throw ourselves on the lawn to talk, to have a nap in the sun, to talk about movies or books or our lives, or politics, of course, it was all completely ordinary, commonplace, we were young students at a public university.

To me it seemed incredible that anybody could think the National belonged to the guerrillas, when from inside the truth was quite different. Most of the students were middle-class or working-class, that's what everybody thought was strange. That the poor should have somewhere to study, that the best university in the country should be for them. That's why they want to see it closed down and the land used for something profitable, like a shopping mall, with a theme park and a hotel attached, that's what some people want, and that's why they dream of seeing it closed down and its students in mass graves. It makes them angry that poor people should have opportunities, that there are good teachers and a high budget, their mouths water thinking of those millions that could be used on contracts or on buying guns and helicopters to defend the Fatherland, but which are actually spent on books and on equipping laboratories, no, the rich don't like that because, to them, sending their children to university, at Los Andes or abroad, costs them a lot, and that's why they feel defrauded, what's this about giving the best to the poor? what's the big deal, then, in being rich? They say their taxes keep the country going, but you know that isn't true. Those who keep the country going are the poor and the middle class, who really do pay taxes. That's why Colombia is a poor and middle-class country. Anyway, Consul, why should I tell you what you already know?

I went around with my group of friends, and in addition there were Brigitte and Lady, who had helped me get involved in that life. Once I met them in one of the open areas in Fine Arts and they asked me about the friends I'd made in the bar, and I told them, very good, excellent contact, thanks, I didn't want to tell them that I was already flying higher, and why, and at that point I got another call from the former Miss Colombia, asking me to her office.

I have something very good for you, she said, not for now, but I'd like you to think it over and let me know, and I said, why all the mystery? I told her I'd really liked Señor Alfredo, that I'd go back whenever he called me, but the former Miss Colombia said, what I'm offering you is much better, it means getting on a plane and going to Japan to work for six months, a year maximum; you'll be in a beautiful residence, with everything thrown in: lodging, food, light and heating, everything. You'll be working with Japanese people, who are timid, clean, and very polite, and in a year you'll be able to earn several hundred thousand dollars, clear, they pay high-class women like you very well there, it's a great opportunity that I don't offer everyone, anyway, think it over for a few days and call me, as soon as you decide you can go, we have a free place.

I walked out, lost in thought. Japan? a hundred thousand dollars? That's what I'd been hoping to get to take Manuel away, but it wasn't going to be easy to justify such a long time to my parents; I'd have to tell them I'd won a scholarship or something like that, it was complicated, too many lies and false papers. The thing sounded good but scared me a little. It had its pros and cons. I thought I'd be able to see how life was in Japan and later fetch Manuel so that he could study Japanese and learn to make films, like Kitano and Kurosawa and Ozu, there are bound to be good universities there, I told myself, but the problem was always the same, how to explain to him what I was doing? Just thinking about it made me dizzy, as if I was having to strip off and open my legs in the middle of a square, while everyone looked at me coldly and menacingly, no, to him I was virtue, I couldn't show him my other side, even though the goal was to save him, or to save the two of us. That was why when he started studying philosophy at the National I stopped him from meeting my friends, it made me nervous to think that for any reason he could meet Lady or Brigitte and find out, it made me panic. How could I be with him in Japan without telling him? It was difficult, but a good opportunity. I would keep it in mind and see if anything happened that would help me decide, or if anything better came along. And there was also the other thing: the promise I made myself and which, in a way, I made to Monsieur Echenoz. His memory was still very much alive inside me.

This is where the story starts moving faster, Consul, because the next thing that happened, sometime later, was that Andrés Felipe called me one afternoon, sounding very nervous, and said, I have to see you, precious, all right? go to room 507 of the Hotel Charleston, I'm registered under the name Boris Salcedo, can you come now? When I got there, he was a bundle of nerves: they were accusing him of having links with the paramilitaries, because in a joint operation of the police and the Secret Service one of Don Fermín's people had been arrested with a computer on which his name appeared, as a contact, and the press already had hold of it, you remember Don Fermín, the one with the ranch in Antioquia? He said that going to that fucking house had been a mistake, that he'd been following orders, that not only the press was on to it but also the prosecutor's department, that in addition Don Fermín had given them three days to solve the problem or he'd start to talk, and the president was nervous; the advisers had told him that the best thing to do was burn him, me! Andrés Felipe cried, doing a line of coke, can you imagine? what my colleagues are suggesting is to throw me to the wolves, the sons of bitches, saying that I met with Don Fermín of my own accord to get money, they tell me the government will stand by me to protect me, and my family, but I have to declare that I went of my own accord, can you imagine? it could mean ten or more years in prison and the end of my career, what am I going to do afterwards? what's going to happen to my wife and children? that's why I wanted to talk to you, precious, I'm going to refuse to make a statement, I'm going to defend myself, but since you came with me it's likely they're going to look for you, they're going to ask you to inform on me, they're going to offer you things or maybe even threaten you, I don't know, that's why I want you to leave the country for a while, if you need money I'll give it to you, and I said to him, well, of course, Andrés Felipe, of course I need it, and he said, look, in that case I have ten thousand dollars, take it but go somewhere else, now, today, and then I asked him, and what did I do wrong? and he said, nothing, but you were there, precious, nothing's going to happen to you, it's just in case they look for you and question you, but if anything bad happens to me, then I want you to remember that when we got back in the helicopter that night, I went directly to the Palace to report on the meeting, do you remember that? and I said, yes, of course, you left me in a taxi, and he said, perfect, the best thing is not to have to say any-thing at all, but if you do you can't forget how it was, right? go somewhere, wait for the heat to die down.

He gave me a hug, did two lines of coke, and I asked him, have you already gone into hiding or what? and he said, no, what's happening is that I can't make appointments anywhere, I don't know what to do, I thought to make a statement to the press from here, my lawyer is coming to talk with me later and then we'll decide, but I wanted to sort things out with you first, did you tell anyone on Don Fermín's ranch your name? and I said, no, not as far as I remember, and he said, thank God for that, that means it'll be harder for them to locate you, well, precious, good luck and don't contact me by cell phone, delete my number and all my calls, okay?

I left feeling nervous and making calculations, what might happen to me? I assumed that Víctor might help, after all he was in the Secret Service, so I sent him a letter, which was the only way, and wrote to him, what's up, stranger? It worked, and the next day he called me, hi, princess, shall I send some-one to pick you up? I said yes, I'll be at the Metro Riviera, and when he saw me he said, the thing is, the heat's on right now, I think Piedrahita is going to be out on the street all week, they're really nervous upstairs, I stole a little moment to see you, princess, but I'm going to have to work later, I'm on a stakeout, and I licked his neck and said, don't scare me, Víctor, who are you following that's so dangerous? and he said, no, he isn't dangerous, he's a white-collar son of a bitch the chief wants to turn, that's what they told me, we have to keep an eye on him to make sure he doesn't do anything stupid, and of course, that got me worried, a white-collar son of a bitch? it had to be Andrés Felipe, and if they're following him they must surely have seen me going in to the Charleston and even heard what we were talking about, but it struck me as strange that Víctor should be so calm with me, so I didn't say anything more and concentrated on what I was doing, a classic fuck, and when we'd finished and he was taking a shower I saw his cell phone vibrate several times, so I stretched over to see the screen and two capital C's flickered on it, CC, just that, once and once again. He dressed quickly, gave me a roll of dollars, and we did a couple of lines of coke; then he saw his phone and said, hey, wait, princess, this is urgent, and dialed and I heard him say, yes, yes, oh, fuck, seriously? okay, wait for me there, have you got everything recorded? no? good, I don't give a damn about them, and he said to me, I have to rush, princess, we need to look for a girl who talked with the man, oh, God, this is starting to smell fishy, how many times have I told you, this country is full of bad people.

We left the motel and he dropped me at Seventh and 140th. I was dying of panic, convinced that girl was me. I started to list what Víctor knew about me, and was relieved to realize he knew almost nothing, not even my name, just my cell phone number, which since it was for this work I'd bought using false papers. But they'd have a description or photographs: of the hotel, of the helicopter that took us to the ranch. I'd have to be very careful.

I felt scared for Manuel and my parents, what would happen

if they went to the house? Víctor and his chief and Secret Service guys in general weren't so fussy, I had to act fast. Then I remembered the offer from the former Miss Colombia. To go to Japan for a year, let things cool down, and then send for Manuel. It was the only solution, but I needed to talk with someone. I was alone, what to do? For some reason a light went on in my brain and I thought, Alfredo the lawyer! he could tell me how serious the problem was and if it was worth going. I didn't have his number and I didn't want to call the former Miss Colombia, so I went straight to his house. Seeing me, the doorman remembered, and immediately lifted the receiver of the entry phone.

He told me to follow him. Alfredo was waiting for me in the elevator, very surprised. To what do I owe this miracle? he said, and I said, I have to talk to you, you're the only person I can trust, I have a problem, I'm sorry, if you're busy I can wait, and he said, don't worry, come, would you like a drink? and I said, yes, please, anything at all, a double, and I started telling him my life story, look, I'm this and this and that's why I got involved with a guy from the Secret Service and then with people from Congress and the government, and that's why I ended up in this and that; I told him about the visit to Don Fermín's ranch and he opened his eyes wide, Fermín Jaramillo? and I said, I suppose so, I didn't ask him his full name, and Alfredo said, damn it, wait, I'll show you a photograph, he looked for a newspaper and showed it to me, is this him? I said yes, it is, I was on his ranch with the adviser I told you about, and Alfredo, looking increasingly grave, continued listening to the story, and I ended with Víctor, and I said, I think they're looking for me, I don't know what I did that was so bad, that's what scares me the most, not knowing, and he said, well, it isn't a crime to go as someone's companion, you don't work for the government, the problem isn't the law but those who are covering their tracks and trying to protect this adviser. Andrés

Felipe? I asked, and he said, yes, the press are investigating contacts between the government and the paramilitaries, the secret pacts, and that young man has become key to the whole business, the likeliest thing is that they'll put pressure on him to plead guilty and say he acted alone, that's what they always do, that's why your problem isn't with the law, let's say, with the legal law, but with the law of those guys and the government, who do what they have to in order to protect themselves. It wouldn't surprise me if they made up some sordid affair your friend was supposedly involved in that would make the visit to Don Fermín seem unimportant.

He stood up, answered a call on his cell phone, and after a while came back. Don't worry, I'm going to protect you. If you don't have a safe place stay here, does your family know I exist? do you want to call them? No, I said, that's no problem, they're used to my being away. I heard my cell phone vibrate and when I looked at the screen my chest contracted. It was Víctor. I said to Alfredo, should I answer? No, he said, better switch off the phone so they can't trace you.

I spent the night in a guest room, looking at the lights of Bogotá and feeling scared. All I could do was wait. There was no mention of the case on the news, but I was sure the whole thing was about to blow up. Three days later, Alfredo arranged for me to travel overland to Quito. He had a friend, a magistrate of the Ecuadorian court, who could put me up until things calmed down. In the end I made up my mind to go home, invent an excuse, and pick up my passport, but when I got there nobody was in, only the maid. Mother had gone out and Manuel, who had no classes that day, had gone to the Luis Ángel Arango Library. It hurt me not to be able to say good-bye to him, but I told myself, it isn't for very long. I left a note saying I was going to Los Llanos, and would call as soon as I could. I took out the money Andrés Felipe had given me. I should go to the apartment in Chapinero for my other savings,

I thought. I caught a taxi and went, but as I got closer I saw two vans similar to Víctor's on the corner of the street. I went back to the Nogal building, shaken, but from Seventh I saw more Secret Service vans in the parking lot of the building. What was going on? had they tracked me down? I stayed hidden for a while on the other side of the avenue, but nothing happened, so I decided to go.

I rushed back to the city center. Now I had nowhere to go, but luckily everything was ready for me to travel to Ecuador. From a phone booth I called my university friends. Tamara reassured me, saying nobody had come looking for me in the faculty. She didn't ask me for any details, she was a good friend. Then I called Jaime, the Aesculapian priest, and said, look, I need you to help me, it's a matter of life and death, I have to hide for a few hours, maybe until tomorrow, but it's very dangerous, are you up for it? and he said, of course, we'll protect you here in the community. I went there, and I think that saved my life, Consul. I was there the whole of the following day, worrying my head off, until in the end I decided that there was no other way out and from a pay phone called Alfredo's friend, the one who was going to get me out of the country. He was anxious, and insisted we should go that same night. I was picked up two hours later and we began the journey. He told me they had arrested Alfredo and put together a charge thanks to some cleverly edited recordings. We crossed Rumichaca Bridge on a false passport.

The following day I bought the newspaper and saw the news: former magistrate Alfredo Conde, arrested in his house. Then I went on the Internet and saw all the news bulletins. A spokesman made a public statement, saying that they would do everything they could to clarify the relationship between the lawyer and terrorism. Behind him, next to the chief of police, I noticed Piedrahita's thin, Indian-looking face, and I thought: they know I was there, they've charged him, and now they're looking for me. I also saw that Andrés Felipe was being kept in detention in a house in La Picota belonging to the prosecutor's department, that they had grabbed him trying to leave the country.

From Quito I called the former Miss Colombia and said, I agree about Japan, but I need you to get me a ticket leaving from Ecuador, and so it was, they sent me on a route that was like a country bus, with stops in São Paulo, Dubai, Bangkok, and finally Tokyo. Five days' traveling.

In Tokyo everything seemed phantasmagorical. I had read Murakami and imagined the city as a combination of cold, sometimes icy sentences that spoke of lonely people, all-night cafeterias, and young people who couldn't find a place in the world and isolated themselves in little towns in the mountains, that's how I imagined it, a place in which everyone lived submerged in his obsessions, and when I arrived, going from the airport to the center in a van, I looked through the window and said to myself, I'm alone and I'm far away, I've left Manuel but I'll go back for him, I couldn't do anything but escape to save myself, to save the two of us, because if I'm in danger then he's in danger too, and my joints and my love lobes hurt at the thought that I couldn't write to him or call him, what could I say to him? what explanation could I give? The best thing was to live through this time as quickly as possible and then look him in the eyes and tell him the truth. It would be painful to be separated from him, but the day would come, I just had to be strong.

Suddenly, in the middle of the city, the van turned in at an underground garage: this was my final destination. We took out the things and went up to an apartment on an upper floor, with a view of rooftops. Then I sat down to wait for things to pass, for the time to go by, that was all I wanted. I asked the woman who received me what was going to happen, but all she said was, rest, girl, you must be dead, do nothing but sleep for at least three days, the first week is for you to get used to it and the jetlag to pass and the bags under your eyes to go. So I was shut in for a week. I wanted to go out but they wouldn't let me, and when at last I went out they gave me an escort. I don't want to tell you names or many details of what I lived through in Tokyo, as I'm sure you'll understand, it's dangerous and there are people who could spend their whole lives tracking you down.

I worked with a group of Japanese who were the clients of the organization of my *mamiya*, a Colombian friend of the former Miss Colombia. It wasn't a traumatic experience, but it was hard. After a while I found the lack of freedom stifling. I couldn't go out on the street alone. I was earning good money but from it they kept deducting the costs of the journey, the costs of bringing me there, arranging my papers, and I don't know what else. Every time I asked, my debt had increased. One day I asked a Japanese for accounts and the guy, a horrible dwarf, gave me a slap and threw me to the ground. I learned that I had to prepare myself for a new transformation: to be the submissive woman, ready to hit back when the enemy lowered his guard. I vowed that that Japanese dwarf would end up with his brain split open, and I began a tactic of seduction. Monsieur Echenoz was right again, and a month later I had him in front of me, naked. I knew what I wanted to do as soon as he forced me to kneel and suck his cock. The killer whale. I clasped him between my teeth but something strange happened: as I was about to cut into his skin the guy moaned with pleasure and ejaculated like crazy. Then he asked me to stand up straight on his back with my high heels on and walk all over him. Strange. Then he grabbed a lighter and held out his arm, which was covered in keloidal scars. I burned him and he ejaculated again, screaming with pain.

I soon realized that he was the local boss, so it struck me as a good idea to go along with him. His name was Junichiro, but

I called him Juni. He knew English, although he didn't speak much in general. He was thirty-four years old. One night he told me that, as a boy, starting at the military school in the province where he was born, his comrades forced him to lick the asses of the ten dormitory heads. For a year they gave him beatings in the toilets, urinated in his face, and of course fucked him thousands of times. From what I understood he felt guilty for having felt pleasure and that was why he liked to be punished. It purified him and excited him. I was with him for about a year. One night I heard noises in one of the rooms in the apartment and when I went to see I found him lying there almost unconscious. He was bleeding from the anus. I asked him what had happened but he said nothing, and a second later I saw Tarek, an Iranian bodyguard, come in with a towel and some drugs to cauterize him. I thought it was horrible and I walked out. I didn't want to see him again and, fortunately, he respected me.

Then I got to know Jaburi, who was also a bodyguard. Whenever I went out I went with him, and one night, coming back to the apartment, I asked him to come with me into the shower. We fucked under the water, which was the start of my making him fall in love with me. The fucking was great. We maintained our relationship until one morning I felt something, a dizziness, my period was late, I was pregnant. It could only have been his, because we fucked without a condom. I think I must have wanted it subconsciously, so that he would get me out of there, to remind me that my life wasn't just that, and it worked. Jaburi paid my debt and went to talk with the local bosses. We got married and they gave me an Iranian passport, because I'd left my Colombian one in the pocket of a pair of jeans and it had faded in the washing machine, maybe because it was false. Soon afterwards we got permission and were able to travel to Tehran, where Manuelito was born. But they don't know that in Tokyo: the organization told the other girls I'd run away; I think they even said I'd been captured and tortured, I'm not sure.

In Tehran I kept putting off getting in touch with Manuel, every day I said to myself: tomorrow, next week . . . I had to gather my strength. I was dying to tell him that he had a nephew, actually a son. Manuelito was our son. I applied for the passports without Jaburi knowing. I hoped to run away somewhere before writing to Manuel, but without my realizing it time passed. I never imagined he'd come looking for me. It's hard to explain what I did, but that's what happened. In Japan I was high on pills most of the time; that's what I chose to escape. I have lots of gaps. Sometimes I looked at a calendar and said, are we already in September? and then, ten minutes later, we were in another month, and suddenly someone said in my ear, happy New Year, and I'd smile and take another pill. Jaburi saved me but I gave him my body and made him happy for a time. I didn't give him a son because Manuelito is mine alone. He hit me once, although you could say I asked for it. I prefer not to talk about that, but the truth is that I didn't hate him, I felt sorry for him. He seemed to me a loser, an inferior animal. I'll tell you what happened, Consul: one night I refused to have sex with him and he said, I'm your husband, you're obliged. I told him that nobody obliged me to do what I didn't want to do and I got up and locked myself in the bathroom. Then I started shouting through the window. The neighbors woke up, and his parents and brothers, who lived on the floors below, came up to our apartment. I started saying that Jaburi was a coward, that he beat me because he was incapable of having an erection and satisfying me, and I said that he wasn't a man because he forced me to put my finger up his ass and rub him, and that, as a wife, I did it even though I was dying from disgust, and I cried that Jaburi was a lousy faggot who couldn't get enjoyment with women and only had erections when he painted mustaches on me with a burned cork. The

282 - SANTIAGO GAMBOA

neighbors started laughing and saying, "Virtuous woman," and at that moment Jaburi knocked down the door and grabbed me and hit me while I screamed and laughed. You shouldn't hit a woman, but I enjoyed it. It was a way of telling him: you may have force and religion on your side, but I'm the one who has what you want between her legs, and I can destroy you. Again I raised my arms and prayed for Monsieur Echenoz.

The rest of the time, Jaburi was fine with me. The payment he'd obtained to save me was more than sufficient. He'll find it hard for a while and then he'll recover and later he'll be happy. That's how it always is in life. The more quickly you suffer, the better it is in the long run.

And that's all, Consul. The rest you already know.

PART III

The urgent communication from Bangkok came as a shock. I was starting to get accustomed to the company of Juana and Manuelito Sayeq when one day, as often happens when you're waiting for something, the telephone rang.

It was Angie, the secretary.

"There's a call from Bangkok, Consul. It's urgent."

It was the lawyer, sounding very upset. He said that for some reason (something beyond his control), the legal authorities had suddenly brought the hearing forward to that very morning, abruptly, and that in court, when given the chance to speak, Manuel had refused to plead guilty, which made everything very difficult.

"Didn't you tell me the young man had agreed?" the lawyer asked angrily, clearly blaming me. "That you'd explained to him what was at stake?"

I was stunned.

I told him I had, but that something had probably changed inside him. I assumed that on learning about Juana and the child his desire to be free had revived. Even though that freedom was utopian and unrealizable.

"And now what do we do?" the lawyer asked. "I remind you that your countryman can be tried under article 27, the old military law with an immediate death penalty, and they don't even have to wait until the end of the trial. Actually they don't need a trial at all, just an order from the prosecutor's department. I told him: from now on they can finish this at any moment. It's very serious, what can we do?"

I found it strange that he should ask me that question (which of the two of us was the lawyer with important contacts in Bangkok?) but I preferred not to get into an argument, so I said to him:

"For now, defend him, do everything you can to defend him and get him acquitted. It's the only option."

"I've already told you that isn't realistic," the lawyer insisted, still nervous, or rather annoyed, as if I had deceived him.

I hung up angrily and called Colombia, but . . . The damned time difference! I had to wait four hours. At last, at around six-thirty, I managed to talk with the Consular Department. I told them it was urgent that I travel to Bangkok, that the trial had begun that morning, without warning. I couldn't tell them my principal idea, which was to ask Juana to persuade Manuel to plead guilty and gain time. I wasn't sure that could still be done, but it was the only way out. The famous lawyer wasn't going to be of much use.

When they saw the file in Bogotá, they told me that if the lawyer had the situation in hand, it wasn't urgent for me to travel, but that they'd set the procedure for a new mission in motion anyway, in anticipation of the next hearing.

I preferred not to say anything to Juana until I had a specific date and a reply from the Ministry, so that night I gave her the excuse that I had a diplomatic engagement, which was actually true: a reception at the Bulgarian Embassy. And that's where I went, in the district of Chanakyapuri, and was able to discreetly drown my nerves in vodka and *rakia* and eat Tarator soup and some splendid sausages.

I got home late and fortunately they were both asleep. I had a last gin sitting on the bed, inside the mosquito net, thinking and thinking. I would have to act fast. The next day I called Bangkok, but wasn't able to reach the lawyer until the afternoon.

He told me they'd heard the testimonies of the police officers who had made the arrest and that the next hearing would be in three days. I asked him to keep me informed of the slightest development.

Then I called Teresa at the Mexican embassy and told her everything. She was pleased to hear my voice, and offered to help:

"Don't worry, I'll try to go to the next hearing with the lawyer, do you think you'll be able to come?"

"I'm working on it, but without a green light from the Ministry I can't move. You know how it is."

After three days the travel authorization from the Consular Department still hadn't arrived, so I decided to ask for leave and pay for the tickets myself. When I told Juana what was happening she looked worried and a tear ran down her cheek. She gave Manuelito Sayeq a big hug, lifted him up, and sang something into his ear. The child didn't cry much, he seemed very peaceful, unlike the two of us. That same night we got on the plane. The child was asleep.

I explained to her how vital it was that Manuel plead guilty and she understood that without having to think too much about it.

"It's crazy not to have done it from the start," she said, "but don't worry, Consul, I'll talk to him and persuade him."

Teresa was waiting for us at the airport, at two in the morning. Oh, those night flights. She gave me a big hug, and I introduced her to Juana and little Manuel Sayeq.

"I wasn't able to speak with the lawyer yesterday," Teresa said. "I did go to the court, but they wouldn't let me in. To be honest, I'm not really sure what's going on."

We got to the apartment in the middle of the night—Teresa had offered to put us up and I'd accepted—and we arranged the guest room for the boy. I would sleep on the couch. It was almost four but nobody seemed very sleepy, so Teresa suggested we have a drink.

"I thought you'd never ask," I said.

She brought out a bottle of Herradura and we started drinking with a certain desperation, as if it were the antidote to a dangerous bite. Then I opted to withdraw and listen to Teresa and Juana asking each other questions, telling stories, getting to know each other.

A Colombian sociologist of thirty-one (how old was she, actually?) with a life of loss, flight, hate, an unconventional, tragic adventure, which hadn't made her resentful but quite the contrary, someone full of life, a strong, hopeful woman, capable of withstanding any hurricane, and next to her Teresa, forty-something, divorced, the mother of two daughters, a comfortable life, and more conventional except for the slightly unconventional aspect of her liking for strong liquor, a diplomat, living a privileged existence in a Southeast Asian country, with a lot of nostalgia and at the same time the desire (perhaps) to meet someone (isn't that what everyone wants? what we all want?), always thinking of the future.

I closed my eyes and fell asleep, not knowing what time it was, and when I woke I was lying on the couch, with clean sheets (smelling fresh, of lavender), and a nice pair of pajamas that weren't mine! (Teresa explained that they hadn't been able to open my case and hadn't wanted to wake me, so she'd gotten out a pair belonging to her father, who had left them behind after a recent visit.)

Dawn was breaking.

Today, Death paid me a visit.

Before, my life was a feast at which all hearts opened, and all wines flowed from glass to glass, from mouth to mouth.

One of those nights, I felt Death on my knees and found him bitter. I cursed him.

"Oh, Death, come and take away the thought of Death," I read in an old book.

"When me they fly I am the wings," he replied, from another poem.

I summoned all my strength. I planted myself in front of him and rejected his terrifying fury. Then I escaped.

Death had a thousand faces. All the faces.

Sometimes it was a young poet gazing at the twilight, in the port of Aden.

Death is here, and oh so punctual.

Lord, your guest is waiting for you in the drawing room.

Entrust my most precious treasures to the witches, to the spirits of poverty, to hate. I have succeeded in banishing any human hope from my soul.

As I already said: today Death paid me a visit. Death, the Grim Reaper.

Death who never rests from his labors, from his sleepless-ness. Who loves us and passes between us like a wind, a *venti-cello*, a slow, dense music, a dark cloud.

I called to my executioners to raise their rifles, I summoned all the plagues to drown me in their sand or their blood.

Unhappiness was my god. My one, beloved god.

Then I lay down on the dusty soil of Harar and saw the young poet again.

He was writing letters, looking southward. Every now and again he sank his hand into the red earth and let it run between his fingers.

We played with madness (were we fantasizing?) until the afternoon gave my mouth the terrifying smile of the idiot.

But I recovered my appetite, and went back to the parties, to the wine. Death was still there, I could not ignore him.

Everything is merely proof that I can still dream.

3

D awn was breaking.
It was almost six in the morning, and Teresa and Juana were still asleep. I sat down in the living room to wait for them, thinking that a confession by Manuel would set things in the right direction. The waiting would be difficult, as would the procedure for the pardon (if the pardon came), but others had done it. They were both young, they would bear it.

I opened my e-mail and found a message from Gustavo:

> What happened to Manuel Manrique? Did you find his sister? You never told me.

I answered, saying that I had found her.

> She's an incredible woman, I'll tell you all about it. She's here with me. She's asleep now in the next room. We're in Bangkok and in a few hours she and Manuel are going to meet. The trial has already started. I hope he'll be able to serve his sentence in Colombia. It'll have to be negotiated with the ministry. Thanks for everything, a hug.
>
> E.

Around eight I managed to speak with the lawyer. He was surprised I was already in Bangkok, and said he would make arrangements for Manuel's sister and me to visit Bangkwang.

"I won't be able to go with you," he said, "I have a meeting with the prosecutor that's key to the trial. It's a big problem."

I told him I would try to persuade Manuel to plead guilty, and asked him if he thought it would still have an effect.

"Well," the lawyer said, "if he makes a confession the trial will end with a sentence that may be a long one, but at least it'll get Article 27 off our backs. The important thing is that he do it in a solemn way, even a bit theatrically. It'd be very important to plan it for Monday's hearing. I can ask to be heard first and announce it. That would go down well. It may even make them reduce the sentence by a few years. Do you think you can persuade him?"

"Yes," I said. "I'm sure. His sister will talk to him."

"That's excellent news," he said. "In that case, go to Bangkwang around ten this morning, I myself will call the warden and tell him to expect you at that hour. And then come to my office in the afternoon. We have things to discuss."

"All right," I said.

When I hung up, Teresa came out of the bathroom, already dressed. She called her office and said that she would be busy until the afternoon, that they should transfer only urgent calls to her. She called the driver to come and pick her up. Juana was in the kitchen: anxious, hopeful. With a touch of fear for what she had to face.

We had a breakfast of bacon and eggs, orange juice, and coffee. The heat kept rising. Soon afterwards Manuelito Sayeq started crying. By 8:45 we were ready. The car from the Mexican embassy was waiting for us outside the door.

Again the bustle of the streets, the smog, the screeching sound of the *tuk-tuks*, the accelerating and braking. And on leaving the city, the other world: paddies, fields with palms and fruit trees, stooping women wearing triangular hats, with their children tied to their backs.

Juana was looking at everything in surprise.

"I suppose I'll have to get used to this," she said. "This is going to be the landscape of my life for a while."

"The next fight will be to try and get his sentence transferred to Colombia," I said.

She looked at me anxiously. "To Colombia? We'll see about that later, Consul, what makes you think it's going to be better there? Anything would be better than that hell!"

Her answer did not surprise me.

"Well, that depends on the two of you and nobody else," I said.

"I could rent one of those huts," Juana said, "grow rice, and visit him at weekends until he comes out. We have time, we're young. Manuelito Sayeq will grow close to his uncle. Or rather, his father. Manuel will be his father."

The walls of Bangkwang didn't impress her. The warden had a visitor from the Australian embassy, so we had to wait, and at last, about eleven o'clock, he received us in his office. Teresa accredited herself as a diplomat, given the task by her Foreign Ministry of following the case of the neighboring country. I introduced Juana as the prisoner's sister.

The man greeted her without looking her in the eyes, and said, yes, his lawyer called a while ago, you have an hour for the visit. He lifted the receiver and a moment later an orderly came to take us to the first cellblock.

I asked Juana to wait, and Teresa went with her to the visitors' parlor. I kept going with the orderly and one of the guards. As this was a special situation they authorized me to go as far as his cell and talk with him for a few minutes, preparing him for the visit. We went through three doors of rusted bars, in the midst of the heat and the flies. The corridor was a damp little passageway.

"It's that one," the guard said, pointing.

There were plenty of stains on the ground, seeping through the cracks in the doors, but as I approached Manuel's cell, I noticed something shiny. I felt a rush of fear and walked more quickly.

My God, it was blood! A bloodstain was spreading along the corridor, from under his door. We ran. The guard took an eternity to get the key in.

At last he opened it.

Manuel was lying in a fetal position. He had cut his wrists with a sharpened spoon.

The guard went back out into the corridor and pressed the alarm button, but I saw immediately that he was dead. His eyes were half open as if he were laughing. I embraced him, clasped him to my chest, cursing. He was still warm. The warmth of his skin told me: not long ago, not very long ago.

On the wall, just above the body, there was a drawing made with his own blood and traced with his finger. A heart-shaped island and a volcano. Two figures sitting on the hillside, a man and a woman, holding hands, looking at the approaching storm, unable to see the monstrous animals that lay in wait below the water. To one side, he had written: *Us*.

By some desperate association of ideas, a poem by Vallejo came into my mind, and I cried out, as I hugged him: "Do not die, I love you so much! But the corpse, alas, continued to die . . ." I cried out until I had no voice left, and my face turned red and filled with tears. At that moment, feeling that part of reality was opening up, leaving a hole for the elements, the irrational, I realized to what an extent this story had become *my* story.

A few seconds later (or maybe minutes, I couldn't be precise), a gurney arrived and they took him out wrapped in a grey blanket. The guards were shouting nervously, giving each other orders. The other prisoners were also shouting; although they were unable to see what was happening, the momentary chaos seemed to excite them. What darkness, what sadness, I thought. "But the corpse, alas, continued to die." Manuel's face, his dignity, seemed to give an unreal light to those dirty, peeling walls.

Going through the second set of bars, the guard went out into the yard and pushed the gurney along a path, right past the visitors' parlor where they were waiting. The noise made both of them run to the window.

Juana saw him and then looked at me.

I saw something collapse in her eyes. More than pain, I seemed to recognize an expression of profound weariness. She came out into the yard without screaming, raising her hands to her face. The gurney reached her and she was able to touch him. The men stopped and Juana swooned over him, kissing him: his blood and his eyes, his pallor. Kissing his skin and his wounded arms. Kissing everything that was kissable on that dislocated, absent face, in which Manuel was no longer there. She wept and I also wept. "Weeping together made us feel a strange happiness."

Teresa also wept, but kept her distance, since she was holding Manuelito Sayeq. The guards said something to each other and continued with the gurney as far as the infirmary (I assumed). Juana hugged me again and for a second we were one and the same. I felt her grief, her guilt, perhaps her anger.

Soon afterwards the doctor came and shook his head, he was dead. I already knew that. We all knew. Then he handed over two folded sheets of paper.

"They were in his pocket," he said.

One was for me, and said:

I told you, Consul, this wasn't going to be a crime story, but a strange love story. Now I'm free, even happy, and with this freedom I abolish myself. At last.

The other was for Juana. She read it and read it, crying, and finally handed it to me.

"Please, Consul, read it."

Dear sister. I wasn't able to see you, I thought I could hold out, but I've been drowning more and more, and now there's a way out and I don't have any strength left. Forgive me for failing you. I asked the consul to look for you but I'm not sure he'll succeed, time is up. Soon they'll be coming for me. I seem to hear them, hear their steps, but they won't find me. My life was always yours, but I have it on loan. I'll give it back to you when you come to where I already am almost, where I will be forever. You don't know the pleasure I feel seeing the liquid come out of my body, at last clean of that blood. This purity will suffice for both of us. With mine, I cleaned yours. I'm waiting for you where you know. If you read this it's because they will have found you. A kiss.

Something bothered me, or rather made me indignant, didn't they pass on the messages? didn't he know that Juana was coming to see him? I went to one side (I didn't want Juana, who was still crying in Teresa's arms, to hear me) and asked the warden of Bangkwang: didn't the lawyer send you my messages? weren't you told the consul had found the prisoner's sister? weren't you told we were coming here? The warden looked surprised, which I didn't understand, and when I repeated my question he said no, he didn't know anything.

Then he called one of his men and asked him, but he just shook his head. Without asking permission I grabbed the phone and dialed the lawyer's number. One ring, two, three. No reply. I couldn't believe it, he hadn't been given the message! They had killed him.

I insisted to the warden: it was important for us to clarify this, but he just looked up at the ceiling with a total lack of interest. I finally managed to speak with the lawyer:

"Of course I passed on the message, I dictated it by phone to the warden's secretary and mentioned it was urgent!"

I told him what had happened and he said he would come immediately, that we should wait for him.

I asked to speak with the warden's secretary, but I was told, which secretary? he didn't have a secretary, there was a woman who took messages. I asked the warden and he said, no, I already told you, I didn't get any message. They called the woman and somebody translated: nobody had left her a message like that, when do you say they called? The woman disappeared after a while and it was impossible to get her back.

At last the lawyer arrived and I said to him:

"Nobody received the messages and he never knew anything. It would have saved him."

The old man chewed something, a leaf similar to a betel, and said, nobody kills themselves for something like that, at least in my country. He must have had his reasons.

"You killed him, you didn't give him the message that would have saved his life, and you deceived us all."

The old man spat through the window.

"I understand how upset you are, Consul, but didn't you tell me the young man was going to plead guilty anyway?"

The blood rose to my head, and I had to make an effort not to hit him. Teresa noticed and came over. She said in my ear: calm down, there's nothing you can do. He's a son of a bitch, but you can't touch him!

I was having difficulty breathing, but I managed to say to her:

"Manuel never knew I'd found Juana, or that she was in Bangkok! He cut his wrists only a short time ago, the blood on the floor was still liquid, do you realize? He killed him!"

"Yes," Teresa said. "But don't forget you're representing your country. Later, you can make an official complaint, or piss in the Chao Phraya, but here you have to keep up appearances. If you touch him you're going to give them the opportunity to kick up a fuss."

We spent the rest of the day in Bangkwang, in a funeral chamber that was quite small but air-conditioned. When they brought in the body, in a coffin made of planks, Juana looked at her brother's livid face for a time that to all of us seemed infinite. It started to get dark and the prosecutor (who had also arrived) said that we had to go, that they would be taking the body to the morgue, where it would be kept while they waited for his sister's decision and the final legal procedures.

"Do you feel better?" I asked the prosecutor. "You must think your city is cleaner now."

Teresa squeezed my arm.

"If only our problems were limited to lost and stupid young people," he said, "although I know I mustn't judge anyone who has taken his own life."

"Doesn't that seem to you sufficient demonstration of innocence?" I said.

He turned and lit a cigarette in a somewhat theatrical manner. "Not really," he said. "To be honest, his death doesn't demonstrate anything."

"The pills weren't his," I insisted. "Someone put them in his case and you know it. Everybody knows it!"

Teresa glared at me again. The prosecutor seemed to lose patience.

"Eleven million tourists come here every year," he said. "Many to have sex and take drugs, others to traffic, and some, simply, on vacation. There are bound to be victims."

Saying this, he got in his car. But immediately he lowered the window and said:

"I forgot to give my condolences to his sister, please convey them to her from me. And please, let her decide quickly if she wants to repatriate him or bury him here. In this heat, bodies decompose."

"I'll tell her, don't worry," I said. "For now I trust in the quality of your cold chambers."

When we got home, Teresa opened a bottle of gin and suggested we go out on the terrace and look at the river, the flow of the traffic, the clouds. Night had already fallen. Juana still couldn't say anything. Around her eyes a purplish ring had settled, as if her eyelids were raw.

The Chao Phraya reflected the hallucinatory lights of the city, its iridescence. Teresa sat down next to me and we drank in silence, one glass after another. When Manuelito Sayeq fell asleep Juana came out again. I put a lot of ice in a glass and offered her a drink.

"I'd like a double, Consul, thank you."

"It's the only thing we can do," I said. "My condolences."

She thanked me for looking for her and bringing her here from Tehran, allowing her to get to him, even though it was too late.

"I can't help thinking," Juana said. "If only we'd come yesterday . . ."

That was nagging at me too: if only the Consular Department had given a rapid answer, if only I'd taken the decision to travel earlier, if only the Thai legal authorities hadn't brought the trial forward. If only, if only . . .

"If only I'd written an e-mail or a Facebook message, or called him on his cell phone," Juana said, "he'd be alive, it's all so . . ."

She started crying again. Teresa hugged her.

"Don't think anymore, Juana," I said, "nothing's going to bring him back. You will have him in your son."

"I have to decide what to do with the body," Juana said, "but to be honest it doesn't really matter. He isn't there."

"Are you going to call your family?" I asked.

"I haven't thought about it," Juana said. "I suppose they'll want to bury him in Bogotá. Manuel would prefer not to go back, but the truth is, none of that matters anymore."

I filled the glasses again and again, until we had to go down to the 7-11 for another bottle. We drank until dawn.

Teresa and Juana went off to their rooms at six and I remained on the couch, near the window, watching the skyscrapers emerge from the darkness into the clear light of morning.

Before going to sleep I grabbed my toiletry bag, took out my toothbrush, and went to the bathroom. I opened the door slowly, so as not to make a noise, and noticed that there was someone inside. It was Juana. She was naked, and was looking at herself in the mirror. I froze. I had never seen a body like that, with strange, enormous tattoos: Japanese ideograms, suns, Buddhist eyes, yins and yangs, and on her belly a genuine painting, what was it? my God, I recognized it: *The Great Wave of Kanagawa* by Hokusai! I felt an irrational force pushing me towards her, but I restrained myself. Lower down on her right thigh, she had a version of *The Raft of the Medusa* by Géricault, and on the left a painting that I identified, not then but a few days later, as *The Ninth Wave*, by the Russian Ivan Aivazovsky, a painting about which the poet Fernando Denis wrote some revealing verses:

It is already almost night in a painting by Ivan Aivazovsky,
the ninth wave,
beneath the magnanimous sky of the world,
beneath the insane light that gives horror and beauty and tar-
nishes the dream
that cries out in its colors.

Three shipwrecks plus an incredible number of religious or mystic signs. Added to these were scars and circular burns that seemed to convey some message. I looked at her without moving a muscle, without breathing, to avoid her noticing my presence. She was very beautiful. She had the same expression of weariness that I had seen in the prison and was swaying her head from side to side, as if in time to a lullaby. Then she started to move to the sides and slowly caressed her hips, her stomach, her breasts. She raised her hand to her pubis, tracing circles, slowly at first, but then a little faster and finally frenetically. I felt my body collapse, but made an effort and supported myself. Suddenly she grabbed the tube of toothpaste and penetrated herself with it, moving her fingers very quickly. Seconds later she shuddered, but her weary expression did not fade, not even at that moment.

She struck me as the most beautiful woman in the world, and I knew I loved her. From a distant and impossible place, I loved her.

Then I withdrew without making a noise and went to sleep, feeling excited, guilty, and sad.

When I woke, there was news. The lawyer called to say that the Ministry would take charge of Juana's stay until she decided what to do with the body, as a courtesy. They didn't want a scandal.

He also said that the head of the Narcotics Squad had informed him of two cases similar to Manuel's, with French and Indonesian people involved. Not at the Regency Inn, but at other hotels in the same area.

"It should help us get to the truth," the lawyer said, "and allow us to file a lawsuit against the state in order to at least obtain some compensation."

And he added:

"Tell Miss Manrique, and tell her also that I'm well-placed to handle that lawsuit. I know lots of people."

I really wanted to insult him, but it was Juana who had to decide, so I passed on the lawyer's words to her. She looked through the window for a moment and said:

"I'd be interested in hearing the conditions. I'd also like to speak with the prosecutor and accept the Ministry's hospitality while I resolve the matter."

Two days later Juana moved to a government apartment with Manuelito Sayeq. Teresa and I walked her to the door and I carried her suitcases. She had spoken with her family in Bogotá (she didn't go into details, and I didn't ask) and they had decided to bring Manuel back.

When we said goodbye she gave me a long hug, and said in my ear:

"I realized you were in the bathroom the other night, Consul. I felt the way you looked at me, how intensely you looked at me. I heard you breathing, standing there quietly, and I liked it."

I didn't know what to say.

"Your tattoos . . . They're beautiful."

"Another day I'll show them to you properly and tell you the reason for each one, although I suppose you can already imagine. Thank you for everything."

I said goodbye and told her I'd call her when I got to Delhi, that I'd be in touch to help her. When they came for her, she gave me another nervous, rapid hug. I wanted to ask her what she was planning to do next, where she was hoping to go, but didn't dare. It had become very clear that Juana wanted to handle her affairs alone and not rely on other people, even when those people claimed to help her. I was also aware of something unusual about her behavior, but was unable to decipher what it was. Then she put the child into the official car, a black Toyota Crown, and I watched them drive away. I waved goodbye, sadly, until the car was swallowed up by the traffic at the end of the avenue.

Had she spoken with her parents? What words had she used to tell (perhaps explain) that difficult story? She realized that the decision wasn't only down to her. Maybe she had decided to go back to Colombia, at least for a time. After all, it was her country.

That same day I had to fly back to Delhi. Teresa drove me to the airport.

"Will you come back here, now that everything is resolved?" she asked.

"I'd like to see you again," I said.

"We'll talk over the phone, we'll write," she said. "I'm with you on this. In any case, I'll keep an eye on Juana, I think we can be friends."

"Thanks for everything," I said. "Without you I wouldn't have been able to get anywhere in this affair."

Teresa looked at me sadly. "But it turned out badly."

I gave her a hug and walked toward Immigration. When I turned to wave to her one last time, I saw that she was gone.

5

A week later, I spoke with Teresa again. I told her I hadn't been able to get in touch with Juana, who wasn't returning my calls, and was no longer living in the government apartment. When I didn't get an answer, I went looking for her and the doorman told me she had left three days earlier. Trying to find out more, I spoke with the lawyer, who said he had not heard from her, but had news about the case. A lieutenant had been arrested and, in order to avoid beheading, had confessed various crimes, including the framing of Manuel. Not that it mattered anymore.

It seemed strange that Juana should have disappeared. I wrote her an e-mail but didn't get any reply.

A month later, the government of Thailand wrote to the Foreign Ministry in Bogotá, expressing its condolences for the death of Manuel Manrique.

Because I had dealt with the matter, the Consular Department sent me a copy marked FYI.

The note emphasized how important it was to fight the international drug networks, "responsible for tragic situations that ruin the lives of good and innocent people."

Bogotá answered, thanking them for the letter and promising to bring forward steps for the speedy opening of an embassy in Bangkok.

ometime later, from my office in Delhi, I wrote Juana an e-mail, without much hope of a reply, asking her where she was and how she was feeling. To my surprise, she replied immediately. "I'm in Paris, Consul, call me at this number." Surprised, my heart thumping, I dialed the number on my cell phone. Within a few seconds, I heard her voice at the end of the line. She told me Manuel's body had been flown back to Bogotá and was now in the Jardines de Paz. It had hit her mother hard and she had needed medical attention, but her father had taken it well. The important news, she said, was that she had been in contact with the Thai prosecutor again, because she had decided to write a book about her brother's case and file a lawsuit at the court in the Hague with a French lawyer who was a friend and associate of the lawyer in Bangkok.

"You won't believe what's going on, Consul," she said. "The prosecutor told the Ministry of Justice and the Royal Palace what I was intending to do, and you know what? They're offering me two million dollars in reparation provided I drop my suit."

I was silent for a moment, then asked, and are you going to accept?

Of course not, she said. For Manuel and for my son Manuelito, for the memories and the pain and so that my child, who is the continuation of my brother, can live a different life, in a different world. No, Consul, I didn't accept the two million.

"Really?"

"I asked for four," she said. "And I assure you they'll give it to me."

At that moment the line went dead, and although I kept trying I couldn't get through again.

8

A few days later I called Teresa and told her about Juana. She thought it strange that Juana had left Bangkok without saying goodbye. Then, my curiosity aroused, I called the prosecutor's office (I'd had his card since our first encounter) and, much to my surprise, he himself answered. I asked him about the new bandits who must be sleeping in Bangkwang, but suddenly he cut me off and said, why are you calling me?

I told him that I had learned some details in the case of young Manrique and expressed my gratitude for the way in which the Ministry was handling it.

"What are you talking about?" he cut in again. "That file's been closed since the repatriation of the body and the official note of condolence. The Ministry hasn't reopened it, or heard from anybody, or had any contact with the lawyers or the family members. The case is closed. What details are you referring to?"

"Forget it," I said. "I think I've been ill-informed."

I immediately called the lawyer and asked him about the supposed lawsuit and the offer of two million dollars.

After a silence, he said:

"I don't have the slightest idea what you're talking about, Consul. The last time I spoke with her you were present . . . Compensation? For heaven's sake, don't make me laugh. You Westerners will never understand anything."

After a somewhat contemptuous guffaw he said:

"Excuse me, do you have any other questions?"

"No, thank you for your time."

I called Juana's Paris number, but there was no answer. I checked on the Internet what district it corresponded to, but didn't learn much: it was the number of a public telephone in a shopping mall in La Défense.

I searched for her in vain through the Colombian Consulate in Paris, and wrote to her again but never got a reply.

My curiosity aroused, I dialed her parents' number in Bogotá. It was the only other thing I could think of. The only thing I hadn't yet done. As the phone started ringing at the other end, I felt my lip trembling slightly. I already feared what I was quite likely to hear. At last a woman's voice answered. It turned out to be the mother. I introduced myself as the consul who had handled the administrative part of her son's case. She thanked me and called her husband ("Come, it's about Manuel, come on!"). The father's voice sounded older than I had imagined: he said the family would be eternally grateful for everything that had been done, and that he had already written a letter to the Ministry. I said I wanted to personally express my condolences to him and to Manuel's mother and sister, but he replied:

"We're very grateful, Consul, although you ought to know that unfortunately his sister also abandoned us."

"I didn't know," I said, "I'm very sorry."

There was a silence. I could have sworn he was wiping away a tear.

"She disappeared four years ago, Consul, you know, this country is dangerous. There are families nothing ever happens to, and others like ours. Things have gone badly for us."

I hung up after more condolences and sat there thinking about shipwrecks, about Géricault, Aivazovsky, and Hokusai.

About Juana.

Once again she had disappeared.

9

INTER-NETA'S FINAL MONOLOGUE

They are going around saying that I am the mistress of silence: that I am the prostitute, the fancy woman, the lover. The whore of silence. But what can I do if every time I think, I prefer to keep quiet, to imagine empty spaces, to smile at nothingness. I am about to do it one more time, like my Sleeping Beauty: to go to a place where the grim heartbeat of the world, the mechanism of this weary planet, can't be heard, to escape to where the air and life are silent matter. I want to absent myself, to leave.

And how is the poem of silence, how can it be?

Oh, it will be a construction of words like zephyrs, a surface made of clouds, a volcano of signs. How do I know?

For a start I have to choose a poem in which to hide myself, a poem whose words will serve as a screen to block the light, its verses like cliffs protecting my little island from disaster and the sadness of the world. I have already lost almost everything. I'm not brave: just a fragile grain of sand.

One day passes, two days, three, and I have decided.

I will hide myself in a poem by Roque Dalton, murdered by his own comrades, his own friends! It's one of the greatest demonstrations of idiocy in history. Oh, the dreams and the words, how they kill. Roque was free and ethereal, as I wish to be. As was somebody I loved very much and who is no longer with us. So now I leave them, perhaps forever.

I take my leave with my poem-home, my poem-world:

LATE AT NIGHT

When you learn that I have died do not utter my name
because death and repose would be delayed.

Your voice, which is the bell of the five senses,
would be the dim lighthouse sought by my fog.

When you learn that I have died utter strange syllables.
Say flower, be, tear, bread, storm.

Do not let your lips find my eleven letters.
I am tired, I have loved, I have earned silence.

Do not utter my name when you learn that I have died,
from the dark earth it would come through your voice.

Do not utter my name, do not utter my name.
When you learn that I have died do not utter my name.

Epilogue

I have already filled six notebooks. I've listened, imagined, walked around Bangkok, and revisited a few places. I have fantasized, remembered, and written.

Tomorrow I shall leave without having really seen anybody (Teresa hasn't lived here for some time now). Nothing except the sound of old words that at the time nobody listened to. Well, only me. Now I have to organize them, reconstruct the story, and try, once again, to give them a meaning.

In *The Last Tycoon*, Elia Kazan's film of the F. Scott Fitzgerald novel, with a screenplay by Harold Pinter, the main character, played by Robert De Niro, twice tells the following story: a woman rushes home and empties the contents of her purse on the table in the entrance hall: change purse, glasses, a nickel, a brush, a box of matches, and a lipstick. Cursing, she grabs the nickel and the box of matches, and then nervously takes off her black gloves and throws them angrily into the gas stove. She lights a match and brings it close to the stove, but just as she is about to light it the telephone rings. The woman hesitates, curses again, and finally answers.

After listening to something she shouts into the receiver:

"I already told you, I never owned any damned black gloves!"

She slams the phone down and goes back to the stove, is about to light it, but at that moment realizes that there is someone else in the room, someone who has seen what she has done.

What's going to happen next? And above all: what is the nickel for? "To buy a ticket for the movie," says De Niro, because that's where the story that has to be told starts.

I go back to my question: have I, in fact, understood anything? The only answer is to keep searching for Juana, seduce her in the distance, maybe in another book or in another city. As Rimbaud said, pointing with his finger to the future: *Et à l'aurore, armés d'une ardente patience, nous entrerons aux splendides villes.* The splendid cities. Stories happen there, maybe at dawn or late in the afternoon, in any case far from the blazing noonday sun. Will we reach them? Maybe we will enter that new city at dawn or before nightfall.

So for now all that is left for me is to take my leave, just as in that old musical: *So long, farewell, auf Wiedersehen. Goodbye.*

About the Author

Santiago Gamboa's debut came in 1995 with *Páginas de Vuelta*, which introduced his unique voice to Colombian readers. His English language debut *Necropolis* (Europa 2012) was the winner of the Otra Orilla Literary Award.